THE THREE KINGS

Forsaken #3

_____

PENELOPE BARSETTI

Hartwick Publishing

Hartwick Publishing

The Three Kings

Copyright © 2022 by Penelope Barsetti

All rights reserved.

Contents

ONE

Huntley

WHEN I STEPPED INTO THE ROOM, I FOUND MY MOTHER on the floor. She lay beside the portrait of my father, as if they were sleeping side by side once again. Her face was distorted from all the puffiness, and her skin had a permanent shine from the rivers of tears down her face. She must have heard me walk into the room, but she continued to stare at the ceiling as if she hadn't.

"Mother."

She slowly turned her head to me, as if she'd had no idea I was there until now.

"I need to show you something."

Her eyes remained defeated, like she didn't care in the least.

"Come on." I extended my hand to her and pulled her to her feet. She was my queen. My commander. The woman who taught me the sword and the ax. It killed me to see her so weak, to witness her heartbreak, the damage she'd carried in silence all these years.

As if she were a frail old woman, she held on to my arm as I walked her to the other side of the basement. We made it to the cage, Faron's head pinned to the back of the chair, the sword sticking out.

She stilled, her breathing deepening.

"Father is avenged. As are you."

Her arm slipped out of mine as she moved forward, her spine straight, her shoulders back, her majesty returned. She stepped through the open door to get a closer look at him, to see him executed the way my father had been. Her breathing grew labored. Her hands came together at her waist. She remained that way for a long time, looking at his dead body, his bloody teeth.

Then she spat on his face. "Delacroix belongs to the Rolfes. Always has, always will." She stepped out of the cage and returned to me, her fingertips dragging down her face to wipe away the shine of her tears. Once she gathered herself, she turned her eyes on me. "Did she grant you permission?"

It was bittersweet to watch my mother get the last word. But the pain immediately followed afterward. All I could muster was a shake of my head.

Her eyes sharpened. "You broke your promise." Judgment was in her voice. Even disappointment.

"It pained me to see you like that. To see everything you've been holding in these last decades. To see everything you've lost—because of him."

Her eyes softened briefly, touched by the love in my heart, but then they returned to disappointment. "I haven't seen his face in twenty years. I did my best to preserve it in my memory, but his features began to fade more with every passing year. To see him again… It shattered me. I hadn't had a chance to grieve. I'd been too busy surviving. Too busy fighting. But I finally had my opportunity to feel the hurt."

"Faron deserved what he got."

"You'll hear no argument from me, Huntley. But your wife deserves a husband who keeps his word. You shouldn't have done that."

It was a shock coming from her.

"Does she know?"

I nodded. "She walked in afterward."

Her whole face tightened in a grimace. "Huntley…"

I knew the situation was dire. It couldn't be fixed with a kiss, by calling her baby, not even with an apology. I knew I was fucked.

She stared at me with her observant eyes, seeing emotions on my face that no one else would notice. "You better hope she loves you enough to forgive you. That's your only chance out of this."

"She's bound to me forever, so it's not like she can escape me."

"She can if she kills you."

My breathing stopped entirely. The thought hadn't crossed my mind. "She wouldn't do that."

"That promise was her condition to marry you. You broke it—so she doesn't owe you anything anymore."

I was glad he was dead, but now I wished I could take it back. "I didn't expect you to feel this way. I thought you would be too pleased with his death to think about Ivory."

"I'm not thinking about her." She was a foot shorter than me, so she always had to tilt her head back to address me, but her presence was just as forceful as mine. "I'm thinking about you, Huntley. I know how important she is to you, and once you find someone you love, your loyalty is to them and them alone."

"My loyalty is also to you—"

"It changes once you're bound to another person. Your promise disappointed me, but I also respected it. Where is she?"

"I don't know." I let her go because she was too upset, and she clearly wanted nothing to do with me. To pursue her would just have made the situation worse. "She needs space right now."

"Keep your guard up, Huntley."

"She would never hurt me, Mother." I said it with a bite, offended that she would insinuate something so sinister.

"Faron killed your father, and a promise to the woman you love wasn't enough to stop you. Now you've killed her father. You don't think she'll be blinded by revenge? You don't think she'll lose her resolve just the way you did? I hope I'm wrong—but proceed as if I'm not."

TWO

Ivory
___

B<small>LINDED BY MY TEARS</small>, I <small>BARELY MADE IT OUT OF THE</small> castle.

Guards watched me as I passed, and even Ryker tried to stop me, but I evaded his grasp and kept going. I made it out the double doors, to the city below the hill, and then to the fields outside the city. "Pyre!" Once the castle was behind me and I could feel the fresh air right on my face, I felt the tightness in my chest release. "Pyre!" I dropped to my knees and sat there, my eyes on the torched patch of grass from earlier that morning. It was almost sunset now, the sky tinged with purple and orange.

A swoop through the air, and then the ground shook once the dark-green dragon landed in front of me. *Are you alright?*

My arms cocooned my body, as if I were shivering from the cold. "No."

He laid his body on the grass, resting his neck and snout on the ground right in front of me so we could be eye level. *What has happened?*

"My husband…killed my father." The tears started again, splitting my chest right in half.

Why would he do such a thing?

"It's a long story… But he promised me he wouldn't."

Why would he break his promise?

"I don't know…couldn't control himself. Doesn't matter. I trusted him. The only reason I agreed to any of this was because he would spare my father's life. He lied to me. If I hadn't done any of this, my father would still be alive."

You can't think that way, Ivory.

"It's true…it's all my fault." I brought my knees to my chest and sobbed harder, the image of my father's dead body forever ingrained in my mind. The sword pierced his throat and the back of his head, grotesquely pinning him in place.

I'm sorry.

My forehead rested on my knees, and I hugged myself.

Pyre curled his body around me and then covered my body with his wing, plunging me into near darkness. *Sleep. You'll feel better when you wake up.*

I lay on my side on the grass, still crying, clutching my knees to my chest.

I'll keep them away.

THREE

Ryker

IVORY FLEW OUT OF THE CASTLE IN TEARS, TEARS I'D never seen her shed in my life. When I tried to grab her, she shoved me so hard against the wall I hit the back of my head against a sconce.

At first, I thought she and Huntley had had a fight.

But I couldn't imagine a fight would end in her fleeing the castle, the castle she'd just taken with two enormous dragons. Whatever it was had to be bad. Really bad.

And that was when it hit me. "Shit."

I moved down the hallway to the stairs in the rear, and I came across Effie on the way.

"Where's Ivory?" she asked. "I haven't seen her yet."

I shoved her aside without answering.

"Ryker?"

I moved to the stairs, took them in a rush, and made it into the basement.

Effie followed me the whole way. "You're scaring me. What's going on."

I made it to the cells in the dungeon and stilled when I saw him.

I was instantly nauseated, instantly sick, but I couldn't look away. My eyes wanted to break contact, but my mind needed to be convinced that this was real, that my father had been executed with a sword through his skull.

"Oh no…Ryker."

I finally pulled my gaze away when I realized it was true.

My father was dead.

And I knew exactly who had killed him.

Effie was on me, her hands on my shoulders, her sad face in my line of sight. "I'm so sorry."

"You hated him."

She flinched at my bitterness. "Doesn't matter. Your feelings are all I care about right now."

Huntley didn't feel the same way about his own wife. I left Effie's affection and headed back to the stairs.

"Ryker."

I took the stairs two at a time to get back to the ground floor as quickly as possible.

"Shit, what are you going to do?"

I emerged from the basement and flew down the hallway. Guards passed me, some in the armor of the Delacroix, some in the dark armor of the Runes. My eyes scanned every room, searching for that asshole in the dining room, the study, the bedchambers, everywhere.

I finally found him.

He was outside the city gates, standing on the grass. Twenty feet in front of him was one of the dragons, wrapped in a ball like there was something in the middle. He stood there alone, in his armor and weapons, staring.

I took off, running down the path to the gates.

"Ryker!" Effie's voice faded behind me because she couldn't keep up.

I made it outside the gates, across the grass, and approached him from behind. "It was all a lie, wasn't it?"

He didn't turn around, as if he'd heard me approach a while ago.

"She never meant a damn thing to you. Just a means to an end."

He slowly faced me, his features hard but his eyes empty.

The dragon remained curled around Ivory, steam coming out of his nostrils as he stared at Huntley.

I came close, drawing my sword. "A man who doesn't keep his promises isn't a man at all. And a man who has no intention of keeping a promise as he makes it is something even worse."

His blue eyes watched me, but his dominant hand remained at his side and didn't reach for his sword. "I'm not going to fight you."

"Then this will be an execution. Get on your knees."

"Ryker, this is between her and me—"

"You killed *my* father, so it's between us now."

"You know he wasn't a good man—"

"And neither are you." I gripped my sword and prepared to strike him. "Now raise your sword and fight me, or let me chop you into a hundred pieces and feed you to this dragon."

He still didn't draw his sword. "I had every intention of keeping my promise. But when I saw my mother—"

"I don't want your excuses." I slashed at him.

He deflected the sword with his brace and stepped back.

"I want your death. I want this blade through your fucking throat." I slashed at him again.

He ducked then sidestepped the next swing. "Ryker, stop this."

I slammed my sword down and finally sliced him across the hand.

He gave a slight grimace but no other reaction.

"As your king, I order you——"

I swung wildly, coming at him for the killing blow.

He skirted away, his armor protecting the worst of the hits.

"Stop." His mother's voice came from behind me, deep and authoritative.

I ignored her.

"Stop, or I'll have you killed."

I kept my eyes locked on Huntley. "You can kill me after I slaughter this piece of shit."

Huntley continued to move back. "Ryker——"

"Fight me!" I swung my blade down on him.

Huntley evaded it.

One of the archers fired an arrow right at me.

Huntley moved in the way and took the hit, the arrow striking him right in between his brace and his armor. "Stop." He held up his hand to his mother and the soldiers she brought with her. "Fire again, and I'll have your head." He turned to me. "Drop your sword, Ryker."

I kept it in hand because this wasn't finished.

Huntley stepped closer to me. "I know you're angry right now, but you're going to get yourself killed. I can protect you, but not from my mother. If she sees someone come after her son, she won't stop until you're dead in the ground. Walk away now. Let this go."

"Did you let it go?" I said as spittle flew out. "Did you let your father's death go?"

His eyes narrowed.

"Then don't expect me to." I sheathed my sword then walked away. I moved past Queen Rolfe and her men and headed back to the castle. Effie had just reached the gate, a sword in her hands.

"Are you okay?"

I grabbed her by the arm and pulled her with me. "I'm fine."

She looked over her shoulder. "You wounded him."

"Not deep enough."

"Don't do anything stupid, okay? You aren't in charge of Delacroix anymore. You could get killed."

"I don't care, Effie."

"Well, I do." She grabbed me by the arm and forced me to a halt. "I can't lose you."

"Ivory will take care of you if I die."

Her eyes squinted with a look of hurt. "That's not why." She rose on her tiptoes and cupped my face, bringing our lips together for a kiss. "This is why. This is why I can't lose you."

FOUR

Ivory

I RETURNED TO THE CASTLE IN THE MIDDLE OF THE night and made it to my childhood bedroom. It was exactly as I'd left it, the sheets in disarray on the mattress, the books from the library still on the coffee table. Ryker must have told the maids to abandon this room, and they clearly listened.

The floorboard in front of the bed creaked when I stepped over it, and then I plopped down on the edge of the bed that faced the window. The curtains were drawn closed, and the bedroom was dark. I hadn't showered in days, but now I was too depressed to care about the oil in my hair and the grime on my skin.

I didn't want to face Ryker.

He would never forgive me.

The night passed and became morning again, and all that while, I remained in the same place on the edge of the bed. I'd slept most of the day in Pyre's embrace, so now I was wide awake throughout the night, but my eyes were still bloodshot from despair. I eventually took a bath and changed my clothes, but I felt the grief weighing me down as if I was still covered in dirt.

I sat on the couch with a blanket on top of me, the curtains still drawn. All our hard work had led to this moment, the first step in securing a future without the threat of Necrosis, but it felt like a defeat.

My bedroom door opened and revealed Ryker.

I shifted my gaze to his, saw the horror on his face, and looked away.

I couldn't take that look, not from him, not after I'd let him down.

He came into the room, Effie in tow.

He pulled up a chair and took a seat, and Effie sat on the couch beside me, looking at me with tender eyes that showed her empathy. Silence ensued, a long stretch of silence packed with anguish.

I couldn't look him in the eye. "I'm sorry… I'm so sorry." My eyes filled with tears.

"Girl…" Effie grabbed my hand.

"He promised me…" I let the words escape as a whisper, my heart broken for several reasons. "I trusted him…"

Ryker stayed quiet.

"I'm the reason we made it this far. I'm the reason we have two dragons in our army. I'm the reason they weren't defeated by Necrosis. I'm the reason they took back Delacroix...and I'm the reason he's dead." The tears continued to well up until they were so thick, they streaked down my cheeks. "I know he did terrible things. But the Rolfes did terrible things too. He said he would consider apologizing to Queen Rolfe, even said he would help us against King Rutherford. We could have moved on from this. We could have started over. But now, we'll never get that chance..." I finally found the strength to look at my brother and accept his angry stare.

But he wasn't wearing one. He was defeated—just the way I was. "Yeah...it's pretty fucking shitty."

"I'm sorry, Ryker. I should have listened to you."

"It's not your fault," he whispered.

"Yes, it is. I trusted him."

"You were trying to make the world a better place. Your heart was in the right place."

He was being so good to me, better than I deserved. "I'm not sure what to do now..."

"I have an idea." He sat with his forearms on his knees. "We flee to the Capital. You're close with one of the dragons. Take him with us."

"They won't be separated."

"Then take them both."

"And then what?" I asked. "We attack Delacroix? That will negate everything we've worked for." I shook my head. "You'll be named duke. The lottery will continue. Nothing changes. And I promised the dragons I would help them, and I can't do that until all the Kingdoms are united and Necrosis is defeated."

"She's right," Effie said. "Everything up to this point will be for nothing. Your father's dead. That's the only thing that's changed. Ryker, you talked to him about altering the way things were, and he made it perfectly clear he had no interest in that. Maybe if he had, things would have been different."

Ryker shook his head. "We made a deal—and that motherfucker broke it."

My heart hurt every time I thought of him. A man I wanted nothing to do with.

"He'll pay for this—eventually." Ryker stared at his hands. "I'll never support a king who can't keep his word. I'll never support a king who uses other people to get what he wants."

I didn't defend Huntley, not anymore.

"We take the Kingdoms, kill Necrosis, and when everything is said and done, we kill him." Ryker lifted his chin and looked at me. "Agreed?"

I kept my mouth shut, my eyes still blurry with tears.

Ryker pressed me. "Ivory."

"And then what?" I asked. "Who rules?"

His eyebrows furrowed together. "You."

"Me?" I whispered.

"You just said you're the reason they got this far. You. Not Huntley. Not Queen Rolfe. You."

When I inhaled my next breath, it burned all the way down.

"Are we in agreement?" he pressed.

Effie stared at me.

Despite all the pain in my heart, that thought had never crossed my mind. "No…" I shook my head. "I can't do that, Ryker."

Now he looked angry. "You can't be serious—"

"I just can't, okay? Drop it."

"I'm not going to fucking drop it. He killed our father—"

"And Father would have killed him if he'd had the chance, even if I begged him not to. The cycle never ends. Now we're talking about killing him, and if we did, his brother or mother would avenge him. They would kill you, and then I would avenge you. It'll never

23

stop, Ryker. I know it's hard, but we have to let this go. Nothing we do will bring Father back. We need to continue on our mission, which is bigger than any of us."

Ryker dropped his chin, releasing his anger in a drawn-out sigh. "Alright."

"So don't try to take down Huntley yourself. He's a strong fighter."

"Really? I find that hard to believe…since he refused to fight me."

I should have known Ryker would go after him. "I know it's hard to let this go, but we must."

———

Days passed, and I didn't see Huntley.

I spent my time in my room or outside the city with Pyre. We'd sit in the field together, talking about his homeland, Storm, the kingdoms, anything but what Huntley had done to my father.

Huntley and his mother moved forward with their conquest of Delacroix, giving an address in the market square as they pronounced themselves the true rulers of the Kingdom. Perhaps some of the inhabitants remembered them from before and rejoiced at their return. But I bet others saw them as the outsiders.

I knew I'd have to face him eventually because we needed to discuss the next steps. Word would get back to the Capital that two dragons were in Delacroix, if it hadn't already. The other Kingdoms would know too. We had to make a course of action sooner rather than later before we were the ones cornered and attacked.

But the idea of facing him... It made me sick to my stomach.

I knew the moment had come when heavy footsteps sounded outside my door. A single knock struck the wood.

I was on the couch, and the second I felt his presence on the other side of the door, my stomach tightened into knots. My eyes remained on the open window, the very window he'd crawled through to get to me last time.

He opened the door and let himself inside.

I could see his outline out of the corner of my eye. His broad shoulders. His powerful chest. His impressive height. Without actually seeing him, I could make out the features of his face based on his energy. His eyes were hard with remorse. His jaw clenched in regret.

He shut the door behind himself and sat in the chair Ryker had occupied days ago.

I breathed harder when he was near, so heartbroken by what he'd done to me.

He was quiet, as if giving me the opportunity to speak first, to look at him once I was ready.

I kept my gaze on the window because I would never be ready.

"I know you didn't want to see me. And I wanted to give you space."

"I still don't want to see you." My knees were to my chest, my arms hooked around them. The sunlight was visible outside the window, the town glowing with midday heat. "If it were possible, I'd never see you again."

He had nothing to say to that, judging by the three minutes of silence that passed.

"Please go." The sadness was in my voice, in the quiet way I spoke, the defeat in my tone.

"I meant that promise when I made it. And I intended to keep it every step of the way. But I found my mother in an old storage room. Your family removed our portraits and threw them in the basement, and when she found them, she broke down in a way I've never seen. I stood there, listening to her sob, holding a picture of my father as if she'd just lost him yesterday." He kept his voice steady, emotionless. "That terrible night came back to me. Your father held her down and forced her—and not once did she cry. Not once did she give him any satisfaction. But seeing her collapsed on the floor...made me realize she'd been holding that in

26

for twenty years. I snapped…and lost it. I can't even remember doing it. I was out of my mind, deranged."

I kept my eyes straight ahead. "I understand why you did it, Huntley. You could have gone down there and tortured him until he begged for death…and I would have understood. What I don't understand is how you can make a promise to the woman you love and not keep it. That's what I can't comprehend."

He said nothing.

"You don't love me. Not enough anyway."

"That's not true."

"It must be true. Because you chose revenge over love. You have to live with that decision now."

He inhaled a slow breath, an audible one that showed his pain. "I would take it back if I could—"

"But you can't. It's done."

He gave another exhale. "I'm sorry."

I didn't forgive him. Would never forgive him.

"You really think if our situations were reversed, you would have done anything differently?"

That got my head to turn, got me to look at him head on for the first time. Now, I saw how he really looked, how sunken his eyes appeared, how bloodshot they were. His expression was tight with tension, as if his entire body had been clenched all week, as if he'd been holding his breath in anticipation of this conversation. There was no confidence. There was no arrogance. Just sorrow. "There's nothing in this world that's worth losing you, Huntley."

He inhaled a deep breath, and his eyes tightened in pain, as if my words were an arrow to his heart. He was the one to look away, to sever the contact too painful to sustain.

"I thought you felt the same."

FIVE

Huntley

_____

I CARRIED THE HEADSTONE TO THE HOLE THAT I'D DUG and set it inside. I compacted the dirt back into place with my bare hands, pressing it tightly so the stone wouldn't come loose and slip in the rain. The stone-mason had engraved it with his name, his title, and the children he'd left behind. Then I grabbed the shovel and dug the hole in front of it, making it six feet deep, seven feet long.

"Son."

I stabbed the shovel into the dirt and rested my arm on top of it.

"What are you doing?"

I dropped my arm and looked at her head on. "Burying her father." I expected her disappointment, even a look of betrayal, but her expression didn't change.

"Your father's headstone is beautiful."

I'd done his yesterday. It was in front of an olive tree, right on the bluff. His body was long gone, but his memory would be revered. He'd been avenged, but other than the thirty-second high I'd felt initially, I didn't feel any better. The most comfort I'd ever felt was in my wife's loving embrace.

"Ivory hasn't forgiven you?"

The mention of her name made me look away, the pain in my chest so raw. In the week we hadn't spoken, I'd felt that agony in my heart, the same agony I'd felt when she was taken by the Teeth. It was a million times more profound now than it was then. I knew when she was asleep because it turned into a simmer.

"I'm sorry."

I grabbed the shovel and got back to work.

"Huntley." She stepped closer to the grave site, coming right beside me.

I tossed the dirt aside then straightened.

"You need to fight for her."

"Mother." I didn't want to talk about it. Didn't want to think about it.

"I've never seen you like this. It's visible all over your face." Her hand went to my shoulder, and she gave me a squeeze.

I pushed her arm down. "I can't take it back."

"Don't forget that she's still your wife. No amount of anger or pain can change that fact. She's bound to you for eternity, as you are to her. Remind her of that. Remind her of the blood you shared, of the vows you exchanged. Even if she doesn't want to be with you anymore, she has to."

I stared at the dirt.

"Use that to your advantage."

I reached for Ivory in the middle of the night, and she wasn't there. I'd done that every night since we'd been apart, even though I knew she was gone. A part of me wished it'd been a bad dream, that I would wake up and it'd be as if it never happened.

"Fight for her."

———

Ivory spent most of her time in her room. If she wasn't there, she was either with Pyre or Ryker and Effie. At sunset, I went to her bedroom and knocked.

It was quiet, but that didn't mean anything.

I opened the door and found her in the exact same place as last time. She sat on the couch, a book in her lap, wearing a nightgown. Her long hair was pulled back out of her face, showing off her elegant neck and the hollow at her throat.

Her look was full of animosity, and her posture was stiff. That look of love in her eyes was long gone.

It hurt me every time I looked at her.

I sat in the chair that faced the couch, the same place I'd sat when she'd said there was nothing I could ever do to fix this. Her attack had inflicted a level of pain I'd never felt before. It was like a fiery sword that cut the skin and burned it at the same time. Never in my life had I known agony like this, and now I understood how my mother had felt every single day of her life since she lost my father. "You know how much I regret what I did. I don't have to tell you that. You can see it all over my face. You can see how miserable I am without you."

Her green eyes stayed on me, her cheeks fairer than they used to be, like she'd lost the rouge that used to bring her color. She glanced down for a moment, taking a second to process my admission.

"I lost my temper. I lost my logic. It had nothing to do with the way I feel about you. If I could love you more, which I can't, it wouldn't have happened any differently. I know this is hard to understand, but my actions have no reflection on the strength of our relationship. I lost my mind…and I couldn't stop it."

"Huntley." She inhaled a slow breath. "We can talk about this a million times, but it's not going to change anything."

Another knife between the ribs. "And you can be as angry with me as you want, but we're still married. You're still my wife. We're still bound together forever. When I die, I'll be waiting for you on the other side, just as my father is waiting for my mother."

Her eyes sharpened, breaking through the fog of sadness. "What's that supposed to mean?"

"It means that we're still together."

"I said we're done—"

"We can't be done, Ivory. Don't you understand that's impossible?"

She set the book aside and straightened. "We can still be married, but that doesn't mean we need to be together, to be in the same place at the same time—"

"Yes, it does." My hand moved over my chest. "Because I can feel your pain no matter how far apart we are. You're the single most important thing in the world to me, and I must protect you always."

"The *single* most important thing?" Her voice dripped with sarcasm. "We both know that's not true."

"I told you my actions had nothing to do with you."

"Clearly," she said, with an even heavier dose of sarcasm.

"We're husband and wife. And now we're king and queen. We're together. Period."

"Excuse me?" That fire that I loved under other circumstances came out as an inferno. "No. That's not how this works——"

"There is no alternative. You will bear my sons. You will bear my daughters."

"And how are you going to manage that? By forcing me? Your mom will love that…"

"I've proven that I'm not that kind of man, so don't insult me again."

"But you're the kind of man to force a woman to be married to him?"

"I didn't force you. You made those vows of your own volition. I'm just reminding you of the lifetime commitment that you made, a commitment that doesn't end, not even in death. I know that I hurt you, and I'm sorry for that. You're entitled to be angry as long as you like, but we still love each other."

"Do we?" she said, her voice full of venom.

"Look me in the eye and tell me otherwise." Our trust had been broken. Our relationship had been broken.

But there was no doubt in my mind that the love we had for each other could never be broken.

She looked so pissed off, but she didn't dare say the words. "I doubt you'll want to be with me if I'm sleeping around."

Just the suggestion made my blood boil. "Don't make empty threats."

"What if they aren't empty?"

"They are," I said. "No matter how much you may hate me right now, I'm still the man you want between your legs every night."

"Wow. Don't flatter yourself."

"I can prove it."

"Yeah?"

"How about I walk into the first pub I see and take a woman home?"

The fangs in her eyes retreated, and her skin turned as pale as snow. Her reaction was involuntary, and she probably had no idea how distraught she looked at the mere suggestion.

I'd taken a gamble I was terrified to lose. Because if that hadn't been her reaction, I would have been crushed. "That's what I thought." I got to my feet. "We sleep together, so grab your things and bring them to my bedchambers."

"No."

"Then I'll come here."

"And I'll throw your ass out."

"If there's an attack on the castle, I need you close. I need to protect my queen."

"I can protect myself, asshole." She looked away, out the window, silently dismissing me.

I stood my ground. "Ivory, this is how it's going to be."

"If I have to sleep in the same room as you, I'll slit your throat in your sleep."

I stared down at her, not believing her whatsoever. "I thought we were done with empty threats."

SIX

Ivory

THE BEDCHAMBER HE'D CHOSEN HAD TWO BEDROOMS, the main one for the royal couple, and another for the baby nurse. I occupied the smaller one, bringing my books and essentials to make it mine. The room had a smaller bed than I was used to, and sleeping alone had been an adjustment. I went from having a bear-sized personal heater every night to sleeping on the edge even though I was alone.

The room had its own washroom, so I really didn't have to interact with him at all.

The door opened behind me, and he stepped into the room.

I could feel his presence, feel his stare in my back, but I ignored him.

"Ivory."

"Don't push your luck, Huntley." He'd dragged me here against my will, and I wasn't in the mood to grant another request. I turned away from the closet and met his look, my face tight with tension.

"I buried your father. He's in the cemetery."

It took me a second to process what he'd said, to accept that my father was truly dead. Sometimes it felt like a bad dream that would fade. But then I remembered him pinned to that chair, his throat stuffed with a sword.

"Thought you'd like to visit." He left my room and shut the door behind him.

I grabbed the closest book sitting on the dresser and chucked it at the door. "Fuck off." Tears welled in my eyes again because it was time to say goodbye, to acknowledge that I was truly orphaned.

———

I crossed paths with Ryker in the hallway.

"What's going on?" he asked. "I went to your room, and your things were gone."

"I'm in the bedchamber with Huntley."

His eyes narrowed in ferocity. "Just like that, everything's forgiven?"

"I don't have a choice."

"What does that mean?"

"He said divorce isn't possible, so we're husband and wife until the end."

"That's barbaric. He's just going to force you every night?"

"No. He wouldn't do that." No matter how much I despised him right now, I knew that wasn't him. "Just wants me close."

Ryker gave a slight shake of his head, furious.

"As much as I hate it, it's necessary. He's the King of Delacroix—and that makes me the Queen."

"So, this is about power?"

"This is about succeeding. I was the one who talked him into challenging the Capital and then uniting all the factions at the bottom of the cliffs. If I really leave, he may not be as motivated to do those things. He might just take the kingdoms like he originally planned and let everyone below suffer."

"So, you care more about people you don't know than yourself?"

"I wouldn't put it like that…"

"That's what you're saying, Ivory."

I ignored my brother's stare because I didn't want to see his pity. "Father is at the cemetery. I'm going to visit if you want to come."

The pain moved into his eyes once again, reminded of our harsh reality. "Yeah. Let's go."

———

His tombstone was beside Mother's. The earth was fresh on top, the tombstone pristine rather than weather-worn like Mother's. A breeze moved through the grass, and the white jasmine flowers bowed with every gust.

I stared at his name carved into the stone and thought about everything I'd never said. "I started to wonder if he was responsible for her death. Maybe he wanted to be unattached. Maybe he wanted to have his whores in peace. I meant to ask him…but never got the chance."

"You don't really think that, do you?" he whispered.

"I don't know…"

"He loved her."

"That's what I tell myself."

"And even if he did, he never would have admitted it."

"I guess."

"And if he did, I wouldn't mourn his death."

The breeze blew into my eyes, making me shut them tight so they wouldn't sting. "Do you think he deserves this?"

Ryker turned to look at me.

"He justified his invasion of Delacroix, and I don't fault him for that. But what he did to Huntley's mother... Do you think he deserves this?"

"Yes."

I turned to look at him, surprised by his answer.

"But not in the way it played out. Not in the way his daughter was used and made a fool."

My eyes closed again in a cringe.

"Even if he did deserve it, that doesn't justify what Huntley did."

I gave a sniff. "I don't want to live in this kind of world anymore. I don't want to have to debate the morality between two men I love—" It made me sick to describe Huntley that way, when his love for me hadn't been enough. "I don't want to be married into a family that deserted everyone down below with impunity. And I don't want to be the daughter of the man who raped the queen just for the sake of torture. I don't want to be a part of any of this."

"Yeah, me neither."

"I don't want children to be sacrificed to Necrosis. I don't want Delacroix's citizens to be tricked into believing they're the winners of a fantastic lottery rather than used as a sacrifice. I don't want any of this."

Ryker was quiet for a long time. "Well, you're Queen of Delacroix now. Soon, you'll be Queen of the Kingdoms. Then you'll be Queen of All. You can make this world into whatever you want it to be."

"Yeah… I guess."

"And if Huntley disagrees…kill him."

I couldn't even entertain the idea, not even as a fantasy. "I would never do that."

Ryker released a drawn-out sigh. "He's forcing you to stay with him—"

"It's more complicated than that, Ryker. I would never hurt him, and I don't want to even suggest it. And I would never want you to hurt him either."

He gave me an incredulous look. "You still love him."

I avoided his stare.

"We're standing over Father's grave, and you still love him."

"Ryker, love doesn't just die—"

"It does when he betrays your trust and murders your father."

"Come on, you know it's more complicated than that."
Maybe I'd had time to reflect on how deeply complicated this was, how there were no heroes in this story,
only villains on both sides. It was all about power. That
was all anyone cared about. There was no right. No
wrong.

"It's not complicated at all, Ivory. You pledged to help
him in exchange for your father's well-being. He took
that promise and pissed on it." He marched off, leaving
me standing alone at the grave site.

The wind whipped in my hair, and the sting moved past
my eyes and into my heart. Now I'd never felt more
alone, standing over my father's dead body, my heart
weeping. Huntley made me feel whole, made me feel
like I had my own family, made me feel like I had my
own person who would be on my side, no matter what.
The loss of that was somehow the worst part.

"I'm sorry for your loss."

I turned at the voice, not having heard her approach.

Queen Rolfe came to my side, dressed in her long-
sleeved black dress, her hair pulled back in a braid.
She'd stared at me with callous eyes on many occasions,
but this wasn't one of them. Her eyes looked sincere,
which didn't seem possible.

"I assume you're here to spit on his grave."

Her hands came together at her waist, her posture rigid and stiff, as if her throne accompanied her wherever she went. "I came only to give my condolences. I lost my parents at a young age. I know your sorrow."

"I prefer your cold truths to your empty lies, Your Highness."

She stared at the headstone for a moment before she looked at me again. "I won't pretend that his death doesn't bring me peace. But I'm truly sorry that it happened. I'm truly sorry that you had to witness that. And I'm truly sorry that my son didn't keep his promise to you."

She'd never spoken to me like that before, in the same tone that she spoke to Huntley. It was straightforward, but it was also embedded with affection. Her blue eyes pierced mine with apology, and when I couldn't take it anymore, I looked away.

"I've never seen my son so miserable."

"I feel a million times worse than he looks."

"I'm sure," she said. "I feel like I'm partially responsible for this because if I hadn't been there weeping over my late husband, I don't think Huntley would have done what he did."

"That's a poor excuse."

"Not an excuse, Ivory. I'm sure you've noticed the bond between us, which is distinctly different from the one I share with Ian. We were both traumatized by that night, and I know Huntley hates himself for not stopping my torture. He went into a blind rampage and lost control over his faculties. He wasn't himself."

"Huntley had every right to exact his revenge for what my father did. He had every right to avenge what happened to you. He had every right to chop off his hand, burn his face against hot coals, carry out whatever torture he deemed fit. All I asked was one simple thing—not to kill him. Don't act as if I'm being unreasonable."

"That was not my intention. I just don't want this to divide you."

"Too late for that."

She was quiet for a long time. "You're the best thing that's ever happened to him—and I don't want him to lose you."

The words were a hook in my chest, and I felt myself turn to look at her once more.

"I mean that."

"I assumed you would be ecstatic at our falling-out."

She shook her head. "Not in the least. When Huntley told me what happened, I was very disappointed in him. A man is only as good as his word—and he broke it. His relationship with you is much more important than my closure. At the end of the day, your father's death doesn't bring back my husband. It doesn't erase what happened. It changes nothing."

I looked at the tombstone again.

"I know you're hurt right now. But please forgive my son."

"I appreciate what you're doing, but this is between him and me."

She turned quiet.

"Will you do something for me?"

Her answer was immediate. "Anything."

I looked at her again. "You said you knew how to break our marriage."

Her eyes immediately turned guarded, and her breaths grew heavy.

"Tell me how."

She held my stare and her silence.

"You ordered for me to be raped. You threw me to the Teeth, and now my body is marked with scars I'll carry for the rest of my life. You owe me."

Her eyes shifted back and forth between mine.

"I healed the dragons. I saved HeartHolme. I gave you Delacroix."

Still nothing.

"Tell me, Your Highness."

"Athena."

My breath halted. "Sorry?"

"Call me Athena."

I'd never heard anyone address her by her first name. Even her sons addressed her as Your Highness most of the time.

"You're a queen now. You're my equal. You're my daughter. You've earned it."

It was one of those rare moments in life when I was speechless. Truly without words. Even my mind was without thoughts.

"I will tell you. But you must wait a year."

"Why?"

"Because I think you'll feel differently by then."

———

I walked into the room with the grand dining table, the place where my family had shared our meals. It had been a nightly ritual, but once my mother was gone, we'd only done it on holidays and special occasions.

Huntley was at the head of the table, his mother to his left. The seat to his right was open. Commander

Dawson was next to Athena, and then there were Ryker and other soldiers.

I took the seat beside Ryker.

Huntley stared at me across the table, his eyes both disappointed and pissed off. The standoff lasted for nearly thirty seconds, as if he was thinking about ordering me into the seat at his side, but he made the right choice by saying nothing at all. We both knew I wouldn't have listened. "Delacroix has been invaded peacefully. No citizen life was lost, and the only soldiers who perished were those who refused to surrender. Our crest flies high on our banners, and this beautiful city is back to its former glory." Huntley was no longer in his black armor. Now he wore the garments of a king, a shirt with the Rolfe crest, a cloak at his back, clothes fitted perfectly to his strong frame. It showed off the bulkiness of his shoulders, his muscular arms, his wide chest.

The seamstress had created my wardrobe, long-sleeved dresses with the Rolfe crest on the sleeves. There was a discreet belt loop at the waist for my weapons if I chose to wear them. The fabric was soft but strong, and the garments were beautiful. Far more beautiful than the ball gowns I used to wear in the Capital.

But I refused to wear them.

I was still in my breeches, tunic, and boots, my sword at my hip.

Huntley continued to command the room. "We should assume that King Rutherford is aware of the conquest and the dragons. We should also assume he's preparing for war—whether it's at his border or ours." He turned to me. "The dragons secured Delacroix by their appearance only. But for the battles to come, they'll need to be prepared to fight. Storm is more malleable, but Pyre is far too skittish."

"Just because they're dragons doesn't mean it's in their nature to be killing machines."

Huntley kept a straight face, but his eyes gave away his anger. "King Rutherford will prepare for the dragons. Wouldn't be surprised if he constructed enormous crossbows to shoot them out of the sky. If you want your dragons to live, they need to be prepared. That's all I'm saying."

"And you want me to prepare them?"

His eyes drilled into me. "You're the only one I trust for the job."

I looked away, severing his attempt at intimacy.

Huntley stared at me for a moment longer before he continued. "We'll organize the Delacroix army and march on the Capital. If they come to us, we're backed against a cliff. Nowhere to retreat. No walls to hide behind. Offense is our only chance of success."

"And of the other Kingdoms?" I asked. "Delacroix can't take on everyone to the north."

"She's right," Commander Dawson said. "I don't know the sizes of their armies, but combined together, it's guaranteed to be larger than ours."

"We'll need to defeat the other Kingdoms before marching on the Capital," I said. "And we'll need to do it quickly. Our closest neighbor is Minora. Nearly the same size as Delacroix, so it could be a swift defeat with the dragons."

"What of Delacroix?" Huntley asked. "How will we defend it if we're invading other Kingdoms?"

"If our armies aren't here, there's no reason to attack," I said. "King Rutherford is an asshole, but he's not going to kill the innocent citizens who have nothing to do with us. And if their armies are in Delacroix, it'll be that much easier to take the Capital."

Huntley gave a slight nod. "Can Minora be defeated as swiftly as Delacroix with just the dragons? We wouldn't need to bring an army at all if that's the case."

"Possibly," I said.

Ryker spoke next. "I can flee to the Capital. Tell them I ran once my father was slain. Can feed them false information about us and our numbers." He turned to me. "And I can send you information as I receive it."

Huntley was quiet.

"I don't know," I said. "It's risky."

"In what way?" Ryker asked.

"They could assume you're a spy," I said. "That's what I would assume."

"If my kingdom was just taken and my father killed, why would I betray them? King Rutherford is unaware of my ideological opinions. If I didn't support your cause and was just a victim in this conquest, that's exactly what I would do. I would take a horse and ride straight there. He wouldn't question it."

But I would. "How will you communicate with us?"

"By crow, like we always do."

"Those letters could be intercepted."

"Not if I send my missives before daybreak."

The last thing I wanted was to lose my brother, not after losing my father. I turned to Huntley at the head of the table.

He stared in stony silence and didn't grant permission or denial.

"I'd have to give King Rutherford—"

"There is one king now—King Rolfe." Huntley sat with his arms on the table, that stony stare terrifying. "King of Kingdoms."

Ryker hesitated before he continued. "I'll have to share information with Rutherford. Otherwise, he'll be suspicious. And the information has to be correct. If it's not and I get caught, I'm dead."

Huntley commanded the room with his silence, his eyes glued to my brother's face, deep in thought. "Queen Rolfe, I appoint you to train the dragons. Prepare them for the war that's to come."

Queen Rolfe. No one had ever called me that before.

"Ryker, I will consider your suggestion," he said. "You will have my answer tomorrow." He turned to Commander Dawson. "We'll orchestrate our attack on Minora and prepare our soldiers to defend Delacroix in my absence. This meeting is dismissed."

SEVEN

Huntley

I OCCUPIED THE STUDY THAT ONCE BELONGED TO MY father.

He used to work at his desk, poring over old maps, drinking his whiskey straight out of the bottle and forgetting the glass. The fire had burned in the hearth, the curtains drawn shut because it was distracting, and I'd sharpened my knife as I'd sat there. My mother had warned that I was too young to handle weapons, to sharpen them with my small hands, but my father always insisted on raising a man—not a boy.

Now I sat there alone and could barely feel his presence.

The room was masked with evil, masked with the faded scent of whores, of spilled scotch that absorbed into the wood. Maybe what I did was wrong. Maybe my family was guilty of the same crimes as Faron. But I still felt like I'd honored my father's memory by stabbing his enemy through the throat.

The door opened and my mother entered. "Am I interrupting?"

I'd been sitting there for an hour, haunted by ghosts. "No."

She approached the desk, her hands together at her waist. "You're in a foul mood."

"I'm always in a foul mood." My elbow was propped on the armrest, my closed fist underneath my chin.

She stared at me for a while. "What is it, son?"

I dropped my arm and straightened in the chair. "It doesn't feel the same."

She took a look around, as if searching for my father's belongings. "I've noticed the same thing. The bedchamber, the hallways, the castle doesn't have the same spirit as it once did. Faron occupied our home for too long."

I stared at the surface of my desk, appreciating how many long years had passed.

"I had a conversation with Ivory this afternoon."

I kept my eye on my wife from a distance. My men reported her whereabouts throughout the day, so I always knew where she was. I knew she could handle herself if danger were to appear, but I also knew she was devastated by grief and didn't carry her sword, even though I'd asked her to three times. Just because the conquest of Delacroix had been smooth didn't mean that everyone accepted my reign—even though I was the true king.

"She wants to know how to break your marriage."

My chin lifted at her words, an invisible sword piercing my heart. "Did you tell her?"

She shook her head.

I knew Ivory was angry. I knew she meant every word she said. But I hadn't thought she'd take it that far.

"I told her I would in a year."

My eyes were on my mother again. "Why would you do that?"

"Because she reminded me how indebted I am to her—and she's right."

"I'm your son—"

"That's more than enough time to fix this, Huntley."

"You don't know how stubborn my wife is."

"She's not as stubborn as you think."

My eyes narrowed.

"I eavesdropped on a conversation she had with her brother. Ryker suggested they use you to get what they want, and once you've served your purpose, they kill you. Ivory becomes Queen of the Kingdoms. And you'll pay for what you've done with your life."

My eyes dropped as my heart tightened into a painful fist.

"Your wife's response?"

I still didn't look at her.

"She said she would never hurt you. Forbade her brother from doing the same."

The tightness in my chest vanished, and I inhaled a slow breath.

"She loves you still—and said it aloud."

I knew she did, but it was still a relief to hear it.

"The marriage remains unbroken. All you need to do is fix it."

————

When I entered the bedchambers, Ivory was already in her room, judging by the closed door. I removed my weapons and set them on the table, and then I unfastened the buttons of the uniform and hung it up in the closet. The material was lightweight and comfortable, but I still preferred my heavy armor. "Ivory." I put on my lounge pants, black and made of soft cotton, and approached her door.

There was no answer, so I opened the door and stepped inside.

She'd fallen asleep on the couch, books scattered around her, and the fireplace had gone cold. I tossed on more logs and stoked the flames as I stared at her.

Her knees were to her chest with her arms wrapped around her body, clearly cold.

I scooped her into my arms and carried her to my bed.

She stirred slightly but never really woke up.

I got her under the sheets and pulled the blankets to her shoulders so the warmth would be sealed around her. I reminded myself of my father when he found me asleep somewhere around the castle then delivered me to bed. The other side of the bed was vacant, and I could probably slip inside without her noticing. All my life, I'd preferred to sleep alone, except when I had a whore in the middle of the night and was too kind to throw her out. But I'd become accustomed to Ivory beside me, to her deep and even breaths, the way she tossed and turned in a nightmare. I was always the first thing she reached for.

But I knew I was exiled from her bed.

Just not her heart.

———

Commander Dawson served the now-elder Queen Rolfe, so I needed my own second-in-command. I selected Brutus, the man who served by my side in every war, who didn't flinch when an army of ten thousand marched on his gates.

Commander Brutus entered the dining room. "Her Majesty said she's not hungry."

I'd spank her ass right now if I could. "If she doesn't get her ass in here, I'll come get her myself. Tell her that."

He nodded and dismissed himself.

I didn't wait for her to join me before I started breakfast. Instead of a ridiculous royal spread of more food than I could ever eat, I requested a simple plate of breakfast meats, potatoes, and sliced toast.

Minutes later, she came into the dining room, dressed in her armor and weapons, like she intended to work with the dragons right after breakfast was concluded. She dropped into the chair across from me, barely making eye contact with me.

A servant poured her a cup of coffee then put a plate of food in front of her. He dismissed himself, leaving us alone together.

I ate my food as my eyes focused on her across the table. "We make decisions together, so when you refuse my request for an audience, you're wasting my time along with everyone else's."

"Don't scold me."

"Don't act like a child."

Her eyes widened with fire.

"You're Queen of Delacroix—act like it."

She chewed the inside of her cheek like she wanted to say something but couldn't find words scathing enough.

I took a few more bites of my food and watched her ignore hers. "You can be pissed at me all you want, but we're in a war right now, so you'd better get your shit together. Keep it separate."

She shifted her gaze away for a while. "Fine. So, what did you want to talk about?"

"Sending Ryker to the Capital. What's your opinion on it?" I stabbed a breakfast sausage with my fork and took a bite. I knew she was loyal to me behind all that rage and resentment, so I trusted her assessment.

"I think it makes sense—if he doesn't get caught."

"You don't think he'll tell Rutherford everything and turn on us?"

"No." Her answer was immediate, without a shred of doubt. "He's not happy about what you did to my father, but he supports our cause all the same. He wouldn't betray me. He wouldn't betray what we're working toward."

That was enough to convince me. "Then I think he should go."

"He should leave immediately. If he waits any longer, Rutherford will be suspicious."

"I agree," I said. "He'll leave this afternoon, and I'll take Storm and some men to Minora. It should be conquered before the Capital has any idea what happened."

"And what about me?" she asked, eyebrows furrowed.

"You'll stay here."

"And do what?" she asked incredulously.

"Rule. I doubt Rutherford will attack Delacroix before I return, and if he does, you can flee on Pyre."

"I'm not worried about me, asshole," she snapped. "You think I'm just going to stay behind while you conquer a city by yourself?"

I did my best to suppress the grin that wanted to appear on my face, but it was impossible. It came through, seeing her love and loyalty bright like a beacon.

"What?"

My grin widened. "Nothing."

"I think it makes more sense for both of us to go."

"I'd rather keep you safe."

"Well, I want to keep you safe too. Every step of this journey has been made together. We aren't separating now."

"Alright. Then I'll have Commander Jerome stay behind and protect Delacroix."

"Minora will concede much quicker with two dragons rather than one."

"One is enough if you ask me."

"They won't separate anyway."

"You're going to have to convince them to eventually."

She gave me a hard stare. "If we won't separate, how can I convince them to?"

I'd never known a woman who could love me so much and hate me so much at the same time.

"It may be imperative for the two of them to be in different places at once. If we claim the rest of the Kingdoms, it'll be easier if we can maintain order by dragon flight. I could visit all Kingdoms in the same day if I could fly to each of them. And I could leave my queen behind, knowing her dragon will defend her."

"They aren't always going to be around, Huntley. Once Dunbar is gone, they have no purpose here."

"Do they have a purpose there?" I asked. "You and Pyre have become close. I imagine he wouldn't want to leave you."

"I'm sure he'll visit, but he'll have his own life. He won't be interested in helping us maintain order. Just because they're dragons doesn't mean they're innately violent and domineering."

"Maybe they are—they've just forgotten."

She finally grabbed her fork and took a bite of her eggs. Her head was down and her eyes were focused on her food, but her mind seemed elsewhere.

"What is it?"

"I worry about my brother. Just when we're together again, we're apart."

"Ryker has more than proven himself. He's capable of taking care of himself."

"You don't know Rutherford. You don't know the Capital."

"You forget that I was a Blade Scion, that I was a spy right under their noses, and they had no idea. You forget that I was selected as one of the greatest fighters for the king, one of the few worthy enough to defend him."

She lifted her chin and stared at me for a while. "Then you know he's intelligent. Really intelligent."

"Are you saying your brother isn't?"

She shrugged. "He's a smartass… I'll say that much."

I gave a slight chuckle then took another bite of my sausage.

For just a brief moment, it felt the way it used to, the two of us against everyone else.

EIGHT

Ryker

I COULDN'T PACK ANYTHING, NOT WITHOUT RAISING suspicion, so all I could take was my armor and a few small supplies.

Effie watched me gather my things, sitting at the edge of the bed. "Should I stay here?"

"You're coming with me."

"I am?" she asked. "How will you explain that?"

I threw my pack over my shoulder. "Effie, once King Rutherford knows the Runes have reached the top of the cliffs and taken Delacroix, he's not going to care who you are or what you are to me."

Her eyes dropped down. "I guess that makes sense. But will they let me stay in the castle with you?"

"Where I go, you go." We grabbed a couple things for her then departed my bedchambers for the front of the castle. It was a sunny day, but a coldness had settled over the surface as fall stepped onto the stage. Soon, there would be orange pumpkins in the fields, autumn squash on the dinner table, pomegranate seeds sprinkled on top of salads.

Ivory was there waiting for us, in her casual clothes like she'd been working with the dragons since the morning. Her hands were together at her waist, a mannerism she'd had since childhood. She didn't do it often, and when she did, it meant she was nervous. Her eyes turned to me, and they flashed with a mother's worry.

"I'll be fine. You think I would have volunteered otherwise?"

"You're an idiot, so that doesn't mean much."

"You think I'd endanger Effie?"

Her eyes softened slightly. "Be careful, alright?"

"When am I not careful?" I asked. "I saved us from the Teeth, didn't I?"

She turned to Effie and gave her a long embrace. "Thanks for going with him."

"Where he goes, I go." She hugged my sister just as hard, as if this journey had made them sisters.

Ivory pulled away and gave me a long stare. "I feel like I just got you back."

My hands moved to her arms, and I gave her a squeeze. "And once you've claimed the Capital in your name, we'll be together again."

"Then we've got to go after Necrosis…" She gave a sigh. "That'll be a whole new pain in the ass."

"Let's cross that bridge when we come to it." I gave her a clap on the shoulder before I pulled her in for a hug.

She rested her forehead against my chest and squeezed me, just the way Mom used to. "I'll see you soon."

"Can't wait to see you fly in on the back of a dragon. Light up the sky and everything below." I lifted my gaze and saw Huntley appear behind her, in the uniform of the king, a black long-sleeved shirt with the feather crest in the center. A cape blew behind him in the breeze, and his broadsword sat on his hip. Ever since he'd taken control of Delacroix, he became a lot more menacing. Hardly said anything, but his animosity was in the energy around him.

Ivory pulled away and sucked a deep breath into her lungs. "I'm normally not so bad at this sort of thing, but after everything that's happened… I just never know when it's going to be the last time."

Huntley's eyes shifted away—like he knew exactly what that meant.

"This isn't the last time," I said. "Even if your piece-of-shit husband has a change of heart."

"Ryker."

"What?" My eyes moved back to hers.

"He's not a piece-of-shit husband. He's an asshole for what he did, but he's always been good to me. Always looked out for me. His crime doesn't erase all the good things he's done."

I'd wanted to take a jab at Huntley's expense, but instead, I'd gotten my sister to recite a goddamn poem about him. "I'll send a letter when I can." I turned around and walked away with Effie beside me, ready to head to the Capital and hope for the best.

NINE

Ivory

WHY? PYRE STOOD IN FRONT OF ME, HIS BROTHER Storm in the distance behind him.

"Don't you want to be able to defend yourself?"

He tucked his wings into his sides. *I don't know.*

"No, you do know. You just don't have any confidence."

If your legs had been sawed off, you would understand.

Every time he mentioned what had happened to him, it was like a fresh wound all over again. With his wings cut off, he hadn't even looked like a dragon anymore, just a large lizard. His pain permeated the air and was absorbed into my lungs. "You're going to prevent that from ever happening to yourself again. Think about it that way."

He turned his gaze away, looking over the plains.

"I know you're scared, Pyre. But you're a fire-breathing dragon. Everyone is terrified of *you*—as they should be. I just want to give you a boost in your confidence, so when the time comes, you're ready to snap spines in two with those razor-sharp teeth."

I wasn't always like this. Young and naïve, I used to think I was invincible. Look where that got me.

"Pyre." I stepped closer to him. "Once we defeat Necrosis and return to your homeland to defeat King Dunbar, what will you do then?"

He dropped his chin and looked at me again.

"You're going to punish him for what he did to you. Right?"

He still didn't say anything.

"You're going to char him alive or break his bones. You're going to rip him limb from limb and toss his body parts to the wolves. You're going to make him shit his pants, alright? You're going to make him pay for what he did to you. For what he did to your mother. That's what you want?"

Yes.

"Then let's prepare you for that. Think of it that way."

Alright.

"I want to hear you say it."

Say what?

"That you're going to make that fucker shit his pants. Come on!"

Yes…I'm going to make him shit his pants.

"Again."

This time, he squatted down and opened his wings, releasing a loud roar right in my face. *Roooooooooooaaaaaaaaar.*

My hair flew back from my face, and I toppled over.

I'm going to make him shit his pants.

I was on the ground with a sore ass, but I never felt better. "Attaboy."

———

I spent the entire day training with Pyre.

Storm did his own thing, spending his time in solitude. He'd always been the more aggressive of the two, so he didn't need any of my pep talks or instruction. He sat in the distance, watching us as he ate one of the farmers' livestock.

"Don't forget to use your tail. It's completely coated in armor with spikes. If you're ever stuck on the ground, you can use that to kill twenty men at once."

If I use my tail, you'll be dead.

71

"Just want to make sure you don't forget."

Ivory?

"Yes?"

With this armor on my wings, does that mean they can't be cut? He lifted one wing and turned his head to examine it.

"Your armor is pretty sturdy, so I assume so. They'd have to take it off first."

Is there a way to lock it in place?

"I don't know. But remember, Pyre. Even if that did happen, which it won't, I can always fix you."

He turned forward once again. *Yes…but what if you perish?*

"I'm not going anywhere, Pyre. I'm a tough bitch, and even if that weren't true, my husband is a psychopath."

Are things well with you?

I wiped the sweat from my forehead before I took a seat in front of him. "Not really."

That makes you sad.

"Of course it makes me sad. Every time I think of my father, I think of what Huntley did. And every time I think of Huntley, I think of what he did to my father. I'm a grown woman who doesn't need anybody, but it's still hard to realize you're orphaned."

You have your brother, just as I have mine.

"I know…"

And if Huntley is your husband, he's your family as well.

"I know that too."

I've seen the way he looks at you. The way he loves you. It's hard for me to understand why he would do that without reason.

"He did have a reason. A good reason. But he also promised he wouldn't do that, so…"

What were his reasons?

"My father murdered his…then raped his mother." As I said it out loud, the shame washed over me.

Pyre stared at me for a while. *Those are horrendous crimes. It's hard for me to hold him accountable under those circumstances.*

"I know. But my father tried to flee the bottom of the cliffs, and when he got up here, Huntley's father denied his entry and forced him back down—even though he knew how harsh the conditions are."

Oh, I see. This is complicated.

"Very."

Both men wanted the same thing—and were willing to do anything to get it.

"Yes."

Your father returned and got his revenge.

"Yes."

And then Huntley did the same.

"Yes. But when my father was in the dungeon, I spoke to him. He said he would help us defeat Rutherford. Said he would apologize for what he'd done. I know an apology is pretty hollow for what he did, but my father isn't the kind of man that apologizes or ever admits wrongdoing, so it means something."

Pyre stared.

"I agreed to help Huntley if he promised to spare my father's life…and he didn't."

Pyre bowed his head slightly.

"What do you think?" Pyre had become my closest friend since we met. Ryker and Effie weren't always around, and I couldn't speak to Huntley about these things. Athena had become kind toward me, but I still didn't consider her a confidante. "Do you think I'm wrong for being upset?"

No.

"So, you think Huntley is wrong?"

I think you're both wrong.

My eyes dropped.

I think this divide between you has always been inevitable. If he spared your father's life, he would have come to resent you for it.

74

Every time he looked your father in the eye, he would have felt like less of a man for doing nothing. And now that he's executed your father, you resent him. This relationship never stood a chance. It was always doomed to fail.

I sucked in a quick breath through my closed teeth.

You said his mother despises you as well. Your brother despises him. Your union is causing grief to each of your families. That's not what a marriage should be. A marriage should be a union, not a divide.

With every word that echoed in my mind, it hurt more.

I'm sorry to have upset you.

"It's okay, Pyre."

———

I took a long bath in the washroom and had dinner alone in my quarters. It was a suite attached to the main bedchamber, only accessible through the main doorway. It gave me privacy, but it also made it impossible to get to me without going through Huntley first. A wall separated us every night as we slept, and as I lay there alone, I swore I could hear his deep and even breaths.

Now I sat in the chair by the fireplace, my eyes focused on the pages of my book without really reading it. I read the same sentence three times because I couldn't concentrate. My mind always traveled to the source of my heartbreak.

75

My bedroom door opened, and Huntley appeared in his just his undershorts, his powerful body commanding the room as if he were in uniform. He approached me by the fire, looking down at me with his arms by his sides.

A sudden urge came over me. A yearning for intimacy. A need for his warm chest against my back. Those thick arms strapped around my body like tight ropes. I inhaled a slow breath then exhaled all those feelings. "Something you needed?" I kept the bite out of my voice as best I could.

He dropped into the opposite armchair, sitting on the very edge of the cushion. "Wanted to check on you."

"I'm fine," I said quickly. "Just reading my book and enjoying my night."

He stared at me with those intelligent blue eyes, seeing past my lies, seeing past my excuses. "A couple hours ago, the pain started." His hand rubbed his chest, right over his heart. "Throbbing. Agonizing. Never-ending." He dropped his hand and kept up his stare. "What happened?"

I forgot about our strange connection, the way we could feel each other's heartache. His started right away and reduced to a low simmer. I got so used to feeling it that I hardly noticed it anymore. I closed the book and set it on the table beside me. "I talked to Pyre."

"Is he alright?"

"He's fine. But he said some things…"

"Such as?"

My eyes dropped. "That we were always doomed to fail."

His stare was hot on my face. Burning.

"Your family hates me, and my family hates you. Even if you hadn't killed my father, you would have resented me. Your mother would have resented you. And now Ryker is angry with me because I defend you…in some ways." I shook my head. "We never had a chance. We married for political reasons, but those were the wrong reasons." I lifted my gaze again.

He was calm but furious at the same time. "We can tell each other that was the reason, but we both know that's bullshit. It was an excuse. It was a way for us to sidestep our differences and be together."

My eyes dropped again.

"Baby, I admit we've got everything stacked against us—"

"I told you not to call me that anymore…"

He went quiet, as if I'd slapped him. "Whether I call you that or not, it doesn't change the fact that that's what you are. You're my baby. You're my wife. You're my soul mate."

"Well, I don't want to hear it, okay?" I raised my eyes and looked at him once more.

His face was tight with tension, like he might explode in a scream. "We have everything stacked against us, but that doesn't matter."

"I think it does matter—"

"It doesn't matter when we love each other. If you didn't love me anymore, then we would be in trouble, but you do. I broke my promise, but your feelings didn't change, and that tells me they'll never change. That tells me that nothing in this world is ever going to rip us apart. So, I don't give a fuck if our families are sworn enemies—that's not going to come between us."

My arms crossed over my stomach, my knees coming to my chest. "My brother hates you—"

"I'm not a fan of his either."

"If my mother knew what my husband did—"

"If she knew her husband raped someone, she'd want nothing to do with him."

I released a heavy sigh.

"Both of our families have done shitty things. Let's move on."

"You broke your promise—"

"And I apologized. I will apologize again if that makes you feel better."

"It doesn't."

"Then I won't bother." His angry eyes stared at me so hard. "I don't care if your brother likes me. He's not the one I'm married to. And my mother has taken you in as a daughter. She could have told you how to break our marriage to finally get rid of you, but she didn't. Elora respects you, whether she admits it or not. We've made progress, Ivory. We're not going to throw that all away now. You really want to replace me with a man you don't love? To spend your years wondering where I sleep at night? To look into your son's face and wish you saw my eyes instead of a man you don't care for?"

I looked away, the image making me sick.

"Then it's you and me—forever. Understand?"

I kept my eyes down.

"Ivory."

I forced myself to raise my chin. "I need to forgive you first."

"Then forgive me."

I gave a slight shake of my head. "I'm not ready to do that."

The anger remained in his eyes, bottled up inside behind his irritated visage. "I'm not living apart anymore. We sleep in the same bed from now on. I'm not having my queen, my wife, sleep in a different room."

"I'm not having sex with you—"

"You bet your ass you are."

My eyes widened at his demand.

"It's been two weeks, and I've been losing my goddamn mind. You must be too."

"My hand works just fine."

"And I bet you pretend that I'm that hand."

My eyes shifted away, trying to evade his accusation.

"So, would you rather think about me or be with me?"

"You're an asshole."

"No argument there." He rose to his feet and grabbed some of my things, my weapons, and my armor. "Grab your shit, Ivory." He carried everything into the bedchamber and left the door wide open.

I wanted to resist. Wanted to be stubborn. Wanted to tell him off for his arrogance. But sleeping alone every night had done nothing to make me feel better. It only made me feel more alone, made me vulnerable to the ghosts of this castle.

I grabbed my books and clothes and stepped into the royal bedchamber. The four-poster king-size bed was in the center of the room, facing the enormous fireplace. Oil paintings were on the walls, of people I didn't know and landscapes I hardly recognized. I hung up my clothes in the closet and took my toiletries into the washroom.

By the time I stepped out, a fire was burning in the hearth and Huntley was in bed. The sheets were at his waist, showing his hard abs and powerful chest. One arm was underneath his head, and his eyes watched every move I made.

I was in my silk nightgown, the material stopping at just above my knees. I hadn't worn one since I'd lived in Delacroix. Ever since I'd met Huntley, his clothes had become my nightgown. Or I didn't wear clothes at all.

The second I got under the covers, he was all over me.

He yanked down one strap then sealed his mouth over my shoulder, giving me a gentle bite with his teeth. It turned into a hungry kiss, his arm hooking around my waist and dragging me to the other side of the bed where he lay.

I felt as if a monster had grabbed me and yanked me into the darkness.

He somehow got the nightgown off me, and it was kicked away to the bottom of the bed.

I wanted to push him off, but it felt so nice to be touched again, to be cocooned in his warmth. His kiss felt like a bite, but it'd been so long since he'd devoured me. He may never have devoured me quite like this.

His hand gripped both of my tits at the same time and gave a squeeze before he hooked his thumb into my panties and tugged them off my ass. Then he yanked my shoulder and rolled me to my back, getting the panties off the rest of the way.

His heavy body moved on top of mine, pressing me into the mattress, dominating me with that ruthless gaze. His arms hooked behind my knees and forced my pelvis into a tilt, and the maniacal gleam in his eyes told me how much he wanted this, how much he missed it. He gave a push, getting past my tightness, and once he was in, he sank into me in one fluid motion. A quiet growl left his lips, just barely above his breath, full of the satisfaction he felt once he touched me, once he was surrounded by me. It was full of possession, like he'd finally claimed what was his. "My queen."

My hands latched on to his arms to hold on, my body shaking with his thrusts. My fingers dug into the hard muscles of thick arms, and with every thrust, I dug deeper and deeper. The reconnection of his body with mine was better than I ever expected it to be, so overwhelming that I couldn't suppress the moan that escaped my throat.

His perceptive eyes watched every subtle reaction I made, every attempt to resist the white-hot chemistry between us. But he knew he had me right where he wanted me. His breaths deepened and came out shaky, and red blotches formed on his skin, all the blood rushing everywhere. "This is how a king fucks his queen."

I resisted the contractions my body naturally made, the way I wanted to tighten around him and slip under the veil of unbelievable euphoria, but I controlled my body, kept it dormant as best as possible.

He moved over me even more, hitting me so deep even though he knew it hurt in the best way, and rocked his hips in a different direction, grinding his body right against my clit. "You're so fucking stubborn."

I released an unstoppable gasp, but the friction was so damn good. My body had gone to sleep these past few weeks, covered in cobwebs, and now it was more alive than it'd ever been. At odds with myself, I couldn't hold out much longer. The only thing that helped me keep it at bay was the potent stubbornness I'd had since birth.

He fucked me harder, the anger mixing with arousal in his eyes. Barely holding on and growing angrier that he had to, he took his rage out on his thrusts, making them deeper and harder. He wouldn't release unless I released first, so this was a very complicated battle of wills—and he refused to lose. "Come on, baby."

"Don't call me—"

"I can call you whatever the fuck I want right now." His hand grasped my hair, and he held on to it tightly, fisting the strands like reins to a horse. He forced my head back, forced my eyes on his. He hit the bed even harder, the headboard smacking against the wall with the pace of a running stallion. "You're my wife. You're my queen. You're mine."

The resistance snapped, and I couldn't hold on any longer. In betrayal, my hips bucked involuntarily, and while the scream remained quiet behind my lips, the tears pooled in my eyes then dripped down my cheeks. It was so good, too. So deep and throbbing. So potent and satisfying.

He couldn't wait for me to finish. His hips gave their final pumps, and he filled me with a masculine groan, conquering my body the way he'd just conquered my homeland. His cock thickened inside, twitched in victory, and dumped all of his arousal deep inside me.

He'd won.

And the look of victory in his eyes made that very clear.

TEN

Elora
_____

After I forged the sword, I tightened its shape with a hammer, making the grooves in the metal very distinctive. Then I plunged it into the pail of cool water, solidifying it. A burst of steam erupted from the bucket, along with a hiss.

The door to the shop opened. Ian appeared, dressed in the garb of royalty, the Rolfe crest on his chest. He gave me a long stare, like that was enough to address his point. "Has he come?"

"If he had, don't you think I would have told you?" I pulled the sword out of the bucket and returned it to the table. Now I had to sharpen the edges, which took quite a bit of time because the blade had to be even on both sides, had to sing as it sliced through the air. "How's being king?"

"I'm not the king. I'm just standing in for the queen."

"Alright…how's being queen, then?"

His eyes narrowed into a pissed-off expression.

I grinned and kept working.

"Assuming Necrosis doesn't attack again, rulership is easy."

"All things are easy in peace." I skimmed the side of the blade and carved out its sharpness. Now that I'd experienced Ice, the regular metal we used seemed dull. If I could get my hands on more of the material, I could make an armory of weapons that people would risk their lives for. "Have you heard from Huntley?" I left the blade on the table and addressed him directly.

"Just got his missive. They've taken Delacroix. Faron is dead."

"Awesome."

His eyebrow cocked. "You okay?"

"Uh, why wouldn't I be okay?"

"Because he was technically your father."

I rolled my eyes. "A father is more than the deed. A father is a guardian, a friend, a confidant. Raping a woman doesn't make you a father. It doesn't make you a man either. I couldn't care less that he's gone, and I hope Huntley made him suffer before it ended."

Ian let the subject drop. "Let me know when he approaches you."

"Where will I find you? At the brothels?"

He walked off. "Fuck off, Elora."

"Oh, that's right. You're queen now. So, they come to you, huh?"

He flipped me off before he walked out the door.

———

My hands were sore from working all day. The knuckles ached, and only a warm cloth could soothe the tension. I turned the lock, tested the door, and then turned around. I halted in place—and came face-to-face with a man.

I considered myself a perceptive person, but I hadn't heard his footsteps, heard the sound of his breaths. Caught off guard without my hilt in hand, I couldn't even draw my sword. I appeared unfazed, even though my heart was loud as a drum. "What took you so long?"

He pushed his hood down and revealed his face, which was on display in the firelight from the torch that hung overhead. He had the same bright-blue eyes, the same chiseled jawline, the same hostile aura. "You prevailed over Necrosis."

"You bet your ass we did."

"But my gift had nothing to do with it."

"No, not really."

His eyes glanced to the door behind me.

"Do I need to let you in?" I asked sarcastically. "Or can you do that yourself?"

Like Ian, he kept the same hard expression. There was no reaction in his eyes, just a void.

I rolled my eyes and unlocked the door I'd just locked, and we entered the forge. It was dark, so I had to light all the candles once again to bring the shop into a nice glow. The fire from my forge was out, and that was usually enough to keep this place lit up like a bonfire. I leaned against the counter with my arms crossed and stared. "Ready to tell me who the hell you are and how you know so much about Necrosis?"

His eyes scanned the room for a moment, but it didn't seem like he actually cared about anything he looked at. His eyes were glossed over, just the way Ian's were whenever he was deep in thought. His black cloak hung behind him, and the opening in the front revealed a hard chest in a tunic, narrow hips, and long legs that gave him a height much taller than mine. "I don't recall agreeing to answer any of those questions."

"You're going to have to. At least, you do if you want my help."

He finally turned his gaze back to me. "That wasn't the deal. I gave you the Ice—and now you're in my debt."

"The Ice wouldn't have saved us from Necrosis. We would have perished—and I wouldn't be alive to owe you anything." We'd lost the battle. I'd felt it in my heart long before Necrosis breached the wall. I could have made a million arrows, and it wouldn't have turned the tide, wouldn't have saved my people, and the feeling of hopelessness was unbearable.

"But it'll be instrumental for the war to come."

"Two swords aren't enough to make any substantial difference. We have two dragons now."

"Dragons that they know about. Dragons that they'll be prepared to fight."

I crossed my ankles. "What are they going to do against two dragons—"

"Shoot them down with crossbows."

"A crossbow isn't enough—"

"Big crossbows." He silenced me with his gaze, in a way that was naturally menacing.

My heart started to beat a little harder as I stared at his face, tried to penetrate that dark gaze. "Who are you?"

His eyes flicked away, as if he didn't owe me an answer.

"You've already shown your cards. You need me."

He ignored me.

"You need me a lot more. I can promise you that."

I stepped closer to him, my arms still crossed over my chest. My eyes dug deep into his cheek, like a blade sawing through flesh to get to the bone. I noticed the definition of his features more, the pronounced angle of his cheekbones, the way his jawline was sharper than the blades I crafted every day. "What do you want?"

After a long pause, he looked at me again. "Asylum."

My eyes shifted back and forth between his, my brain trying to understand the request. "Asylum from what?"

He held my gaze this time. "Necrosis."

"What do they want from you?"

Now he looked away. "It's not what they want from me. It's what I am to them."

"Which is?"

He was absolutely still, not even drawing breath. His eyes were focused on my cold forge, just a few hot embers still visible underneath the ash. "I'm one of them."

———

I'd never felt threatened by anyone, not friend or foe, but now I was aware of the danger I was in. Just a few feet away stood one of the vilest creatures in existence, something of the void, a monster that fed on human souls to satisfy his atrocious hunger. My instinct was to reach for my sword, but he was armed as well, and the second I moved, he would do the same.

When I said nothing, his eyes met mine. "I'm not going to hurt you."

"I know—because I would never allow you to."

He stared for nearly a solid minute, his eyes locked on me like an archer focused on a target. Then he stepped away, as if the distance between us would prove he meant me no harm.

Now, my eyes scanned his body for signs of darkness. But since most of his body was concealed, I couldn't see his bare skin. He could be starving this very moment, or he could be satiated after just feeding on a soul.

I wasn't sure which one was worse.

Once he was near the stone forge, he regarded me. "It's not just me. There are others. Others who want to be free of them."

"But you *are* them."

"Not by choice. They turned me a long time ago."

"They…can do that?" When Necrosis invaded our lands, it was always to feed. No other purpose. I'd never heard of someone being turned into one of them.

"Yes. It's rare, but it happens."

"Why did they turn you?"

He never answered. "Yes, I'm Necrosis. But I'm not an Original. And because I'm not, I'm different. The same is true of others, others who ask for asylum as well. I warned you they were coming, and I gave you Ice to increase your odds of survival. You prevailed, so now I ask you to open your lands to us."

"I'm not the queen."

"I know."

"She would never agree to help you."

"Then you know exactly why I chose to come to you." He pivoted his body toward me, looking me straight in the eye. "She would strike me down the second the words left my mouth, which would be a detriment to your people since I can be an asset to HeartHolme."

"At least you claim to be…"

His eyes went still, sharp like daggers. "If that were true, you should be afraid of me. And you don't look the least bit afraid."

"Don't flatter yourself. I'm not afraid of anything."

"We're all afraid of something. Maybe it's not me, but you have fears just like everyone else."

My arms tightened over my chest as a shiver moved along my skin. "If Necrosis knew we'd granted you and the rest of your people refuge, they would come after us even more."

"You already have that problem." He took a seat at the edge of the stone, his posture perfectly upright, his knees far apart. He took his gaze off me and looked elsewhere. "Now that they know you have dragons, you're even more of a threat than you were before. They won't stop until HeartHolme no longer sits on the map."

Was I naïve to think they wouldn't return because of our dragons? Was I naïve to enjoy our victory longer than I should? "I don't think the warning and the Ice are enough to earn you entry into our lands."

"We'd fight with you."

"How many of you are there?"

He took a long pause. "Twelve."

"That's not enough to make a difference."

"I know everything about Necrosis—and can share every detail."

"What kind of details?"

"How to enter their lands unseen. Details of the Three Kings. Weaknesses."

"The Three Kings?" I asked.

"They're brothers. And they've ruled Necrosis since the beginning. Age has driven them into madness. All living things are only meant to live one lifetime. Existence is so unbearable it shouldn't go on longer than necessary." His forearms rested on his thighs, and he dropped his eyes to examine the floor at his feet. "The reason why you've never discovered Ice before is because it doesn't exist in your lands—only in ours."

"So there is more."

"But it's inaccessible to your kind. Give us refuge, and I will share all the details of Necrosis—how to slip past their borders and retrieve the Ice, how to give you the best chance to defeat them once and for all."

"I still don't understand what's in it for you."

He lifted his chin.

"If they're gone, you'll be the last of your kind."

"I'm not one of them. I'm just a very poor imitation."

"Even so…you could live forever."

"Like I already said, living forever is overrated. Every time the body grows weak, I have to suck the soul out of an innocent person. Every time the process starts, I vow to let myself starve to death. But when the hunger takes over…I become a different person. I can't override it. I can't ignore it. I have to feed."

"Whether Necrosis exists or not, that's still your fate."

"But it'll punish them for what they've done to me—and they won't be able to turn more people."

"You do realize that we can't allow you and the twelve others to live, right?"

His expression didn't change—as if he weren't the least bit surprised.

"Can't allow you to take away someone's soul, someone's afterlife. All Necrosis will need to be eradicated—and we can't make an exception for you."

"Never asked for one."

"So…this is basically going to get you killed."

"I'm aware."

"And you still want to do this?"

His confident stare was his answer.

"There's nothing after this for you." I didn't know this man, didn't even know his name, and I pitied him.

"After everything is said and done…I hope I can get my soul back."

"How?"

"By taking the souls of the Three Kings—and giving them to the Bone Witch."

———

I passed the guards at the entrance to the castle and made my way inside. There was a fire in every hearth, warmth in every stone, in every fiber of the rugs that lined the hallways. I made it to the top floor, where Ian occupied the guest quarters.

Asher made me wait for him in the dining room until he was ready to see me.

Ian emerged, in a black tunic and breeches, his clothes and hair a bit disheveled. He dropped into the chair at the head of the table, filling his role as king of Heart-Holme perfectly, as if Queen Rolfe had never occupied the throne. "What did he say?"

"How'd you know that's why I'm here?"

"It's nine in the evening. Why else would you wake me?"

"You're asleep before nine?" I asked in disbelief.

His scowl deepened. "I'm up at sunrise, overseeing this Kingdom. I don't have the luxury to sleep in every morning like you do."

"Still…nine is pretty lame."

He gave an aggravated sigh. "Elora, what did he say?"

"It's quite the story…" I told him everything that transpired in my shop just an hour ago.

Ian listened intently. Didn't ask any questions. Just sat there with his arms on the armrests, hanging on to every word, his blue eyes focused on a single spot on my face.

"He seeks refuge in HeartHolme in exchange for our help—along with twelve others."

Ian was quiet, his expression hard, as if I hadn't told him that wild tale.

"I've never been that close to a Necrosis without striking them down…"

"He seeks an alliance—and his request is denied." He straightened in the chair and shifted his body forward, his arms moving to the surface of the wood.

"Uh…what?"

"We can never trust him."

"Doesn't matter. His information is vital. Through him, we can get more Ice for our weapons."

"No."

"I'm sure we can keep them isolated to a section of HeartHolme—away from everybody else."

"That's not why."

"Then why?" I asked.

"Because he could be a spy."

"A spy?" I asked.

"So Necrosis will know everything about us. Did you tell him the dragons have vacated HeartHolme?"

"No. And he didn't ask."

He released a quiet sigh. "We've got to catch this guy. Next time he contacts you, capture him or kill him. He can't roam this city freely like he's one of us. He could be feasting on our people, and we'd have no idea."

"Why would he tell us Necrosis was coming if he was a spy?"

He gave me a cold look. "So you would trust him—and that's clearly worked."

"I don't trust him, alright? But I think he could be of great use to us."

Ian looked away.

"He gave us Ice. We never would have known it even existed if he hadn't told us about it. Maybe warning us about Necrosis could have been a ploy, but not the Ice. There was no reason to give us that information."

Ian kept his gaze averted. "He wants to betray his own kind, get himself killed, all for what?"

"To get his soul back."

"Or he could just live forever and not have to worry about it."

"Maybe. But if it were me, I'd probably do the same."

"Why did they turn him in the first place?"

I shook my head. "He didn't say. But he did say he didn't get a choice in the matter."

"And what's so special about him that Necrosis would convert him rather than eat him?"

"Look, I don't know. But I don't expect the guy to give me his entire life story during a clandestine meeting. His personal story isn't any of my business. All that matters is, we have a common enemy. We help him take down Necrosis, and he might have a shot of taking the souls of the Three Kings."

"Wait," Ian said. "I thought Necrosis didn't have souls."

"I didn't either, but it looks like these guys do. He gets his soul back, Necrosis is defeated, and he's free and so are we. It makes sense."

"You say you don't trust him…but you're really in his corner."

"I just think it makes sense, is all."

Ian looked away, and quietly, his fingertips started to drum on the surface.

"I think we should try it."

His fingers continued to drum. "It's not my decision to make."

"But we have no idea when Queen Rolfe will return."

"I'll send her a missive."

"And risk it being intercepted?" I exclaimed. "They're in the process of conquering the Kingdoms. That information could be taken by anybody, including King Rutherford. Too risky."

"Then we wait until she returns."

"We don't have time for that. Ian, you're king of Heart-Holme until she comes back. You have the opportunity to forge an alliance with somebody who can help us defeat Necrosis, and we can't wait months to take advantage of that offer. You need to run HeartHolme like she's not coming back."

"If she were here, I know her answer would be no."

"But she's not here—and we both know her stubbornness knows no bounds."

Ian looked away.

"I think we should do it."

"It's too risky—"

"It's riskier if this guy is telling the truth and we don't use him."

"Can you imagine how the Runes would feel if Necrosis was among them?" he asked incredulously, his eyes shifting to me.

"They don't need to know."

"And once they start feeding on people, what then? How do we explain that?"

"They won't."

"If they don't feed on us, then what are they going to feed off?"

I remembered what he'd said, when he got to a point of intense starvation, he couldn't control his senses anymore. His body acted on instinct, did whatever was necessary to survive. "I'm sure we can come up with an alternative."

"Like what?" he asked. "Cows? Do animals have souls?"

"Yes. But I don't think that would work. We can make them hunt in the wild."

"So, hunt other innocent people?"

"They're gonna do it whether they're in HeartHolme or not, and since their help will spare so many lives and afterlives, I don't think we should get too hung up on it. A few for the many, right?"

He gave a slight cock of his head then a shrug. "I need to speak with him before I make my decision."

"Alright, I'll talk to him."

"When?"

"I don't know. Whenever he finds me again."

ELEVEN

Elora

"PAY UP." I SNAPPED MY FINGERS THEN OPENED MY PALM wide.

Hugo gave a loud gruff in irritation. "You already took a hundred coin—"

"I don't care what I took. No one forced you to raise the stakes. Now, pay up, or I'll make you pay up."

He gave another gruff along with a glare.

I stood my ground in the bar, surrounded by men who stared at our confrontation.

He finally reached into his pocket and dropped the coin pouch into my open palm. "Cheat…"

"What was that?" I snatched the bag of money and stepped in front of him. "If you've got something to say, you should grow some balls and say it loudly. You know, what I'm doing right now."

He sidestepped me and marched out of the bar.

"Little bitch…" I opened the drawstring and counted the money before I sat on one of the stools at the bar. "I'll take a pint."

"You got it, sweetheart." The barmaid smiled at me before she filled the glass and slid it across the table toward me.

"Make that two." He sat in the chair beside me, in a black long-sleeved shirt and dark pants, his short brown hair combed back. He received a smile from the barmaid before the pint was placed in front of him. He was well-kept and well-dressed, so it was clear he didn't roam the streets all night with nowhere to go. He grabbed the mug and took a drink as he continued to face forward.

"I was wondering when you'd turn up again."

"I turn up when you stop wondering."

I pivoted on the stool and faced him, my hand resting over the top of the mug. "If we're gonna drink together, we should be on a first-name basis."

"You're obsessed with my name like it'll tell you anything about me."

"It'll tell me a lot. A name is a powerful thing. It's your identity in words. If your mother had named you something else, you probably would have been an entirely different person. It can change destiny."

"You believe that?" He turned slightly on his stool, giving me more of his direct stare, more of his hard jawline and ruthless eyes.

"Yes."

"So, if your mother had named you Rose, you think you would have been a passive flower that waits to be pruned? That relies solely on her looks to manipulate the emotions of the person who has your full attention?"

My logic had been turned against me, but I was too stubborn to admit it. "I do that every day." I grabbed the mug and took a drink, my eyes on him all the while.

A very subtle smile moved on to his lips, just enough to reach his eyes. "Bastian."

I'd never heard the name, but it somehow suited him.

"What does that tell you?"

"You're strong."

He took a drink.

"But broken."

He flinched before he set the glass down. It was a quick movement that he tried to cover up, but I noticed it.

"I relayed your message to my brother. He wishes to speak to you face-to-face."

He stared into his glass. He smelled of birchwood and fresh leaves. The thick muscles of his body pulsed with vigor, with the fuel from heavy meals of meats and breads, not souls. In every way, he looked like a man of HeartHolme, a man who worked his hands raw in the carpentry shop he owned. But he wasn't alive. He was dead. "And I should expect to walk out of there as a free man?"

"He has no intention of harming you."

"A Necrosis walks freely in HeartHolme. He'd be a poor king if he trusted me."

"Never said he trusted you. The weight of his decision is heavy, and he can't make a good one if he's never seen you in the flesh."

"What is your opinion?"

"My opinion is irrelevant."

"If you convinced your brother to even entertain this idea, then your opinion is anything but irrelevant. It has the power to influence kings and queens, which is why I came to you in the first place. You're stubborn but open-minded. You're smart but not arrogant about it."

My eyes narrowed. "You speak of me like you know me."

He faced forward and took a drink. "I've watched you for a long time, Elora."

"Strange. Because if we were in the same room together, I would have noticed you."

He turned to me, looking at me head on with eyes the color of the ocean. "Why is that?"

In the moment, I didn't think before I spoke because my mouth didn't come with a filter. I spoke my mind, and if someone didn't like it, that was their problem and not mine. But now, I actually regretted the slipup—because I didn't know how to answer the question. "You don't look like a Rune."

"What do I look like, then?" He pressed me, as if he knew I was cornered and he wanted to back me into the corner even further.

I sidestepped it altogether. "My brother said your proposal was risky, but I said it would be far riskier if your intentions are genuine and we deny your aid."

"My intentions are genuine—but there's no possible way I can ever prove that."

"My brother is a pretty good judge of character."

"Really? He's not outspoken like his elder brother, and he is certainly subdued compared to his mother."

How did he know that? "Don't mistake his quietness for weakness. Ian chooses to observe life rather than partici-pate in it. That makes his opinions more solid than the stones of our keep. Huntley makes rash decisions, like when he decided to fall for the enemy, when he declared war on the Teeth to save a single person. Queen Rolfe is too traumatized to lead a kingdom of people because her emotions guide her decisions more than her intelligence. Ian is the only one calm with logic, who can consider the stakes of any situation with real deliberation."

His eyes shifted back and forth between mine. "I always assumed you were closer to Huntley."

"I am. But that's because I'm also rash and impulsive. And I'm more stubborn than he is. My relationship with him is different because he looked after me when Queen Rolfe chose not to."

He must not have been surprised by that because he didn't ask any questions. "Would your brother be willing to meet on neutral ground? Outside HeartHolme?"

My eyes studied his face. "You know, if I were an enemy to the Runes, that's exactly what I would do. Lure King Rolfe outside his kingdom and assassinate him."

"I've been living among you for a long time. If I wanted him dead, I could have lifted a poison arrow from your storage and climbed to the roof of your shop. All I'd have to do is wait for him to visit you thirty minutes after sunrise."

My blood turned to sludge in my veins. The man had been everywhere, through my private storage in the basement, had watched my brother come visit me from a vantage point that no one saw coming.

"If I meant you harm, we wouldn't be drinking together this very moment. We wouldn't be on a first-name basis. I wouldn't admit that I know everything about you, from where you sleep to who you're sleeping with."

I held his stare, growing furious. "Are you trying to piss me off? Because the tip of my dagger has your name on it."

That slight smile returned. "Just wanted to prove a point."

"That you're an asshole."

"That no man would drag out an assassination this long."

"Ian suspects that your aid has just been a ploy to gain our trust."

"To what end? If I said nothing, Necrosis would have been at your gate before you raised the alarm. They would have poured over the top like water through a broken dam and flooded HeartHolme. Even if your dragons came, it would have been too late to battle the infestation. They would have already invaded every home and alley, killing the Runes in their sleep. The Ice is the greatest hope you have against Necrosis. It gives every Rune a fighting chance against my kind. Your trust isn't worth everything I've already offered you. Your paranoia is misplaced."

His words humbled me because I knew HeartHolme would have been lost without him. "I think it would go a long way if you met him at the castle. If you request to move the meeting, he'll only grow more suspicious, and that suspicion will cloud everything you say."

"What if he imprisons me?"

"He won't."

He stared at me.

"I won't let him."

The stare continued.

"That was why you came to me, right?"

He looked forward again. "Sounds like you believe me, then."

"I wish you would tell me more. But yes, I believe you."

———

Bastian and I walked together through the lit streets, heading to the castle that stood as a beacon of hope to all the Runes. He left his weapons behind, but he marched me to the gate like a man about to go to war. His posture was rigid and contained despite the large strides he took, and his head was always up high, as if he balanced a crown on top. "He's not good enough for you."

I turned at the comment, my eyebrows raised. "What are you talking about?"

"The man in your bed."

"Are you literally watching me through the bedroom window?"

"No. But I've seen him come and go in the middle of the night. That can only mean one thing."

"You need to get a hobby that doesn't involve stalking people."

"I've accomplished what I've set out to do—so no more stalking necessary."

"Thank the gods."

"But I'm still right—he's not good enough for you."

My head turned back. "He's just a good lay. Not that it's any of your business."

"And that's all he is to you?"

My eyes narrowed. "Why are you asking me these things?"

He never answered.

"How would you feel if I asked you something so personal? You wouldn't even tell me your name."

"Who I'm sleeping with is a lot less personal than my name."

"Damn, that's cold."

"Not as cold as you, considering the guy is enamored by you."

"He is not enamored by me——"

"For a smart girl, you aren't that observant."

I raised an eyebrow. "Who are *you* sleeping with?"

"No one."

"Really? A guy like you?"

He halted.

Shit. I halted too.

He stared at me for three hard seconds. "What's that supposed to mean?"

"I don't know… You're dark and mysterious. All you're capable of is a nighttime bang."

"Really? Because it seemed like you meant something else."

"Nope." I'd lie through my teeth until the end of time.

He moved forward again. "Cut him loose."

"Did you just try to tell me what to do?"

"No. I *told* you what to do."

"Motherfucker, who do you think you're talking to?"

He stopped again. "A woman with a heart. I've seen the way you've protected your people. I've seen the way you love your brothers. I know the guy is putting up a front because he doesn't want it to end, so you can't see it. But this relationship means a hell of a lot more to him than it does to you. You're not selfish. You aren't sadistic. So just take my word for it and end it before he really gets hurt."

All I could do was stare at him now because this man was so acquainted with my life as if he'd been a part of it for a long time. "Why do you care so much?"

"I don't," he said coldly. "But I know you do."

The conversation died, and we both continued on our way to the castle. The guards checked him for weapons, and once he was clear, we entered the main doors and stepped into the large foyer. Since he was an unwelcome visitor, a team of guards escorted us up the stairs to where the throne sat with the windows behind the chair.

The guards blocked the path of retreat, so there was nowhere for Bastian to flee.

Asher was there, his eyes always judgmental. "I'll retrieve His Highness."

It was still weird to think of Ian as a king—even if it was temporary.

If Bastian was nervous about the situation, he didn't share it. He was as calm as he was in the bar, as if our heated conversation hadn't just happened. With his arms relaxed by his sides, he stood there, his eyes on the windows that gave a view of the sky beyond.

It seemed as if I was more nervous than he was—and my neck wasn't on the line.

After minutes of silence, Ian emerged. Dressed in the garments of a king, the feather crest on his chest, he entered the room with the energy of a Rolfe, as if he owned this castle and everyone in it. He ascended the steps then slowly dropped onto the wooden throne, his arms sprawling across the armrests, his fingers curling over the edges. His broadsword was at his hip. Just like Queen Rolfe, he handled executions himself. Didn't hand the responsibility off to someone else.

Bastian stared.

Ian stared. His gaze was more perceptive, probably trying to gauge any evidence that Bastian truly was Necrosis. Without the dark marks on his skin and the strain of hard features, there was no way to recognize him for what he was. He'd fooled me. I was sure he would have fooled everyone else too—if he hadn't told me.

Ian continued his hard stare, looking a bit like Huntley with a hooded brow and angry eyes.

Bastian didn't speak—as if he refused.

Whoever held their silence longer retained the most power, and neither of these men was going to cave.

Finally, my brother did. "Speak."

Bastian remained quiet.

"You want my aid—then ask for it."

I could already tell that Ian didn't like him. But that feeling seemed to be mutual.

After another bout of silence, Bastian spoke. "I know Elora has already conveyed my desires. Without my warning, HeartHolme would have been swarmed by Necrosis, and your dragons would have arrived too late to stop it."

"Where were you when all of this happened?"

I turned to Bastian, curious to know his answer.

He finally spoke. "Watching."

"You attack us, then ask for asylum," Ian said. "Funny way to show your allegiance."

"I wasn't part of the army."

"Then what is your purpose?"

Bastian's expression remained stony.

"Do you want me to help you or not?" Ian asked. "There can be no secrets between us."

"Every detail of my life is irrelevant. I single-handedly saved HeartHolme by warning Elora, and I gave her the Ice she used to make the blade you wielded in battle. My allegiance is not to you. It's to anyone who has the power to end Necrosis forever. And the Runes seem to be the only ones with that power—and desire."

"Why would you destroy your own kind?"

"Because they aren't my kind—at least, not by choice."

"You do realize that if we wipe out Necrosis, we can't continue to let you live? Every single Necrosis must be wiped from this world. There can be no chance they can turn others and rebuild their army—and threaten our eternal salvation."

Bastian's eyes remained impassive. "We're in agreement about that."

"Even if you're instrumental in winning this war, I will kill you myself."

"If I can't get my soul back, I don't want to live anyway."

Ian stared for a while before he shifted his gaze to me. "Elora said you have to kill the Three Kings to accomplish this?"

Bastian gave a barely perceptible nod. "It's more complicated than that…but yes. I can share all my knowledge about Necrosis and lead you to victory. All I ask is, once their army is defeated, I have the opportunity to tackle the Three Kings before you kill them."

"If I grant you asylum, Necrosis will know where you stand," Ian said. "Won't that complicate things?"

Bastian gave a slight nod. "They'll want to kill you even more than they already do."

"And why do they want to kill us in the first place? For generations, Necrosis has wanted to feed on us and nothing more. Now, they want to annihilate us." Ian remained stiff in the chair. "Why?"

"Because they know you're a threat to the Kingdoms."

Ian dropped his hard expression, the bewilderment setting in.

My features mirrored his because that statement didn't make any sense.

Ian sat forward slightly, his fingers sliding forward. "Why would they care about the Kingdoms?"

There seemed to be hesitation on Bastian's part because he didn't say anything. "Do we have a deal or not? Because I'm not giving you any more information until I'm guaranteed asylum."

Ian shifted his gaze to me, silently asking my opinion.

"If we say yes, you need to tell us everything. No secrets." I stared at the side of Bastian's face.

He turned to regard me.

"We can grant you refuge behind our walls. We can give you shelter, allow your people to become Runes. You won't feed on our people, and the instant one of you does, the contract is void. You'll have to leave Heart-Holme to feed. Your identity must remain a secret. If the Runes know what you really are, they'll panic. You'll have to satiate your hunger before your skin has the chance to darken—otherwise, everyone will know. Do we have a deal?"

Bastian stared at me for a while before he looked at Ian again. "Citizens of the Kingdoms have blood much purer than those below. They have better food. They're exposed to abundant sunshine. All these factors create happier individuals, which makes their blood superior to anything that can be found at the bottom of the cliffs. That, in turn, makes their souls pristine. That's where the Three Kings feed, along with their elites."

The world was a fucked-up place—but it just got more fucked up. "You're saying that Necrosis does exactly what King Rutherford does? Sacrifices the poor to the poor. Feeds the rich with the rich."

Bastian gave a subtle nod. "Yes. Pure blood makes them more powerful."

Ian went rigid in his seat, unable to process the weight of the revelation. "How is Necrosis feeding on these people without being caught?"

"There're only a few Necrosis in the Capital," Bastian said. "No one knows they're there, so when people are murdered under suspicious circumstances, that's the last thing on their minds."

"How do they get there?" I asked. "They climb?"

"No." Bastian gave a slight shake of his head. "They fly."

———

The meeting turned informal, the three of us moving to the dining table. Wine was served, along with wild boar and roasted garlic potatoes. Bastian sat across from me, while Ian occupied the head of the table, where Queen Rolfe would normally be.

When Bastian had offered his help, I was excited by the advantage to beat Necrosis. But his revelation made me realize how sick this world really was. How everyone was just out for themselves.

I poured my third glass of wine and took a big drink.

Bastian watched me from across the table, one eyebrow slightly cocked.

"What?" I asked. "Never seen a woman drink before?"

"Never seen a woman drink like a man." He pulled the bottle toward himself and refilled his glass.

Ian stared straight ahead, his plate still stacked with the meat he hadn't touched. "This whole time, I thought Rutherford and Faron were the enemies. In actuality, it's Necrosis. It's always been Necrosis."

"Necrosis didn't make Faron conquer Delacroix and kill your father," I said.

Bastian took a drink. "But they helped him do it."

Ian and I both turned to look at him.

"What are you saying?" Ian asked.

I stared at Bastian, seeing a man who looked indistinguishable from other humans. "No one knows how Faron made it up the cliffs…"

"Now you know." Bastian said it simply, like this age-old mystery was of no consequence.

Ian slouched back into his chair and ran his hand across his beard, his eyes defeated. "Curse the gods…"

"Why would Necrosis do that?" I asked. "Why would they forge an alliance with Plunderers?"

"Because they continue to sacrifice soul-rich people to Necrosis," Bastian said. "Through the lottery. And Rutherford conceals the identity of the Three Kings and the elites. They walk among the citizens of the Capital, and no one has any idea what they really are. They feed on whomever they choose. It creates the perfect ecosystem."

"So…" Ian's eyes shifted back and forth across the table. "Necrosis has no interest in invading the Kingdoms."

Bastian gave a quick shake of his head. "No. Not when the power dynamic works in their favor. They can get what they want without risking open war. If the citizens of the Kingdoms knew what really transpired right under their noses, they would take up their swords and fight. Necrosis doesn't want that. They want everything to stay the same."

"And the rest of Necrosis doesn't care that only the Three Kings and the elites get the best souls?" I asked.

"They do," Bastian said. "That's why they aspire to become elites. It's the perfect system. Keeps them obedient."

I turned to Ian. "We have to warn Huntley."

"I was thinking the same thing." He brought his wine to his lips and took a drink. "But if that missive were intercepted…it would be catastrophic."

"It would be more catastrophic if he didn't know," I said. "That he's about to kick the hornet's nest."

"They don't know that Queen Rolfe has taken the dragons," Bastian said. "But once they do, HeartHolme will be vulnerable."

Ian turned to me, accusation in his eyes.

"I didn't tell him," I snapped. "He's been watching us a long time."

Ian turned to Bastian. "You never answered the question."

"And which question is that?" Bastian asked in a bored tone.

"Why Necrosis wants to wipe us out," I said. "You said they know we're a threat to the Kingdoms. But how do they know that?"

He relaxed back into the chair and crossed his arms over his chest. "Ivory."

"What does she have to do with anything?" I asked.

"They know you took her. They know you have a path up the cliffs. They know you intend to take Delacroix for your own. They know it won't stop there, and you're prepared to challenge King Rutherford. And what happens after you take down King Rutherford? Your eyes will turn south—to the final enemy. You've made yourselves very dangerous."

My heart sank into my chest because all of that was true. Huntley and Ivory were in Delacroix now, oblivious to the threat that lurked in the shadows. We were even more vulnerable without the dragons. Once Necrosis found out we were unprotected, they would come for us again.

And this time, we would die. "What happens when they know you've switched sides?"

"They'll be even more threatened."

"Will they be surprised by your betrayal?" I asked.

"Initially. But they'll quickly realize it isn't surprising at all."

"Why is that?" I asked.

He looked away for a moment, like he didn't want to answer my question.

"No secrets."

"This secret has nothing to do with you or Heart-Holme," he said. "It's mine—and I'm going to keep it." When he looked at me, there was a viciousness to his gaze, as if he was prepared to go head-to-head with me.

I let it go.

Ian spoke. "It's because they turned you against your will."

My brother, perceptive as always.

Bastian gave no reaction, so it was hard to tell if that was the truth. "Once they know my allegiance has changed, I won't be privy to their maneuvers. I think it's best that I continue my position with Necrosis as long as I can—just for appearances. I didn't suggest it before because I assumed you wouldn't allow that. That requires a level of trust that I can't earn in our short time frame."

Ian looked at me, silently asking my opinion.

I didn't have an opinion to give. "What do you do for them, exactly?"

Bastian pulled his hand away from the stem of his glass and brushed his palm across the surface of the wood. "I'm a scout. I keep an eye on all the independent factions and report back to the First King."

"Why him?" I asked.

"He's the First King—the king I'm bound to serve."

"Why is he first?" I asked.

"Because he's the eldest of the three brothers."

"They're brothers?" It was hard to imagine Necrosis having any sense of family, not when they fed on the souls of the innocent. "That's why you've spied on us so much." I felt the betrayal, knowing he walked through the streets of HeartHolme with the intention of destroying it.

There wasn't a hint of apology in his gaze. "I've kept most of your secrets to myself. I only shared what I had to in order to deflect suspicion. I've been aware of Queen Rolfe's departure since the moment she left in the middle of the night, but I kept that information to myself. I knew your dragons were gone too, but I didn't say a word. In order for this to work, I'm going to have to continue sharing details of HeartHolme. If I don't, or I get caught in a lie, then we'll all be doomed."

I looked at my brother again, knowing the line we walked was very thin.

"I'm sure they know by now that Huntley has retaken Delacroix. That means they'll know the dragons are there too. I know you wanted to keep the dragons' location a secret, but that was a secret too big to be contained."

"Fuck." I dropped my forehead to the surface of the table. "What do we do now?"

"I'll have to tell Huntley to return one of the dragons," Ian said.

I continued to speak into the wood, my voice muffled. "He said they wouldn't separate."

"Well, they're going to have to."

I sat upright again. "Are you going to send a missive?"

Ian sighed. "I'll send a rider."

"That's even riskier," Bastian said. "A lot could go wrong along the way. The crow is safer."

"And faster," I said. "By the time the rider gets there, Huntley will already be marching to the next Kingdom." That man didn't wait around. He got shit done. Once he had the momentum, he rode with it. "In the meantime, we need to protect HeartHolme. How are we going to do that?"

Ian didn't say anything.

Bastian was quiet for a while. "Ice."

Ian turned to him. "You said there was no more."

"No more outside Necrosis," he said. "There's plenty more, but it's dangerous to reach."

"Where is it?" I asked.

"Inside the caves," Bastian said. "Away from sunlight."

"Is that where Necrosis lives?" I asked. "Underground?"

"No." That was all he said.

"If I had more Ice, I could do a lot more to protect HeartHolme. If I had enough to make hundreds of arrows, we could take them down before they reached the wall. Show me where it is." I'd never ventured farther south than HeartHolme. There was nothing toward Necrosis, just death.

Ian looked at me. "Elora."

"We need it," I said. "Without the dragons, we need something."

"He can go get it himself," Ian said.

"He may not always be around."

Bastian had no reaction to that.

Ian grew annoyed. "We'll discuss it later, Elora." He turned back to Bastian. "We have a deal—don't break it."

Bastian gave a nod.

"You're dismissed."

Bastian gave me a hard stare before he rose to his feet and left the room. The guards parted to let him pass.

I stared at my brother. "You want me to keep an eye on him?"

"Yes," he said. "But keep your guard up. He's still Necrosis—and I don't like him."

"Is there anything he can do to change that?"

He shook his head. "Never."

TWELVE

Elora
———————

I CAUGHT UP TO HIM IN THE DISTANCE, HIS SILHOUETTE noticeable in the light from the burning torches. "Where are you staying tonight?"

He didn't break his stride. "With you, I'm guessing."

"Excuse me?"

"Ian asked you to watch me, right?" He looked at me, his cloak billowing behind him. "It's the only reason he would let me walk out of that castle without chains on my wrists and ankles."

I sidestepped the accusation. "You have a place here?"

"Yes. Just a few streets over from yours."

"And how did you get that place?"

"I paid for it."

"With what money?" I asked.

"I didn't steal it, if that's what you're asking."

"How do you earn money? What are your skills?"

"I can build things—like you."

"What kinds of things?"

"Doors, tables, homes."

"So, you're a carpenter?"

"Yes. That's what I was in my former life."

We made it to the residential area, the streets lit up with more torches. "How long ago was your former life?"

He turned down the street, as if he was heading to my place. "I know what you're really asking."

"I hadn't considered it until now."

"About a hundred and fifty years ago."

He didn't see my reaction because I was directly beside him, but I was stunned. Necrosis had always been mysterious, more of an entity than a real being. That made them mythical. But now that I knew a Necrosis, I viewed them in a new light. They were immortal, but that fact had never seemed important before. I'd never considered their age, how long they walked this earth, everything they'd seen through the years.

We reached my humble dwelling, a two-story home that was narrow and long, wedged between two bigger homes. In my small yard, I had my own garden and a chicken coop so I could have fresh eggs every morning.

I got the door unlocked, and we stepped inside. It was dark, so the first thing I had to do was light all the wax candles positioned throughout the bottom floor. Bastian helped himself to the fireplace and threw on a couple logs before he got the flames going. Soon, my home was lit with light, and I was able to uncork a new bottle of wine. "Want some?"

He sat at the dining table and relaxed in the chair, as if the answer was obvious.

I poured two glasses and left the bottle on the table.

He held it by the stem but drank it like it was ale or water. His gaze remained fixed on me, half of his face lit up from the glow of the fireplace. His dark hair reminded me of the walnut wood of the table at which we sat. "You're alone in a house where no one can hear you scream—and you aren't afraid."

I picked up my glass and took a drink. "Don't flatter yourself. I'm not afraid of anything."

The corner of his mouth crooked in a smile. "Then you weren't as comfortable around me as you are now."

"Well, you were a stranger."

"And I no longer am?"

I took another drink just to cover my silence.

"I don't think your brother fears me either. Otherwise, he wouldn't want me anywhere near you."

"No. My brother just knows I've got bigger balls than all of his men."

The subtle smile returned, as if he found my crassness amusing rather than off-putting.

"So…what was your life like? Before it happened?"

His eyes dropped to his glass. "I lived in a small village to the east. My father was the steward, my mother was a midwife, and I built cribs for newborns, homes for newlyweds, tables for holidays dinners. It was a simple life. A simple time."

"So, you were a Plunderer?"

"Technically. If put on the spot, that's what we'd say. But like other scattered Plunderers, we were something entirely different. We were just people, working from sunrise to sunset, telling stories by the fire, finding joy in the little things."

I pictured a place I'd never seen, heard the lumberjack chopping the wood, saw Bastian in his shop sanding the wood of a crib before he gifted it to a family. The cold air was on my face, the peace was in my lungs. "Sounds nice…"

"It was." He took a drink and looked at me again.

"Is it still there?"

After a long pause, he gave a shake of his head.

"What happened to it?"

"Nothing lasts forever." That was the only answer he gave.

If he was a hundred and fifty years old, that meant his parents were long gone. "Do you have any siblings?"

He stayed quiet, his eyes dropping again. The silence that followed was so heavy it didn't seem like words could break it. "A sister."

That meant she was gone too. "Did she have any children?"

"No."

He was truly alone. I didn't really have parents, but I had my brothers, and they never felt only half related. "I'm sorry."

He drank from his glass and brushed it off.

"I've been thinking…"

His blue eyes stayed on me, clear and so bright.

"I want you to take me to the Ice."

His gaze remained hard, unsurprised.

"We're going to need it."

"I agree. And you're right, I may not always be around. Haldir is not only intelligent, but in a state of permanent suspicion."

"Haldir?"

"The First King. Over the span of decades, I've convinced him of my allegiance, but one false move and that veil will be pierced. Without the Ice, HeartHolme is vulnerable. Another attack by Necrosis will wipe out your people for good."

"Then you need to take me."

"It's a dangerous road."

"You think I care? HeartHolme is at risk."

"Your brother could send someone else in your stead."

"He doesn't want me to fight, and if I don't have Ice, any weapon I make is pointless. Besides, we can't trust anyone else to keep your secret."

He gave a slight nod before he abruptly stood up. Then he headed to the front door.

"What are you doing?"

As if someone had knocked, he opened the door and stared into the night.

Both of my eyebrows rose up my face, unsure what was happening.

Then Victor appeared, sizing up Bastian with a look of rage he'd never shown before.

Did Bastian hear him before he even got to the door? I got to my feet and rushed over.

Victor eyed me next. "What the fuck is this?"

I was just about to make introductions and explain Bastian's visit, but Victor's words took me aback. "Excuse me?"

Victor looked at him again. "You've been gone all day, and then this asshole opens the door?"

"Whoa...hold on." I moved in front of Bastian. "Excuse me?"

Bastian whispered below his breath before he walked away, "Told you."

Victor turned on me. "Told you what?"

"None of your business," I snapped. "That's what. Bastian and I are working on something for my brother. That's all. But one, I shouldn't have to explain that. And two, even if our meeting were romantic, it's still none of your business. We agreed this was no-strings-attached, no-commitment, just good ol'-fashioned fun. You have no right to act this way. I don't belong to you. I don't belong to anyone."

He was a meaty guy who possessed war in his eyes, and he gave me that look that told me he was about to snap. But he took a breath and let it out slowly. "Elora—"

"We're done."

"No, we aren't—"

Bastian spoke from his seat at the table. "That was the wrong thing to say, man."

I stood closer to Victor, sizing him up like one of the guys at the bar. "Asshole, you don't tell me what to do. Try it again, and I'll throat-punch you so hard you won't be able to breathe. Got that?"

He opened his mouth to speak. "Elora—"

"Goodbye, Victor." I shut the door in his face and locked it.

Bastian drank his wine at the table, acting as if nothing had happened.

I returned to my seat and refilled my glass.

A slight smile moved on to the corner of his mouth.

"Shut up."

He took a drink of his wine.

"You can hear that well?"

"Yes."

"So, you can hear people outside right now?"

"No. If they come closer to the house, I can."

"That's a Necrosis thing?"

"Yes."

"What else do Necrosis have?"

"Night vision. Increased strength and agility."

"Can Necrosis have children?"

He hesitated before he answered. "No. That's why we protect our kind so fervently. When you turn someone, it's like siring a child. You're connected in a way that you can't really explain."

"Who turned you?"

"Haldir."

"The First King?" I asked, surprised the most powerful Necrosis was interested in Bastian. "Why?"

He finished his glass and left it on the table. "Story time is over." He left the table and walked over to the couch. The couch faced the fire, so he took a seat at the edge, his arm on the armrest.

I lingered at the table for a while before I joined him, sitting at the opposite end. "You can sleep on the couch."

"I can slip away in the middle of the night, and you wouldn't even know."

"Not if I'm on the other couch."

"I'm quiet."

"Well, I can hear almost as well as Necrosis, so…"

He gave a slight smile before he looked at the fire. "I know there will always be this unease between us… because of what I am. But I have no ill intention toward you or any of your people—and I know you know that."

I stared at the fire and felt my heart clench into a fist.

"You'd look weak if you admitted it, so I get it."

With my knees pulled to my chest, I turned to regard him.

"But it's smart not to trust me. At the end of the day, my very existence is a threat to your afterlife. That will never change."

————

"Are you insane?" Ian rounded on me, his boots loud taps against the floor. "Are you literally fucking insane?" We were in his study, maps and letters across his desk, a fire in the hearth. "He's Necrosis—and you have a soul."

"We need the Ice—"

"He can retrieve it himself."

"And if Haldir kills him tomorrow, what will we do?"

"Haldir?"

"The First King."

He stopped his pacing. "Looks like he's more interested in sharing with you than he is with me."

My eyes narrowed. "What's that supposed to mean?"

His stare continued, along with the silence.

"You told me to keep an eye on him. I asked him a few questions. You know me, I never stop talking."

He resumed his pacing, his big shoulders heavy with defeat. "The answer is no, Elora."

"I'm sorry…did it sound like I was asking permission?"

He turned back to face me. "This no-nonsense attitude is fine when I'm just your brother, but I'm king now."

"Queen."

He gave a slight growl. "I'm not in the mood for this."

"And I'm not in the mood for Necrosis to get their asses over here and take HeartHolme. Are you?"

"We'll send someone else."

"Someone else?" I asked incredulously. "Is there someone else we trust enough with this information? We'd have to admit that Bastian is Necrosis, and how do you think that will go?"

Ian wore a stern look.

"I'm our only option."

"I would rather go and leave you behind to rule than let that happen."

"Queen Rolfe appointed you—not me."

"And I can decide who to leave in my stead."

"People are already on edge with Queen Rolfe, Commander Dawson, and Huntley being gone. The last thing they need is another switch. Besides, people don't respect me as much as they respect you."

"That's bullshit, Elora."

"Look, I don't take it personally, alright? You're from the royal family. I'm…I don't even know."

His eyes dropped like it was too hard to look at me.

"I need to do this."

"He could not only kill you, but claim your soul and take your key to the Undying Kingdom."

"He wouldn't do that."

"He said himself that when he gets hungry, he can't control it."

"Well, he's not hungry right now. And he still wouldn't let that happen."

"Why do you trust him so much?" He stepped toward me. "Because he's good-looking?"

"You think he's good-looking?"

His stare hardened. "I'm not in the mood for this, Elora."

"If you swing both ways, that's totally fine—"

"Knock it off."

I crossed my arms over my chest and sighed. "I never said I trusted him—"

"You're willing to travel with him alone into Necrosis territory. If that doesn't mean you trust him, then I don't know what does. He's stronger than you, faster than you—"

"I deserve more credit than that."

"I never said you were weak, and the fact that you refuse to acknowledge him as a serious opponent only makes me more concerned."

"Ian, if I don't do this, I put all of HeartHolme in jeopardy."

"I care a lot more about you than HeartHolme, Elora."

My arms tightened over my chest. "You don't mean that…"

"Damn right, I do. Kingdoms rise and fall. Family is forever."

I gave a subtle shake of my head. "You're king, Ian. That means you put HeartHolme first, above all else, exactly as I'm doing."

My brother looked away and headed toward the window. His heavy cape hung over his massive shoulders and down his back, reaching the floor behind him.

"You know I'm right."

He ignored me.

"I didn't come here to ask your permission. I came here to tell you that's what's happening."

"You've always been stubborn and stupid."

"I prefer selfless and heroic, but whatever."

He slowly turned back to me. "I really don't like this, Elora."

"I'll be fine, Ian. I have my Ice sword."

"If Huntley were here, he would never allow this."

"Then good thing he's not here because he's dramatic as hell."

———

Victor appeared out of nowhere, intercepting me on my route back home.

I gave a dramatic roll of my eyes when he came to my side. "What do you want?"

"To finish our conversation." He grabbed me by the arm and halted me.

I flipped my arm over his and evaded his hold, then I gave him a shove in the chest for good measure. "Don't fuck with me, Victor."

He raised his hand in a gesture of surrender. "Just want to talk to you."

"About?"

"Come on, Elora. Everything was fine between us until this pretty boy showed up."

"You know, you aren't the first guy to say Bastian is hot."

His eyes narrowed.

"We agreed this was casual, alright? I'm sorry if I hurt you because that wasn't my intention, but I'm not sorry for walking away because there was never a commitment between us. It's over—so take it like a man."

His eyes widened slightly. "Then let's discuss a commitment."

"Victor, I'm just not in that place."

"Give it time, and you will be."

"Look, we barely survived the Necrosis attack, and we just plunged into a war that will probably kill us all. There's no time for this."

"Really? Because it's made me realize what's important."

My heart deflated. "You deserve to be with someone who feels the same way, Victor. Look at you." I gestured to his body, from head to toe. "You're hot. You've got nice eyes. You come from a good family. Are a great provider. You could have anyone you want. Don't waste your time on me."

His eyes dropped down for a moment. "I feel like everything changed when that guy walked in here." He looked at me again, the accusation in his eyes. "If that's true, I'd like a chance to earn you."

"Victor…" I shook my head. "Even if that were true, why would you want to be with me? Why would you want to be with a woman who wants someone else?"

"So, it is true."

"That's not what I said—"

"You got a thing for him or not?"

"Why does everyone keep assuming that—"

"Just answer the question."

"I'm not going to lie and act like he's not hot, because he is. But that's it."

His eyes gauged me, shifting back and forth as he stared.

"Victor, it's been a long day, and I'm pretty tired." A part of me felt cold for ending things so callously, but if I gave him any leeway, I was afraid it would just make it harder. There was never a time in this relationship when I thought about him when we weren't together. When Necrosis attacked, I'd hoped he was okay, but I was far more worried about my own family than I ever was about him.

"Yeah."

"You can find a girl so much cooler and hotter than me. Trust me, you're going to look back on this with relief."

All he did was stare. "Take care, Elora."

"You too, Victor."

With that, he turned around and left.

I watched him walk down the street before I unlocked my front door and stepped inside. Once I hung my coat, I gave a slight jerk, seeing the man seated at my kitchen table. With dark hair and those piercing eyes, he stared, a bottle of scotch in front of him.

"I don't know the customs of Necrosis, but in Heart-Holme, we don't just enter people's homes." I sat across from him at the table and pulled the bottle toward me. Didn't even bother with a glass. Just took a drink straight from the bottle and gave a cringe as it burned on the way down.

"Victor isn't taking the breakup well, is he?"

"It's not a breakup," I said quickly. "We were never together in the first place. And you heard all that?"

He pulled the bottle toward him, gave a slight nod, and then took a drink.

Which meant he'd heard everything else. Shit.

"So, who else thinks I'm hot?"

Gods, the humiliation. "Ian."

His eyebrows immediately furrowed. "That's flattering."

"He's straight. Meant it in a different context."

"Good." He took another drink. "Glad I don't have to break his heart the way you just broke Victor's."

I rolled my eyes. "He'll be fine. I just made another woman very happy."

He slid the bottle back toward me then rested his arms on the table. Those vibrantly colored eyes stared into mine with a quiet stillness, a depth that couldn't be perceived by the naked eye. He held the contact effort-lessly, his eyes not shifting back and forth, absolutely motionless.

I grabbed the bottle and took another drink, mainly just to brush off his heated stare. "Ian agreed to the plan."

"Really? That seems unlikely."

"Are you calling me a liar?"

"Yes. Just trying to be gentle about it."

I set the bottle down and slid it back toward him. "He knows it's our only option."

"There's always another option. If our positions were reversed, my decision would be the same. Would never allow my sister to travel alone with a monster that feeds on souls to retain his own immortality."

"But you aren't like them."

"That's what I say—but how can you ever really trust me?"

"Well, I think it'd be pretty lame for you to jump through all these hoops just to eat me at the first opportunity. Seems like a lot of work for a very small payoff."

He cracked a subtle smile but pulled it back instantly.

"And I'd like to see you try. I'd kick your ass."

The smile returned, bigger than it was before. "You underestimate my strength."

"No. You underestimate mine."

His lips returned to their straight line, and his eyes focused on my face with greater intensity than before. "When do we leave?"

"Tomorrow?"

"How will you handle Ian?"

I shrugged. "We'll just leave."

"I think your brother deserves better than that. He deserves the chance to say goodbye."

My eyes narrowed on his face, taking in the somber expression. "Why do you care so much?"

"Because I know what it's like to be an older brother. We don't leave until we have his permission, and we don't leave until you say goodbye."

THIRTEEN

Elora

THE NEXT MORNING BEFORE THE SUN WAS UP, BASTIAN and I entered the castle and found my brother in his study.

He finished his note with his quill before he rolled it up and stamped it with a seal. "I sent the missive to Huntley this morning. Not sure if it'll make it there in time." He rose to his feet and gave me his authoritative stare. He was different when someone else was in the room, especially someone of Necrosis.

"Make it there in time?" I asked.

"His last letter said they would take Minora immediately," he said, moving around the desk. "They may have already departed Delacroix."

Shit, I hoped not.

He stopped in front of us, giving Bastian a cold look. "I gave you my answer, Elora. If you're here to convince me otherwise, you're wasting my time as well as yours. And we both know we have more important shit to do." The accusation was in his gaze, as if Bastian were responsible for this meeting.

"I wanted to sneak out this morning, but Bastian refuses to leave without your permission," I said. "So, you can stop looking at him like he's an asshole."

Ian turned back to me. "I never would have forgiven you if you'd pulled that stunt."

"Your forgiveness won't matter if we all die." All the pieces on the map were in motion, and we only had a finite amount of time until disaster struck. "I need to do this, and you know it."

Ian shifted his gaze back to Bastian.

"If Bastian meant me harm, we wouldn't be here right now." He'd have no problem sneaking out of the gate and getting me alone.

Ian stared at me for a long time, his expression hard the way Huntley's was. An entire minute passed, and he said nothing. "How long is the journey?" His eyes shifted to Bastian.

"A week there," Bastian said. "A week back. Maybe more, depending on how much Ice we collect."

"And if you're caught?"

"The only distinctive feature of Necrosis is the darkness of their skin when they need to feed," Bastian said. "There's no reason for them to suspect she's not one of them."

"But they won't recognize her either," my brother said.

"There're a lot of us." Bastian held his stare. "More than you realize. I can vouch for her."

Ian turned his attention back to me. "I still don't like this, Elora. But your instincts have always been right. I trust your judgment."

It was the nicest thing he'd ever said to me. "Thanks, brother."

He brought me into his arms and gave me a hard embrace, his palm on the back of my neck the same way Huntley did. His chin rested on the top of my head, and he gave me a squeeze before he released me. "Be careful."

"I will."

He looked to Bastian next, and all that warmth he'd just given me disappeared. "Touch my sister and I will carve your eyes out of your face and feed them to the pigs."

Bastian didn't flinch at the threat.

"And if you kill me first, Huntley will take my place. Trust me, you don't want to fuck with him."

"Your threats fall on deaf ears, but lucky for you, I mean her no harm. And she made it very clear she would kick my ass if I tried."

―――――

We grabbed four horses and packed the saddles. One horse was tied to each of ours, so we'd have more room to pack the Ice we would harvest. I wore my riding boots and my heavy cloak to shield me from the sun and the cold. We were traveling south, where it should be a little warmer, but windstorms swept through our lands periodically.

Bastian was dressed in all black, wearing his armor and weapons. His heavy cloak hung behind him, and the hood was bunched at the nape of his neck. His short hair was combed back, and he already had a shadow on his jawline because he'd skipped the shave. He guided his horse forward by the reins then mounted him in a single fluid motion. "Ready?"

I mounted the horse beside him and gathered the reins in my hands. "Lead the way."

He kicked his boots into the horse and took off at a run, heading east around the mountain that protected HeartHolme.

I followed behind until I caught up to him, the four horses pounding the earth with their hooves. It was early morning, the sun barely over the horizon. The sky was an array of pretty colors, and the coldness pressed right into our cheeks as we sped across the wildlands. We stopped for a short break at midafternoon, barely enough time to eat and do our business, and then we rode hard once again.

We traveled until twilight. The sky turned dark blue, and the stars blanketed the heavens. The horses couldn't travel any farther without injury, so we stopped for the night, in a shelter of trees. We hadn't spotted anyone on our travels, so the world felt empty except for the two of us. I unpacked my bedroll and flattened it on the ground, and then I searched for pieces of wood to make a fire.

"No fire."

I dropped the logs onto the stones. "We didn't see anyone."

"Doesn't mean they didn't see us." He unrolled his bedroll then laid his short sword on the ground beside it.

"Well, I like to end a long day like that with a hot piece of meat and some warm bread."

"I have dried meat in my bag."

I shook my head. "I prefer it juicy." I pulled out the striker from my bag and got the first piece of wood to smoke. After a couple breaths, I was able to make the flames appear, and soon they grew into a full fire.

He sat in his bedroll and watched me.

I put the meat on the spit and started the roast, along with a couple slices of raw dough that I'd packed. Juice dripped from the meat and sizzled on the hot rocks, and the bread started to glow as it turned a golden brown.

With his forearms on his knees, he watched me, his eyes a lighter color in the glow from the fire.

I removed the meat and bread and divided them between us. After my first bite, my stomach gave a growl of approval. "Worth it."

He ate in silence, chewing his food slowly while keeping his eyes on the fire or me. Then he reached into his bag and pulled out a canteen. He removed the lid, took a drink, and then an amber droplet missed his mouth and streaked down his chin.

"Now we're talking." I reached my hand across the fire.

He handed it over and resumed eating.

I washed down my dinner with a healthy swallow of scotch, feeling all the aches in my body fade immediately.

In silence, we ate, eating everything until there was nothing left.

"Why do you eat food if you already eat souls?"

He wiped his hands on his trousers. "They fulfill separate needs. Food is fuel for our daily activities. Souls feed the curse."

"That's what you call it?"

"It's the most fitting."

I rinsed our dirty plates with the water from my canteen then wiped them down with a rag. "Do you feel bad every time you do it? Feed on someone?"

He stared for so long it didn't seem as if he would respond.

"Sorry…that was an intrusive question."

"Since I don't feed until my breaking point, I don't remember it. But I see the aftermath. Once I'm satiated, that's when all the guilt kicks in. The shame. The self-loathing."

"Have you ever tried to kill yourself?"

He shook his head. "I've considered it."

"Why haven't you done it?"

He looked away.

"Sorry, that was an asshole question. I just meant—"

"Because I have something to live for." He looked at me again. "It's just not an option."

"Something or someone?"

He never gave an answer.

"Are you married?"

"No. I already told you that."

"I asked if you were with anyone."

"Same thing."

"Sometimes it's more complicated than that. Can Necrosis get married? Since they don't have a soul."

"Not in the sense you have marriage. But we can be bound to each other."

"Have you ever been bound to anyone?"

He gave me a hard stare. "No."

"Why do I feel like there's something you aren't telling me?"

"Because there is."

I pulled my knees to my chest and rested my chin on top of my folded arms. Instead of pressing him with more questions, I let the conversation end. The flames in the pit started to die down, slowly shrinking back to the rocks. "If it's because you don't trust me, just remember where we are right now. I'm traveling with you, alone, prey and predator."

"It's not that I don't trust you."

"Then what is it?"

His eyes dropped down to the fire. "Just too hard to talk about." He dismissed the conversation by pulling back the blanket of his bedroll. His boots kicked the rocks into the fire, putting out the flames and bringing us into pure darkness. Then he lay down and looked up at the canopy of trees.

I decided to lie down too. "You want me to take the first watch?"

"No need. I can hear in my sleep."

Good. Because I was dead tired. I got comfortable in the bedroll, and almost immediately, I was out for the night.

———

I woke up to his boot nudging me. "It's sunrise."

"Ugh." I rolled over and pulled the sheet over my head.

He nudged me again. "I said get up."

I swatted him in the shin.

"Get your ass up, or I'll pick it up myself."

"Asshole…" I forced myself upright as I rubbed the sleep from my eyes. It took me a moment to fully awaken, to take in the gentle sunlight that appeared through the branches of the trees. The cold air hit my skin immediately, like a piece of ice against my face. I reached for my pack and pulled out the first snack I could find, nuts and berries, and munched on that to get my brain to stir.

A mug appeared in front of me, steaming hot.

"Oh my gods...is that coffee?" I took it from his hands and brought it to my lips for a drink. Bold in taste and aromatic with a multitude of flavors, it was warm and delicious. "This is the best shit I've ever had."

"The beans are from Necrosis."

"Necrosis drinks coffee?"

"We aren't that different from you—as hard as that is to believe."

"Really fucking hard." I drank it all before I got up and packed my things.

He was already ready to go, standing at the edge of the clearing to keep an eye out. One foot was propped on a rock, and he stood with his shoulders back, surveying the scene ahead of him with the intelligent eyes of a hawk.

I pulled on my boots, tightened my cloak, and then mounted my horse. "I'm ready."

He continued his stare for a while before he mounted his horse. "We're changing course."

"What? Why?"

"A group of riders is headed in our direction."

I scanned the world around us, seeing no disruption in the serenity. "I don't see anyone."

"I don't see anyone either. But I can hear them."

"What?" I asked incredulously. "How?"

"Because they're on horses—and there're a lot of them."

"Must be Plunderers."

"My same assumption." He kicked his horse and took off.

I did the same and rode beside him. "Do you have a hard time sleeping at night?"

His hands gripped the reins as he turned to look at me.

"Since you can hear everything?"

He looked forward. "I have a hard time sleeping for a lot of reasons."

———

Days passed without incident. Sometimes we camped at night without a fire. Sometimes we talked before bed, and sometimes we went to sleep right away. But throughout the journey, he never gave any indication that he was a threat. I felt comfortable with him, but I was smart enough not to let my guard down—at least not fully.

We traveled south farther than I'd ever gone before. So far that I actually felt the change in temperature, saw vegetation I'd never seen before. The dirt was even a different color, somewhat red and rough in texture.

When we stopped at sunset, I saw the outline of the mountains that marked the border to Necrosis. They stretched as far as the eye could see, from one point of the continent to the other. Unlike the red dirt, the mountains were dark in color, and as the night deepened, there was a distinct shine on part of the surface. It was slightly blue, a gentle glow. "What is that?" I asked, pointing.

Bastian followed my outstretched finger. "Bioluminescence."

"I'm sorry…am I supposed to know what that means?"

He sat across the fire from me, a roll in his hand. "The minerals and vegetation absorb sunlight during the day then give off that glow throughout the night. Not sure why. Perhaps it's to attract pollinators."

"Do you guys use it for anything?"

"We use the minerals for weapons. The plants are used for herbal remedies and tea."

"Does Necrosis need remedies?"

"We're vulnerable to flesh wounds just like you."

"What about illness?" I asked.

He gave a shake of his head. "Since our bodies aren't truly alive, we don't progress in that way."

"Lucky…"

He took a bite of the roll and chewed as he stared at me. "I can go in alone and meet you out here."

"Excuse me? Why are you trying to change the plan?"

"Just giving you a way out."

"Did I ask for one?"

"I wouldn't blame you for being scared, Elora—"

"How many times have I told you I don't get scared? I'm traveling alone with one of you—so there's your proof."

"You know I wouldn't hurt you, so that doesn't count."

"Do I?" I challenged.

He gave me that hard stare, his eyes so focused on mine they seemed to have their own fire. "Yes." It was as if he dared me to doubt him. "I can harvest the Ice myself and return with what I have. It's less risk on your part."

"That defeats the whole reason I came with you—"

"It's just an option—if you want it."

"I'm good."

He continued his stare. "I wouldn't let anything happen to you, if that's any comfort."

He was the only ally I had. Once I crossed into their lands, he would also be my only lifeline, my only way out of there. "So, if they discovered what I really was, you would fight them so I could get away?"

He gave a nod.

"Aren't some of these people your friends?"

"The twelve I mentioned before."

"And they're there now?"

He gave another nod.

Silence returned to the campfire, his eyes on the flames.

With my arms around my knees, I stared at his face, studied his high cheekbones, the beard that took up his entire jawline. It grew thicker by the day, just the way my brothers' did when they were too busy to shave. "Is your sister still alive?"

The question seemed to provoke him because he lifted his gaze and looked into my eyes. The stare was unlike any kind he'd shared before, which had been guarded and impenetrable. Now his eyes were clear as a sunny day, the path to his missing soul visible. "Why do you ask?"

"You aren't married, and you aren't seeing anyone…but you're living for something. She must be the thing you're living for."

There was no confirmation or denial. Just that stare.

"She's Necrosis too."

He was quiet.

"And you're trying to free her…"

He dropped his eyes.

I knew I was right. "I'm sorry."

His eyes stayed on the fire, his heartbreak on the surface. "When Necrosis came to our village, they slaughtered everyone. Fed on their souls like an all-you-can-eat buffet. I survived, discovered my parents' corpses, but then I realized my sister was missing. Haldir set eyes on her and decided to keep her for himself."

My stomach dropped, absolutely sickened.

"He turned her. Made her into one of them."

"Gods…"

"Her beauty was indescribable. She had soft features like a rose petal, but she also had wildfire in her eyes. All my friends wanted her. Every boy in the village wanted her. At some point, I just got used to it. But Haldir never did."

She wasn't just turned against her will. Something even worse happened to her.

"I followed them into their lands and drew my sword. It was a suicide mission, but I'd rather die trying to save her than live a life of grief. I wasn't the swordsman I am now, so I was no match for the First King. Before he could eat me, she begged for my life, agreed to succumb to all of his demands…" He took a deep breath and let it out slowly, his eyes focused on the fire with a tint of rage. "That was when he turned me. I went there to save her…and all I did was make our situations worse."

The fire crackled in the silence. The nighttime sounds of the forest were audible. The cracking of branches. The hoots of an owl. The wind through the leaves. It was the sound of silence—and it was so heavy.

"For the last one hundred and fifty years, I've amended my relationship with the First King. I've pretended to embrace my new life as Necrosis. I've followed all his orders, even the ones that made me sick. But I've been biding my time, waiting for the right moment when I could save us both." He suddenly rose to his feet and stepped away, his visage hidden in shadow as his backside was lit up by the glow of the flames. He departed the campsite and took refuge behind a tree, withdrawing from me and the conversation.

I remained behind, swamped by the burden of despair. My heart hadn't felt this heavy since I'd thought we were doomed to be defeated by Necrosis. It was the kind of hopelessness that I could taste on my tongue, could feel in the pit of my stomach. The more I got to know Bastian, the more I realized he was just as human as I was.

I left the campfire and approached him where he stood. He leaned against a tree, his arms crossed over his chest, one foot planted against the trunk. His eyes were forward through the opening in the trees to the empty plains ahead, ignoring me beside him.

I stared at the side of his face, a face that was tight in a blank expression.

"I'm sorry."

It was as if I wasn't even there.

Now it all made sense, why he paid so much attention to my relationship with my brothers, why he was so adamant about Ian's blessing before we left. My hand instinctively reached for his arm. My fingers touched the thick muscles before taking note of the surprising amount of warmth. A lot of heat for someone who wasn't technically alive.

The second he felt me, his face tilted slightly, giving me a look.

I could see the heartbreak in his eyes despite all his efforts to hide it. I could feel the pain radiating from him like heat from a fire. I could feel the despair as if it were a void inside my own chest. It made me reach for him like it was a cure for the pain, like I needed to console myself rather than comfort him.

My hand cupped his face as I moved in and pressed a kiss to his mouth. The second we made contact, the thick arms in front of his chest dropped, and they circled my waist instead. His big hands spanned the small of my back, and he tugged me close, bringing my chest to the top of his stomach.

His mouth didn't just reciprocate my kiss. It devoured it. I'd made the first move, but he quickly took the lead, parting my lips with his before releasing a deep breath into my mouth. His hands tightened on my little body, and after he turned his head slightly to change the orientation of our mouths, he gave me some of his tongue, expertly executed.

My fingers felt the coarse hair of his chin, savored the taste of his lips. I was wrapped in the arms of a man who could eat my soul at any second, but the fear never took hold, not when this felt like oblivion.

One hand dug into my hair next, while his other arm wrapped around me and pulled me flush to his hard body, my stomach right against the distinct outline of his dick inside his pants. It was clearly intentional, wanting me to know that he was just as capable as a living man, that he was big enough to make me forget every other man who had been inside me.

Damn, he was a good kisser.

Our breaths were heavy, and soon they turned into quiet moans as we grabbed on to each other with desperation. The kiss was spontaneous with no ulterior motive, but now things were moving fast, so fast that I wouldn't be surprised if I ended up buck naked against that tree with his big dick between my legs.

Then it stopped.

He was the one who withdrew, who took away the fuel that fed our inferno. He looked away for a second, as if he couldn't look me in the eye and face what had just happened. His hands left my body, and with every new withdrawal, I felt even colder. "That can't happen again."

It was like being slapped in the face with a brick of ice. "What…?"

"Let's go to bed." He stepped away from the tree and headed back to the campfire. "We have a long day tomorrow."

I stood there as I watched him walk away, still shocked by how quickly it started and ended. "Who kisses someone and then just stops?"

"You kissed me."

"Yes. A beautiful woman came on to you, and now you're running away."

He kicked the fire and snuffed out the flames, bringing the forest into darkness.

"Who does that?"

He ignored me and climbed into his bedroll.

"Asshole, we're in the middle of a conversation—"

"I don't want you." He sat up again, looking at me in the darkness. "Is that what you want me to say?"

The sting was packed with venom, paralyzing me for an instant.

"Then I'll say it again. I don't want you." He lay flat. "Let's go to bed, and when we wake up in the morning, act like nothing happened." He lay still and closed his eyes, as if he really did forget about it that quickly.

I stood there for a while because the whiplash was so strong it brought an ache to my neck. It took me a moment to hold my head high and walk to my bedroll, to pick up my humiliation off the ground and put it back inside my chest. I got under the blanket and lay there, my lips still warm from his kiss. My heart was beating so fast. Beating with rage. Beating with pain. "You don't kiss a woman like that unless you want her, so I'm calling you out on your bullshit."

FOURTEEN

Elora

When I woke up the next morning, the coffee was already made, and Bastian had already packed his horse for the journey. The second I sat up, flashbacks of the night before hit me, the way he kissed me better than any man had ever kissed me before. I'd bedded some amazing lovers, and I'd had men devour me like a feast —but Bastian was definitely the best out of them all.

And it was just a kiss.

A kiss that had only lasted a couple minutes. A kiss that could easily have accelerated into a passionate hump against the trunk of a tree in the middle of the woods, both of our pants around our ankles, our moans like the sounds of wild animals.

Didn't want me…yeah fucking right.

I poured myself a mug of hot coffee and sat by the fire as I drank it. No amount of caffeine would wake me up today, not when I'd hardly gotten any rest last night. Hot dreams kept pulling me from sleep, and then I'd be up for hours, thinking about all the images that had faded from my mind.

He avoided me, sitting against the trunk of the tree closest to his horse. He was ready to go, his sword at his hip, his bow and quiver of arrows beside him on the ground. His eyes were focused on the open plains, seeing the sun slowly inch farther and farther over the grasslands.

I had a quick breakfast of fruit and nuts then poured out the remainder of the contents of my mug. My things were packed away, and then I was ready to ride. "Are we just not going to talk about what happened last night?"

He turned to look at me, holding my gaze like a man. "I stand by what I said."

"You mean, you lied."

His hard expression didn't change.

"Because we both know you're full of shit." I stuck my foot in the stirrup and grabbed the saddle by the pommel before I hoisted myself onto the horse. "A guy doesn't press his rock-hard dick into a woman's stomach like that unless he's interested. I've been around the block a few times, so don't fucking gaslight me. Just be a man and give it to me straight." I clicked my tongue and pulled on the reins to get the horse moving. "Or don't. I'm not sure I care anymore anyway."

———

It was a long day of riding, and by the end of it, the mountains were right on top of us. The trees thickened at the base, so we had to bring the horses to a brisk walk so we wouldn't get our heads chopped off by low-hanging branches.

The closer we got to approaching Necrosis, the more nervous I became, but I wouldn't admit that out loud. Ever.

Bastian dismounted his horse then tied him to a tree branch, giving a lot of slack in the rope so both horses could move around.

I copied him and dismounted my horse. "Are we going in?"

"Not yet." He stopped at the tree line and stared at the rocky terrain before us, seeing something my weak eyes couldn't catch. "We'll wait until just before sunrise, when the guards change their watch."

"They guard their lands?" I asked in surprise. "As far as I know, no one has ever had any interest in paying them a visit."

"That changed the moment you drove them off with your dragons." He turned back to his horse and pulled out his bedroll and his supplies. He laid everything on the ground then got to work making a fire.

"Won't they see it?"

"This is a blind spot to their towers." We tossed the logs on top and got a steady fire going.

I took my seat across from him, tired from all the riding, missing my bed at home. I leaned my back against a tree and stretched out my legs in front of me, my ankles crossed. During the darkest part of the night, there was always a deep chill, but it was welcome after sweating all day.

I played with my pocketknife, shaving the skin off a twig I'd found on the ground. I sliced it into a point, a makeshift weapon that could do little damage. My eyes were down, but I could feel his heated stare.

I ignored it for a while, but when it didn't abate, I lifted my eyes and met his look. "Yes?" I wasn't sure why I was so pissed off. Was it because my pride was wounded? Was it because it was the first time I'd been rejected? Or was it because I was so painfully disappointed that my feelings weren't reciprocated?

With his forearms resting on his knees, he sat with a straight back, the fire lighting up the masculine features of his face. "It's nothing personal."

"Nothing personal?" I asked, my eyebrow cocking. "Not being attracted to someone is very personal."

He looked away, his shoulders falling with the breath he released. "It's not you—"

"Grow some balls and just say it—"

"I want to eat you." He looked at me again, and this time, his eyes were deadly, like the desire coursed through his veins that very moment.

I shut my mouth.

His stare continued, fixed in place, unblinking.

"You said you weren't hungry."

"I'm not."

My sword was right beside me, but I didn't reach for it right away. But I was ready to slice his head clean from his shoulders.

"When we came together, I could feel it."

"Feel what?"

"Your soul. It's like a bonfire. It has the energy of all the gods in the heavens. It's brighter than the stars that light up the night sky. It's the single most powerful thing I've ever come close to. I've never felt anything like that in my life, and when I felt it…I wanted it for myself."

The disappointment hit me harder.

"You and I…it's never going to happen."

I was in danger that very moment, but I still didn't feel as afraid as I should. "Do you want to eat me right now?"

"A little bit." He looked away, as if too ashamed to look me in the eye as he said those words.

"Have you always felt that way?"

"No."

"So, it was only after——"

"You drove me fucking crazy against that tree." His eyes remained averted, looking into the shadows of the trees around us. "I only stopped because I had to. Only stopped because I was afraid if I didn't, I would suck your soul right out of your chest and leave your dead body on the ground."

"Is that how you always feel with your lovers?"

"I've only been with Necrosis—so, no. But if I were with a Rune or a Plunderer, I doubt that would happen."

"Then why did it happen with me?"

After a long pause, he turned back to me. "Because you're strong. Because you're fearless. Because you're unlike any other woman I've met." His eyes remained hard, just like a drink of scotch. "Because I've wanted you from the moment I saw you."

Bumps formed up and down my arms, but they weren't provoked by the chilled air. It was an internal discomfort, an anxiety that started in my stomach then slowly seeped out.

"It's not every day you meet a woman who can forge weapons better than any man. A woman who can hit the bull's-eyes in darts every time. A woman who can hustle men twice her size to pay their debts. I respect Queen Rolfe and consider her to be a selfless ruler. I respect Huntley and Ian as well. But you're by far the smartest one out of all of them. I knew you were the only one who would consider my words with logic rather than fear."

I'd felt this heat between us the moment we met, noticed the way he stared at me every time we spoke. There had been a tension in the air almost immediately, but it also felt as if we'd always known each other. There was a familiarity that shouldn't exist, not when I was alive and he was dead.

"I had no intention of ever pursuing you. But I didn't anticipate you would ever pursue me."

"Why wouldn't I? Look at you."

He held my gaze for a long time, his hard gaze etched in stone.

"I know you heard what I said to Victor."

He still didn't give any reaction. "You know what I am. You know I'm dangerous."

I gave a shrug. "How many times have I told you I'm not scared of anything?"

He didn't crack a smile, not this time. "You should be."

"Well, you wanted to eat me and you didn't, so I'd say I'm safe."

"Doesn't mean I'll have that same restraint again—especially if I'm hungry."

"Then we won't be together when you're hungry. Problem solved."

He continued to stare. "This isn't a debate, Elora. I'm Necrosis and you're a Rune. It would never work."

"What would never work? I'm attracted to you, and you're attracted to me. I'm just looking for a midnight romp in the woods. No commitment. No expectations. Nothing. Not all women fantasize about wearing a wedding dress. You're making this more complicated than it needs to be. All you need to do is not eat me. It's that simple."

He looked away again, dismissing my comment.

I knew I'd lost the argument by the way he withdrew from me.

"I appreciate your trust, but it's misplaced."

"I don't think it is."

"You don't understand how it feels. To feel a soul that powerful and not consume it. I loathe myself every time I feed, and if I fed on you...then I probably would take my own life. So, this can't happen. I'm sorry."

It was the first time I hadn't gotten what I wanted—and it stung. It stung because my desire was genuine. I pretended it wasn't there, but it'd always been bubbling underneath the surface. The second I'd laid eyes on him, I forgot about Victor. That relationship was over before Bastian spoke his first word.

He turned back to me. "And don't even think about putting me in that situation again."

Damn, he read my mind.

"Because I'll kill you."

———

We took the horses as close to the mountains as we could, then made the rest of the journey on foot. The night had officially passed, but the sunlight was so faint that it felt like twilight. With Bastian in the lead, we took a rugged path in the hills and moved toward the base of the mountain.

My eyes scanned everything around me, as if Necrosis would emerge and reach for my throat. Nothing was known about their lands. We didn't know if they had cities. If they had castles. If they grew crops. Nothing.

Bastian kept a quick pace most of the time, but he would abruptly stop or slow his steps, as if he'd heard something I could never detect with my average ears.

I had a notepad in my hand, and I took notes as best I could, in case I ever needed to return alone.

Bastian blended in with the darkness and the color of the mountain in his clothes. He was also strong like the crags that surrounded us, his enormous back and shoulders blocking the view of the sky up the hill.

"How much farther?"

He halted and turned back to me, his pissed-off eyes telling me to keep my mouth shut.

"Sorry…"

He moved forward again, racing against the rising sun. It grew brighter as we traversed the mountainside, and greater details were revealed of the landscape. The mountains were made of rocks and dirt, not grass and foliage found in the rest of the world. My lungs strained to breathe, like the air was too heavy. It was a very different climate from what I was used to.

Bastian made a couple turns before he approached the entrance to a tunnel. It was small, barely big enough for two people to fit inside. He went in first before he pulled out a torch and lit it.

We descended the dark path, a bluish glow from the minerals in the walls. Deeper and deeper we went, traveling far under the surface of the mountain. It was just a jagged and broken path of loose rocks and dirt, so we had to be careful not to slip.

"Can we talk down here?"

He held the torch high and extended outward, the hot oil missing his hand and arm. "Yes."

"You said Ice grows here?"

"Yes."

"So, it's a living thing?"

"Yes."

"How can something be living and be solid?"

"I'm not the person to ask."

"Just doesn't make sense."

He traveled farther, and the path leveled out, reaching a large cavern. He stuck out his arm and stopped me before I could go any farther. "Careful." He raised the torch higher and illuminated the scene.

Black ivy stretched across the floor of the cavern and up the walls, and little balls of Ice hung from the limbs of the plant. It looked like pieces of fruit, round apples and nectarines, only it was a solid piece of glass. It was clear all the way through, perfectly round like a sphere, and it reflected the light from our torches.

"Whoa…" I took a look around, seeing a sight that defied my entire understanding of the world. "How does something grow without sunlight and water? And if it's such a threat to your people, why don't you eradicate it?"

"It's a weed. You can kill it, but it's just going to come back." He dropped his pack and pulled out a smaller sack from inside. "Necrosis tried to wipe it out years before I was born, but it just pops up in other places." He took out his dagger and sliced it into the soil, cutting around the root of the ivy in the dirt.

"What are you doing?"

"The horses can only carry so much Ice. It's smarter to grow it yourself." He sliced it clean from the earth and placed it in the sack. "All we need is for one root to attach to the ground. Others will follow. Then you can grow and harvest your own in abundance." He cut a few others and added them to the bag.

"You think it'll grow in HeartHolme?"

"You have caverns."

"But our soil is totally different."

He dropped the sack back into his pack. "All we can do is try."

I dropped my pack and got to work, slicing off the spherical balls of glass and dropping them inside.

Hours passed as we worked in silence, harvesting all the Ice and carefully placing it into our packs. We'd each brought two packs, and while it was a lot of weight to carry, it wasn't enough Ice to make every soldier a weapon. If the ivy didn't grow, I'd have to make several trips out here until we had enough.

"What's your sister's name?"

He stilled at the question then looked at me across the cave. "Avice." He dropped his head and got back to work, slicing another ball and dropping it inside his pack.

"What's she like?"

"She's a lot different now than she used to be. When we were young, she was fun and outgoing. Always told me I was an old man, even when I was barely a man."

"I believe that," I said with a chuckle.

"But once she became bound to Haldir, she's become far more somber. Listens more than she speaks. Alienates herself from everyone around her. The conversations we share are stale. We can't discuss our past lives, so there's little to talk about."

"Why can't you?"

"Just too hard." He stood upright and pulled both sacks over his shoulder. "I can't fit anymore."

"Neither can I." I dusted off my hands then picked up both sacks, but I only lifted them halfway because they were far heavier than I'd realized. I dropped them back to the ground then lifted them one at a time.

Bastian pulled one off my shoulder and added it to his own load.

"I can carry it."

"I got it." He headed out and grabbed the burning torch from the ground.

I followed behind him, and just the single sack was enough to make my shoulder scream from the weight. On top of that, we were going uphill, so my thighs screamed too. I wore armor and carried a sword and shield, but the sacks of glass had to be ten times heavier than all of that. I lagged behind him, the distance growing between us, and soon, I was sweating so hard I could feel it soak through my shirt.

He turned back to look at me. Without judgment in his eyes, he extended his hand. "Hand it over."

"I said I'm fine."

"You don't need to prove anything to me."

"Are you kidding me? I have to prove myself to everyone—always."

He grabbed the sack and pulled it over his shoulder, now carrying all four on his own. "Elora, you never have to prove anything to me." He turned back up the path, moving with the same briskness as before.

I actually had to stop and catch my breath for a few seconds.

We continued our journey to the surface, the light from the tunnel visible at the very end. All we had to do was get back to the horses, and the steeds could carry everything the rest of the way.

When he reached the opening, he set the sacks down and took a seat on one of the rocks. "We wait until nightfall."

"Oh, thank the gods." I sat on a rock on the opposite side of the cavern, the distance between us just a few feet. "Have you always been that strong?"

"Yes. But becoming Necrosis has amplified those qualities." He had thick arms like my brothers, powerful shoulders that were packed with different layers of muscles. Even his forearms were ripped.

"I need to work out more."

He cracked a small smile. "No, you don't."

"It's pretty pathetic I couldn't even carry one sack…"

"The Ice has a high density. That's why you could construct two swords out of the small amount I gave you. It's a lot heavier than weapons and armor. I'm surprised that you could pick it up at all, if I'm being honest."

"Well, that's me, always surprising people."

He looked out the entrance of the tunnel, peering through the sunlight to the rest of the hill.

"Is your city on the other side of these mountains?"

"Yes."

"What's it like?"

"No different from what you're used to. Each of the Three Kings has his own castle in separate areas of the valley. The rest of Necrosis reside in their homes. We have to contribute to our community like everyone else, so some are farmers, others are carpenters, and so on."

"So, you're just like us…except you live forever."

He gave a slow nod. "Pretty much."

"And you can't have children, right?"

He shook his head.

"So, nothing ever changes. Old generations don't die out. New ones aren't reborn."

"When our population is on a decline, that's when we turn people. They become our children…so to speak."

"But that's not the same thing."

"I agree with you."

It was a sick and twisted reality. Living out the same day over and over, making no overall progress, and feeding on other people's afterlives just to postpone their own deaths. "That's disgusting."

"If our bodies didn't give in to the feeding frenzy, I suspect there would be fewer of us."

"Why?"

"Living forever is overrated."

I noticed the despair in his eyes, dull like storm clouds.

"It's like staying at a party too long. When you get there, it's fun. You don't want it to end. People start to file out. The fun dies down. But you linger because you don't want it to end. But at some point…it just becomes sad."

My eyes didn't leave his handsome face. Now I noticed the subtle expressions he made, the way his lips pressed tightly together like he cleaned his teeth behind his skin. I noticed the way his pupils grew full, that blue glow fading into darkness.

"We're meant to live a single lifetime. Without a dead-line, there's no urgency to do anything. There's no reason to have children. There's no reason to plant the next harvest. There's no reason to even leave your home. We're meant to die, and without that fear hanging over your head, there's no motivation to live."

"So, if you get your soul back…you're just going to kill yourself?"

He dropped his gaze. "Probably."

"But Necrosis turned you so young. You've never really had a chance to live."

He shrugged. "I suspect my sister won't want to go on, and if she doesn't, I'm not sure how I can."

"It's not your fault this happened."

His eyes lifted again.

"You can't hold yourself accountable for everything."

"I'm her brother. It was my job to protect her."

"And that's exactly what you did, Bastian. But at a certain point, you need to relieve yourself of this responsibility. If you salvage both of your souls, you aren't responsible for what she decides to do with it. You can start over. You can find happiness. You can live the life you were supposed to live and then die at the end of it."

He brought his palms together and rubbed them slightly, his eyes down on the ground. "I've got to get my soul back first. Then I'll decide what I want to do with it."

FIFTEEN

Elora

AT NIGHTFALL, WE LEFT THE CAVERN AND RETURNED down the rocky path we'd come from. With only the light of the stars to guide our path, Bastian took the lead, carrying hundreds of pounds in Ice.

It was easy to keep pace with him when I was completely unburdened by the weight. All I had to worry about were my sword and bow.

Bastian suddenly halted.

I halted too.

He moved to the edge of the trail and gently set all the sacks on the ground, doing his best to be as quiet as possible. The rocks shifted slightly, nothing that caught my ears, but it could have caught someone else's.

"What's—"

His hand sealed over my mouth, and he brought my face close to his. "Someone's coming." He spoke so quietly, I could barely hear him. "They're headed this way. I can hear it." He pulled his hand off my face and looked past my shoulder.

"How many?"

"I'm pretty sure it's just one."

"I'll take the Ice and keep going."

"No. They'll hear you."

"Then should we kill him?"

"No. That's the worst possible thing we can do."

"Then what?"

"You hide. I'll try to talk my way out of it."

"How are you going to explain——"

"Just hide. And don't come out until I tell you to." He let me go then faced the direction from which we'd come.

I moved farther down the path until there was a bend in the trail. I took a seat there, just barely able to make out Bastian where I'd left him. He took a seat on one of the boulders and pulled out his canteen to take a drink.

I heard the footsteps a moment later, followed by the outline of a large Necrosis.

Bastian continued to behave casually, like he didn't even notice.

The large man came closer into view, the details of his face impossible to decipher in the limited starlight. But he was tall like Bastian, ripped like him too. He was in armor with short swords on his belt and a big dagger too, so he didn't look like a civilian. Then a deep voice emerged, hoarse as if he'd smoked too many cigars. "Bastian."

Bastian finished his canteen then rose to his feet. "Damien."

"What are you doing over here?"

"Passing through."

"On this trail?"

"You know what it's like when you want to slip out without a fuss."

"And who's making this fuss? Beatrice?"

Bastian never answered. "Is there something you need? I need to get on my way. Haldir wants a full report when he returns from the Capital."

The First King was there right now?

Damien looked him over, like he saw the holes in Bastian's story but couldn't piece them together. "Use the main gate next time."

"Will do."

Damien walked back the way he came.

Thank the gods. I wouldn't have been able to move without him hearing me.

Bastian took a seat again and drank from his canteen. Minutes passed, and he stayed that way, waiting until the right moment to move forward. He eventually stowed his things, picked up the sacks, and continued toward me.

I rose when he came near. "That was close."

"He didn't believe me, so we've gotta move."

"Yeah, I could tell."

Bastian took the lead again, this time moving faster than he had before.

"So…who's Beatrice?"

"Looks like I'm not the only one with good hearing."

"It sounds like you do have a girlfriend."

"I don't do girlfriends. I'm not a boy."

"Whatever you want to call it."

"I was seeing her a while back. Didn't work out."

"Uh-huh."

He stopped in his tracks and turned back to face me. "I'm not a liar." His expression was hard, but his eyes flashed with fury. "I'm loyal, so if I'm committed, I don't flinch. But I wasn't committed to her, nor to anyone else. I broke it off a while ago, and it's not my fault she doesn't know how to let it go." He faced forward again and took off faster than last time.

"Damn, sounds like you broke her heart."

"More like her pride."

We reached the bottom of the mountains then crossed into the tree line where our horses were tucked away. Bastian had marked the bark on the trees, so we'd have a map to get us back to where we started. The horses were still there, a bit spooked when we approached.

Bastian dropped the sacks on the ground then stretched his arms and shoulders, like the weight had made his muscles cramp up along the way. It was sometime in the middle of the night now, the nighttime sounds of the forest amplified, and my eyes were heavy with exhaustion. I was a tough bitch who could endure a lot, but I was ready to return home and sleep in my own bed again. Ready to take a shower every day. Ready to start my mornings with a fresh sticky bun from the bakery.

"Do you happen to know a shortcut back?"

He tossed me one of the bedrolls and grabbed his own. "No."

"Damn." I set it up on the ground then moved to make a fire.

"No fire tonight." He was already on the ground in his bedroll, ready to fall asleep the second his head hit the pillow. "Damien and the others are suspicious now. We can't risk it until we're farther north."

I didn't put up an argument. Far too tired for that. "Alright."

We lay there together, the forest loud with all the creatures, the predators hunting the prey. The horses released quiet neighs and chewed at the grass near us. Sometimes I would hear a twig snap, but Bastian never stirred, so I assumed the sound was inconsequential. It took me a while to drift off, but once I did, I immediately began to dream.

We rode hard every day, trying to cut down our travel time because we were both anxious to be rooted in one place. We both wanted a hot meal in our bellies, a hot shower to wash off all the travel, an ale from the pub. I was also in a hurry because I didn't want the ivy we'd harvested to die. If we managed to make it grow, it would be invaluable.

Bastian was quiet throughout the entire journey. He never started a conversation, and if I ever tried, his responses were short and cold. That bond we'd had before I kissed him was long gone, and now he kept me at an artificial distance like he wanted nothing to do with me.

Like I might rip off his shirt and kiss him harder than the last time.

We weren't even friends anymore.

Maybe we were never friends.

Our journey to the south had taken seven days, but our return journey was only five because we booked it so hard. I waved the customary red flag as we approached, and the high gates immediately began to swing open for our entrance.

We rode through the open doors and entered the city, where the destruction of the war was still visible. The soldiers repaired the cannons and cleaned up the dead, but the debris from the attack was still visible.

We handed over our horses to the stables and went the rest of the way on foot.

"Are you going to see Ian?"

"No. Going to the caves first. Got to get these plants in the ground as quickly as possible."

He grabbed the sacks of Ice and hoisted them over his shoulders. "I'll drop these off at your forge."

"You don't have a key."

He'd already walked away. "I don't need one."

I went to the caves on my own, the same caves where Pyre and Storm had stayed during their visit. I went far underground, taking the tunnel that was reserved for an emergency evacuation. With a torch for light, I made my way deep down, far away from the afternoon light, and found a flat spot that seemed as good as any. I took out the ivy plants from the sack, which were already shriveled from the airless compartment in the sack. I did my best to plant them in the soil, to get their roots in the shallow dirt, and then poured some water on top in the hope it would make them look less wilted.

I stared at them for a while, wishing there was more I could do to ensure their survival. I didn't know anything about plants. Just how to forge steel and turn it into a weapon. How to make plates of strength and turn it into armor. Inanimate objects were all I knew, not fragile living things.

I returned to the entrance of the cave and came face-to-face with Ian. "Whoa, what are you doing here?"

"What are you doing not at the castle?" His eyebrows furrowed in that same angry way Huntley's did. "I told you I wanted to see you the second you returned to HeartHolme. And where is Bastian?"

"It's a long story, but I needed to plant some Ice in the cave."

"Ice?" he asked. "It's a plant?"

"Ivy."

His eyes glanced past me to the cave entrance.

"Bastian said if we can make it grow, it'll spread, and then we'll have a lot to harvest ourselves. It's a lot smarter than making several trips back and forth. We almost got caught when we were there."

"Thank the gods you didn't." His hand reached for my shoulder and gave me a squeeze. "I was worried."

"I told you not to waste your time being worried."

"You never answered my question. Where is he?"

I shrugged. "Went to drop off the Ice at my forge. It was heavy. I could carry it…but he moves a lot quicker than I do."

"Did he hurt you?"

I gave him a cold look that told him how tempted I was to roll my eyes. "Of course not."

"So, nothing happened?"

Well…not technically. "He's a good guy, Ian. He's everything he says he is. If he wanted to harm us, that would have been the perfect opportunity. He's earned our trust. He's earned mine, at least."

Ian stared for a while before he gave a subtle nod.

"I'm exhausted and really want to take a shower, so I'll see you later."

"I want to speak with Bastian."

"We've been traveling for two weeks straight." I rolled my eyes before I walked away. "You can wait until tomorrow, Your Highness."

I fell asleep sometime in the afternoon, but I slept through the rest of the day and all of the night. I woke up bright and early the next morning, my body truly relaxed for the first time since I'd left. The bed was so soft and comfortable that I never wanted to get up again. "Girl, I'll never take you for granted again."

I got a sticky bun from the bakery down the road and made my way to the forge a couple streets over. I was tempted to take the day off and spend it in my bed, but I was too excited about the Ice we'd harvested. There was too much shit to do, and I was the only one skilled enough to create what we needed.

I walked through the door with my cup of coffee and gave a subtle jerk when I realized I wasn't alone.

Bastian was there, dressed in a long-sleeved shirt and trousers, his short hair slicked back slightly. The beard that had thickened over our travels was gone after a shave, and now all the bones in his jaw were visible. His eyes were brighter than they had been before, like a shower and a long night of sleep had erased the dullness.

"What are you doing here?"

"Waiting for you."

"You know where I live." I walked to the table where he sat and set down the mug of coffee on the surface.

"Didn't want to bother you."

I saw right through that lie. The forge was a public place, not a private residence with a four-poster bed. "You're bothering me when you sneak up on me in my forge."

"Didn't sneak up on you. You just weren't paying attention." His knees were spaced apart as he sat in the chair, one of his muscular arms on the surface of the table. He'd already helped himself to some coffee because his mug was empty with a dark rim at the bottom.

There were a few balls of Ice on the table, so I took a seat and rolled one back and forth. "Ian wants to speak to you."

"I saw him this morning."

"How'd that go?"

He leaned back in the chair and propped his arm on the armrest. "He'll always be suspicious of me, regardless of my actions. It's disappointing but unsurprising. You can't expect the sheep to trust the wolf." The sunlight came through the window and blanketed him in a golden glow, showing the sharp angles of his face, the roundness of his shoulders. "But I guess it doesn't matter." His eyes shifted back to me, a light blue color that could be seen in the clearest of skies. Once his eyes were settled in place, they didn't move, as if stuck.

I was stuck too, paralyzed by that stare, my throat a little dry. Flashbacks flew by, my palm scratched by the coarse hair of his beard, his hot mouth yanking the reins from my hand and seizing all control. He had big hands, hands that he used to build things, hands perfect for enfolding a woman in his arms, holding on to all her curves.

I dropped my gaze and grabbed one of the spheres sitting on the table. They were cool to the touch, perfect circles. My thumb brushed over the surface, and I peered inside the clear, gold-flecked substance. The fragments were easy to melt and shape, but once they cooled, they held their position like steel. "I've got a lot of work to do. Not sure where to start."

"If you make enough arrows, you could take down a lot of them before they even reach the wall."

"That's what I was thinking too."

"I think your best fighters should have compounded swords. The more Ice, the less damage they take. You should be able to make blades that can take them down with a single hit."

I stared at him, the cogs in my head turning. "Not a bad idea."

"Daggers would be helpful too."

I nodded.

"I suggest you have an army on the ground next time. You have to keep them away from the wall as much as possible. Once Necrosis breaches the city, they'll be impossible to get out. The war will be over."

I nodded again.

"I can help."

"I thought you were a carpenter."

"I've been around a long time. Know a bit about everything." He rose from the chair and took one of the spheres with him.

I took another sip of my coffee then joined him at the forge. I got the fire started, coaxed it until the flames were white-hot, and then melted the first batch of Ice in the pot. The color deepened once it came into contact with heat, the clear appearance becoming murkier and turning blue in color.

Bastian pulled on gloves and poured the liquid into the blade mold, the fluid slowly filling it out until the shape was defined.

I did the rest, cooling it so it hardened and then attaching the hilt.

Unlike the other blades I made, these were a deep blue, dark like the nighttime sky just before the sun officially set. The other blades I made were silver, subtle and bright. The potency of the Ice was visible, and once Necrosis understood we were armed with their destruction, they would fear these blades even more.

I got to work, smashing it with a hammer, compacting it even more, shaping the blade so it could slice through the thickest rope, cut through a piece of stone. Once it was completed, I held it by the hilt and tested it out.

I wasn't prepared for the way it maneuvered through the air, so I'd spun it on my wrist far quicker than I'd expected.

Bastian stepped aside. "Careful."

"I know what I'm doing." I steadied the blade again and examined it further.

"Didn't look like it." He took it from my hand and laid the blade across his open palms. He turned it over and examined the other side, inspecting the blue material that comprised the blade. "Necrosis will know exactly what this is the second they look at it. Not only will you have the element of surprise, but also fear." He flipped it back over and returned it to me. "This blade should be yours."

"It is pretty, isn't it?"

"I know you loaned your sword to Ian during the last battle. I'd prefer it if you kept your own this time."

I stared at the blade in my hands but felt his stare right on my face. Felt those blue eyes blanket me with warmth. "Ian doesn't want me on the battlefield, and I don't have enough Ice to make everyone a sword like this, so it should go to a soldier." I lifted my chin and met his look.

His eyes were exactly as I expected them to be. "I risked my life to get this for you—so you will do as I ask." His stare burned into my face a little longer before he stepped away and approached the sacks on the table. The single blade had used ten spheres of Ice, and at that rate, it would go quick.

I set the blade down before I approached him. My eyes were on the side of his face, and I stood at his shoulder, almost close enough to touch. With the same intensity he gave me, I stared, knowing he could feel my look.

He ignored my stare. "Don't."

My hand reached for his arm, and my fingers immediately grabbed on to the bulk of muscle underneath his sleeve. I felt it the second I touched him, that rush of energy, the first spark of a fire.

He inhaled a slow and deep breath.

I gave a tug, trying to get his body to turn and face me.

He was as unmovable as a mountain.

My hand cupped his cheek, and I forced his face to turn. I rose on my tiptoes and reached for his mouth with mine.

He snatched my arm and threw it down. "What part of I want to kill you don't you fucking understand?" He stepped away, his shoulders rigid with tension, and his shirt fit him differently because his entire back was coiled with rage. He moved several feet away before he turned around and looked at me again, a thunderstorm in his eyes. His look was just as intense as it'd been before, but now it was tinged with unspeakable anger.

"But you won't—"

"You have no idea what the fuck I will or won't do."

The rejection was just as painful as last time. I was the kind of person that wanted what I couldn't have, but this was different. It hurt a lot more. "Yes, I do. You're strong enough to control it."

He gave a loud sigh that sounded like a growl. "You wouldn't say that if you could feel what I feel. If you could feel the torment as it wraps around your entire body and drowns you. It's suffocating. Unbearable."

"You'll get better at it—"

"It's not worth the risk. You could have any man you want—"

"But I want you."

He looked away, his jaw clenched tight with rage. "I have nothing to offer you."

"I didn't ask for anything."

"You're risking your afterlife for someone who's not even alive. I'm not worth it."

"I think you are."

This time, he turned around and released another growl. "Stop it."

"No."

He turned back to face me. "I accomplished what I set out to do. I've been granted asylum from your king and handed you the weapons you need to win this next battle. That means you and I are finished."

My arms crossed over my chest, and I maintained a hard expression, refusing to acknowledge how much that hurt.

He walked out. "Goodbye, Elora."

———

I carried on in the forge for the rest of the day. Whenever I was down, I liked to stay busy. I liked to work with my hands, keep my mind entertained, act like there wasn't a weight in my heart.

I forged the blades for the soldiers and made a few arrows, but once the sun was gone, I was too tired to keep going. I went to the pub across the street and sat at the bar. The ale was delicious, even better than I remembered, and I realized I never wanted to leave HeartHolme again.

When I looked across the bar, I noticed Victor sitting there with a woman. They laughed over their drinks, their faces lit up in the candlelight. Victor was so entranced by the pretty woman, he didn't notice me sitting there.

"Good for him." I paid my tab and headed home, the ale in my belly enough to keep me warm against the cold, to make me feel weightless enough that the pain didn't reach my bones. I made it inside the house, engulfed in warmth from the fire that burned in the hearth.

The fire that I didn't make.

I stripped off my jacket and tossed it on the table as I made my way farther inside. That was when I noticed him in the armchair, blending in with the darkness of the shadows, his knees apart, his elbow on the armrest. His eyes caught the light and glinted as they followed my movements.

My heart dropped into my stomach and bounced back up into my throat. Men hadn't made me nervous since I was a teenager. I grew out of that phase with an armor of confidence. But his presence made me weak from top to bottom, made my mouth forget to swallow. Maybe it was because he was dangerous. Maybe it was because he was the most handsome man I'd ever seen. Maybe it was because he gave me a thrill that no living man ever could. Or maybe it was because I was stupid.

He rose to his feet and approached me, a head taller, at least a hundred pounds heavier. He had to tilt his head down to regard me because of our height difference. Closer he came, his footsteps quiet against the rug.

When he halted in front of me, my heart stopped altogether.

"Are you sure you want to do this?"

My eyes stared into his.

"Because I meant every word I said."

I'd always been reckless and stupid, but this was probably the stupidest thing I'd ever done. There was still a chance to get out of it, but I didn't want to take it. When I saw Victor at the pub, I didn't feel anything. Anything at all. And come to think of it, I'd never felt anything for any man I'd ever been with. But with Bastian…I did. "Yes."

He released a slow, drawn-out breath, like my answer was the cause of his misery and his joy simultaneously. His blue eyes flicked back and forth between mine before his hand slid into my hair and his arm gripped me by the waist. In one fluid motion, he pressed his mouth to mine as he tugged me flush against his hard body.

I felt it again, that inferno. It started at my mouth and spread everywhere else, making me burn hotter than I ever had. My arms locked around his neck as I rose onto my tiptoes, our lips moving together like it was our hundredth kiss rather than our second.

He fisted my hair and gave a slight tug as he growled into my mouth. His arm squeezed my back harder, locking me in place against him. His lips deserted mine and rested against my cheek, his deep breaths loud against my ear.

I should want him less, not more. I should have been terrified in that moment, but I wasn't in the least. I either had a death wish or I really was the most fearless person who ever lived. My fingers dug into his hair, and I directed his lips back to mine.

His kiss was instant, more aggressive than it'd been before, and through purposeful embraces with just the right amount of tongue, he took charge. He kissed me like he had against that tree, kissing me better than any man had ever kissed me before.

I felt it against my stomach again, the outline of a dick he should be very proud of. My hand brushed up against it, feeling the bulge with my palm, tracing his size with my fingertips.

His hands suddenly dove underneath my shirt, pushed my chemise up, and he gripped my tits with his massive palms.

I moaned against his mouth when he took me like a man, when he squeezed me so hard it hurt a little bit. His fingers gave my nipples a pinch before he tugged my shirt over my head and pulled the chemise off with it.

I went for his shirt next and got it off, revealing the rock-hard body that had been tucked away. A hard chest was separated from a tight stomach by grooves that bisected all his muscles. His core was strong like the trunk of a mighty oak. All the lines separating the muscles made him look as if he'd been carved with a knife.

My lips kissed his chest as I undid his pants. I sank to my knees as I pulled the pants off, taking his underwear too. On my knees on the rug, I came face-to-face with the big dick I'd only felt through fabric.

With a hard expression, he looked down at me, the excitement and conflict written all over his face.

My hands gripped his thighs as an anchor, and I brought his dick into my mouth, gave the head a kiss with my tongue.

He sucked in a deep breath and closed his eyes.

It was a big dick, and I had to open my throat wide to get it in.

He sucked in another breath then released a loud moan.

I flattened my tongue and took him in, pushed him as deep as I could take him, but there was only so much I could handle without choking. I pulled him out and moved him in again, feeling him take up every single inch of my airway.

His fingers gripped me by the neck and gave me a squeeze.

I kept going.

His fingers squeezed me a little harder, cutting off my circulation altogether for a moment. With a shaky hand, he held me there, his eyes open and filled with desperation. His hand didn't let me go, continued to squeeze me.

I should be scared.

Damn scared.

But I stayed calm and kept going, pushed his dick inside my mouth and pulled it out again.

His fingers finally released their hold.

I took my first breath in thirty seconds.

He moved away and took a seat on the couch, his pants still at his ankles, his dick against his stomach. His head was tilted down, and he breathed hard, like it took all his strength to stop himself from doing what he feared most.

I got to my feet and pulled the drawstring to my pants. They came loose around my hips and started to shift down my waist. My thumbs scooped inside my underwear, and I pulled everything down.

His eyes lifted and stared.

I kicked off my boots then stepped out of my bottoms, naked except for my socks.

With a clenched jaw, he combed his eyes over my naked body, the fire burning directly behind me. He started at my tits, dragged his eyes over my flat stomach, and then stared at the bare skin between my legs. I preferred a manicured look, and judging by the desire in his eyes, he did too.

My knees hit the couch, and I straddled his hips.

He inhaled a deep breath when I climbed on top of him, and he let out a growl when I lowered myself over him, my wetness against his.

My hands clutched his shoulders, and I leaned into him, my back arching, my nails clawing at his skin. I dipped my head to his and planted my lips on his once more.

One hand gripped my ass hard, while his other hand dove into my hair again. He kept it from my face as he kissed me hard, as he gave me his breath and his tongue, as he ground his hips slightly so his dick slid through my wet lips.

I could feel him throb against me, feel the pleasurable friction right against my aching clit every time he moved. My nails scratched down his chest and left little marks in their wake as I rolled my hips and ground right against him.

He squeezed my ass harder then moved his lips to my jawline and neck. He kissed me everywhere, his hand moving to my tit so he could palm it and flick the nipple with his thumb. He grabbed at me and squeezed as he plastered me in kisses, as he panted against me as if I was the sexiest woman he'd ever been with.

The wait was killing me. Driving me mad. Making me insane. I pushed him off me then rose higher, grasping his dick from behind. I held it upright then wiggled myself onto his head before I slowly sank.

"Gods…" It was so good. Better than I'd ever imagined. I closed my eyes as I rolled my hips slightly, feeling every inch of that big dick inside me. My hands were planted against his chest for balance, and I let out a moan because it felt so right.

That was when I noticed how still he was. That he hadn't moved. That he hadn't released a moan of his own. I opened my eyes.

His skin was discolored. Blotches of black were visible in random places, up his arms, down his chest. They looked like soot marks, like someone had grabbed the ashes from a cold fireplace and rubbed them all over his body.

His breathing was deep and ragged as he looked down at himself.

It was the first time I'd seen the darkness up close. We'd been at war with Necrosis before, but I was always in the rear, in charge of armoring all the men who risked their lives for HeartHolme. But now, it was right in my face.

He lifted his chin and looked at me again, his eyes still the same beautiful color. "This is what you do to me…" He dropped his forehead against mine and continued his even breaths. His hands gripped me by the hips, and he closed his eyes.

His hardness never changed. He continued to stretch me like his arousal couldn't be abated, not even by the sight of his Necrosis.

Minutes passed, and he remained that way, and gradually, the dark marks on his skin started to fade. His beautiful skin returned, unmarked by the curse that had claimed his soul. Soon, he was himself once more.

His lips caught mine, and he resumed the kiss, his hand on my ass again. Then he guided me up and down, telling me he could handle this—at least for right now.

My hands anchored against his chest, and I moved over him, rolling my hips at the same time, taking his dick as deep as I could handle it. The fire between my legs made me forget about the threat right in front of me, the monster that could snap my neck and harvest my soul straight out of my chest.

He thrust his hips up to meet me, his hands gripping me by the hips. "Fuck." The word left his mouth in a heated whisper, his skin shining with sweat. He moaned with me, mirrored my breaths, got lost in the connection between our bodies.

It didn't take me long to reach my crescendo, not when it came to Bastian, not when he looked at me like that and fucked me like that. My fingers fisted his hair as I writhed, as I started to buck uncontrollably against him. My eyes locked on his as I came, saying his name over and over. "Bastian…"

His skin started to darken once again, and the focused expression on his face showed how hard he worked to fight it, to stay in the moment with me, to not kill me then and there. Both hands gripped my ass and guided me at the quick pace he wanted. His hard face had never looked so handsome as it did when he was in the throes of pleasure. I knew the moment he released because his entire body tightened, his eyes hardened like daggers, and he let out a moan that he couldn't suppress. He anchored me to him as he filled me, as his hips continued to grind while he moved inside me.

My arms circled his neck, and I stayed against him, unafraid of the dark marks that had spread everywhere.

My forehead rested against his, and I closed my eyes, leaning into him with complete relaxation.

He scooped me into his arms and held me there, his breaths fast and uneven, but slowly coming back to a normal pace. The fire burned in the hearth, the heat still warm against my back. As the minutes passed, the darkness in his skin faded, coming back to normal.

I pulled away so our eyes could meet. "I knew you'd never hurt me."

His eyes darkened as if that was the worst thing I could have said. "You have no idea how close I was—several times."

"But you prevailed. I want to do it again."

"You're fucking crazy—"

"I like being crazy."

He sucked in a slow breath, still wearing that pissed-off expression.

"It was worth it."

The anger slowly faded, his handsome face returning to normal.

"You were worth it."

SIXTEEN

Ivory
___

"You're getting a lot better at this." I pulled back my bow and fired, and Pyre swiped it away with his massive claw. I fired more, shooting off multiple arrows at once, and Pyre either swatted them away with his palm or flung his tail to hit them aside.

I'm gonna make them shit their pants.

I gave a laugh. "And you will. Trust me."

Storm lay on the grass, eating the sheep that had been given to him for lunch. He was much more advanced than Pyre, either by experience or instinct, and he rarely joined us in our sessions.

Pyre looked toward Delacroix. "Commander Brutus approaches."

I returned my arrows to the quiver and strapped my bow over my shoulder. "What do you need, Commander?"

In his full armor and weaponry, he stopped in front of me. "Your Highness, King Rolfe requests your presence."

Your Highness? I would never get used to hearing that. "I'll be there in a minute."

"It's urgent." He turned around and walked back.

"I'll see you later, Pyre."

Can I have a sheep?

"Yes. A sheep. Not a horse, alright?"

Sorry about that…

I hiked up the dirt path and headed back to the castle at the top of the hill. I made it through the double doors, up the stairs, and straight to his study—the study my father used to occupy.

When I walked inside, the guard shut the door behind me.

Huntley leaned against his desk, an open scroll in front of him.

"What is it?" I stepped forward. "Has HeartHolme been attacked?"

He tore his gaze away from the missive and met my look—and it was clear he was pissed.

"What happened?"

"I got a letter from Ian. I'm gonna read it to you."

"Okay…"

He unrolled the parchment and began to read. "Huntley, I hope this letter arrives before your departure, and I hope it's made it into the right hands as well. Sending you this information is risky and reckless, but it would be even riskier if you were unaware of the truth about the world you now occupy."

My blood went cold.

Huntley continued. "Despite what we've always believed, the cliffs don't separate us from Necrosis. They're among you in the Capital as we speak."

Now it went even colder.

"Necrosis is led not by a single king, but three. They're called the Three Kings, and the first goes by the name of Haldir. Everyone except King Rutherford and his most trusted advisers is unaware of their presence. I know you're wondering how they manage to go back and forth between Necrosis and the Capital, and I assure you the answer is utterly terrifying. They can fly."

"What…?"

Huntley ignored my outburst. "Only the Three Kings have this ability, but this makes them far deadlier than we realized. When Rutherford and Faron planned their coup to take back the Kingdoms, they forged an alliance with Necrosis. The Three Kings agreed to help them with their conquest in exchange for feeding on the blood-rich citizens of the Kingdoms. I know this is a lot to take in because everything we knew about our world is now shattered. Rutherford is no different from Necrosis. As far as I'm concerned, they're one and the same. We're all just food and labor to the two of them. They want the world to stay as it is, and the reason Necrosis attacked us in the first place is because they realized we're a real threat to their order of the world. Be careful, Huntley. I imagine the dragons are powerful enough against one of the kings, but I really don't know. Good luck." Huntley tossed the scroll onto his desk and looked at me again, furious.

I was so overwhelmed, I couldn't speak.

"You owe me an apology."

My eyes dropped to the rug at my feet, the truth too much to bear. My own father did this. He sold out every person in this world for power. He agreed to be their pawn just to rule. It was the most sickening thing I'd ever heard.

"Ivory."

My eyes flicked up again.

"On your fucking knees."

We were all just a bunch of sheep. Some of us worth more than others. Some of us tastier than others. It wasn't the world versus Necrosis. It was the powerful versus the weak.

Huntley moved toward me, more livid than I'd ever seen him. "Whether he had a soul or not, your father was Necrosis as far as I'm concerned. He was one of them—and never one of us. And you made me feel like shit for giving him what he deserved. Look me in the eye and say it. Say you're fucking sorry."

I dropped to my knees on the floor, not out of remorse, just weakness. That was the moment I knew I had no idea who my father was. I'd never known.

Huntley stood over me, bearing down on me with that pissed-off expression.

"I'm sorry…" I dropped my head and kept my eyes on the floor. So much hit me at once that I didn't have a reaction. I didn't know whether to weep or throw back a hard drink. "I'm sorry for everything." All I could see were his boots in front of me, scuffed from constant use. They were a little shiny, and I could see my disheartened expression on the surface.

He kneeled in front of me, bringing our eyes level. The pissed-off expression was gone. "Now, forgive me."

I inhaled a painful breath and gave a nod. "I forgive you…"

His hand slid into my hair gently and pushed it from my face. It was a soft touch, the kind he hadn't given me in a long time.

It made me close my eyes, and the tears fell.

"Baby."

"I can't believe it…" My hands cupped my face, needing something to cover the shame. "I can't believe he did this." The sobs cracked my chest. Burned my throat. Made me feel dead inside.

Deep and gentle, his voice reached my ears. "Baby." He grabbed my wrists and tugged them off my face.

I yanked them back and cupped the bottom of my face with my hand. My eyes turned away to avoid his.

He moved his head into my line of sight, forcing his blue eyes on me. "This is not your fault."

"I feel…so sick." The horrors my father committed felt raw in a whole new way. He killed my father-in-law. He raped my mother-in-law. He took over Delacroix and sat on a throne that didn't belong to him. I enjoyed a room in the palace like a princess when I was just a thief's daughter. We sacrificed people to Necrosis. We served Necrosis. We lied to the people we ruled and let them believe they were safe. "I feel…so ashamed."

"You have no reason to be ashamed."

"My family—"

"He's not your family because you're a Rolfe. You're my wife. You're my family. You're the rightful queen of Delacroix. That's not who you are anymore."

"How can you love me after everything he's done to you?" Tears continued to pour down my cheeks.

His hand reached for my face and caught a tear with his thumb. "It's pretty fucking easy, baby."

"I'm so sorry—"

"I know. You don't have to say it ever again—because I know." His arm circled me, and he pulled me in close, his chin resting on top of my head. He held me there on the rug in his study, listening to me cry my heart out. "I know."

———

I sat alone in the dining room, with a cup of tea and a sandwich that I hardly touched. It was hard not to look back over my memories and search for the evidence I didn't notice at the time. Evidence that my father was an evil psychopath.

Was that genetic? Did that mean I would be an evil psychopath too?

"May I?"

I looked up at her voice, seeing Queen Rolfe standing at the back of one of the chairs. "Of course."

She took a seat, her back so rigid she didn't even touch the support of the chair. "Huntley told me the news."

I looked into my cup of tea, the milk making the contents murky.

"Are you alright?"

I grabbed my spoon and gave the cup a stir even though it'd gone cold a long time ago. "No."

"I can only imagine how you must feel."

"No, you can't. Because I can't even tell you how I feel." I continued to stir my tea, playing with my food. "I feel stupid, you know? I asked Huntley not to kill him—and that makes me sick. I let it interfere with my marriage…"

"Your husband still loves you, so no harm done."

"But still…I said some harsh things."

"Huntley still made a promise to you based on the information you both had at the time. Let it go. I know he has."

"Still feel like shit. Huntley told me how honorable his father was. I see how strong his mother is. And I… My father is a fucking rapist. A murderer. A liar. I hate to think about all the other terrible things he did. Things I don't even know about."

Queen Rolfe directed her gaze out the window, having nothing to say to that.

"I'm sorry. This isn't your problem."

"You're a Rolfe. Your problems are my problems."

"That's...kind of you to say."

Her hand reached for mine on the table, and she gave it a squeeze.

I looked at our joined hands, stared in disbelief at her touch.

"My daughter."

I heard the words as loud as a ringing bell, but my brain could not process them.

Footsteps sounded behind me, and then her hand pulled away.

Huntley entered the room. He was behind me, but I could feel the way the room changed once he entered, the way the energy transformed. I was sitting in his seat at the head of the table, so he took the seat on my left across from his mother. "You didn't eat your lunch."

"Not hungry."

He grabbed the plate and pulled it toward him. Then he helped himself.

I loved that he didn't pester me to eat. When I was upset, he let me be upset. When I needed my space, he gave it to me.

He finished the sandwich in a few bites. "The game has changed. Now that they know both dragons are here, they'll realize HeartHolme is unprotected. Ian wants to send one dragon back to defend it."

I snapped out of my sadness. "They won't separate."

"Then you'll need to convince them otherwise."

"It's impossible." Pyre and Storm couldn't be more different, but they came as a pair.

"Baby, we can't abandon HeartHolme."

"That's not what I'm suggesting. The only way Necrosis finds out about the dragons is if they leave the Capital and travel south. So, if we take them down before that happens, the secret is safe."

"Even with two dragons, that seems like a stretch," Huntley said. "We can't depend on that."

"I should return to HeartHolme as soon as possible," Queen Rolfe said. "If war is on our doorstep, that's where I need to be."

"Ian did say something cryptic in his message," Huntley said. "He was obviously concerned that the missive would be intercepted, so whatever he's trying to tell me must be substantial."

"What was the message?" Queen Rolfe asked.

"They have a good chance of getting more of what we already had." Huntley turned his gaze on me, as if I would be able to figure that out.

"He said nothing else?" I asked.

He shook his head. "Said HeartHolme is about to be strengthened. That was the last thing he wrote."

I dissected that in silence.

Queen Rolfe figured it out the quickest. "The Ice."

Huntley and I both turned to her.

"They found more of it," she said, more to herself than to us.

"Elora said there was no more," Huntley said.

"Well, that mysterious man obviously lied," Queen Rolfe said. "And then revealed where we can find more. If that's the case and the entire army is strengthened by these weapons, then we can take Necrosis head on in battle."

Huntley rested his arms on the table, his body shifted forward as he held his mother's gaze. When he was deep in concentration, he didn't have the sternness of a king, more of a soldier ready to kill. "A war on two fronts. That's our best chance."

"What?" I asked in surprise. "You say they attack Necrosis while we take the Kingdoms?"

Huntley turned to me. "The Three Kings can't be in two places at once. It'll divide their attention. If what Ian says is true, they won't need the dragons anymore. They'll be equal in battle."

"But they're still outnumbered," Queen Rolfe said. "They need the men of the Kingdoms in order to challenge them."

The same thought crossed my mind. "I think we need to finish our work here as quickly as possible so we can join them. With the Ice, the men, and the dragons, Necrosis won't stand a chance."

Huntley continued to stare, his expression hard as he remained deep in thought. "I suppose you're right."

"If Necrosis attacks HeartHolme, we'll be able to defeat a chunk of their army," Queen Rolfe said. "That'll make the next war easier to win."

"Ian said they have a good chance of getting more," Huntley said. "He never said it was a done deal. I suspect they know the outcome of that venture by now, but he sent this letter prior to that revelation."

Queen Rolfe gave a nod. "I shall return to HeartHolme at first light. I'll take a few men with me. My son has regained his birthright, so my job here is done." She looked at her eldest son, the pride in her eyes.

Huntley held the look momentarily but dropped his stare when it became too much. "We should begin our acquisition as well. We've already wasted too much time." He turned to me. "Has Pyre improved?"

"Dramatically." He would always be more timid than Storm, but at least now he was confident in his own scales. Instead of seeing himself as a prisoner of abuse, he saw himself for what he truly was—a powerful dragon.

"Then he's ready to fight?" Huntley asked.

I nodded. "He's ready to burn everything to the ground."

Huntley abruptly rose to his feet. "Then I'll prepare the men for our departure. Baby, will you join me in battle or rule HeartHolme in my stead?"

He'd called me baby right in front of his mother, would say it in front of anyone because he didn't care. "I'll ride Pyre. You'll take Storm."

He stared at me for a moment longer, his hard gaze growing in intensity, as if he didn't just approve of that answer—but relished it.

SEVENTEEN

Huntley

COMMANDER DAWSON WOULD DEPART WITH MY MOTHER in the morning, so I was grateful to have Jerome, whom I trusted to stay behind. Jerome had served alongside me at HeartHolme and the outpost for many years. He was selfless in combat, as if a glorious death in battle was the way he wanted to go. I trusted him to execute my orders in my absence, and I trusted him to carry on if I fell. I ordered him to prepare half the army to leave for HeartHolme in the morning. The other half would remain behind and defend the city if the Capital were to attack. It would be a pointless move on their part because I would just take it again when I returned— with my two dragons.

By the time I got back to the castle, night had fallen. The humidity in the air gave it a warmer climate, so even on a cool night, it was infinitely warmer than it was at the bottom of the cliffs.

I ordered dinner to be sent to my room and stepped into my bedchamber a moment later. The second I walked in the door, I noticed the difference.

Ivory's presence had filled the emptiness, had filled the silence. Her jacket was over one of the armchairs, her slippers were at the edge of the bed, and she sat on the couch near the fireplace, an open book in her lap. She needed to finish her sentence before she acknowledged my presence, and after a couple seconds, her green eyes flicked up and met mine.

Her long hair was over one shoulder, soft because she'd brushed it after she bathed. She was in a silk nightgown, stopping just above the knee. A fierce look of authority was normally in her eyes, but when it was just the two of us, her features softened.

I stared at her a moment longer before I headed into the washroom and took my evening bath. Instead of letting the heat relax my muscles, I rushed through it, getting clean as quickly as possible so I could return to my queen in the next room.

When I returned, my dinner was already set on the table, along with the small bottle of scotch I requested.

I sat at the table, and she remained on the couch, her eyes down on her book again.

She was still a bit shaken by what she'd learned about her father. A bit unsure of herself. I didn't blame her. Wasn't sure what I would do with myself if I found out my father was the biggest asshole who ever lived instead of being the most honorable man I'd ever known. I was in just my pants, so I planted my foot against the opposite chair and gave it a push. The legs of the chair dragged across the rug.

She looked up.

I stared at her as I grabbed my fork.

She slipped the bookmark between the pages before she took the seat across from me.

My dinner was a juicy steak, potatoes, an entire loaf of bread, a side of green beans. I cut into the meat and took a bite. Her face was my entertainment.

"Are you nervous?"

"For?" I took another bite.

"You're about to conquer a Kingdom."

"My entire life, I've been at war. With the Teeth. With Necrosis. With Delacroix. It's just another day."

"Have you been to Minora?"

"When I was a child."

"So it's a place you've basically never been."

"I have a good memory."

She reached for the bottle of scotch and took a quick drink, giving a little cringe as it went down. "What's the plan for tomorrow?"

"We lead the army to Minora."

"Do we fly? If we do, they'll know that the dragons aren't at Delacroix."

"Doesn't matter," I said. "You're not to dismount Pyre —for any reason. Those are my orders."

There was a flash of irritation in her eyes, an instinctual reaction.

"Do not land. Not for me. Not for anything."

"I can fight—"

"Those are my orders. You burn that place to the ground until they surrender."

"Even the innocent people—"

"Doesn't matter. It's war." Assholes made a deal with the dead to take my homeland away from me. Ian and I had been just boys. I didn't give a damn about innocent people. It was called war for a reason—because it was bloody and brutal.

She looked as if she might challenge me, but she made the smart decision not to.

"If the duke cares about his people, he'll surrender immediately. The battle will be over, and we'll have another force to take to the Capital. And then we'll do it again—and again. I don't expect the Capital to be conquered so smoothly. They'll have a trick up their sleeve."

Her hard stare quickly dropped, and then her features tightened into a look of fear. "Shit."

My eyes narrowed.

"Ryker…I totally forgot."

He was probably at the Capital by now—Necrosis in his midst. "You can't warn him."

"Then what am I supposed to do?" she asked incredulously. "Just not tell him that he's walking around with a bunch of dead things that want to eat his soul?"

"He has information about us, so he's the last person they would consume."

"Not if they don't believe him…"

"And if that's the case, it's already too late."

Her eyes immediately dropped, and she gave a quiet gasp. "Fuck."

"Baby, I'm sure he's fine. They have no reason not to believe him."

"What if this was your sister?"

My answer was immediate. "I wouldn't be worried. She can handle herself better than anybody."

She looked away, as if she didn't believe me. "What if I travel to the Capital—"

"No."

"Huntley—"

"You'll blow his cover if you get caught. I know this is hard, but you need to have faith that he's okay. I'm not worried about him. His story is solid, and Rutherford and your father knew each other a long time. He's not going to hurt his friend's son. You're overreacting."

She stared at me for a while before she nodded. "You're probably right…"

"When we receive his first letter, you'll get the assurance you need."

She gave another nod.

I ate the rest of my dinner as she stared at a random spot on the wall behind me. Her eyes glazed over as she remained deep in thought, the consternation subtle on her face. She eventually turned her attention back to me. "How do you feel about your mother leaving?"

"She can take care of herself."

"I meant not having her by your side."

I'd stayed at the outpost for long periods of time to help Ian, so we were often apart. But now that I ruled Delacroix and soon the Kingdoms, we would always be far apart from each other. It would be hard for her to leave her people. It would be hard for me to leave mine. Ian could go back and forth and visit, but not her. "Everything has changed—and it saddens me."

Her eyes softened.

"The distance between us will be so great that I'll probably never see her. The only connection we'll share is the missives we send back and forth. She'll make a special trip to see our children when they're born, but that's it."

Her eyes remained sorrowful, saddened for me. "When she gets to a certain age, she'll need to retire, right? Hand the throne to Ian? Maybe she can live with us then."

"There's only one way my mother will leave the throne —through death." I'd watched my father die right before my eyes, and then my mother became two parents. My attachment to her had grown since she was the only parent I had left. She raised me to be the man I was today, and not seeing her anymore would be like losing her too.

"I'm sorry, Huntley."

I grabbed the bottle sitting in front of her and brought it to my lips. "Things change. My children will need me the way I needed her, and they'll become my priority. I won't be a son anymore. I'll be a father. That's the way of life."

"I know this isn't the same thing…and it doesn't mean as much, but you'll always have me." She watched me with heartbroken eyes, and her hand reached across the table to rest on my wrist. Her fingertips were callused like mine now, so her touch was abrasive.

I stared at her hand before I rested mine on top. "It means a lot, baby."

———

My hand gripped her by the back of the neck, and I shoved her face into the mattress, her ass high in the air, the curve in her back pronounced because of the way I pinned her. Her wrists were together in my hand and fixed in place with my grip.

I fucked her deep and hard, listening to her muffled moans as they tried to escape the mattress in her face. I fucked her like she didn't have a choice. I fucked her like I'd picked her out of a lineup and paid top coin. We left for war in the morning, so I should spend that time making love to her, but I wasn't in the mood for that, not after the dry spell she'd put me through.

I'd fantasized about all the dirty things I wanted to do to her all day long during our separation. When I walked to the military barracks, I imagined my dick in her mouth. When I ate breakfast alone, I imagined her pinned down just like this, taking my big dick with tears in her eyes.

I knew she loved it, so it didn't matter.

The screams came next, her tears soaking the sheets against her face.

This wasn't the first round of the night, and it probably wouldn't be the last. I added another load to the previous and gripped her hard as I finished. The moan that escaped my lips was unstoppable. It felt good to release, to fill my wife with all the seed she should have been getting the last few weeks.

I finally let go of her and lay on the bed.

She stayed that way for a few seconds before she rolled over and joined me. She was on her side facing the other way, her skin moist with sweat even though her only job had been to lie there and take it.

My arm hooked over her stomach, and I dragged her into my chest, the two of us sharing a single pillow. The body heat was uncomfortable because I was already warm, but I wanted her anyway. My chest to her back, my lips to the back of her head, I held her. "I missed you."

Her body softened against me. "I missed you too."

"I'm glad you're coming with me."

She turned her face over her shoulder to look at me. "Where you go, I go."

———

My body was fitted with the heavy armor Elora had made just for me.

For a king.

The armor was midnight black with the feather crest in front, but it was a masculine version of the image. The design was monochromatic, making me blend into the darkness when the sun went down. It had to add fifty pounds of extra weight for me to carry, but swords and arrows wouldn't be able to penetrate.

Ivory had her own armor, and the second I saw her in it, I had to do a double take.

She'd never looked sexier.

Her armor matched mine, the same color and same design, and it was fitted to her small body perfectly. Her brown hair was pulled back in a tight braid so she could tuck it inside her helmet, and that was sexy too.

When she noticed my stare, she met my look. "What?"

I looked her up and down and walked out.

I crossed the castle until I made it to the entryway. My mother was where I expected her to be, fashioned in her traveling gear, ready to return through the secret tunnel back to HeartHolme. Her expression was stern and heartless, devoid of all emotion, back in her role of authority.

But that expression disappeared when she saw me.

Her eyes softened. Her lips pressed together. She looked grief-stricken, this goodbye as hard for her as it was for me.

I walked up to her, soldiering the pain like a man. "Travel safely."

Her eyes flicked back and forth between mine, her emotions right on the surface. "Take back the Kingdoms. Burn all that resist you."

"I will."

Her hands cupped my cheeks, and she brushed her thumbs across my skin. "I'm so proud of you, son."

My eyes dropped because it was too hard to look at her. "I know."

"I can't wait for you to return to HeartHolme and help us defeat Necrosis for good."

I nodded, her hands still on my face.

"I just wish your father were alive to see this."

"I wish that every day."

She withdrew her hands. "I'll wait for your missive."

"I'll send it whenever I can."

"Take care of your wife."

It meant the world to me that Ivory was included. It was something my mother would have said about Ian—

because he was family. "With my life."

"Good. Because she will give you powerful sons and daughters raised to be powerful sons."

I nodded. "Goodbye, Mother." I'd said goodbye to her before, but this was different. Our world had forever changed, and we both knew it.

"Goodbye, son. I love you."

"I love you too."

She gave me another look of longing before she turned around and walked off with Commander Dawson and the men who would escort her back to HeartHolme. Her dress trailed behind her, and her long hair ran down the center of her back. She held herself tall and proud, like she was the queen of the world.

I continued to stand there, watching her move down the hill toward the stables at the bottom.

Ivory came to my side and followed my gaze. "Are you okay?" Her hand reached for mine, our fingers interlocking.

"My mother was devastated when she lost my father. It could have broken her, and no one would have blamed her. But she became the most fearless woman I've ever known. Strong. Resilient. Powerful. I wish my father knew everything that she accomplished. I just…wish he knew."

Her hand squeezed mine before she drew near. "I think he knows."

I turned to look at her.

"And I think he's proud of all of you."

———

Commander Brutus had the soldiers organized in their lines outside Delacroix on the field. The two dragons were there, part of the army with their matching armor. Ivory was already at Pyre's feet, her helmet covering most of her face, but the rest of her curves were still noticeable.

I walked to the front, my sword at my hip, my shield and bow on my back. It was a sunny day, the perfect weather to storm a castle. They would see us coming from miles away and be powerless to stop it. They'd have time to prepare their defenses, but they would also have time to panic. "Are you ready for this?"

Storm lowered himself to the ground so it would be easy for me to climb up. *I'm always ready to kill.*

"That makes two of us." I climbed up his side and reached the saddle secured to the armor that protected his spine. Elora had made a pommel too, something for me to hold on to when in flight. I turned to look at Pyre.

Ivory climbed to the top and got herself into the saddle. Her beautiful hair was hidden under the helmet, but her eyes still sparkled when they were directed at me. She gave me a nod, telling me that she was ready.

"Let's go."

Storm pushed off the ground and opened his wings wide. They caught his weight immediately, and he soared higher into the sky, almost going straight up. He righted himself once again, and that was when Ivory came into my view.

The dragons flew side by side, gliding through the air, while the soldiers rode their horses below.

I didn't wear my helmet. Instead, I kept it hooked to my armor. I needed my men to see my face, needed my enemy to know exactly who was coming for them.

Ivory shouted to me from Pyre. "I can't believe this is real."

I could. It'd been real in my head for a long time. I'd imagined how I'd take the Kingdoms so many times, but doing it on the back of a dragon had never been a scenario. The siege would be better than any I'd ever imagined. I could already feel the victory in my palms, feel the vengeance in my heart. I shared my father's likeness. I forgot how similar we were until I saw his portrait in the basement of the castle. I had his blood in my veins, his strength in my muscles, his heart inside my chest. I would take everything back in his name—and do it as brutally as possible.

———

The dragons circled over the army, keeping watch from the sky. The horses couldn't match our stride below, so we doubled back many times, keeping an eye on the action on the ground. We set out first thing in the morning, so we'd arrive at Minora at sunset. It would make the fire from our dragons that much more terrifying. The night would deepen, the flames would grow brighter, and if they didn't surrender, their entire city would be engulfed in the inferno.

Right on time, we approached the gates. Minora was northwest of Delacroix, the Kingdom farthest away from the Capital. It was similar to Delacroix because it was situated at the edge of a cliff, but not one of the cliffs that divided the continent. Below was the ocean, the waves beating the rocks and the cliff face.

When the army left the cover of the forest, we could see that the city was preparing for our arrival. They'd probably spotted the dragons hours ago, but that wouldn't be enough time for them to make a difference. The Capital would have enough time to construct large crossbows to pose a threat to the dragons, but not Minora. They probably had no idea that Delacroix had been seized in the first place.

What did they expect to do against us?

"Huntley."

I turned to look at my wife on the other dragon.

"Shouldn't we ask them to surrender first?"

"Why?"

Ivory's face paled slightly. "I just don't think it's necessary to start burning and killing unless they refuse to surrender. Isn't that the proper way to do it?"

"Did your father give my family the opportunity to surrender?"

Her eyes went dull. "My father isn't here, Huntley. You executed him. And Rutherford is at the Capital, waiting his turn. The people of Minora did nothing to you. I know you're better than this."

"I'm sorry if I gave you that impression." I faced forward again.

Ivory didn't say anything for a long time. "Huntley—"

"This discussion is over."

So, we burn?

"Yes. We burn."

Storm flapped his wings and took off, approaching Minora ominously with his powerful wings outstretched. He dropped his head and released a line of flame, burning the grass that led into the city, just to show Minora what was coming.

Ivory's voice came again. "Is that the kind of king you want to be?"

I ignored her.

"Because that's not the kind of king your father was."

That got my attention, and I was forced to meet her look.

"He would have asked for their surrender first—even if they deserved to burn. Save your wrath for the Capital. Rutherford is the one who deserves it. Not these people."

The gates opened, and two riders rode out—holding white flags.

"Huntley." Ivory's voice came from beside me.

I watched them ride out then bring their horses to a stop. The cannons of the city were loaded and ready to fight, and I could see the archers along the walls. Terrified men who hoped that the white flags would be enough to spare their lives so they could return home to their families.

"Accept their surrender and spare their men as well as ours," she said. "If you burn them first, they'll never be loyal to you when you take the Capital. You want these people to respect you, not fear you. If you do this, you'll be no different from Rutherford."

The power blindsided me. I wanted to punish these people for crimes they didn't commit. I wanted to unleash the force of my dragon on a city that didn't deserve it. It took me a moment to abandon the blood lust and think objectively. "Let's go down, Storm."

Relief flooded Ivory's face.

We lowered to the earth and glided until we landed.

Ivory did the same.

I dropped down from Storm's body and hit the earth with my boots. The two riders maintained their position on their horses, holding nothing but the white flags. They didn't carry weapons, symbolizing their peace-fulness.

I let Ivory join me before I moved forward to the men who awaited my presence. The horses gave a slight stir as I approached, releasing neighs of discomfort. They had the height advantage, so when I stopped several feet away, I made my demands. "Dismount your horses if you wish to speak to me."

The two riders obeyed my request. They removed their helmets as well.

I could feel Storm and Pyre behind us, their snouts just a few feet away.

Perhaps that was why it took the riders so long to approach us, because they could barely walk when they trembled so hard. They stopped a short distance from us, looking at the dragons behind us more than at me.

"Huntley Rolfe, King of Kingdoms." Their duke was too much of a coward to show his face, so he'd sent these two commanders to speak on his behalf. If this was who he selected to represent his power, then he was weaker than I imagined. "You may refer to me as King Rolfe. And this is Her Highness, Queen Rolfe."

Ivory removed her helmet to show her face.

Both men stared at her for a couple seconds too long.

"I accept your surrender," I said, bringing the attention back to myself.

The man on the left spoke. "King Rutherford is the King of Kingdoms. Does this mean you've defeated the Capital?"

"Not yet," I said. "But I will. And as part of the accep-tance of your surrender, you will aid me. I will spare Minora and all its subjects in exchange for rulership of your Kingdom—and the pledge of your army."

"What of the duke?"

"He's spared as well—if he yields."

Both riders dropped their flags and gestured to the men at the top of the gates. The doors opened a moment later. "Your dragons will have to stay out here. We don't have room for them in the city."

"That's fine. Send two cows. They're hungry."

Four.

"Make it four," I said. "The duke is to remove his belongings from his quarters because Queen Rolfe and I will reside there now."

"Yes, sir," one of the riders said.

"Yes, *Your Highness*," I corrected. "Make that mistake again, and I'll have your head."

"Yes, Your Highness," he said quickly. They both turned around and headed inside the open gates.

Ivory turned to me when they were out of earshot. "We don't need to take his room—"

"Yes, we do."

"I'm sure they have spare bedchambers—"

"Doesn't matter."

"We won't reside here, so—"

"Doesn't matter, Ivory. I'm the King of Kingdoms, and I have the best of everything."

"A bit egotistical…"

"Damn right it is. If you don't demand the best, then people will assume you don't deserve the best. Minora is mine, and I must occupy it as such." I stared her down, making sure she had no more objections. "I will fuck my queen in his bed and rule Minora as if he never existed. That's how it's done, baby."

———

The duke was a fat, middle-aged man with an ugly moustache. Duke Edgerson was his name. Now it was just Edgerson, my personal adviser to Minora. We were greeted with a full meal in the dining room, while our army was given food and housing until we departed for the next Kingdom.

I sat at the head of the table with Ivory on my right. Edgerson took the seat on my left, quiet and submissive the moment we walked in the door. The table was covered with a feast that we didn't need because the adrenaline had killed my appetite, but I ate anyway, just to establish myself as the owner of this castle.

Edgerson looked at me, his hands together on the table. "I assume you're the son of the late King Rolfe."

"Yes."

"I'm sorry for your loss."

"Are you?" The sarcastic quip escaped my lips like an arrow from a string.

Ivory gave me a warning with her eyes.

"I'm sorry…" Edgerson immediately glanced back and forth between us. "Did I say something wrong?"

"Yes," I hissed. "You just fed me some bullshit. And I don't eat bullshit."

Edgerson still looked confused. "I'm sorry...I'm not following."

"If you gave a shit that my father was murdered, you would have done something about it. But no one did a damn thing. Rutherford and Faron moved in, and no one blinked an eye over it." There were no repercussions. No loyalty. Their king was murdered, and they'd made no objection.

Now Edgerson didn't know what to say.

I went back to eating, letting the silence fester.

Edgerson looked past Ivory toward the guards standing at the doors behind her, and then with his eyes down gave a nod so slight it was almost unnoticeable.

But I noticed it because I noticed everything.

That was when the guards started to move in.

Ivory's back was turned, so she didn't see.

Before Edgerson could react, I pulled out my dagger and stabbed it right into his hand on the table, pinning him in place so he couldn't do anything to Ivory across from him. Then I was out of my chair, my sword out.

The guard jerked back with his sword in hand, not nearly as confident when his foe was aware of the attack.

I came at him and the other guy at the same time, swinging my blade and taking on both of them. After a couple hits and a flurry of attacks, I sliced the throat of one and stabbed the other through the stomach.

When I turned around, a guard had a sword to Ivory's throat.

I stopped in my tracks.

Her head was tilted back so her eyes could barely lock on mine. Her hands gripped his arm, and she breathed hard, her eyes watery.

Edgerson must have lost consciousness at the sight of the blood coming from his hand because he was passed out on the table.

"Surrender." The guard pressed the blade into her throat. "Or your queen dies."

I spoke through a clenched jaw. "Drop your sword, or everyone you've ever known dies." I took a step forward, my sword still at my side. "Your children. Your parents if they're still living. Your wife. Brothers. Sisters. Aunts. Uncles. Friends. Acquaintances. The butcher who sells you meat at Christmas. I'll kill everyone you've ever known, and you'll know the true meaning of loneliness."

He stilled at my words.

"Get that fucking sword away from my wife, or I swear to the gods—"

Ivory stomped her foot into his boot and pushed back down on his arm at the same time.

That's my baby.

She ducked so I could throw my sword and stab him into the wall by the neck.

He went limp and collapsed, but the blade went into the wall so deep that it kept him in place.

Still distressed, she dove right into my chest and grabbed on to me.

I squeezed her to my chest and pressed a kiss to her forehead. "It's alright, baby. I'd never let anything happen to you."

She pulled away. "So, was the whole thing a setup?"

"Probably thought they could kill me, then take my army."

"What about the dragons?"

"They couldn't do anything if they tried. It was an isolated event. Edgerson was stupid enough to think he could outsmart me." I grabbed the dagger from his hand in the table then stabbed it right through the base of his skull.

He collapsed forward, his face in his plate of food.

Ivory crossed her arms over her chest and looked away. "Now what?"

"We hang their bodies for the rest of the town to see, so they know not to fuck with me."

She turned the other way and paced, her eyes on the ground.

"What is it?"

She stopped, her eyes on the other wall. "I just didn't realize how hard this conquering thing would be…"

"Love and war aren't supposed to be easy." I grabbed their bodies and dragged them into a pile in the center of the room so my men could take care of it. "I'll evict Edgerson's men from the castle and put our men on duty. They'll be able to guard us as we sleep tonight."

"*You can sleep?*" she asked incredulously. "After all this?"

I held her look without a hint of hesitation. "Like a baby."

———

Just as a conqueror should, I fucked my wife in the royal bedchambers that now belonged to me and infected every inch of the castle with my power. I didn't wear a crown upon my head because the only people who did were those who sat on their asses all day. My father never did—because he was too busy doing shit.

As was I.

Sometime in the middle of the night, I stirred. Sleep evaded me, and I went to the armchair in front of the enormous window. The lights lit up the city and the empty streets, and far into the distance, I could make out the outline of our enormous dragons, curled up and asleep on the field, guarded by my men who surrounded them.

I could use a drink, but I didn't want to wake up my wife.

Thirty minutes later, her quiet voice pierced the darkness. "What are you doing?"

I kept my eyes out the window.

"What happened to sleeping like a baby?" She left the bed and came to me, wearing my clothes to keep warm. When she moved to the other armchair, I grabbed her hip and tugged her into my lap.

"I'm a grown-ass man. That's what happened."

Her arm slid around my neck, and she folded her legs underneath her to keep warm. "Bad dream?"

"No. Just anxious."

"Anxious for what?"

"To reach the Capital and smash Rutherford's skull in with just my fist."

Her fingers moved into my hair, and she lightly brushed through the strands, her sleepy eyes on my face. "We'll get there."

"I don't want to wait."

"You know we need the other Kingdoms first."

"And I'll take them. Just wish I could take a shortcut."

Her fingers continued to caress me. "I know."

My head turned away from the window, and I looked at her head on, watching her love me despite my uncontrollable blood lust. She caressed me like I was a gentle soul, not the barbaric murderer I'd become. "A queen has never accompanied her king in war—at least not here in the Kingdoms."

"I'm glad that's changed."

I wanted her to be safe, but there was nowhere safer than by my side. I couldn't leave her at Delacroix when the Capital could storm it. I couldn't let her return to HeartHolme when Necrosis could attack any moment. Right here on my lap was where she belonged.

Her hand cupped my face, and she leaned in to give me a kiss. "Come back to bed."

My hand slid up her thigh and underneath the fabric of her shirt, feeling the warmth inside the clothing. I inched up, finding the cotton of her panties that I wanted to yank down again. "I'll come back to bed—but I'm not tired."

EIGHTEEN

Ryker

THE CAPITAL WAS EXACTLY AS I REMEMBERED IT.

The salty air blew in from the ocean and combed through the heat of the city. The harbor was filled with sailboats after the fisherman finished their catch for the day. The city was a mix of homes and olive trees, of cobblestone streets with markets that sold the best produce in the Kingdoms. The homes closest to the water were painted solid white, just like the castle. At night, you could hear the waves beat the white sand of the shore.

Effie was amazed by it all. "It's the most beautiful place I've ever seen."

"It is." We rode our horse right through the streets even though it was prohibited, bypassed the guards who tried to stop us, and then made it to the main gate that led to the entryway of the castle. That was where we were stopped, but after a quick explanation, we were granted entry.

Effie remained close to my side as we entered the castle and made our way upstairs. The castle at the Capital was far grander than the one in Delacroix. With chandeliers made of crystal, expensive rugs, jewels on the walls, it was a place of luxury. All the portraits we passed showed King Rutherford and his family, none of his predecessors. There were individual portraits of his sons, some of the queen. I'd seen it many times, but it had a new meaning now after everything that had happened.

Effie looked at everything with paleness in her cheeks, looking just as terrified as she'd been when we were trapped with the Teeth.

Once we reached the top, we met with Rutherford's right-hand man, Scoros. He guided us into the throne room where King Rutherford was waiting. Once we stepped inside, I could feel the tension, feel the stares of everyone in the room. His sons, his queen, and the other advisers and servants who served him.

I approached the throne with my heart in my throat, terrified to come face-to-face with this man. I was a spy in their midst, and the second they realized that, I would be dead. Effie, too.

I stopped several feet away, Effie at my side. "Your Majesty, I bring terrible news from the south—"

He raised his palm to silence me, regal in his king's uniform. A crown sat upon his head, filled with so many jewels that the endless sparkle was distracting. He was a decade older than my father, and his face hung a little lower because of it. He was also heavier, enjoying sumptuous meals that we didn't have in Delacroix. He rose to his feet and approached me.

I stilled and held my breath.

Then he opened his arms and embraced me with a hug.

I let out the breath before I was ready, and my lungs deflated with a squeeze.

"My scouts told me the news. Delacroix has fallen to foreign invaders." He pulled away, his hand still on my shoulder. "I can only assume that means your father has been executed." Fatherly affection was in his eyes, like he viewed me as a son.

I couldn't say the words, so I just gave a nod.

"I'm sorry. Faron was an honorable man."

My heart gave a twinge for a different reason.

He dropped his embrace. "Tell me what's happened."

"The Runes took the city. They have two dragons—so there was nothing we could do. We weren't prepared for an attack, and even if we had been, we had no defense against such beasts. The gates were open."

King Rutherford gave a nod. "How did they make it up the cliffs?"

I wasn't sure if my father had told him about the secret passageway, and I couldn't be caught in a lie. "I don't know. They have dragons, so obviously, some of them flew."

He didn't seem suspicious.

"My dad told me to run, so I did."

King Rutherford glanced at Effie. "We can put her to work here. We always need help in the kitchen and the gardens." He must have judged her based on her clothing, which was modest compared to mine.

I didn't want us to be separated, and the only way I could ensure that was by telling a bald-faced lie. "Effie is my wife. We married last week."

I couldn't see Effie's reaction, but I bet her eyes doubled in size.

King Rutherford couldn't contain his surprise. "I didn't realize you were betrothed."

"It was spontaneous. My father wanted me to marry Elizabeth, but I'd already fallen in love with Effie. My father didn't approve, obviously. So, we wed in secret. I know he was hurt when he learned the news, but he quickly accepted her as a daughter."

King Rutherford addressed her differently now. "The two of you are welcome to stay in the castle until we reclaim Delacroix. You're officially the duke now. When the Runes arrived, did they have your sister with them?"

I shook my head. "Haven't seen her. I assume she's dead."

He gave me another pat on the shoulder. "You're probably right. I'm sorry for that."

"Thank you, Your Highness."

"Now, I need you to tell me everything you know about these people—because we're going to destroy them when they arrive."

———

We were given a spare bedchamber, and the servants brought both of us clothes to wear. Once the door was shut and locked, Effie rounded on me. "We're married? Are you crazy?"

"What else was I supposed to say? And keep your voice down. We can't afford to let anyone hear us."

She crossed her arms over her chest, dirty and weary from our travels. "What happens when they find out that's a lie?"

"How will they find out? We wed in secret."

"All secrets come out—one way or another."

"If I didn't do it, we would have been separated. Servants don't have the same rights as we do, so you would have been raped or beaten. I wouldn't have been able to protect you at that point."

"Well, if the Capital wins, we're going to have to stay married forever."

"That's fine with me." The words tumbled out on their own, like a boulder released from the top of a cliff.

The irritation left her face instantly. Now her eyes were wide again, pregnant with emotion.

My relationship with Effie had started with a bolt of lightning. We'd been moving at full speed since, galloping through time with the speed of the fastest stallion. We'd been through so much, survived so much, and that created a relationship unlike any other I'd experienced. The suffering bound us together—at least it did for me.

She remained stunned.

I gave her time to process what I'd said, because in the last five minutes, we'd gotten married, and now she was a duchess.

"Then maybe we should actually get married…"

My heart skipped a beat when I heard those words.

"But Huntley and Ivory have two dragons... I imagine they'll burn this place to the ground. It won't matter then."

"I'd still like to get married...if you do."

"Did you...did you just ask me to marry you?"

"I did...if your answer is yes." I didn't have a ring to offer her. I didn't even have a home to share with her. Right now, I didn't have anything but myself.

Her eyes shifted back and forth between mine, as if she didn't believe the question was sincere. "You could have a lady—"

"I don't want a lady. They're stuffy and boring."

"But I don't have anything to offer you—"

"I don't have anything to offer you either. Not anymore, at least."

Her eyes softened. "That doesn't matter to me."

"Does that mean your answer is yes?"

Her arms tightened over her chest, and her eyes watered slightly. "I think so."

Now I was in disbelief because I'd manifested my own future. I'd lied about our marriage, but now I would make it real.

"I want to be by your side as we fix this world. As we make it whole again."

I loved it when she looked at me like that. With pride, not despair. "There's no one else I'd rather have at my side as we do this. And I promise, we'll still find your family. When this is all over."

Her eyes watered a little more, but she blinked it back. "I know we will."

———

We weren't married, but it felt like we consummated our marriage that night. We were in a new place, in a room we'd never been in before, but we made it ours, made it home. We stopped sometime late into the night, and when the sun woke me up just hours later, I knew that our rendezvous had taken far longer than I realized.

I had to start my day, falsely serve King Rutherford in whatever way I could, and wait for Huntley to take the Capital. I could sabotage the city from the inside out. I just wasn't sure how to do that yet. I wanted to send a missive, but I didn't have any information worth relaying.

I got dressed and prepared to depart.

Effie did the same, putting on one of the dresses that were supplied in her closet. With her hair clean and dry and her skin free of the grime from our travels, she looked brand-new. She wore a blue dress with thin straps over her shoulders. It showed her legs from the knees down. She looked like a princess without a crown.

Now I didn't want to leave. "You look nice."

"Thanks." She looked down at herself. "Never worn a dress before…"

"It suits you."

A knock sounded on the door.

Effie stepped out of sight before I opened it.

It was one of Rutherford's advisers. "His Highness has assembled his commanders. He requests your presence in the grand hall."

"I'll be right there." I shut the door and turned back to Effie. "Wait here until I return."

"Wait?" she asked. "I want to see the city."

"I'll take you tomorrow."

"What if you're busy with Rutherford?"

"I promise I'll take you. I don't want something to happen to you in my absence. Royal ladies don't go places unaccompanied, so you'll stick out like a sore thumb. Wait, alright?"

She finally caved and gave a nod.

I departed the bedchamber and headed to the grand hall. When I walked in, I saw Rutherford at the head of the table, his eldest son Maddox to his right. His commanders and generals were there as well.

Maddox and I made eye contact then we exchanged a subtle nod before I took a seat. Half of the table was empty because it could easily accommodate twenty for a grand feast. The room was silent, and there were no drinks on the table.

Since no one spoke, I didn't either.

I waited and waited, but nothing seemed to happen.

We must be waiting for someone. Or several someones.

Thirty minutes came and went, and I glanced at every person at the table, wondering if they were as impatient as I was. Rutherford didn't speak to his son Maddox. He didn't speak to anyone. I wouldn't have rushed here so quickly if I'd known other guests were en route.

Who was so important that Rutherford would continue to wait? There were enough people here to start the meeting. He had his commanders and the person who had fled Delacroix. So, who was he waiting for?

A few minutes after that, the double doors opened as the servants allowed someone inside.

The man who entered was tall, taller than me, and that was saying something since I was already six-foot-three. He wore a dark blue jacket with a black undershirt and black pants. With lifeless eyes, he walked toward us, as if he was bored the second he stepped into the room. His skin was close to being fair, but it was a slightly deeper color…almost gray. With pronounced cheekbones and a heavy jaw, he looked almost inhuman. The skin around his left eye was slightly discolored—as if he'd been punched recently.

He was accompanied by a woman. With dark hair, fair skin, and bright-blue eyes, she looked distinctly different from him because of her beauty. She looked like a rose garden, and he looked like a swamp.

He took the seat at the opposite end of Rutherford. The woman took the seat beside him and stared straight ahead at the empty chair opposite her. Her clothing was dark blue as well, almost midnight black. Her dark hair was tucked behind her ear, revealing her slender neck and delicate skin.

Two more men filed into the room and took their seats at the opposite end of the table, leaving all the chairs between us empty. There was a distinct line in the center, a divide between them and us.

I'd never seen these men in the Capital, and I had no idea who they were.

The man stared down Rutherford across the table and, as if he were the king, spoke first. "How did this happen?"

Rutherford didn't have the answer, judging by his silence.

"First, they thwart us at HeartHolme. Now, they've taken Delacroix with two dragons. They'll take the other Kingdoms before they turn their eye on the Capital. How do you plan to defeat them?"

It took all my strength not to react to his words, but that was impossible when my stomach clenched so tightly it made me sick. Now my eyes took in his appearance differently, especially the color around his left eye. I'd never seen one in the flesh, only heard stories told by my father, but that simply couldn't be. It was impossible.

Rutherford spoke sparingly, and that could only mean one thing—that he was afraid. "We'll arm our cannons and shoot their dragons out of the sky."

The man brought his palms together on the table, his arms and hands covered by clothing. "You'll need something stronger than cannons. You'll need crossbows, something to pierce their scales and secure them to the ground. Have your engineers make this as quickly as possible."

Rutherford nodded—as if he wasn't the one in charge anymore. "Even if we take down the dragons in the skies, their combined army will still dwarf ours. We need men. We need soldiers."

The man stared and said nothing.

Rutherford squirmed under his gaze, as if he regretted the request he'd just made.

"The Runes were only victorious in battle because of the dragons. Now that they've vacated HeartHolme, my men will crush them as we should have done during the first attack. We will feed on the weak and imprison the strong for later use. HeartHolme will be no more. I have no men to spare."

My breathing increased on its own, and it took all my strength to keep it normal, to appear unfazed by the information I'd just learned. I'd fled Delacroix to act as a spy, knowing I would be putting my life at risk. But I had no idea that I would put my afterlife at risk too. Because Necrosis was here.

Right under our noses.

"You must turn to your ally in the north and request aid."

Rutherford dropped his gaze.

"You must ask for Regar. The Runes will arrive with their arrogance, and their morale will be crushed once they see the sun and the moon are obscured by black wings."

Black wings?

"They will grant your request," Necrosis said. "They will do anything to keep peace in their lands." As if the meeting was finished, he rose to his feet. The woman and the men who accompanied him did the same.

Rutherford recovered enough to speak. "Yes, Haldir."

———

I returned to our bedchambers, finding Effie standing at the window that had a view of the water.

She turned when she heard me and faltered slightly when I crowded her against the wall. "What happened?"

I pressed a single finger to my lips, asking her to lower her voice. I didn't believe we were being watched, but with treasonous words like this, I couldn't take the risk. "I just met with Rutherford and his advisers." I spoke in a whisper, our faces just inches apart. "He's working with Necrosis."

A quiet gasp escaped her lips, and her eyes looked horrified. "Oh my gods…"

"They're here. I saw them in the flesh—or whatever they have."

Now she had the reaction of cold steel, which was no reaction at all. It was just shock in its purest form. Terror. She didn't know what to say.

"I have to tell Ivory."

"How?"

"A letter."

Her voice broke from a hushed whisper. "You can't."

"I can't not tell her. They have no idea what they're up against."

"How many were there?"

"Four in the room, but there may be more elsewhere."

"What does this mean?" she asked. "Is Necrosis running the Capital?"

"Yes." That was exactly what it seemed like. I'd spent the whole afternoon piecing it together. "Humans and Necrosis are both segregated. The strongest come to the top of the cliffs. The weakest remain at the bottom. The Kingdoms believed they were safe from Necrosis, but in actuality, they walk among them. They're fed upon—and they have no idea."

"Gods…this is terrible."

"Yes."

"Why?" she asked. "Why would Necrosis want this?"

I shook my head slightly. "There's not enough room up here for everyone, so only the best of the best get to reside. The Kingdoms sacrifice their people in lotteries, so they're constantly feeding those below. It's a system—

and they want that system to continue. We're basically sheep—and they're herding us."

She crossed her arms tightly over her chest, her breathing uneven now.

"They also said something else…talked about black wings."

"Black wings? What does that mean?"

"I don't know, but they said they would use it to defend the city against Ivory and Huntley."

Her eyes frantically shifted back and forth between mine. "You don't think they mean…a dragon?"

It was the first assumption I'd made, but I didn't want to say it out loud. "I have to tell Ivory."

"Ryker, it's too risky. If you get caught, we'll both be killed."

"Then what do I do?" I asked. "Let them attack the Capital, having no idea there's a black dragon about to burn them alive? Effie, I can't do that."

"They seemed to have accepted us with open arms, but that doesn't mean they aren't secretly suspicious."

"Rutherford and my father were friends a long time."

"Still, we have to be careful."

"Our only other option is to flee the city and find them."

"Won't Rutherford's men search for us once they realize we're gone?"

"Probably."

"And we have no idea where Ivory is. I doubt they're still at Delacroix. They must have moved on by now."

I gave a nod.

"We should wait until they take Minora," she said. "Rutherford will know once the city has been claimed, and then we'll know exactly where they are. We can choose to send a missive or travel there ourselves."

I gave another nod.

"Either one is risky...and makes me uneasy."

The last thing I wanted to do was put Effie in danger, but I didn't have any choice. Ivory and Huntley needed to know exactly what they were up against. "Then we'll wait. In the meantime, we'll lie low."

"Should we still get married?" she asked, her voice turning quiet again.

My heart was racing in terror from what I'd just learned, but it amazed me how quickly it turned calm once I heard her question. "I'd like to—if you still do."

———

Unlike the streets of Delacroix, the Capital was blessed with electricity everywhere. All the cobblestone walkways were well lit, and it made the journey along the narrow paths easy to maneuver. The road away from the castle was windy because it was straight down from the top of the mountain, but the view of the homes and shops as they trailed toward the water was indescribable. The docks were lit up, showing the sailboats that bobbed on the water. The air was warm, filled with excitement, and the people we saw were always merry.

"This place is nothing like Delacroix." Effie held my hand, her dress dragging behind her on the cobblestones.

I'd noticed the spire that pierced the sky when we were at the castle, so I made my way down until we reached the double doors that led to the church of Adeodatus. He was the god of souls, of love, of promise.

"You think anyone is inside?" she whispered.

I grabbed the brass knocker and banged it against the large door a couple times.

No answer.

I twisted the knob, realized it was unlocked, and let myself inside.

"Can you do that?" she said.

"It's unlocked, right?" With her hand held in mine, I stepped inside the massive shrine, seeing the sculpture of Adeodatus right in the center, in the middle of a fountain. Monks in robes walked about, oblivious to the two of us by the door even though they must have heard us. "Guess these guys never take a day off." We approached the fountain in the center and watched them work at tables, their noses buried in dusty textbooks. "You sure you want to do this?" I looked down at her, her hand small in mine. "Because now is the time to say something." There was no going back. Once our souls were bound, they couldn't be ripped apart. We would walk this earth together forever, until our souls traveled to the light.

She held my gaze with such confidence that she didn't need to give a verbal answer.

"Alright, then."

———

After I pleaded with the high priest to marry two young people deeply in love, he agreed. The three of us stood in front of Adeodatus as the fountain trickled in the background, harp music coming from one of the great halls.

Our hands were together, our eyes locked in place. My heart kept a quick pace like a drum, but it was more from excitement than nerves. There was also regret because my sister couldn't be there. I hadn't been to hers, and now she hadn't been to mine. I imagined Effie felt the same way—and she didn't even know the fate of her family.

The high priest read from his text, but his words were drowned out in the background. My entire focus was on the woman to whom I pledged my entire existence. Her blond hair was framed around her face, and her green eyes were deep like the leaves in the forest. She was more than just beautiful, but brave and kind, with a heart that could love far deeper than mine ever could.

When I'd found her in the woods, I never expected us to end up like this.

But it felt right, nonetheless.

The priest handed me the dagger. "Her blood is your blood."

I took the dagger and swiped across my palm, making the blood spill out and drip onto my shoes and the floor. I handed the blade to her, and she did the same thing, giving no sign of discomfort.

Our palms were bloody as they came together, transferring between the two of us.

"You'll walk through this world as husband and wife, and you will enter the afterlife as souls forever intertwined."

———

We didn't make it back to the castle.

We ended up in a quiet alley between two buildings, shielded from the lights down the main pathway. Her dress was hiked up to her waist, her panties were tugged so hard to the side that the seam ripped just a bit, and I had her pinned against the wall with her leg over my hip.

Heavy breaths filled the space around us, muffling the rest of the world. My eyes were locked on hers, hers locked on mine. We suppressed our moans in the beginning to keep quiet, but after the minutes ticked by, we abandoned our restraint and just lived in the moment.

Her hand cupped my face, and she kissed me as she moaned at the same time, taking my big dick as she was held in place. Her nails cut into my skin slightly, not enough to bleed, but enough to make me burn as the sweat breached the surface. "Ryker..." She said my name exactly as I imagined my wife would, with desperate need, with lustful longing. I knew my wife wouldn't be some prude who would only get it on behind closed doors. I knew she'd be free, unapologetic, would fuck anywhere, anytime.

I knew she'd be like Effie.

My pants were just at the bottom of my ass, and her hand was underneath my shirt, clawing at my back. Her gown was dirty from the road, and now it was covered in sweat from our midnight rendezvous. The maids would take one look at it and know exactly what had transpired.

She looked so beautiful with a coating of sweat on her skin, with that beautiful shine, and it took all my strength to keep it together instead of blowing this grand moment prematurely. I wasn't going to start off this marriage on bad terms. I was a husband who put his wife first, a man who put his woman first.

But thankfully, she released a moment later, her nails deep in my skin, her face against mine to muffle her screams.

I could feel how tightly she gripped me, feel the depth of her climax. "Sweetheart…" I knew the whores faked it with me sometimes just to boost my ego, so I knew what was real and what was just a show. This was real. Every time with her was real. I barely let her finish completely before I released, coming deep inside her as her husband.

It felt so good, better than it ever had.

We remained tangled together against the wall, our breaths deep and uneven, our skin coated with sweat. Now we had to walk uphill back to the castle because we hadn't thought this through.

Her eyes were as bright as ever, gazing at me with that look of longing she'd shown when we first got together. "I guess I can just tell you the truth since we're stuck together. I love you."

My eyes shifted back and forth between hers.

"That's why I was so heartbroken…because I loved you the moment I saw you."

My feelings hadn't risen to that level, not until we stepped before the high priest and vowed to love each other for all eternity. But it hit me then. "I love you too, sweetheart."

NINETEEN

Ryker

A WEEK CAME AND WENT.

There was no news about Ivory and Huntley. But if there had been, I wasn't privy to it.

The Capital was a glorious city known for its beauty and ambiance, but it quickly transformed into a battle-ground. The engineers worked on large crossbows to take down the dragons from the skies.

I didn't see Haldir or the rest of Necrosis, but I suspected they were still around, waiting to find out if Rutherford had secured Regar. Effie and I spent our time together in bed most days. I would take her on walks through the city, and we would have lunch at our favorite cafés. If we weren't at war and Necrosis weren't in our midst, I'd think we were on our honeymoon.

Effie and I were playing a game of chess at the dining table when a knock sounded on the door. "King

Rutherford requires your presence in the grand hall." The servant's footsteps grew loud as he ran away then disappeared altogether.

My eyes locked on Effie's.

Her eyes immediately fell. "They must have taken Minora."

"Yeah."

"This is really happening, then…"

"Unfortunately." I gave her a kiss goodbye then headed to the grand hall. I was the last one there, and I felt the piercing gaze of Haldir as I moved to my seat. He hadn't paid me attention before, but now he stared me down as if I didn't belong there.

I feigned ignorance, as if I had no idea what he really was.

Rutherford spoke. "They've taken Minora. Edgerson surrendered."

Haldir was stiff in his chair, the placement of his arms blocked by the table. The beautiful woman was beside him, her eyes hazy like her mind was somewhere else. "Coward."

"They had two dragons, and Minora is a small Kingdom."

"Doesn't matter. Now the Runes have two Kingdoms at their backs—and two dragons."

Rutherford dropped his gaze, too intimidated to meet Haldir's stare straight on. "King Dunbar has agreed to loan us Regar. He should arrive any day."

Haldir should have been pleased, but he didn't seem to be. "We should strike when they least expect it."

"If they're holed up at Minora or Supertine, we'll be at a disadvantage, even with Regar," Rutherford said. "They're going to strike the Capital with arrogance, so when they see the mighty black dragon, they'll be knocked off their feet and unable to recover. The plan doesn't change. When will you return to the north?"

Haldir wore a stony expression, as if he didn't owe him an answer. "When Regar arrives, we'll return and prepare to invade HeartHolme. That city will fall before your battle commences, so the dragons can't come to their aid. We'll defeat them in both the north and the south simultaneously. They'll be our livestock, and all the remaining free folk will not dare to oppose us."

This was end-of-the-world shit.

Rutherford nodded. "The Capital will not fall. We'll return the Kingdoms to their former glory once this is over."

———

I sat in the armchair in front of the fire, my hands together on my knees.

Effie sat beside me, paralyzed by her shock.

"I have to send a letter." It would take them a few days to vacate Minora, and if I could send the crow first thing in the morning, it would arrive by nightfall. "Huntley needs to know what's going on. His home is about to be destroyed."

"I thought you didn't like him."

"That was before I realized Rutherford and my father had forged an alliance with fucking Necrosis."

"You don't know that—"

"I do fucking know that, Effie." This alliance had existed a long time. Necrosis played all of us like puppets. My father knew and never told me. He served the undead and didn't blink an eye over it. "And it doesn't matter if I don't like Huntley. I respect him. HeartHolme is home to my sister, so it's important to her, and she's the Queen of the Kingdoms now. I have to tell her."

Effie dropped her chin.

"Rutherford doesn't seem suspicious of me."

"But if he were, you think he'd make that known?"

No. "But we've been close since I was born."

"Delacroix was taken, and you were the only person who fled. A good king would take that with a grain of salt."

"Even if you're right, it doesn't matter. I have to do this. Huntley and Ivory need to know what's going on."

"What will happen if you get caught?"

I looked away. "They'll probably kill me."

"And worse."

I pictured Haldir staring at me one last time before he killed me and ate my soul. "Then I won't get caught."

Effie still looked scared, her breathing deep and even, her eyes pleading with me.

It was my job to alleviate all her suffering, but there was nothing I could do. "I have to do this. Even if it gets me killed…I have to."

She dropped her chin.

"And you know that."

———

I finished the letter and rolled the parchment into a scroll. I looked it over a couple times to make sure I hadn't forgotten anything, because this would be the only letter I would ever send. If I managed to get away with it, I wouldn't be stupid enough to roll the dice once more.

I purposely waited until the very end of night, just before the sunrise crept over the horizon. There was no daylight, just a lightening of the sky, making it blue rather than black. I'd be able to slip in and out of the aviary before anyone noticed. If there was a guard there, I'd try to sneak past. If I didn't have any other choice…I'd have to kill him.

But then Rutherford would know someone had been in the aviary who shouldn't have been.

It wouldn't take long for them to assume that person was me. Effie and I would have to take a horse from the stables and run for our lives.

I slipped the scroll into my sleeve and let out a long, slow breath.

"What if I go?"

I looked at Effie, my wife.

"I could say I'm sending a note to my family."

"And what happens if they read the scroll?"

"You could pretend you had no idea that I was a traitor. Your life is a lot more valuable than mine."

I stared in disbelief because her words couldn't be more untrue. "Effie, you became the single most important thing to me last week. If anyone is going to lose their head, it's going to be me. And I would gladly have it be me instead of you." I glanced out the window again, seeing the sky lighten just a little more. "I have to do this now."

"Then I'll come with you to stand guard."

"I don't want to implicate us both—"

"I'm going with you. End of story."

"Is that how this marriage is going to be?" I asked. "You bossing me around?"

She looked at me with a straight face. "Damn right."

It took all my strength not to let the smile break through, but it did, like the sun poking out from behind the clouds. Once it was unleashed, it took up my entire face, a full-on grin. "That's pretty hot, so fine by me."

———

The aviary was at the very top of the castle, so I had to make it outside without the guards spotting me. That was easy because, at this time of night, the security was pretty relaxed. The guards were ready to be relieved by the morning crew, so they weren't exactly paying attention.

With Effie behind me, I made my way up several floors before I reached the staircase on the outside. It wrapped around the tallest tower until it wound up to the highest roof. Cannons and guards were spaced along the different rooftops, having a great vantage this high above the gate.

We stuck to the wall as we walked up the staircase, our shoulders brushing along the wall as we moved farther up. Once we were close, I raised my hand and told her to stay back.

Her eyes flashed in anger.

My hand cupped her face, and I gave her a kiss against the wall before I left her there and kept going. I nearly made it to the top and peeked over the edge of the stairs to count the number of guards watching the messenger birds.

There was no one.

The birds were in their cages, inside replicas of the Kingdom they were trained to visit. There were several Minora castles, each with a different kind of bird. One was a falcon, one was a crow, and another was an owl. I glanced around again, surprised no one else was there.

I let a minute pass, just to make sure my assumption was true, and then proceeded forward. The sky was lightening with every minute, slowly passing from sheer darkness and into twilight. The birds gave a stir when I drew near, sitting on their perches inside their replica cages.

The falcon was the fastest, so I opened the cage and slipped the scroll inside the little casing at his ankle. I twisted the cap into place so it wouldn't fall then watched him hop onto my arm, ready to fulfill his duty.

"Thanks, buddy." I walked him from the aviary toward the edge of the rooftop.

"Ryker!" Effie's scream split the night. "They're coming!"

My heart somersaulted into my stomach. There was no one on the rooftop, but they had eyes elsewhere. It'd been a setup the entire time. "Don't let me down. This has to be worth it." I heard the thumping boots behind me and threw my arm up, watching the falcon jump and take flight.

"Shoot it down!"

I grabbed my bow, nocked an arrow to the string, and shot the archer before he could release his arrow.

Now I was in deep shit.

The guard fell while the other unsheathed his sword.

I pulled out my broadsword and prepared to fight, knowing more were coming. "Effie, run."

"No—"

"I said run! I'll meet you where we consummated our marriage."

With that, she took off, taking the other set of stairs.

When the guard turned to grab her, I struck with my sword, slashing him along the brace.

He couldn't do both, so he had to focus on me. He spun his sword around his wrist then came at me. Steel on steel. Man versus man. Our blades danced for a moment, but I was the superior fighter, and his throat was sliced a moment later.

I turned to leave, but the way was blocked.

By Rutherford and his army.

The other stairway was blocked too, so there was nowhere for me to go, not unless I threw myself over the tower wall.

Fuck, it'd be really convenient to have a dragon right now.

Rutherford wasn't armed, but he was the first one to approach. He didn't even wear armor, probably stirred from bed by his men. He apparently saw me as no threat because he walked right up to me, wearing the same disappointment my own father had worn from time to time. "Ryker, I couldn't believe it when my men told me the news, yet you stand before me, sword in hand. I pray you have an explanation for this."

I didn't hear Effie's screams, so I assumed she'd slipped from their grasp. That was all I cared about. I was totally fucked. "I sent a message to my father in Delacroix."

"You said he was dead."

"I said I *assumed* he was dead. His allies were supposed to break him out of prison once the Runes departed their lands. I wanted him to know they were in Minora, so he could flee to the Capital if he had the chance." I wasn't much of a liar, but my life was on the line and I had no respect for Rutherford anyway—not anymore.

Rutherford stared me down before he stepped closer. "You have no idea how much I want to believe you. I've loved you like a son."

My knees would be kicked from underneath me and my head would be sliced clean from my shoulders, but it would still be worth it in the end. My sister would have my warning—and she would be prepared for the danger that awaited her.

"Where did you send that letter?"

"I told you—"

"Don't lie to me. Only cowards lie."

I stared him down. "You're the coward. You're the one who's become a little bitch to Necrosis."

His bushy eyebrows hiked up his face, and his furious eyes narrowed.

"King Rutherford is not the King of Kingdoms. It's Haldir—King of the Undead. You've served him instead of your own people. You've turned your kind into livestock, plump for the butcher. Everything we know about our world…is a lie." It stung to say the words out loud, knowing my father was equally respon-sible for it. "At a moment's notice, Haldir can destroy us all. And you would let him."

Rutherford stepped closer. "Like all things, it's complicated."

"It's not complicated at all. How could you do this?"

He had the humility to actually look ashamed.

"How?"

He lowered his voice so the others wouldn't hear. "The asshole that used to rule this place abandoned us down there. Wouldn't grant us asylum. Didn't give a shit about us. Sent us back to that frozen hell without blinking an eye. So we made a deal with Necrosis. If they helped us secure the Kingdoms, we would let them be a silent partner."

We. "As in…you and my father?"

He didn't nod, but his stare was confirmation enough.

"There was no other way."

"The people below are still cursed, and now the citizens of the Kingdoms are also cursed. But you sit on the seat of power, so that makes it all okay."

"Judge me all you want, but I doubt you'd do anything different."

"I would." I'd never believed anything more in my life.

"Ryker, don't make this harder than it needs to be. Where did you send that letter?"

I kept my mouth shut.

The silence passed for a while as he continued to stare. He seemed to reach an epiphany because he let out a long, drawn-out breath. "The Runes returned to Delacroix—with your sister."

I kept a straight face.

"That's why you're helping them."

I held his gaze.

"Ryker, you don't realize what you're doing. Even if the Runes take the Kingdoms, you'll never defeat Necrosis. And even if you do, King Dunbar will sail to our shores and conquer us instead."

"I'll conquer him first."

His eyes shifted back and forth between mine. "I'm going to give you one more chance. Tell me everything you know about the Runes...or Haldir will have to deal with you."

There would be nothing after this. It would just be black—for eternity. "I'm not going to say a damn word. And let that be a lesson to you, Rutherford. That's what loyalty is—because you've clearly forgotten."

TWENTY

Ivory

THE CITIZENS OF MINORA WERE SO PETRIFIED BY THE way their Kingdom had been seized, they put up no resistance whatsoever. It was a peaceful surrender, so no lives were lost, and there would be no change to their customs or laws.

All that changed was the person in charge.

Huntley stood in front of the gathering of citizens who had come out to see his speech. Tall and proud, he wore the uniform of a king, his battle armor on top, the feather crest right in the center of his chest. He wore no crown, but he didn't need one to distinguish his unchallengeable power. "My father, King Rolfe, was assassinated, and my ancestral line of kings was destroyed by an outsider invader. That wasn't the worst of his crimes. He forged an alliance with Necrosis in order to do this. They live among us in the Capital—unbeknownst to the rest of us." It had been silent a moment ago, but conversations suddenly erupted. "I come here to take it back, starting with Minora, then moving to Supertine next. Once every Kingdom is under my command, we'll take the Capital and assassinate Rutherford the way he did with my father. I govern with honor and respect, not fear, so I ask for volunteers to join our army. Those who pledge their lives will be handsomely rewarded upon their return, and those who don't return, that reward will be handed to the people you leave behind." He stood on the rise, arms by his sides, his sword at his hip. He looked at the sea of faces, people he didn't even know but would rule for the rest of his days. "There will be no changes to Minora. Life will exist as it always has. But Rutherford needs to be destroyed first—and then Necrosis. Queen Rolfe and I will depart first thing in the morning, and in my stead, I leave Commander Tomas to keep you safe."

I watched him from the side, watched my husband assume the role of king immediately. He hadn't acted kingly when we met, but he now stepped into the spotlight like it was in his blood. He had his mother's silent authority. Possessed an innate honor that everyone could see and feel.

I'd never been prouder to be his wife.

Huntley finished his speech and stepped off the platform. His eyes locked on mine for a brief moment then he walked away with his men to organize the army before our early departure in the morning.

I looked back at the crowd, seeing the effect he had on everyone already.

I knew his father would have been proud if he could have seen this moment.

I knew his mother would be too.

————

I sat alone in the bedchamber, Huntley gone all day working. While I'd offered to help, I had no experience with military strategy, so I'd probably just get in the way. I could hack and saw in battle, fire an arrow cleanly through an eye, but that was it.

You haven't been down to see me.

My eyes flicked to the window, seeing the shadow of the enormous dragon in the distance. "I can hear you. Can you hear me?" For a second, I felt like a crazy person talking to myself. If Huntley walked in, he would think I was mad.

I can hear your words from your mind.

I tried to talk without speaking aloud. *Can you hear me now?*

Yes.

Whoa… So we could speak and nobody would know.

Yes.

Sorry, Pyre. Things have been busy at the castle. We're leaving tomorrow.

I assumed so, based on all the movements. The soldiers are like ants on a hill.

His voice comforted me in the silence, like having your best friend right beside you. I wished we could be together more, but because of his size, he couldn't fit inside the castle or behind the gates.

I want to finish this quickly.

I do too. But I think we have a long road ahead of us. Once we take the Kingdoms, we have to take Necrosis…and that may take a while.

Yes.

The door opened, and Huntley stormed inside. I could tell it was important based on the way he barged in and headed straight toward me.

We'll talk later, Pyre. I rose to my feet and looked my husband in the eye, knowing something had gone wrong. He didn't break down doors and get in my face like this, otherwise. "What happened?"

He handed me the scroll. "This just arrived by falcon. It's from Ryker."

My hand shook as I took it. "It's not good news…"

Huntley stared for a while before he gave a subtle shake of his head.

"Is he okay?" I unrolled the scroll and looked at my brother's scribble.

"He's fine. We're the ones in deep shit."

I started to read.

Ivory,

Yeah...I've got some shitty news. Rutherford is just a puppet. Necrosis is running the show. The main guy goes by the name Haldir. He's got a few men with him, one woman. I've been to the Capital many times, but I never spotted this guy in the castle, so this has obviously been a secret until now.

Oh, it gets worse.

Now that Haldir knows the dragons are in Minora, he's going to destroy HeartHolme in your absence. He said he'll leave after Regar arrives.

Who's Regar, you ask?

Oh, just a big-ass fucking dragon with black wings. Rutherford asked to borrow him from King Dunbar. I didn't realize dragons existed, let alone could be put on loan.

So...we're totally fucked. You better hurry your asses up and attack the Capital before the dragon gets here. Maybe divide your forces between Supertine and Eagleton? Conquer both at the same time and immediately move for the Capital.

In regard to HeartHolme, I have no idea what to do. May the gods bless their souls…

Don't write back.

-Ryker

PS: Effie says hello. Oh, and she's my wife now. Long story.

I lowered the scroll and stared into Huntley's steady eyes. "Shit…"

His features were calm on the outside, but I knew an inferno raged within him. "Ryker's right. We need to divide our forces. I take Supertine. You take Eagleton."

"You want us to split up?"

"You'll have the dragons. I'll take Supertine the old-fashioned way."

"I still don't like the idea of us splitting up…"

"I don't either, baby. But we're racing the clock now. I can't let one of my commanders conquer a city in my name. The Rolfes do their own dirty work." His blue eyes watched me for a while, taking in my look. "I have complete confidence in you. The second you arrive with those dragons, they'll surrender. Kill the duke and take charge. Once I'm done with Supertine, I'll pick you up on the way."

It still didn't feel right. "We've been separated before, and I don't want to go through that again."

He studied me again, harder and deeper. "If you're afraid, then you can stay with me."

"I'm not afraid," I said quickly. "Don't insult me like that again."

"It wasn't an insult. It wasn't an insult when I said it at the island either."

"The last time we were apart...it was so hard. Now that we're king and queen, I thought we'd never have to do that again." All the lonely nights. The fear that he'd been killed or hurt. The terror that we might not be reunited. It was horrific.

His hand slid into my hair, and he cupped my cheeks, directing my stare to his face. "I would never suggest this if HeartHolme's fate weren't on the line. Our family and our home are in danger."

I knew he was right, but the separation was still a knife between the ribs. I gave a nod.

"I wish I could see you take Eagleton atop of a fire-breathing dragon." His hand slid back down my cheek and to my neck, where his thumb pressed over the front of my throat and gave a gentle squeeze. His eyes watched his movements, watched his hand trail farther down the front of my dress until his palm stopped right between my tits. "You'll have to tell me about it next time we see each other." His eyes lifted again, looking at me with that same domineering stare he'd shown the crowd earlier. He wasn't just the King of Kingdoms. He was the king of me.

My eyes stayed on his as I unclasped his cloak, as I loosened the chest plate of his armor and the belt that carried his heavy sword.

His arms remained at his sides as he watched me strip him down to his naked skin. It was a stare full of power. Authority. Intensity. He wasn't doing a damn thing, but he somehow had control over the entire situation.

I removed what I could, getting him naked from the waist up. His body had become more muscular throughout our travels. His pecs were the size of shields, his abs were hills before the mountains. "Are you going to fuck your wife?" I tugged on his belt, and there was a loud clatter as the sword hit the floor in the scabbard.

"I will after she sucks me off." His hand gripped my shoulder and pushed down, forcing me to my knees in front of him. Then he stepped closer, untying his pants and revealing his hard cock a second later. His hand was back in my hair again, controlling the placement of my head and neck, and he swiped his thumb over my bottom lip as he beckoned it to open.

My bottom lip dropped and my tongue flattened.

He shoved himself deep into my throat and fucked my mouth like it belonged to a whore rather than his wife.

The tears started in my eyes and soon dripped down my cheeks. I had to fight for breath, had to fight the fatigue in my muscles to keep my mouth open and my tongue flat. He fucked me like I had no rights, like he'd paid for my time and he wouldn't stop until he got his money's worth. But I reveled in it.

His hand fisted my hair, and he continued to thrust. "This is how a queen serves her king."

————

Huntley stood in his full armor, speaking to his commander Tomas near the windows. They finished their conversation, and Tomas gave a slight bow before he dismissed himself. I was in my armor as well, identical to his, but my hair was in a long braid down my back. I walked up to him, my heart racing in both anticipation and fear.

When I came to his side, he turned and regarded me, giving me his focused stare.

I hadn't thought our relationship would change after marriage, but it did.

I hadn't thought our relationship would change now that we were king and queen.

I'd been wrong about that too.

Our relationship was deeper, having another layer of foundation that hadn't been there before. It was easy to love each other despite our differences, but it was a unique challenge to trust each other as we ruled side by side. But that came naturally. Our ideologies were identical. Our hearts were too.

He continued to stare, his intense eyes shifting back and forth between mine. He must have known that words failed me because he said, "I'm sending Commander Brutus with you. His one and only job is to protect you —with his life."

"Will he ride Storm?"

He shook his head. "Storm won't allow anyone to ride him besides me. The duke will surrender the instant he sees you in the sky. Once you enter the city, kill him and his advisers."

"But if he surrenders—"

"Look what happened with Edgerson. You can never trust them, regardless of what they say. All they have to do is kill you and take back control of the Kingdom. I'd judge them as a ruler if they had no interest in doing that."

"It just seems barbaric—"

"I don't care how it seems. You're a queen now. Act like one."

"A queen is merciful—"

"And you will be merciful to all the subjects of Eagleton."

"Can I exile the duke instead?"

He inhaled a slow breath, his anger simmering on the surface of his eyes.

"I can't just kill someone unless they deserve it."

That breath he sucked in released as a heavy sigh. "You aren't going to listen to me, are you?"

"Have I ever?"

He moved in closer and grabbed me by the wrist, jerking me close. "I don't give a fuck about the duke. I don't give a fuck about his wife. His children. The only person who matters is you. It's not worth the risk. If you can't put him to the sword, then Commander Brutus can handle it. I'm not letting my wife, my queen, be in danger. Is that understood?" He released me and stepped back.

I gave a slight nod.

"Good." He nodded back. "It's time. I'll take my forces northeast. You head east. I'll meet you in Eagleton once I'm finished."

The longer I drew this out, the longer it would take to be reunited. "Please be careful."

"Baby, I have two forces at my back. They don't stand a chance. They've no doubt heard rumors about the dragons too. They'll surrender the second I arrive."

I nodded.

His hands cupped my cheeks in his gloves, pushing my hair out of my face, and his eyes locked on mine. "Nothing is going to stop me from returning to you. I promise." He pressed a kiss to my forehead then abruptly let me go. He turned his back and walked away, careful not to look at me again.

If he did, it would be too hard.

———

I sat upon Pyre, soaring through the night as we approached the lights of Eagleton. It was slow progress because we had to let the horse and foot soldiers keep their stride, so we glided in circles, flew to the rear of the army, and then flew back to the front just to waste time.

But then we drew close, finally seeing the details of Eagleton. Like Delacroix, its gates were not guarded. The Kingdoms had never been at war with one another. The citizens were simply spread out among the different territories, all united under one banner. There was no need for military protection, not when the only enemy was at the bottom of the cliffs.

Storm wants to burn everything.

"We won't be burning anything."

When he agreed to fight in wars, he assumed he would be burning things.

"He'll get his chance. Trust me."

What do we do now?

"When we conquered Minora, they immediately surrendered. But I don't see that now."

Then I burn?

"No. Fly over the city."

Pyre dropped down low and glided over the settlement, seeing the soldiers on the ground, all looking up to see the mighty dragon in the sky.

"Roar."

ROOOOAAAAAARRRR. The power of his voice shook the air around us, made the ground vibrate with the force of an earthquake.

A large crossbow was fired, and the sound of metal hitting metal was so loud it hurt my ears.

ROOOOAAAARRRRR.

"What happened?"

Pyre jerked away then righted himself, his eyes down on the people below. *They shot me.*

"Gods…are you okay?"

It bounced off my armor.

"Thank you, Elora…"

Pyre opened his snout and released the stream of fire, roasting the soldier stupid enough to declare war on an armored dragon. The fire was so thick and hot that I couldn't see anything past the inferno. Then another stream of fire joined, coming from Storm across from us. All the houses in the vicinity burned, and the culprit had been dead for minutes.

"Enough."

The dragons closed their snouts.

"Get lower."

Pyre dropped down and glided directly over the town.

I raised my voice, calling out to all the people as we headed to the castle. "Surrender, and I will spare you all. In the name of King Rolfe, I seize your Kingdom for my own." No more crossbows were fired. Everyone below screamed and fled, trying to get away from the two dragons.

When we reached the entrance to the castle, Pyre hovered, ready to open his snout again and release the blaze that would engulf them all. "Surrender, or I will burn this place to the ground. What say you?"

Soldiers continued to stand guard in front of the castle even though it was a pointless exercise. Their arrows would do nothing to Pyre, even if he didn't wear armor. But they kept their arrows trained on us.

The doors finally opened, and the duke emerged. He seemed to be the one in charge, based on the fine clothes he wore. He looked up at us, and he had the good sense to appear terrified.

"What say you?" I repeated.

"Eagleton is yours, Your Majesty. Spare my people." He lowered himself to his knees, begging for his life with his hands clasped together. "And if you have it in your heart, spare me as well."

———

Commander Brutus invaded the city peacefully and immediately set up barracks for his men and horses. While the city had an army, it was reserved for King Rutherford to call upon for aid. Other than that, it served no other purpose. It was an agricultural site that produced most of the produce for the Kingdoms.

I landed Pyre and Storm outside the city, and Commander Brutus and his finest soldiers surrounded me as they escorted me into the castle in the rear. We entered the stone keep then found the duke in the entryway, the crown he'd been wearing earlier already gone.

The second Commander Brutus saw him, he pulled his sword out of his scabbard.

"Whoa, steady." I grabbed his wrist and halted it.

"King Rolfe gave his instructions."

"I'm Queen Rolfe, and I'm telling you to back down." I stepped toward the duke. "Eagleton is now under the rule of King Rolfe, King of Kingdoms. You have one hour to vacate the castle. You may remain in the city if you wish or leave it altogether."

He was a middle-aged man, a thick beard along his jawline, kindness in his eyes. "And who are you, m'lady?"

"Queen Rolfe."

"I've never seen a queen lay siege to a city."

"Well, I'm not like other queens. King Rolfe is taking Supertine as we speak."

"Divide and conquer." He gave a nod. "I received a letter from King Rutherford—"

"Rutherford. My husband is king now."

"Of course. He warned you would come with two drag-ons. I appreciated the warning, but he must have known there was nothing we could do. Our Kingdom is not built for military response."

"Then I'm glad you surrendered. His Highness bears no ill will toward the individual Kingdoms and their people. His only issue is with Rutherford at the Capital, which we will take now that all the Kingdoms are unified."

"King Rolfe…I remember that name." He gave a slight nod. "He was killed more than twenty years ago. I assumed the princes had been killed as well. Guess I was wrong."

"My husband can't be killed." He was too stubborn to be killed.

"So, this is about revenge?"

"More than revenge. This is about removing a dictator from power and defeating Necrosis."

Now his face paled.

"Rutherford and Faron were working with Necrosis. They live among us as we speak—because they allowed it. This is our land, and we will dispel the evil once and for all."

The duke didn't voice an argument, but it might have been because he was too shocked. "I wish you all the best, Your Highness."

Commander Brutus unsheathed his blade and moved in to strike.

I smacked his arm down. "What are you doing?"

"Following orders."

"His surrender is peaceful."

"Doesn't matter."

The duke stepped back. "I'll vacate the castle now. Just let me collect my wife and children."

Commander Brutus lunged at him.

I pulled out my own blade and struck down the commander with a force I didn't even know I had. "Stand down, Commander. Or I'll lock you up until King Rolfe arrives."

He stepped back, unable to retaliate because I was the queen. "He'll be furious—"

"He's always furious. I'm the one in charge here, so delegate your men to escort the duke and his family from the castle. Those are my orders, and you'd better follow them. Is that understood?"

He stood there with his blade in hand, conflict written all over his face.

"You will receive no punishment. My husband will know I was the one responsible." I was the one who would be punished with a salty speech and then a violent fuck, both of which I could handle. "Escort the duke."

———

Once the duke and his family left, the power exchange was easy. I remained in my armor and cape just to distinguish my status. Men followed my orders, and Commander Brutus and his best men stayed with me wherever I went. If I was in my quarters, they remained stationed outside.

The dragons were in the field outside the Kingdom, eating all the sheep they wanted to reward them for the long day and night. It was chaos in the city because there were so many new soldiers and so little space. Camps were erected outside to house everyone.

And we still had more that were about to join us.

Despite the exhaustion, I couldn't sleep. My nerves were wired, and I was worried about my husband in the north. He didn't have dragons for his siege, but I believed Supertine would still surrender.

But he didn't return the following day. Or the day after that.

The worry that had been simmering underneath the surface rose into a boil.

What if he'd been captured? What if he was hurt? What if he was... I couldn't even think it.

When the worry suffocated my every waking moment, I put my armor back on and prepared to depart. *I need you and Storm to come with me to Supertine. Huntley hasn't returned.*

We will burn it to the ground until we find him.

Thank you. I stormed out of my room and righted my helmet on my head.

Commander Brutus was hot on my tail. "Your Highness, where are you going?"

"To get my husband."

"His orders were to wait—"

"I don't wait." I turned around and faced him head on. "Huntley should have been here by now. He's not—so I am going to go get him. Just as he would go get me. I'm taking the dragons, and I'll burn that place to the fucking ground until I find him."

"His orders were very clear. If he didn't return, we move forward and take the Capital."

"You're a pain in the ass, you know that?" I snapped. "I'm going to save my husband, and you can't stop me. Get in my way, and I'll cut your fucking head off." I stormed off again, and this time, he didn't follow me.

I made it out of the city and down to the field, where both dragons were waiting. Storm still had blood around his snout from the last sheep he'd eaten. Pyre had wiped off the evidence of his lunch on the grass. "Let's go." I climbed on top of Pyre and held on to the pommel. "Head northeast."

Pyre leaped from the earth, the shift of his weight like a tidal wave through all my bones. Then we were in the sky, the blue ceiling coming down on me like rain. Storm was there too, his cobalt-blue scales contrasting against the pines below.

Pyre kept low to the ground just above the trees, and the three of us searched for signs of Huntley's army. I'd been to Supertine before, but never from Eagleton, so I didn't exactly know the way. But if we traveled north-east, we'd be able to see it up ahead.

I see something.

"What?"

An army. Far into the distance.

"Get closer."

He flapped his wings hard and flew at full speed, crossing the earth quicker than a crow could fly. We traveled leagues in minutes, and my less powerful eyes could finally see what Pyre saw long ago.

An army was headed our way.

When we came nearer, Pyre glided down, getting close enough for us to see but not close enough to put us in danger.

I saw it—the feather crest on his chest. "It's him. Oh, thank the gods."

Pyre glided down until we landed on the grass. Storm continued to fly around.

I slid down his scales to the ground and ran to Huntley across the empty space that divided us.

Huntley dismounted his horse, removed his helmet, and watched me run at him at full speed. There was no smile, just his commanding blue eyes.

I ran into his chest and immediately circled my arms around his neck.

His hand was immediately on my ass, his mouth kissing me like we were alone together. He groped me right in front of his men as if he didn't give a damn who saw. His mouth devoured mine, and once he was finished, he gave my ass a hard smack. "I told you to wait for me." His blue eyes pierced mine, showing their anger along with their power.

"I don't care. I was worried."

"Eagleton is under our rule?"

"Yes."

"And you killed the duke?"

I stared.

He stared back.

"Will you take Storm back or—"

"So, it's impossible for you to do as I ask." His eyes shifted back and forth between mine, furious.

"You knew what you signed up for when you married me." I stepped away. "Don't act surprised."

"I'm surprised that you could convince my commander to disregard my orders as well."

"I threatened to kill him, so…"

His gaze hardened.

"Are you taking Storm?"

"No. I'll ride back with my men."

"Alright." I turned away, knowing this fight would continue once he reached Eagleton. "I'm glad you're okay."

———

I heard him before I saw him. "Were my orders unclear?" His voice echoed off the stone of the keep, was loud enough to snuff out any nearby lit candles. He seemed to be downstairs, but the power of his voice rose all the way to the next floor. "Kill the duke. And not let my wife leave. Pretty simple fucking instructions."

I rushed down the stairs and found him in the foyer, Commander Brutus standing with his arms behind his back. "Huntley, leave him alone."

My husband didn't look at me. "I can't rule the Kingdoms if I can't trust my own men."

"You told me to take Eagleton while you took Supertine, which means I'm in charge. Or am I wrong?"

After a loud breath, Huntley turned to look at me.

"Or am I wrong?" I repeated.

He stayed quiet.

"Commander Brutus serves me in your absence, which means he takes orders from me, not you. If you want me to stay your queen, then you'll need to learn to share power, to respect my decisions, and to not barge in here like you own the place—because I own it too." I turned to Commander Brutus. "You're dismissed."

He gave a nod before he walked off.

Huntley continued to stare, tall and proud in his armor, a few scuffs from the swords that had scratched his plates in battle. He rounded on me as if I was the enemy, his arms by his sides.

"Is that understood?"

His stare only intensified.

Everyone else was afraid of this man, but I sure wasn't. I turned my back on him and returned upstairs to the quarters that were vacant when I arrived. They had a bed big enough for the two of us and a private washroom. I took up residence immediately, looking out the window often to check on the dragons.

He entered the room a moment later, slamming the door behind him.

I'd changed out of my armor into a dress once I'd returned to the castle, and the second all those things were off my body, I felt so much lighter. My muscles were stronger now after being strained under the weight. I turned around to look at him, not responding to his intimidation.

He stared me down for a while before he tossed his helmet to the side and dropped the various pieces of armor that protected his body. More of his skin was revealed as he came closer, and that was when I saw the deep scar in his arm, like a boulder had struck him from the side and bruised him badly.

He got the rest of his clothes off, stripping down to nakedness.

He was rock hard.

His mind hated my defiance, but his body was aroused by it. He stalked closer and backed me up into the bed, his head dipping down to look me in the eye. When my ass touched the bed, he fisted my hair and kissed me, kissed me hard. It was a crushing kiss, like he wanted me but was also pissed about it at the same time.

It drew me out of my anger, and my hands found their way to his chest, feeling the slabs of stone that protected his heart. His skin was searing hot as if he were standing in the middle of a fire but didn't get burned.

His hand gave my ass a hard smack before he grabbed my hips and yanked me back onto the bed. He gathered my dress and hiked it up to my waist before he ripped off my underwear. Then he dragged me into position and shoved himself all the way inside me, hitting me deep and hard like he wanted to hurt me.

He could never hurt me, not when it felt so good.

His hands grabbed on to the tops of my thighs to keep me in place—and then he fucked me so hard it sounded like the bed was about to break. The legs wobbled with every thrust, and at any moment, they were about to splinter.

But he carried on like he didn't even notice. "Baby, you drive me fucking crazy."

TWENTY-ONE

Huntley

I WAS UP AT THE CRACK OF DAWN.

First thing first, I fucked my wife.

It was the way I liked to get my day started.

Half asleep, she just lay there, moaning incoherently, climaxing with quiet sighs rather than screams. Her eyes barely opened most of the time.

I threw on my king's uniform then entered the great hall, where I found Commander Brutus and my advisers drinking coffee and poring over maps. When I entered the room, they all rose to their feet to greet me in silence.

I took the seat at the head of the table, and they lowered back into their seats.

One of the servants immediately brought me coffee and a breakfast tray without my having to ask. It was eggs, breakfast sausage, and freshly baked toast—my favorite. I suspected Ivory had told them exactly what to make me yesterday.

"We don't have time to waste. We must make our attack on the Capital immediately." The Capital was a short distance away, less than half a day's ride. That was how I had mapped it out, to take the Kingdoms in that specific order so the final journey would be the shortest. Our army easily dwarfed theirs, and with our two drag-ons, the siege would be easy. Except for one fact—they may have a dragon of their own. "Make sure all the soldiers are well-fed and well rested before tomorrow. We take everyone and leave the Kingdoms with just enough people to keep them functional in our absence."

Ivory walked in the door, in a dress similar to the one my mother wore, the feather crest on her chest. She must not have been able to get back to sleep after I ravished her, so she had brushed her hair and decided to join me. Her eyes were still sleepy, like she would be a bit dazed all day. She approached the table and prepared to take a seat at the end.

"Move." I looked to Evan, the adviser on my right.

He jerked upright at my command and immediately vacated the chair.

"Baby." I pulled out the chair for her.

Evan moved to the end of the table where she had been planning to sit, and Ivory approached the chair I'd just commandeered for her. She took the seat and scooted forward until her arms rested on the table. "What's the plan?"

"Have you told Pyre and Storm about the black dragon?"

She shook her head. "Hasn't been on my mind for the last few days."

"If we can get to the Capital before Regar arrives, we can take the city easily. If he's there…it'll be more challenging."

"We'll need crossbows."

"I was hoping our dragons could defeat him since there are two."

Her eyes remained on the table, as if she wasn't convinced. "We don't know anything about Regar. He could be bigger. Could have more experience in battle. I wouldn't put all the burden on Pyre and Storm. We need to have our own plan to eliminate him."

"Never killed a dragon before, so I don't have much to offer."

"Do you think he'll have armor?"

I gave a shrug.

"If he doesn't, the crossbows will do the job."

"The crossbows are only effective at close range, so unless Regar is where we want him to be, it's not going to work."

She was quiet for a while, and as if the thought struck her like a bolt of lightning, she perked up. "Pyre and I can speak across distances. When he's outside on the field and I'm in the castle, we can still communicate."

I'd never tried that with Storm. "Your point?"

"We can tell Pyre and Storm where to lure Regar so we can shoot him down."

It was a great plan, and I was immediately struck with pride that she had suggested it. "That's perfect, baby."

———

We sat together in front of the fire in our bedroom, my shirt covering her to her knees. She lay across my lap, her feet propped on the armrest, so the shirt slid up her thighs and exposed just a bit of her panties. Her hair was across my lap, and she looked up at me with tired eyes. Beautiful eyes.

My fingers moved through her hair, feeling the softness of the strands. I looked down at her as she looked up at me, lost in her eyes like she was lost in mine. My hand left her hair and traveled over her chest to her belly. "I want to put a baby in you."

"We're about to march on the Capital, and that's what you're thinking about?"

My hand slid underneath the cotton and felt her soft belly. "I'm always thinking about it."

"We've got a long road ahead of us…"

"But it'll end. And once that ends, we begin." I was the king the way my father had been, but I didn't have a son like he did. My wife was more than just the woman who would birth my children. She ruled alongside me, and she would make the perfect mother. I wanted that picture to be a reality, to have children to teach, to be a role model to someone. My father had been stolen far too young, and now that I'd taken his role, there was no one to take mine.

"You don't want to enjoy each other for a while?"

"We'll always enjoy each other, baby."

"Well…my body will be different. I'll be different."

My eyebrows furrowed in confusion.

"Just in case you don't realize it, I might have scars on my belly. My skin might be loose. My tits might not be as perky as they are now."

My eyes remained narrowed on her face. "Your body is going to grow me a son or daughter. It's going to battle so they'll live, so they'll be healthy, so they'll leave your

325

womb and survive. If I returned from battle covered in scars, would you love me less?"

"No…but that's not the same thing."

"It is the same thing, baby. Nothing will change, except that I'll love you more."

Her eyes softened.

"I love you more because you'll give me my sons and daughters."

"Then, when this is all over…we can talk about it. We've got to survive the Capital. Then we've got to survive Necrosis. It's all uphill from here."

"We'll make it, baby."

"You know what they say. Don't count your chickens before they hatch. I don't want to think about the future too much, not when I'm not sure if we're going to have one." Her eyes dropped down to the fire, the hardness settling into her face.

My fingers flattened across her entire abdomen, feeling a child we hadn't even created.

"We will. I promise."

TWENTY-TWO

Ryker
_____

I woke up in a pool of my own blood.

I blinked a couple times, the red color dull at first, but slowly becoming more prominent as my mind sharpened. I felt the ache in my mouth and realized the source. My hands pushed against the stone floor, and once my arms shook, I knew how bad the damage was. My entire face hurt. The rest of my body too, I quickly realized.

It all came flooding back to me.

Rutherford's cronies beating me until I talked.

But I didn't talk.

I passed out instead.

I wasn't sure how much time had passed. Had I been in here for days or weeks? Had Huntley already attacked the Capital and lost? Where was Effie? Did she escape? Or was she subjected to the same torture in another cell?

I leaned against the wall and rubbed my temple, the subdued migraine coming back to the surface. There was a plate of food on the other side of the cell. Not sure how long it'd been there or if there was much point in eating it.

Footsteps sounded in the hallway outside the door. They grew louder and louder until they stopped.

My cell door unlocked, and a man entered.

Not a man, actually.

Necrosis.

With intense blue eyes and rigid movements, Haldir was exactly as I remembered. Neither alive nor dead, his existence operated on a different playing field. He was like the stone of a sculpture, permanent and unmoving. When he entered my cell, he stood there for a long time, just staring.

I stared back. "Want to join me for dinner?" I glanced at the meager tray. "I've got the food, and you just need to bring the wine. Or scotch…that'd be nice." My arms rested on my knees, and I had no fear, not when my fate was sealed. I could beg and give in to the terror, but that was a terrible way to spend my final moments. Refused to give my killer that satisfaction.

Haldir stood there like I hadn't said anything.

"Or we could just stare at each other all night… That works too."

"This is your last chance, Ryker."

Most of his skin was concealed, even his hands, so if he was covered in dark marks, I wouldn't know. But he was probably no different from a human, where he could eat even when he wasn't hungry.

"Tell us everything about our enemy—and I'll spare your soul."

"What do you really need to know?" I asked. "You know they're taking the Kingdoms one by one, and you're the final destination. Prepare for battle. The rest of the details don't matter if you lose."

He stared down at me over the end of his nose, releasing a quiet breath. "They're approaching the gate as we speak."

"Then why the fuck are you talking to me?" I asked incredulously. "Go out there and fight."

"Who commands their army? What did you tell them?"

He was going to kill me and eat my soul no matter what I told him, so it didn't matter. "I'm not telling you shit, so just get on with it." My soul had touched another for the first time, and then it had been brutally taken away. If I thought about it too hard, I would choke up. I'd leave Effie alone, a widow, unable to remarry even though we'd only been married for a few days. It was a fucking travesty.

He stepped closer to me then squatted down so our eyes could be level. "You want to die on your feet like a man? Or on the ground like a dog?" He reached for his dagger, displaying a thick blade that would pierce me right through the heart.

"Makes no difference."

He stared at me as he changed his grip on the hilt, prepared to stab me right through the heart.

But before that happened, he gave a sudden jerk, and a loud thud sounded.

A rock dropped to the floor, and he lost his balance momentarily.

I reacted on instinct and seized the blade from his hand before I stabbed it deep into his chest. I knew that wouldn't kill him, not when Necrosis were rumored to be the most powerful beings on this earth, but it would be enough to flee. I kicked him, and he fell onto his side.

Effie stood there, her eyes locked on mine with shock.

I was shocked too, but I couldn't remain that way.

I jumped to my feet, grabbed her by the hand, and slammed the door shut. The key was still in the keyhole, so I turned that into place.

It was just in time too, because Haldir threw his body against the door and almost broke right through it.

"Come on." I grabbed her by the hand, and we took off, running down the hallway deep underneath the castle. I'd never been down there before, so I had no idea where I was or how to get out of there. "Do you know the way?"

"Yes." She took the lead and ran up the stairs. When she was close to the top, she stopped when we both heard the sound of voices. "We've got company."

"How many?"

She took a peek. "Two."

"That's nothing."

"Ryker, you should see how you look right now…"

"I've got the adrenaline. That should be enough to get out of here." I sprinted up the stairs and took out the first guard while he was unaware. Snapped his neck and heard the bones crack. With his sword in my hand, I stabbed the other through the throat and killed him before he could make a sound.

Effie took the other guard's blade and continued to lead the way. Higher up we went, making it to the next spiral staircase so we could get to ground level. She was running at full speed when a cannonball slammed through the stone and made a hole the size of her in the floor. She screamed and fell back.

Right into my arms. "Fuck, the war has started."

She caught her breath, weak in my grasp. "Oh my gods…"

"I got you, sweetheart." I scooped her into my arms and helped her back to her feet. "Let's jump across and keep going. We've got to get out of here."

She took a running jump and made it across, and then I followed and did the same. We made it to the next floor, and since chaos was erupting throughout the castle, we were able to slip out without anyone giving a damn.

The Capital was in chaos, smoke was in the sky, and then I heard it.

ROOOAAARRRRR.

"Gods, I hope that's my sister."

We made it down the path and into the street, people screaming as they ran for cover. Once the immediate threat had passed, I felt the weakness in my body, felt it everywhere. I leaned against the wall and stopped for just a second.

Effie turned back to me. "Are you okay?"

"I'm fine. It's just…hitting me."

"You should see how bad you look… What did they do to you?"

That was my secret to keep. "Doesn't matter."

"You can't fight, so maybe we should take a boat and sail away."

"We've gotta get to Ivory and Huntley."

"How? The gates will be closed, and they'll be on the other side."

"There are other ways besides the front gate…"

"I think we should take the boat or hide out somewhere."

"Their dragons are going to burn this place to the ground until Rutherford is dead or he surrenders. And I'm telling you, he's not going to surrender." I took a couple breaths. "How did you pull that off anyway?"

"I studied the guard times and waited for the right moment to sneak by them. Then I hid in another room until I heard your cell door open."

Speechless, I stared at her, realizing how capable she really was. "Damn…that's hot."

"I wasn't going to abandon my husband."

"My husband… Now that's really hot." I gave her a small smile.

She smiled back at me, bright like the sun, like the rest of the world wasn't in chaos around us.

"Come on. We gotta get away from this castle as quickly as possible." I pushed off the wall and took her by the hand. "It's gonna be the first thing to go."

TWENTY-THREE

Huntley

An army as wide as the sea marched on the Capital and dwarfed it in size.

The throne was mine.

There was no offer of surrender because I knew Rutherford would never accept it. Necrosis pulled his strings, so that wasn't an option even if he wanted to take it. I wasn't sure how many Necrosis were in the Capital, but there were probably at least a dozen, and they would be harder to kill than the rest, especially since we didn't have any Ice.

But that didn't matter. The castle was on fire, several walls of the keep had collapsed, and there was so much smoke in the air that the stars were obscured. Their army fired down arrows on my men, and while some fell, there were so many others to replace them that it didn't matter.

I knew they felt the way Ian had felt when Necrosis marched on HeartHolme.

Except there was no one coming to save them.

We reached the Capital before Regar's arrival, and that made the defeat that much cleaner.

My eyes looked up, seeing Pyre and Ivory fly over the castle and release a line of fire that burned every stone and window. She flew away, Storm coming in next to add his flames to the fire.

Commander Brutus rode the line toward me upon his black steed. "The gates have been breached. What are your orders?"

"Spare the civilians. Spare the soldiers that surrender. Kill all those who resist."

He turned around on his horse and took off.

I spoke the word out loud but in my mind as well. "Storm."

Ready to kill?

"Yes." I dismounted my horse and stepped onto the field behind the line of soldiers that fired upon the wall.

Storm flew through the smoke then glided down to me on the ground. He landed with a thud and released a mighty roar.

I could see all the scuffs from the arrows that had tried to pierce his armor. They bore marks from swords as well, but there was no injury to his hide or scales. My sister's skills didn't just protect Ivory and me, they protected my greatest asset as well.

I climbed into the saddle on his back and grabbed the pommel. "Take me to the castle."

Storm pushed off from the ground and soared into the sky, beating his powerful wings and releasing roars that shook the shaky foundations of the remaining buildings. He circled the castle until he landed on the very edge. *Want me to watch your back?*

"No. Stay off the ground." I dismounted and drew my sword.

Storm took off again, blending in with the darkness and the smoke.

I pulled my sword out of my scabbard, spun it around my wrist, and then entered the castle through the side door. Once I was inside, I heard the shouts of the men higher up, barking orders to one another. "Where are you, Rutherford?" I took the stairs and went up, jumping across the broken gaps from the cannonballs my men fired. I moved farther up, sweeping through abandoned corridors until I finally made it to my destination.

Rutherford looked out the window as he watched his city burn down around him. Despite his uniform and the crown of jewels upon his head, he looked nothing like a king. His home was under attack, and he chose to hide inside rather than lift a finger to stop it. He refused to surrender because he was pinned under a thumb far bigger than his.

But even if surrender were an option, I wouldn't take it.

This motherfucker deserved to die.

"Coward."

The men who guarded him turned at the sound of my voice, too busy looking out the windows to notice the assailant who had just entered their territory. "Your people need you—and you stand there and do nothing."

It took him a moment to turn and look at me, to face me like a man. When he finally did, there was no anger, no spite, nothing at all. As if he'd known this was coming. Had known long before I took Delacroix. "This is all pointless. It doesn't matter who sits on the throne, who calls himself the King of the Kingdoms. Because there is only one ruler—Necrosis. They can't be defeated, and now you've doomed us all."

"You doomed us when you allied with them for power. Necrosis wasn't in my lands when my father sat on the throne. The only reason they're here is because you invited them. You're the coward."

He looked out the window. "You don't understand what you're up against."

"I'm the one who's been fighting them for nearly twenty years. I know exactly what the fuck I'm up against. I'm going to kill every single one until this land is rid of their evil. I'm going to do what you should have done."

"What I should have done?" He turned to look at me. "What about your father? Why didn't he do it?"

I gripped the hilt a little harder.

"He could have marched on Necrosis decades ago. He could have saved us all. Only, he didn't. Don't pretend your father wasn't just as selfish as I am. He only looked out for himself, and you know it."

"My father never would have allied with Necrosis."

"Because he didn't need to. He already had everything." He turned to face me, and this time, he stepped toward me as he left his sword in his scabbard. "He had everything, while we had nothing. My family was killed by Necrosis. My friends… Everyone I ever cared about. I told your father this, straight to his face, and he didn't give a shit."

I was proud of the blood in my veins despite all this, because I knew if I'd asked my father to champion this cause, he would have done it. If I'd asked him to fight for the freedom of everyone, he would have given his life for the effort. "It doesn't matter now. I'm here to do what neither of you could. I'm here to remove this fucking parasite from our lives forever. You can still help me, you know."

He stood there and stared, as if it wasn't possible to do anything else. "I can't."

"Because of him?" I asked. "He's not here."

"He's not in this room—but he's here. And if I betray him now, he'll take my soul, not just my life."

"I'm going to kill him, so you don't need to worry about that."

"It can't be done."

"Watch me." I spun my sword around my wrist. "Where is he?"

"The last I heard of him, he went to the cells to kill a prisoner."

"This is your final chance, Rutherford. Coming or not?"

His men stayed at his side, not that it mattered. When the castle crumbled, they would all perish.

Rutherford looked out the window again. "You'll still kill me if I help you."

I should slay him where he stood for the coup he'd staged against my father. But he wouldn't survive the night anyway. I would rather he watched his kingdom crumble around him until he was crushed under stone than give him a swift death. "You're right." I turned to the stairway and made my descent, the castle shaking every few minutes as the battle continued. Where cannonballs broke through the walls and destroyed the staircase, I had to jump clean over and nearly roll the rest of the way.

I went down another level and stopped at the next hole in the wall. The staircase was still intact, so I could stand there and look at the fires and smoke. A man stood on the roof of the next level, dressed in all black, taking in the view. He didn't wear the armor of the guards, didn't carry himself like he was an inferior.

Without seeing his face, I knew his identity.

I unsheathed my blade and stepped forward.

He must have heard me or sensed me, because he slowly turned around and regarded me with ice-cold blue eyes. His thick body was protected by armor the others didn't possess, created from a material we didn't have access to. I knew Elora would give anything to know about its fabrication.

I spun my sword around my wrist and sized him up. I'd killed Necrosis for decades. Subdued their feeding frenzy as they swept through our lands and inhaled innocent souls. I never underestimated their strength, especially when they were in a group. One Necrosis was the equivalent of five men. Haldir must be the equivalent of ten.

I stared at his pronounced cheekbones, the darkness around his left eye.

"You look hungry." I came closer, my sword still spinning around my wrist.

"And you look like dinner." He unsheathed his weapon and did a dance with the sword around his wrist, the blade ripping through the air so quickly it made a high-pitched whoosh.

"This is the beginning of the end for you. You know it."

"There is no beginning or end—not when you're dead." He rushed me and swung his blade with the force of several men.

I blocked the hit with both hands and parried it before I headbutted him so hard he stumbled back.

I took advantage of his moment of weakness and struck my blade on his arm, slashing through the bracers and getting to the skin underneath. Blood oozed out, blue instead of red. Then I kicked him in the chest, and he rolled back. "That's the best you got, *Your Majesty*?"

He was on his feet a moment later, but instead of attacking me, he stayed back, his forehead dripping with blood, his eyes vicious. Then a smile appeared, sick and twisted, showing teeth that were sharp like those of the Teeth.

I heard the sound of flapping wings before I saw the dark outline in the sky. The heavy dragon slowly lowered itself, easily twice the size of Pyre, and the fire in his mouth grew deeper and brighter as he hung above Haldir.

Shit.

Another cannon struck the castle, and the floor where Rutherford and his men had been just moments ago collapsed. The earth shook beneath us as everything came apart and slid back to the earth.

Our platform remained, but there was nowhere for me to go. If I jumped, it'd be suicide.

Fuck.

Regar opened his mouth wider, and the fire started to spin in his throat, building up momentum before it would shoot out and burn me to a crisp. I continued to grip my sword even though there was nothing I could do with it. I thought of Ivory and the promise I'd made to her, the promise I couldn't keep.

She would lead the Kingdoms without me.

My queen.

Haldir sneered with joy, knowing he'd won the battle.

ROOOOAAAAAARRRRRR

The green dragon appeared in the darkness and slammed into Regar, knocking him hard in the flank. He tumbled slightly, the fire snuffed out, and he let out a roar of his own. Then Storm appeared from the other side and hit him again from the opposite direction, his claws ripping at his wings and scales.

"Thanks, baby." I rushed Haldir and swung my blade down right for his neck.

He caught it with his blade, and then we were locked in a deadly exchange of swords, both of us fighting to survive. This time, he came at me with everything he had, moving faster than I could because of his unparalleled strength, knowing he had to fight for his right to live.

I met his blade left and right, threw my fist down when he least expected it. He landed a blow. I landed mine. Our armor began to tear in places where the other had landed their blows. Just to be spiteful, he headbutted me the way I had with him, making me falter backward just the way he had.

Rutherford wasn't kidding.

This motherfucker was strong.

The battle continued, and he was by far the greatest opponent I'd ever faced. Decades of experience weren't enough to prepare me for it. I could take on ten men at once, but not when they were concentrated into a single person. His skills were potent. His rage unmatched.

But I had to destroy this asshole, so I kept going. He would tire out eventually.

His skin started to darken more and more—like he really was hungry.

I had to finish this and finish it quickly. A jolt of energy shot into my body from nowhere, and I rained down a flurry of blows, striking his blade, his chest plate, and getting close to his neck. I faked to my left then spun around and slashed right for his neck, putting in enough force to swipe his head clean from his shoulders.

But he was gone.

My body slammed into the stone keep, and my blade slid away.

I pushed to my knees quickly and reached for my sword before I could lose my own head. I rolled out of the way of his possible attack and finally got to my feet. I looked forward then back, but he was nowhere.

Then my eyes lifted to the sky.

There he hovered, enormous wings spanning out on either side of him. They flapped as they kept him in place, just as Regar had moments ago. With irritated eyes, he stared down at me.

"Coward."

"Once HeartHolme is mine, your mother will be the first to go. Then your brother. Then your sister. My belly will be full of the souls of everyone you love." He flapped his wings and disappeared into the night, camouflaged by the darkness and the smoke, by the screams of chaos in the streets.

TWENTY-FOUR

Ivory

I saw his massive form, clear as day despite the night, his enormous wings keeping his heavy body off the ground. "Pyre, look."

Pyre finished burning the archers on the walls before he lifted his body higher from the ground. He circled until he could see the enemy dragon. He was quiet as he stared, gliding over the broken parts of the castle. *Regar.* Venom was in his voice, fire in his tone.

"You know him?"

King Dunbar's dragon. The one that forced my mother.

"Oh shit…"

He circled again and came closer, and that was when I recognized the man standing on the roof, the one who was about to be charred to ash. "Pyre, that's Huntley down there."

Yes, I see.

"We need to do something."

He's twice my size.

"But there're two of you. He hasn't spotted you yet. Now's the perfect time to catch him off guard."

Pyre remained quiet.

My heart raced, seeing the fire in Regar's throat, the fire meant for my husband. "Pyre, hit him from the left. Have Storm hit him from the right. Then we'll claw that motherfucker to death."

Pyre still didn't say anything.

"Think of your mother, Pyre. Do it for her."

Pyre made a sharper turn and headed straight for Regar.

Oh, thank the gods…

Storm is ready.

"Let's do it. I'll aim my sword for his eyes."

Hold on.

I gripped the pommel and saw the dark form grow closer and closer. I kept my body low, as flat against Pyre's body as possible. Now the black dragon was right up against us, like it was right in front of my nose.

ROOOAAAAARRRR.

My body gave a jerk at the collision, and I nearly flew off the saddle. We started to free-fall, and then I landed back into the saddle. I couldn't even pull at my blade, not when I could barely hold on.

I looked above me and saw Storm hit him from the other side. The hit was hard enough that Regar toppled toward the ground, Storm slashing at his scales and biting at his neck. "Finish him!"

Pyre spun around and dove like a bird.

My hair streaked past my face and tears burned my eyes, we were going so fast. Pyre lifted at the last minute and landed on the black dragon on the ground. I could hear the screams, hear the scales ripped from his body, the sound of breaking bones in his wings.

Then everything went quiet.

He's dead.

I collapsed onto the saddle, my body suddenly exhausted after the battle was finished. "Good job, Pyre…"

———

Pyre landed on the roof of the section of the castle that was still standing, and I slid to the surface. I moved too quickly and my knees buckled, but I got back to my feet and sprinted toward the man who was waiting for me.

I jumped into his arms, and he caught me. With my feet above the ground, he held me, held my body as well as the weight of my armor and weapons. My eyes closed as I held on to him, as I clutched the man I'd almost lost.

"You saved my ass, baby." He lowered me to the roof so he could look at me, his helmet left on the ground behind him. He pulled my helmet off my head and dropped it before both hands slid into my hair.

"Pyre and Storm did."

"But I know you had something to do with that." He pressed a kiss to my forehead. "Did they kill Regar?"

"Yes. He's the dragon that was forced on their mother."

"Then he deserved the death he got."

I looked past him to what was left of the castle, which wasn't much. "Rutherford?"

"Dead."

"You executed him?"

"I let him be buried underneath his own castle."

"And Haldir?"

"Got away." All the relief left his face when he was mentioned. "Opened his wings and took off."

"That's right...he can fly."

"And he's hard to see, unlike a dragon."

I turned around and surveyed the rest of the city. Some buildings were on fire, and the distant sound of fighting was still audible. But the cannons had stopped, and the smoke was traveling out over the ocean. "He must have been afraid of you."

"I almost had his head. But I admit, he's the most powerful opponent I've ever taken on."

That left a stone of dread in the pit of my stomach. Huntley was the best fighter I'd ever seen, and if it was a struggle for him, then no one else could handle the Three Kings, let alone a single one.

"Haldir said he would take HeartHolme. Then kill every person I love, one by one…" The way his voice faded away, weak and broken, told me this wasn't a threat he took lightly. It was potent in his blood, heavy in his heart.

"Then we need to return to HeartHolme as soon as possible."

"I just conquered the Kingdoms. I need to rule these people now. I need to let them rest. I have no idea how I'm going to get the army to the bottom of the cliffs for this war. At least not if I want to make it in time."

I didn't have a single idea either. We could take the secret path, but that was a three-day journey, and we couldn't bring supplies or horses. We could only bring men, and once we made it to the bottom, they'd have to make the rest of the journey on foot. If time wasn't of the essence, we could figure this out. But we didn't have that luxury. "I have an idea."

As if our victory was now far in the past, he stared at me with cold eyes, the stress already getting to him. "I'm all ears."

"The Teeth."

His eyebrows furrowed.

"We take Pyre and Storm to the Teeth and convince them to fight with us."

"And why would they do that?"

"So they don't get eaten by two pissed-off dragons."

"They are allies to Necrosis."

"But if Necrosis is trying to beat us to HeartHolme because the dragons aren't there, they aren't going to have time to travel to the Teeth in the north."

Huntley stared at me for a long time as he considered it, his expression hardening as he became lost in thought. His jaw was clenched. His eyes were empty. After a minute of silence, he gave a nod. "Let's do it. And do it fast."

TWENTY-FIVE

Elora
___

"Elora." Bastian's deep voice flowed over me like warm water.

I pulled the sheet farther up my body then pressed my face into his shoulder, keeping my eyes closed. He was warm to the touch, like the fire in my forge. I released a drawn-out breath and hooked my arm around his chiseled stomach.

"Elora." He grabbed my hip and gave me a gentle shake. "You need to wake up."

"Fuck me if you want…just don't wake me up."

"Your brother is pounding on the door."

"So?" Now I was awake, but I kept my eyes shut. "Let him."

"He seems worried."

"Whatever…" I kissed his chest and then let my mind drift back to sleep.

This time, I heard my brother's voice from downstairs. "Elora!"

Bastian gave a sigh. "Told you."

I released a groan before I kicked back the sheets. "Gods, Ian. What do you want?" I grabbed the first piece of clothing I could find, an old shirt that had been sitting there for days.

His voice became louder as he moved up the stairs. "You aren't at the forge, and you weren't answering the door, so I got worried. Bastian is nowhere to be found, and my mind assumed the worst."

Oh, trust me, it didn't. "Give me a second." I pulled on some pants then trudged downstairs, gripping the handrail because I wasn't fully awake yet.

"It's almost noon." He stood there by the couch, dressed like a king with his sword on his hip. "Why are you still asleep? You never sleep this late." He turned toward the fire, and he must have spotted Bastian's clothes and shoes on the floor because he stilled briefly before he turned back to me. Now he wouldn't make eye contact with me. "Anyway…"

"Yes, I have a fabulous sex life. And I don't have to pay for it." I walked into the kitchen and got the hot water going so I could make a pot of coffee.

Ian moved to the kitchen table and ignored what I said. "Where's Bastian?"

"Why?"

"Because I still don't trust him."

"I trust him as much as I trust you, so you need to get over it."

"Why?"

"Why what?"

"Why do you trust him so much?"

"Because I actually know him." I placed the mug of coffee in front of him.

"Like I said…" He pushed the mug back at me. "It's noon."

I scowled at him over the rim of my mug. "Don't break in to my house again, alright? Bastian isn't going to eat me, so you need to chill out."

Ian shifted his gaze out the window. "Queen Rolfe has returned."

"When?"

"An hour ago. Another reason why I came to get you."

"How is she?"

"Afraid for HeartHolme. I told her about the Ice, but she still fears the city will fall. I expected you to be in the forge working your ass off, but you're sleeping off a hangover like a fucking teenager."

I ignored the insult. "How's Huntley?"

"Bloodthirsty. Last time she saw him, he was about to depart for Minora. Hasn't heard from him since. I imagine he's taken all the Kingdoms by now…or perished."

"Don't say that."

"That's reality, Elora. Hope for the best, expect the worst."

"Did you tell her about Bastian?"

"Yes. That's why I'm looking for him. So, hurry up and get dressed so we can go."

"I'll find him and bring him to the castle."

"Her orders were very clear—escort him to her."

Talk about a shitty situation.

"And I don't want you to be alone with him when you tell him this news."

"What's the guy gotta do for you to chill out?" I spat.

Ian glared at me. "Be alive, for starters."

"Ian, I'll meet you at the castle with Bastian shortly."

"I'm coming with you."

"Gods, can you just get out of my face for two seconds?" I pushed the chair back and carried the mug back to the sink. I tossed the contents down the drain and left the mug on the counter.

Ian got to his feet then moved back to the couch. His eyes dropped to the clothes on the floor.

Shit.

He stared for a moment before he turned to me, his eyes vicious.

This was going to be bad. "Just let me get dressed—"

"You kidding me with this, Elora? Are you fucking stupid?" He raised his voice like he hadn't before, marching toward me like he was about to pull out his sword and behead me. "What the fuck is wrong with you?"

"Calm down—"

"I'll calm down when you pull your head out of your ass."

"Wow…okay." My hands moved to my hips, and I released a drawn-out sigh. "Ian, this is none of your business. You wouldn't have even known if you hadn't barged into my house like you own the place."

"Thank the gods I did. You could be dead right now."

I rolled my eyes, dramatically and ridiculously.

"Elora—"

"Just go."

"That pussy shit doesn't even have the balls to—"

Bastian appeared at the bottom of the stairs right on cue, wearing his pants but bare-chested and bare-footed. His hair was ruffled from my fingers, and his jawline had that five-o'clock shadow even though it was only noon. With a hard expression, he looked at Ian, ready for my brother's fiery wrath.

Ian somehow looked even angrier. His gaze shifted back to me. Bastian wasn't the only one he wanted to murder. "I know you've done a lot of stupid shit in your lifetime, but this has to be the dumbest thing—by far."

"Just get out, Ian."

Bastian continued to stand there, unapologetic with his gaze.

Ian stormed toward the door. "I'm stabbing this moth-erfucker in the heart when he leaves." He walked out and slammed the door behind him.

I let out a heavy sigh as my fingers massaged my temple. "Oh gods…"

Bastian moved for the coffeepot and poured himself a mug. "I warned you."

"You warned me that you might kill me. Not that my brother would catch us."

He took a drink as he stood at the counter. "I warned you this was a bad idea."

"It didn't feel like a bad idea last night." I turned my body and leaned against the counter, looking at him head on. "And it still doesn't feel like a bad idea."

He held my stare as he stood in front of me, tight skin over strong muscles, his eyes quiet and mysterious.

It didn't matter how wrong this was. It felt right. Had always felt right.

"I'm not worth it, Elora."

"Worth what?"

"Dividing your family."

"*You* aren't doing anything. Ian is just being a brat."

"His horror is justified."

"No, it's not." I shook my head before I dug my hand into my hair. "You would never hurt me."

"Doesn't mean I don't want to—and that's bad enough."

———

After we bathed and got ready for the day, we walked out the front door.

Ian was there like he said he would be. He pulled his sword out of his scabbard and faced off with Bastian.

Bastian didn't reach for his and continued his slow walk, his arms relaxed at his sides, not the least bit provoked by the angry man who wanted his head on a pike.

I rolled my eyes so hard. "Ian, knock it off."

Ian kept his eyes on his opponent and ignored me.

"I mean it."

Bastian stopped when he was near, but he still didn't arm himself.

"We never should have agreed to this." Ian rushed him, his blade slashing.

Bastian still didn't move.

I withdrew my sword and met Ian's. I launched an attack and drove him back. "You're acting like a child. Stop it. You were the king of HeartHolme, and now you're an embarrassment to the position. Bastian has given us the means to protect our army if Huntley doesn't return with the dragons. He's the reason we actually have a chance to survive this war. Knock it off."

Ian continued to hold his blade, and his eyes shifted past my shoulder to the enemy that stood behind me. My words obviously meant nothing to him because he faked to his left then jumped to the right to get around me.

I anticipated all of it, so I hit his sword with mine, parried his swings, and spun around to take his sword right out of his grasp. It happened so fast that he didn't even realize he was unarmed until a couple seconds had passed.

Ian's eyebrows were high on his face in surprise.

I tossed the sword on the ground. "I told you to let me fight." When I looked at Bastian, he didn't have that somber look anymore. There was a hint of approval in his gaze, impressed by my sword-fighting skills. "I'll take Bastian to Queen Rolfe now. Come with us if you want. Or take some fighting lessons—because you need them."

Bastian came to my side, and we walked together, leaving Ian behind us.

I could feel Bastian's stare on the side of my face, feel his blue eyes pierce my flesh.

I met his look.

"Not going to lie…that was pretty hot."

"I build good weapons because I know how to use them."

"Damn right."

We walked awhile longer, spending that time in silence.

"I'm sorry about my brother."

"I'd act the same way if I were in his position."

"I doubt that."

"I'd probably be worse, actually."

"His concern is unwarranted."

"Except it's not, Elora." He stared at me harder. "I want you more than I've ever wanted another woman—but that makes me want things I shouldn't. It's ironic. The first time I feel something real for somebody, it's accompanied by this animalistic hunger that I've never had to combat. It's not fair."

"It won't be this way forever, Bastian."

He looked forward again. "I can't ask your family to capture rather than kill the First King. They would put themselves in greater danger by not taking the killing blow when they have a chance. It's far more likely that this won't work out in my favor."

"It will if I ask them to."

"And I'd rather you not."

"After everything you've done for us, it's the least we can do."

He continued to stare ahead.

"We want you to have your soul back."

"But not at the expense of yours."

We entered the castle and moved past the guards toward the next floor. Queen Rolfe was there, sitting on her throne in her full uniform, the feathers woven into her hair as if she'd never left.

Her eyes were immediately on Bastian. A long stare ensued, her look calculating.

Ian appeared behind us then came to our mother's side, acting as her guard.

Queen Rolfe continued her stare, as if she didn't know what to make of him. "My son tells me that you've asked for asylum in exchange for the powerful Ice to use in our weapons. It's not something I would have agreed to, but since my son was the ruler of HeartHolme in my absence, I will honor it."

Ian glanced at her, her disapproval clearly stinging him. He always had a chip on his shoulder because of her. A bigger chip than I had.

"But make no mistake," she said. "I don't trust you."

Bastian gave no reaction. "I understand."

"He's fulfilled his end of the bargain and has pledged to fight with us," I said. "What more do you need?"

Ian gave me a scowl.

Queen Rolfe finally shifted her gaze to me. The stare was cold, but there was never a time when she looked at me with warmth. It was always with indifference, because I literally meant nothing to her. It was as if she hadn't carried me in her womb for nine months, as if we shared no biological relation. "He's the predator and we're the prey. A fact we can't ignore."

"If he captures the First King Haldir, he can get his soul back."

Bastian turned to me, clearly annoyed.

"Then he wouldn't be a predator anymore. He could be at peace."

Queen Rolfe turned her gaze back to him. "Is this true?"

Bastian tore his gaze away from me. "Many years ago, Haldir became infatuated with my sister's beauty. He took her from my village, made her into his own kind. When I went after her to rescue her, he nearly killed me, but my sister pleaded for an alternative. I became one of them—and I've been stuck ever since. However, if I can get him to the Bone Witch, I can reverse what was done to us. And not just us, but anyone who's ever been turned by him. That's my objective, and I need Heart-Holme to accomplish it."

Her fingers started to drum on the armrest repeatedly, her stare unmoving and cold.

Ian glanced at her then continued to look at Bastian, the rouge of rage still coloring in his cheeks.

"I don't want to be Necrosis," Bastian said. "I've never wanted this. I've tried to starve myself to death, but my body will put me into an uncontrollable eating frenzy. So, I stopped doing that. But the self-loathing grows with every meal. If I had my soul back, I could take my life and join my family in the Undying Kingdoms."

My heart broke when I realized what he truly wanted. "If we do this, we could save a lot of innocent people, Your Highness."

Her eyes didn't shift back to me. "The dead are not my responsibility."

"But among those dead are Runes," I said. "And dead or alive, they're your responsibility."

She turned to look at me again. A long stare ensued.

"The only reason she cares is because she's sleeping with him." Ian shared business that wasn't his own and stabbed me in the back. It was out of character, so his emotional turmoil must have been responsible for his betrayal.

I didn't refute the accusation.

Queen Rolfe's stare hardened slightly more, her disapproval written on her face. "You sleep with the enemy."

"Well, Huntley is married to the enemy, so anything goes, apparently." Gods, she was my half sister, even looked like me. It was so fucked up.

It was clear Queen Rolfe rejected that statement, tightness appearing around her lips. "Ivory is the Queen of the Kingdoms now. HeartHolme still stands because she healed the dragons and brought them to the fight. You would do well to remember that."

I was in disbelief. Sheer, unbearable disbelief. "I've done nothing but serve HeartHolme since I could walk. I've outfitted our soldiers with the weapons that have kept us alive this past decade. I went behind enemy lines to retrieve the Ice and risked my soul in the process. I've built your armor with my own hands. I've built armor for two dragons. My life has been in service to your reign, my loyalty unquestioned, and you've never once looked at me like I'm anything more than your biggest regret. I'm your fucking daughter, but you still look at me like a damn rat."

Bastian turned his head to regard me, his blue eyes still with sadness.

All of Ian's anger disappeared, and his face immediately tightened as if he regretted instigating the entire thing.

Queen Rolfe was the only one who had no reaction. No reaction whatsoever.

Why did I expect that to ever change? "Bastian will retrieve the twelve allies we promised asylum. He'll also be able to give us an update on Necrosis. But I suspect we should prepare for war. It's coming—whether it'll arrive tomorrow or a week from tomorrow." Without waiting to be dismissed, I turned my back to the queen and walked off. I expected to depart alone, but I heard him behind me.

———

He walked beside me the whole way back to my home. His eyes turned to me from time to time, but he didn't say anything.

The second I walked into my house, I headed straight for the booze. I grabbed an unopened bottle of scotch and poured two glasses, assuming he wouldn't make me drink alone. I slid the glass across the counter where I stood then tilted my head back to down the entire contents in one go. My thumb swiped the drop from the corner of my mouth and caught the liquid my tongue had missed.

Bastian didn't reach for his glass. He stood in front of me, his concerned eyes reserved for my face.

"A gentleman never makes a lady drink alone."

"You aren't a lady." He lifted his glass to his lips anyway and took a drink. "You're a woman—and that's how I like you." The glass returned to the counter, and he stared me down once again, his eyes flicking back and forth subtly. "I'm sorry."

"Don't be. The last thing I want is for you to feel bad for me."

"Why?"

"Because that's pussy shit." I refilled my glass and took another drink.

"Feeling your feelings because I care about you is not pussy shit." His voice was warm and thick like honey when it poured out of a bottle. "It's not my place to have an opinion about Queen Rolfe's behavior, but I have the right to feel your sorrow—and I do."

"I don't feel sorrow—"

"You don't have to put up a front with me. I find this no-nonsense, no-bullshit attitude sexy as hell, but we're past that. There's more to you than meets the eye, and I can see all those layers now. It's okay to be hurt. I would feel the same way."

My eyes dropped back to my glass on the counter. It was easier to stare at the amber liquid sitting at the bottom than his arresting eyes. "Most of the time, I don't care, but there are moments when I hope things will change. I've seen the affection she shows my brothers. She's a good mother. There are times when I grow envious…and then resentful." My fingers rested on the rim of the glass as I felt the ache in my chest. "But now she's embraced Ivory like a daughter, and she still won't look at me as anything less than dirt? It's fucking bullshit." I threw the glass against the wall and heard it shatter into a million pieces.

Bastian didn't flinch.

"I've defended this Kingdom as much as Ivory has. Just because she rolled in here with a couple of dragons doesn't mean I haven't killed hundreds of Necrosis with weapons made by my bare hands." I grabbed another glass and filled it.

Bastian stayed quiet.

I took a drink and stared at him over my glass, seeing the patience in his eyes. When the glass was empty, I returned it to the counter. There were no tears in my dry eyes, but there were cracks in my broken heart. "Whatever... Fuck her."

"As difficult as this is, you mustn't take it personally. You were born out of trauma, and every time she looks at you, she must relive that trauma. She could have aborted you but she didn't, and you should be grateful that she gave you the chance to live."

I lowered the glass and stared at him incredulously. "You're really going to say that to me?"

He held his silence for a while. "You don't strike me as the kind of woman that wants to be told only what she wants to hear. And I'm not the kind of man that doesn't mean what he says. I hate seeing your pain. I hate seeing you abandoned. But if my sister bore Haldir's child from rape…it would be hard for me to love them unconditionally. And I know she would struggle as well."

I took another drink and felt the burn all the way down.

"If she can let Ivory into her heart, perhaps she can let you in as well."

"That's never happened before. I doubt it'll ever happen."

"But she has embraced the daughter of her rapist. People change, Elora."

Not Queen Rolfe. "I don't want to talk about this anymore." I set the glass on the counter.

"I'll leave for Necrosis at first light—"

I waved off his words. "I don't want to talk about that either."

"Alright." His hand rested on top of his glass on the counter. "Do you want me to leave?"

I gave him a stony look, like that was the very last thing I wanted.

His eyes shifted back and forth as he stared me down. His head tilted slightly, his eyes glancing to the lips that yearned for his kiss. The pause lasted only a few seconds. After that, he stepped closer to me, his hand sliding into my hair, his lips catching mine in a soft embrace.

The second I had his kiss, a soft bubble formed around us, blocking out the bullshit that existed outside the house. I wasn't despised by my mother. HeartHolme wasn't vulnerable to Necrosis. Ian wasn't pissed off at me.

My arm hooked around his neck, and I rose on my tiptoes so our mouths could move together in fluid motion. It was one of those slow and passionate kisses, where the heat rose from a couple small flames to a full inferno. My other hand cupped his face, slid into his short strands of hair, felt their softness as I kissed him like my favorite lover.

His thick arm encircled the small of my back, and he tugged me against his chest before his fingers spread out across my ass. He squeezed one of my cheeks with a man's grip, just the way I liked to be touched. I wanted to be gripped and tugged, not handled with the fragility of thin glass.

He backed me up into the counter, his big dick pressing against my lower stomach. His hand fisted my hair, and he tugged it back so my neck would be open to him. His hungry lips kissed me, his tongue tasted me, his teeth even gave me a playful bite.

My eyes closed as I felt him kiss me everywhere, tug down the front of my shirt so he could kiss my collar-bone, the base of my throat, my jawline.

I got his trousers loose, and then I yanked his shirt over his head.

He broke away to let the clothes leave his body, and that was when I took him in.

His eyes had darkened with hunger, and the black splotches sprinkled his large shoulders and thick arms. The marks were on his chest and stomach. Like ash had fallen from the sky and stained his skin, he was marked by soot.

In a very sick way, I liked it.

I liked that he was dangerous.

I liked that the only reason I lived was because he allowed it.

He pulled my shirt over my head and removed my chemise before his lips devoured my tits. His hands were on me again, squeezing me tightly as his tongue delved into the valley between my breasts.

He didn't pause to restrain himself like last time. He powered through, letting his skin darken more and more as the urge to feed deepened in his veins. I never once thought I was in danger. I fell into the moment, my only discomfort the wetness in my panties.

He lifted me and positioned my legs around his waist before he carried me upstairs to my bedroom. Our kisses continued all the way up the stairs, until he got me on the bed so he could remove my bottoms. He took the trousers and underwear at the same time and pulled them free.

I was fully naked on the bed, anxious for his narrow hips to fit between my thighs and his big dick to sink into my wetness. I watched him lower over me, felt the mattress sink as his weight dispersed the support, and then finally, he moved on top of me. My palms felt his hard chest pass by me as he got into position, his skin even darker now that he was so close to having me.

He settled between my thighs but didn't sink inside me. "You should be afraid right now."

I grabbed on to his hips and tilted my pelvis, wanting to drag him inside me. "Bastian…" I gave him a tug. "I've never wanted you more." I felt his length catch my slit, and I pulled him inside, directing him into a slow and deep sink. My eyes closed, and I moaned the whole time, like sex had never felt this good—because it hadn't.

When he felt me, his reaction was the same. A deep groan escaped his throat from all the way down in his chest. Once he was fully inside me, he released a heavy sigh, a sigh full of so much desire and need.

I grabbed on to his shoulders as I started to rock.

His thrusts synced with mine, and he moved deep and slow, his eyes locking on mine. Even his eyes were a different color now, black like the nighttime sky. He'd never pushed himself like this, but he seemed in complete control.

"I've never wanted a man the way I want you…" My hand snaked up his chest as those words tumbled out. He was the most dangerous man I'd ever been with, but somehow, he felt the safest. Every man who'd come before him wasn't even a memory. This just felt right, from the moment I saw him…like love at first sight.

Those words sank deep into his flesh and chased away the darkness. The color faded completely, his skin the same fair shade it'd been before he kissed me. His eyes were blue once again, clear and fathomless.

Our first time on the couch had been driven by insatiable attraction and desire. It was a means to an end. But this time was different. It was slow and deep, raw with emotion. He didn't have a soul, but I swore I could feel it as our bodies joined.

Hot breaths filled the bedroom as our slick bodies moved together. Our shadows danced across the wall, and my nails sliced his skin deeper and deeper. With my ankles locked around his waist, I got to lie there and enjoy him, feel him do all the work to make my toes curl, to push me to the edge and make me writhe with a breathless moan. "Bastian…" I gripped him tightly as I came, my thighs squeezing his hips, tears damp in my eyes and blurring my vision. It felt so good, better than last time, better than any other who'd preceded him.

As if he had something to prove, he kept going without needing to stop. All his effort was geared toward me, getting me to climax again and again, as if the first two weren't enough. His skin never darkened again. He stayed in the moment with me, his hunger not even registering.

I grabbed on to his ass and tugged him inside me. "I want you."

His body slowed for an instant, his expression hard.

My lips felt his in a short kiss, our breathing too deep for a full embrace.

A loud moan escaped his lips, and he gave his final thrust, feeling the same satisfaction he'd given to me three times in the last hour. His eyes closed for a moment as he felt it, as he writhed just a bit. When it passed, his eyes opened once more, locked on mine.

"You should be afraid right now."

His fingers moved into my hair, sliding through the strands and pulling them from my face. His eyes took me in for a long time, wearing that intense expression that could burn me from across the room. "Yeah?"

"Because I'm never going to let you go."

———

I woke up to him next to me, his chest softly rising and falling with his even breaths. My lips traveled over his hard body and woke him up in the nicest way possible, my head under the sheets with my lips sealed around his shaft. It led to a beautiful morning with my ankles locked around his waist again.

We made it downstairs for coffee and muffins, the two of us sitting together at the dining table. The sunlight came through the open window and warmed the wood underneath our mugs. Little dust particles were in the air, gently hovering in the perfect stillness. I devoured my pecan muffin, but he didn't touch his.

He hadn't said a single word all morning.

I didn't regret what I'd said, but I feared I'd come on too strong. It was one of my faults. I spoke my mind right in the moment, oblivious to any ramifications from my spontaneity. But that was who I was. You never had to wonder what I was thinking because I would give it to you straight. "I'm not sorry about what I said, but I'm sorry if I made you feel weird."

His eyes lifted from his coffee and locked on mine. "I don't feel weird."

"You're quiet."

"I'm always quiet." He held my gaze, the confidence in his stare.

I chose to accept his words as fact. "Well, I'm glad it didn't bother you."

"Why would it bother me?"

"You were the one trying to ditch me, remember?"

One side of his mouth quirked up in a smile. "Not because I wanted to."

"Still…"

"I tried to be a gentleman, but I quickly realized that's not what you're looking for."

"You're catching on." I took a drink of my coffee.

Now the other side of his mouth quirked up. "I want you the way you want me. You can tell me that a million times, and I'll treasure every single time you say it. I've felt this way since the moment I saw you, and I think you felt the same way."

I did.

"But before this goes any further, there's something we should talk about."

"I thought you were quiet?" I teased.

His eyes remained intense like the quip had never happened. "I can't have children." He just came right out and said it, straight to the point. "It's impossible for Necrosis to sire children, as I mentioned before. If having a family is important to you, then I'm not the right guy for you."

"You won't always be Necrosis."

His stare hardened. "There's a very real chance that we'll defeat Necrosis and the Three Kings without breaking the spell. Even if your family allows my existence, I'll be unable to put a child in your belly. That's a reality you'll need to consider."

"I'm not going to let that happen, Bastian."

"I don't question your determination, Elora. But the Three Kings are different from me and the other Necrosis. One Necrosis is the equivalent of five men. A king is the equivalent of twenty."

"We'll figure it out," I said. "I know we will."

"When this is all over, we can revisit this conversation. You can make your decision then."

"Even if you remain Necrosis, it's not going to change the way I feel. If we can't have children, we'll still have each other. We'll still have nieces and nephews from my brothers. It'll be alright."

He stared for a long time, his expression so hard it was impossible to know his thoughts. "As much as I want you, you shouldn't have to settle."

"Being with you is not settling."

His eyes dropped.

"I don't want to waste my time talking about a future that may not even happen. We stay together, no matter the outcome of this war. But I believe we'll accomplish everything we hope to. The Runes are the mightiest people on this continent. We have two dragons. And we have Ice—something they don't know about. The odds are in our favor."

———

I walked with Bastian down to the gate, and somehow, Ian was aware of his impending departure. Queen Rolfe had been reinstated as the ruler of HeartHolme, so Ian had returned to his former post. The gates remained closed, and I knew that was his doing.

Bastian was dressed in his travel gear, his horse at his side. He gave me a heavy look, like this separation would be as challenging for him as it would be for me. He didn't extend any affection, as if he knew my brother was watching us like a hawk.

Ian approached us, his stare cold and hard. "What's happening?"

Bastian faced him head on. "I'm traveling to Necrosis to grab the twelve allies we discussed before. While I'm there, I'll also collect as much information about their plans as possible. After I leave, they'll quickly realize that my allegiance has changed, and you can expect a much swifter attack."

"Then you should stay." Ian was back in his old uniform, but he still had the presence of a king. The garment fit his muscular arms well, and the fancy hilt of his blade showed his royal status.

"I have to evacuate my people," Bastian said. "And I figure I can still get information you'll need."

"What if they already know of your betrayal and kill you?"

My heart did a somersault.

"Then you don't have to see my face ever again." Bastian said it simply, as if he didn't care if that was his fate. "Elora and I checked on the Ice this morning. The roots have dug into the ground, and the wilted leaves have stiffened. Within a couple weeks, there will be a harvest."

"A couple weeks from now, we might all be dead," Ian deadpanned.

"It's still better that it's attached instead of not attached," I said. "Who knows what the future holds."

"I'll return as soon as I can," Bastian said. "I'll only stop to sleep when absolutely necessary. I know we don't have a lot of time."

Ian still looked annoyed. "When you return with your twelve men, how do we know it won't be a coup?"

Bastian was quiet for a long time. "If you still suspect me after everything that's happened, there's nothing more I can say, and I'd rather not waste my time. Now open the gate so I can depart."

Ian stared him down for a while before he nodded to his men. Then he walked off.

The gates creaked as they started to open, and slowly, the walls parted wide enough for Bastian to pass through.

Bastian stared at the open gates before he turned back to me.

"I wish I could come with you."

"This is where you belong, Elora. With your people."

"You're my people too, Bastian."

He stared for a while longer before he hooked his strong arms around my body and embraced me harder. "Even if I lose my life with what's to come, the destruction of Necrosis will still bring me joy. So, if we don't see each other again…kill them all. Kill them for me."

I latched on to him tightly and didn't want to let go. "You have to come back to me, okay?"

"I'll do my best." He pulled away, his arms still around my back. "Slay Necrosis, Elora. Slay every single one without mercy." He moved farther away, forcing the contact to end.

I moved into him again and pressed a kiss to his mouth.

He was hesitant at first because we had an audience, but he didn't reject my affection. He kissed me back then abruptly let me go. His hands gripped the reins of his horse, and he walked out the gates, never looking back to see me one last time.

———

I worked in my shop, making compounded arrows for the archers. I didn't move at my usual speed, my broken heart slowing me down. Once I made another, I added it to the barrel in my forge, making each one individually. If the archers could kill waves of Necrosis before they even reached the gates, that could turn the war. Might even end it if we had enough. If only those Ice plants produced more frequently.

The door opened, and Ian walked inside.

I'd just dropped an arrow into the barrel and taken off my gloves. "What brings you here?"

He held up the scroll. "A message from Huntley."

My mood immediately perked right up. "He's alright?"

"Both he and Ivory survived."

"Did they take the Kingdoms?"

"Yes."

A full-on grin moved over my face. "Huntley is so badass. King Rutherford?"

"Dead. Haldir was there."

"The First King?" The blood immediately drained from my face. "Did he kill him?"

"No. He took off. But Huntley said it was the most challenging fight of his life. Warned me not to underestimate the kings if I come into contact with any of them. One of their dragons was about to burn him alive, but Ivory got there first with Pyre."

"Thank the gods…"

"Yeah."

"Now what?"

"He said they're going to lower as many men as they can with the pulley system they repaired in Delacroix. While that's happening, they're going to fly to the Teeth and try to coerce them to aid in the battle against Necrosis."

"Really?" I asked. "I doubt the Teeth would ever help us."

"But I don't think they'll have a choice when two dragons can burn their entire city."

"True…"

"Depending on when they sent this letter, all of that may already be in motion."

"That also means that Haldir left the Capital already…"

Ian nodded. "I'm sure he's returned to Necrosis by now. That means that we can expect them any time —literally."

I got the chills. "At least we know the dragons are coming."

"Just hope they come soon enough." He put the scroll back into his pocket. "How are things here?"

"I've used nearly all the reserves of Ice. But I've made a lot of good stuff. The arrows are potent, so they'll kill a Necrosis in one shot. Our best soldiers will have compounded swords, so they'll be able to slice through Necrosis like stalks of wheat. Even if we're outnumbered, we have the upper hand."

Ian nodded. "I'd say we have this battle in the bag… except for one problem."

"What?"

"The Three Kings can fly."

Necrosis was already hard enough to defeat, with the strength of five men in one, but now our opponents could also fly. The only beings that could challenge them were Pyre and Storm. "Shit… Forgot about that."

Ian fell into one of the chairs, his thick body hanging heavily. "I hate the wait. I just want it to be over with. Whether we win or lose, I just want it to end." He rubbed his fingers across his jawline. "Necrosis has been our enemy since I can remember. Hard to imagine a life where that's not the case."

"Yeah…" I sat in the other chair.

He turned his head to look at me. "I'm sorry I ratted you out like that. Just pissed off about the whole thing."

"It's fine. I don't care."

His eyes narrowed.

"It was going to come out. The sooner, the better."

"The sooner, the better?" he asked incredulously. "You can't expect to stay with this guy."

"It's really none of your business, Ian."

"You're my sister, and he's Necrosis. Damn right, it is my business."

I rolled my eyes.

"You know when Huntley gets here, he's going to chop his head off."

"He won't because he actually listens to me—unlike you."

His eyes darkened, as if that offended him. "What in the gods do you see in him?"

I ignored him.

"Elora."

"I see a man—not Necrosis. I see a man who lost everything to save someone he loved. I see someone who needs our help. I see someone who deserves a second chance. You're so closed-minded that all you can focus on are the dark marks on his body, not his story, not who he is. And I'm sick of it. I don't give a damn if you don't like him—because I do."

My brother stared for several heartbeats, his expression slightly overwhelmed.

I rose from the chair. "Let's get back to work. We've got a lot of shit to do."

TWENTY-SIX

Ivory

_____

"Ryker!" I rushed to him when I found him in the medic tent. He was beaten badly, clearly tortured. Effie was at his side, no scars on her skin, like she'd been spared from the punishment. I suspected Ryker was the reason for that.

He sat up in bed, his face blue and bruised from all the damage. His movements were slow, as if every single part of his body hurt. Just the smallest gestures were enough to elicit a moan from his lips. "You okay?"

"I look like a rainbow compared to you." I wrapped my arms around him gently and held him close. "I'm so happy to see you..." Once the castle started to come down and the sky was filled with smoke, I worried about my brother, worried that he was trapped somewhere. "I was so concerned."

He gave me a pat on the back before he let me go. "I saw you flying around in the sky. Badass."

I hugged Effie next. "Girl, you okay?"

"I'm fine," she said. "Just glad it's all over."

Well, it wasn't *all* over. "You going to be okay?"

He nodded. "You know I've had worse."

I was pretty sure he hadn't. "So…you guys are married?"

"Yep," Ryker said. "Thought it was time for this stallion to settle down."

Effie rolled her eyes.

I chuckled at her playfulness. She was good for Ryker, understanding his sense of humor.

"It's a long story," Ryker said, turning serious. "It was the only way I could keep Effie in the castle with me. Rutherford wasn't going to host Effie when she's not a royal—so I made her a royal."

It was a big sacrifice on his part, so I assumed his motivations were deeper than that. "I'm happy for you guys. Congratulations."

"Sorry you couldn't be there," Ryker said. "But you know how it goes…"

"Yeah," I said with a nod, thinking of my own nuptials.

The flap to the tent opened, and Huntley stepped inside, regal in his special armor, his helmet left at his tent so his hard face was visible, his brown hair matted from the sweat of the battle. All his armor and weapons must have added close to fifty pounds of weight to his frame, but he continued to carry himself like it was featherlight. His eyes went to me first, like they always did when he stepped into a room where I was present, and then he looked at my brother. "Glad to see you're still here, Ryker."

My brother stared at him for a while, his look uninviting, but then he cleared his throat and shook off the animosity. "Congratulations on your conquest, King Rolfe. The Kingdoms are now led by the rightful ruler."

The last time these two men had been in the same room together, Ryker had wanted to cut him down and leave him as a bloody mess. But my brother obviously had had a change of heart. Knowing that my father betrayed all of humankind must have shaken him to his core—just the way it shook me.

Huntley stared for a while, his eyes open and unflinching, processing my brother's unexpected stance of loyalty. "Rulers. None of this would have been possible without my wife, Queen Rolfe." He shifted his gaze to me and stared at me hard, even possessively, despite the current company. "I conquered the ground, and she conquered the skies." He stepped forward and extended his hand to Ryker. "Your letter prepared us for battle, and I can see that there were consequences for your actions. Thank you for your loyalty."

Ryker didn't hesitate before he stood up and returned the gesture.

I could hardly believe their new kinship. Didn't realize how important it was to me for them to get along until I witnessed it with my own eyes.

Huntley dropped his hand first. "Haldir and Necrosis are headed to HeartHolme, so time is of the essence for our departure. You need to lower as many men and horses as you can to the bottom of the cliffs with the pulley system, and in my absence, you will rule the Kingdoms."

Ryker's eyebrows immediately hiked up his face in surprise.

"You're next of kin. I trust that you'll take care of my people if I don't return, and you'll be prepared to destroy Necrosis in the event Ivory and I fail. Do you accept?"

Ryker took a few seconds to process this before he gave a nod. "It would be my honor."

"I know you're unwell at this moment, but Commander Brutus is here to serve you. I've told him to return the soldiers to their respective Kingdoms and then to reside at the Capital to keep things in order. You'll rule from Delacroix."

"Yes, Your Highness."

Huntley turned to me. "We leave first thing in the morning. Say your goodbyes now." He departed the tent and left us alone.

A silence settled on us for a while. Ryker stared at the entrance to the tent as if Huntley might return and say more. Effie remained in the chair, her arms crossed over her chest.

I looked at my brother. "I know the Kingdoms are in good hands. If the Runes fail, you'll be our second chance for victory."

"Can we not talk like that?" he said quietly, his eyes averted. "I don't even want to think about that…" He stared at the ground for a while before he finally looked at me. "You better kick ass, Ivory. Because I can't live a life where you don't exist."

My face had been stoic a moment ago, but now I battled the dampness that formed in my eyes. "I believe in Huntley. He'll win this war. He's the strongest, smartest person I know."

"Really? Because you're the strongest, smartest person I know."

"Ryker…"

His arms embraced me, and he held me for a while, his arms strong like the grip of a viper. With his chin on my head, he squeezed me, his breaths deep and uneven. "I love you." It was something he never said, only when our parents forced him. But now, he said it freely, from his heart.

"I love you too."

———

The fires had been put out, but smoke still filled the dark sky. The deepest part of the night had passed, and the sky had turned a light blue, the color of twilight. Stars would normally blanket us overhead, but they were invisible behind all the destruction the battle had caused.

I moved across the camp until I spotted the royal flags that marked our tent. The perimeter was lined with guards on duty, protecting Huntley from any enemies that hadn't been killed. We would normally stay in the castle—but there was no castle anymore.

I stepped inside the tent and found Huntley sitting in a chair at his desk. His armor had been removed, and now he was shirtless, scribbling on a piece of parchment in dark ink. He finished his thought then added his signature at the bottom.

Huntley rolled it tightly before he secured a ribbon around the scroll. "I've explained the plan to my mother, so she knows we're coming. Doesn't matter if it's intercepted at this point. It won't make a difference anyway." He rose to his feet and marched out of the tent to hand it to one of his men then returned a moment later.

That was when I saw the beating his body had taken. He didn't bleed from flesh wounds, but large areas of his skin were bruised from all the hits he'd taken from swords and axes. Black and purple marred his normally tanned skin color. It pained my heart just to look. "Are you okay?"

He dropped into the chair again, his knees wide apart, his heavy shoulders slack. "Just anxious."

"No." I stepped toward him, my fingers lightly coming into contact with the large bruise on his arm. "This."

He didn't turn to look. "Didn't even notice."

"They're everywhere…"

"I'm fine, baby."

My fingers continued to outline his hard body, to glide over the deep discoloration from the blood underneath his skin. He didn't have time to rest and heal. He had to keep moving, barely getting a full night of sleep. "Is there anything I can do?"

That intense expression was on his face, his thoughts immediately going to the one thing he cared about most. I was still in my armor, and my hair was matted from the sweat caused by all the fires, but he looked at me as if I'd just stepped out of the shower buck naked. He untied his pants as he got to his feet, pushing them down and kicking off his boots at the same time. Then he lay flat on the bedroll on the ground, his hard dick against his stomach.

I heard his orders loud and clear and shed my armor and weapons. I got down to my bare skin then straddled his narrow hips. His large hands immediately kneaded my ass as he lay there. Then they snaked up my body, over my stomach, and latched on to my tits. He squeezed them hard before he flicked his thumbs over the nipples. "Fuck me, baby." He propped himself up on his elbows, bringing his torso closer to me. "Fuck me hard."

I rose up and widened my knees before I directed his fat length inside me. I pushed my sheath over his head and sank lower, forcing my body to take his throbbing length. Farther and farther, I sank, going as far as my small body would allow.

He closed his eyes briefly, feeling even more like a king when he was inside me.

I grabbed on to his shoulders and moved up and down, rolling my hips every time he was inside me fully. Whether this was our hundredth time together or our thousandth, it felt like the first time, all the desire bubbling on the surface.

"Harder." The command in his voice filled the tent as if he'd raised his voice, only he hadn't.

My speed had been slow because I was getting used to it, letting my body stretch a little more before I quickened my pace. But I followed his orders and moved faster, forgetting about all the horrific bruising on his hard body.

"I said harder."

I moved even more rapidly, going as fast as I could. I quickly became breathless, felt my skin moisten with sweat. Even that wasn't enough for him, because he grabbed my hips with his big hands and guided me hard and fast onto his length, fucking me harder than he ever had before.

I couldn't keep up with the demand and tired out quickly.

He rolled me onto my back and took over, ramming me into the bedroll like I was his favorite whore. He took me so hard it hurt, his hand fisted in my hair, his arm hooked behind one of my knees. He dominated me ruthlessly, like I somehow had forgotten that I was his.

Like he would ever let me forget I was his.

———

"Pyre." He was dead asleep in the field, his body curled in a circle with his snout near his tail. His enormous body rose and fell with the deep breaths he took.

"Pyre." I rubbed my hands over his hard scales, trying to gently coax him into waking.

No.

"I know it's early and we had a long night—"

No.

I gave a loud sigh and watched Huntley approach Storm.

"Let's go, Storm. We have more people to burn."

Storm opened one eye then immediately straightened, like he'd gladly get up early to continue his killing spree.

I gave Pyre a shake. "Come on, let's go kill people."

His eyes opened, but it was in annoyance. *I killed a lot of people. I killed a dragon. Now let me rest.*

"I wish I could rest too, but we don't have the time. We have to move quickly if we want to reach HeartHolme in time."

Storm must have said something to him because Pyre finally got up.

"You'll be able to rest as long as you want when this is all over."

He sat upright and stretched his spine as well as his wings. *What's the plan?*

"We're going to the Teeth. Demand their alliance with the threat of fire."

What are the Teeth?

"Monsters that live off the blood of humans."

Can I eat them?

"Sure. Go for it."

I've had a big appetite lately.

"You've earned it." When I looked at Huntley, he was already in the saddle, fully dressed for war.

I climbed up Pyre until I made it into the saddle. My hands gripped the pommel for dear life because it was the only thing keeping me in place when Pyre made sudden dives and unexpected turns. I'd gotten better at it, but one wrong move and I could be bucked off. "Head southwest."

Pyre jumped from the ground and opened his wings wide, taking to the skies immediately. The smoke had finally blown away after the battle, so there was nothing but clouds and the sun.

Storm did the same and flew beside us.

Once we were above the clouds, it was a whole different world. Just the beaming sun and a sea of blue. Silence stretched for a long time, the two of us just enjoying the flight. Eventually, I spoke. "You did a great job with Regar."

Wouldn't have been possible without my brother.

"You worked together, which means it wouldn't have been possible without you either."

I guess that's true.

"How do you feel?"

I'm glad he's dead. But I still worry about my mother.

"We'll get to her soon. Once we've defeated Necrosis, we'll have the forces of everyone on the continent. They won't be able to challenge us."

I hope so.

The same journey on foot would have taken weeks. Weeks in addition to all the unforeseen obstacles that would make that journey even longer. On the back of a dragon, we had no obstacles, just light and darkness.

At sunset, we lowered beneath the clouds and looked at our location.

Huntley says we're close.

I could see the stark white of snow, the coldness of this forsaken world. The temperature dropped the closer we moved toward the surface. My armor kept me warm, but it wasn't enough when I felt the snow land in my hair.

As we traveled farther east, there was a respite from the cold. My fingertips began to thaw, and my skin no longer prickled with bumps. The land turned green instead of white, and then the territory began to look familiar.

Burn?

"Yes."

Pyre dropped his head and dove straight for the ground. The wind whipped through my hair and strained my eyes as we fell from the sky. Then Pyre released the line of fire from his mouth, and it exploded over the buildings and the trees, igniting on contact.

Storm did the same, turning a different way and making a straight line of flames that burned through the city.

Other people knocked when they arrived. We burned.

Soldiers poured out of the buildings to fight us, but without crossbows, there was nothing they could do but run around and put out the fires and pull burning men from the flames. They were paralyzed by the attack, absolutely helpless.

I'd actually feel bad…if Klaus hadn't scarred my thighs forever.

Enough.

Pyre flew back to the field in front of the city and landed next to Storm. Huntley was already off his dragon, standing in the field, waiting for our enemy to ride out and meet us. I slid down Pyre's scales and met Huntley on the ground.

The gates opened and riders emerged. It took minutes for them to reach us, even with their horses running at full speed. Two black horses were in the lead, followed by a few others, but it wasn't their full contingent. It was less than a dozen Teeth.

When they came closer, Huntley placed his body in front of mine.

The horses came to a stop, Klaus in the lead, looking silently livid. He stared at Huntley for a moment, restraining his fury as best he could, and then hopped off the horse to meet him head on.

His teeth were retracted behind his mouth and throat, but his eyes looked bloodthirsty. He stopped in front of Huntley and stared him down, his eyes shifting back and forth angrily.

"Your city and everyone in it will turn to ash unless you comply with my demands."

Last time I saw Klaus, he wore a gloating smile. Then he feasted on my flesh until I reached the brink of death. He taunted me with his arrogance. Now his world was crumbling around him.

"We travel to HeartHolme to help the Runes defeat Necrosis. The Teeth will be our allies in this battle."

"Necrosis is our ally—"

"Not anymore."

"Once we've fulfilled our purpose, you'll just kill us."

"We can coexist peacefully. We'll draw up a truce. You have my word."

Klaus studied him closely.

"My offer is not only gracious but merciful. Accept it with gratitude." Huntley didn't raise his voice, but he sounded absolutely terrifying, his rage bubbling just beneath the surface.

Klaus finally gave a nod.

"On your knees."

Klaus inhaled a slow breath, furious.

"I said, on your knees."

Klaus's mouth started to shake, as if his teeth wanted to emerge but it took all his strength to keep them locked away. A minute ticked by before he brought himself to the ground, on his knees as Huntley asked. "I accept."

"Good. Now appoint your new king."

The anger on Klaus's face started to fade, replaced by a whole different look. "Why?"

Huntley stepped closer and stared down at him. "You know why."

His breaths immediately deepened and turned uneven. He dropped his gaze to compose himself, but he couldn't hide the fear that crept into his features.

"Did you think you could touch my wife and get away with it?" Huntley pulled his sword out of his scabbard. "Did you think you could feast on her flesh and keep your head? Did you really think I wouldn't fixate about it every day, every moment, until I had you on your knees just like this? Now select your successor."

He dropped his gaze, breathing hard. Through clenched teeth, he spoke the name. "Gunter—"

Huntley swung his sword in a flash, decapitating Klaus with one fluid stroke. The head rolled away, and the body crumpled to the ground. He sheathed his blade and spat on the corpse. "You have one day to prepare your army. We ride for HeartHolme tomorrow."

————

We sat across from each other at the campfire, the dragons asleep on either side of us. We were out in the open, far away from the Teeth but still vulnerable to the world and the elements.

Huntley didn't seem concerned.

I'd caught our dinner that night, and it roasted over the fire. It was like old times, when we were distrustful but unable to keep our hands off each other. When the meat was done, I divided it between us, along with the roasted potatoes. I always gave Huntley the bigger half because his body needed more than mine did. I loved food, but I could exist off much less than he could. "I can take the first watch."

He shook his head. "We both need our sleep. The road ahead of us will be arduous, at best."

"What if they sneak up on us?"

"They aren't going to sneak up on me and two drag-ons." He wiped his fingers on the cloth then rinsed his plate with his canteen. "Gunter may be their new ruler, but I'm the one running the show. They won't fuck with me."

Huntley had always been a brooding, no-bullshit kind of guy, but his coldness had deepened, and so had his authority. He didn't need to be decorated with hand-crafted robes and a crown of jewels to look like a king. He was kingly in every aspect of his life. He dominated everything around him—and not just me. "I'm worried."

He looked at me across the fire, his blue eyes attentive. "Why?"

"Everything you said about Haldir…all those bruises on your body."

"He's my problem, not yours."

"Your problems are my problems, Huntley. Because if he kills you…I'll lose everything."

He kept his same stare, not giving me a glimpse of empathy. "He won't."

"He almost did."

"His dragon almost did—because he's a fucking coward. I'll get him, baby. I'll get all of them."

"I just… I know I can't help you." I was good with a sword, could take on a man twice my size, but one of the kings… I was simply no match for them. Huntley was the strongest swordsmen I'd ever encountered, and I'd watched them knock each other around on top of that roof like two puppets. "At least not without Pyre."

"Then keep Pyre close—always."

TWENTY-SEVEN

Elora

_____

There was nothing to do except sit and wait.

Bastian had been gone a week. A very long week. A week that left me lonely and crippled with anxiety. Necrosis hadn't struck HeartHolme, and our scouts hadn't reported the approach of their army.

Like sitting ducks, we just waited for war to knock on our front door.

I sat at the bar with a pint in front of me, Ian beside me. Now, he was always in his full battle armor, his sword, dagger, and shield, ready for the bells when the alarm was raised. Others in town were dressed similarly, shopping in the market with their bows across the backs and their axes in their belts.

Everyone was waiting.

Ian drank from his beer but didn't say anything.

I hoped Bastian would return. If he didn't, I wouldn't know what to do with myself.

"It's weird," Ian said. "I feel like every night is our last night on this earth."

"Yeah…I know what you mean. I double-check everything every morning, but I realize there's nothing more for me to do."

Ian nodded. "The wall is prepped. We're ready. Just wish Huntley were here…"

"Yeah."

"He wasn't here last time, and I felt it. Everyone did."

I nodded. "But according to his note, he should be here soon."

"I expected him to be here by now, actually." He stared into his glass.

"He'd just conquered the Kingdoms when he wrote that. I'm sure he had a lot of stuff to take care of. He's armed with two dragons, and he survived not just one battle, but several. I'm not worried. You shouldn't be either."

He stared for a moment longer before he gave a quick nod. "You're right."

We returned to our tense silence.

Then I heard it—the bells. The sound was distant, not coming from the main gate, but from the opposite end of HeartHolme. It was so faint I wasn't sure if I was imagining them, but when I looked at my brother, the look on his face told me he heard them too. "Fuck."

———

We ran through the streets toward the castle in the rear, the bell tolling at the very top of the keep. Other soldiers were running too, trying to answer the call before the emergency became worse.

Before we reached the double doors, the bells went quiet.

Wasn't sure if that was a good thing or a bad thing.

We pushed through the doors, and both of us stilled when we saw what lay behind.

Dead soldiers—everywhere.

Ian immediately pulled out his sword. "Elora, stay here."

"Fuck off, I'm not staying anywhere." I did the same, pulling out the Ice sword that Bastian had asked me to carry.

He gave me an irritated look but didn't have time to berate me, so he moved on. He climbed up the steps, finding more of the dead along the way. The castle was silent, so the attackers had been killed…or they had already killed everyone else.

We made it to the next floor—and found Commander Dawson dead on the stairs.

Fuck, this was not good.

We moved farther up and stilled at the sight.

Queen Rolfe was on her knees, a blade pressed so hard against her throat she bled a few drops. Her head was held high even though she was confined to the floor, and her eyes were still as steely and cold as ever.

I'd never seen the man holding her hostage before, but I knew who he was.

One of the Three Kings.

Because he had wings. They were folded against his body but not completely tucked away. He'd flown right into HeartHolme without anyone noticing—and had taken the queen by the throat.

Neither one of us knew what to do. We were both in such shock.

The king was garbed in armor similar to ours, most of his skin hidden from view, but he had hard features just like Bastian. High cheekbones. Sunken eyes. A jawline clenched tight. He was taller and bigger than Ian, and that was terrifying, considering my brother was a pretty big guy.

Even two against one, we didn't stand a chance.

Queen Rolfe spoke despite the cut it caused to her throat. "Run. Now."

Ian was rooted to the spot.

So was I.

Queen Rolfe spoke again. "Ian…that's an order."

He ignored her pleas. "Release her."

With unblinking eyes, he stared. "Open the gates."

It was either the discomfort of the blade or the fear for her son's life that caused her breaths to deepen.

Ian kept his eyes on Necrosis. "I will if you let her go."

"No—" She sucked in a hard breath when he pressed the blade harder into her neck.

"Open the gate first." His voice was deep like a man's, but it had an animalistic quality to it, like a wolf that had learned to speak but couldn't quite master it.

"Ian." Blood dripped down her neck. "I'd rather die— so let him kill me and run."

If only I could sink my blade into his flesh, this would all be over. Regardless of how powerful he was, my blade should be more powerful. But her body blocked every good shot.

Ian's intellectual ability was completely compromised by the situation. He saw his mother in duress, and all he could do was respond emotionally. I didn't blame him, but it was bad for all of us. "I'll open the gate." He backed away.

Queen Rolfe started to fight her restraints, as if she were trying to get killed. "No! Don't let them in, Ian!"

The king shut her up by slicing her across the cheek.

Another one stepped out of the hallway—another king.

Now it was two on two. We didn't stand a chance.

The second one moved toward us and stopped, as if he expected us to lead the way to the gate.

Ian backed away, and so did I.

Queen Rolfe started to weep. "I'm not worth it. I'm not worth what they'll do to our people."

We stepped out of the room and took the stairs, the enormous Necrosis hot on our tail. We made it outside into the darkness and kept going.

"She's right," I said quietly. "We can't do this."

Ian ignored me, walking quickly.

"She wouldn't want this."

With singular focus, he set his determination on the gate and nothing else. "I didn't help her before… I can't do that again."

Huntley had told me the story years ago. They were just boys. Huntley stayed behind, and Ian ran for it, altering their bond with their mother forever. Huntley became the favorite, the revered one, and Ian was always second best. "It's not the same thing, Ian. They're going to kill her anyway." I glanced behind me, seeing the king still following us. "I know this is hard—"

"She's my mother. She would do it for me."

"I don't think she would." I knew she'd sacrifice either one of her sons for the sake of her people. One for the many. "We don't know what's waiting outside the gate, but it's not good. We can't do this—"

"I've made up my mind."

We moved down to the gate where the soldiers were prepared for war.

The King hung back, trying to escape everyone's notice.

Ian raised his head and gestured to the men. "Raise the gate."

I couldn't believe this was happening. "Ian, we might be able to take him."

"We don't know how he communicates. He might tell the other one to kill her."

"He's going to kill her anyway! Don't you understand that?"

411

The soldiers didn't listen, so Ian made the request again. "I said, open the gate. Now."

"I understand what happened in the past is really shitty, but this isn't what she wants. This isn't a test."

The doors started to open.

Now it was too late.

Twelve Necrosis entered on horseback, fully armored.

At least it wasn't the entire army.

As they drew closer, I recognized the one in the lead.

My heart did a somersault as it sank, and once it hit the bottom of my stomach, it sent tremors throughout my body. The shock overwhelmed me. All I could do was stare.

Bastian dropped from his horse, as did the others. Then he walked forward, right past me, and moved toward the castle. He didn't turn his head to acknowledge me. As if he didn't even know I was there.

Ian turned to look at me, derision heavy in his face. He didn't say a single word, but he didn't need to. The punch from his fist hit me right in the cheek without him moving an inch. He was so pissed off he could strangle me right now.

I averted my gaze. For the first time in my life, I was ashamed.

412

Truly ashamed.

———

We were escorted back to the castle, which was now fully under Necrosis rule.

Queen Rolfe was still on her knees with the blade held to her throat, her eyes now glazed over in defeat. She didn't look at us as we entered, like she really didn't care whether she lived or died at this point.

Bastian was there, speaking to the other king. "Haldir has left Necrosis with the army. They'll be here shortly, Kronos."

Kronos, the second king, nodded. "They'll walk through the open gates and have their feast."

Unable to mobilize against the enemy, the Runes would have no choice but to fend for themselves. But that wouldn't last long, not when they were overrun and cornered with nowhere to go.

Gods…please help us.

Queen Rolfe cringed on her knees, feeling the pain of her own people.

Ian stepped forward. "You said you would let her go."

The king holding the knife to her throat stared at Ian for a few seconds. He was the Third King, a king that hadn't been named yet. He gave a slight smile before he removed the blade from her throat and kicked her in the back.

The queen fell forward and didn't catch herself.

"You'll watch HeartHolme fall—and then we'll eat each one of you."

My eyes flicked to Bastian, although he didn't deserve my stare.

His look was elsewhere, pretending I wasn't in the room even though I was just a few feet away.

Queen Rolfe got to her feet, and the first thing she did was slap Ian across the face. There was enough force in her hit that his head turned with it. "How dare you?"

Ian kept his head turned as he breathed hard, as if he couldn't look at her.

"I'd rather die a million times for HeartHolme than betray it." She slapped him again. "How dare you take that away from me? How dare you do this to our people?"

The fallout took the attention of everyone in the room, including Bastian. It gave me a moment to pull out my dagger and tuck it into my sleeve near my wrist. The only way to save HeartHolme was to kill every person in this room—including Bastian. The dagger was reinforced with a concentrated dose of Ice. It would take out Bastian and the others in a single strike, but I wasn't sure about Kronos and the Third King.

I was going for it.

Kronos issued his orders. "Secure them in the castle grounds. I want them to watch."

The Third King moved forward and grabbed Queen Rolfe again, restraining her arms behind her back. Another Necrosis moved for Ian. Thankfully, Bastian stayed with Kronos, and another Necrosis moved for me, his skin dark with hunger.

I ignored him and moved for the Third King because his death was more important than the other two Necrosis. I gripped the hilt and stabbed the dagger deep into his flesh, right in his torso where it would pierce him the easiest.

There was a collective pause in the room, as if no one could believe what had just happened.

I didn't hesitate before I stabbed him again.

He still stood—and released an angry breath.

That was when chaos broke out.

Ian took out the Necrosis on him with his sword, and Queen Rolfe broke free from the Third King's hold. She was weaponless, so she attacked the Necrosis that came after me with her bare fists.

I stabbed the Third King again, hoping he would die this time.

He went weak, his knees collapsing.

Yes.

I stabbed him again, and that was when he fell.

One down. Two to go.

Kronos was on me, moving so swiftly my eyes couldn't even follow him. His face came into my vision—and then everything went dark. I felt no pain, but I knew he'd hit me so hard that the world turned black.

TWENTY-EIGHT

Ian

THE CHAIRS WERE ANCHORED IN PLACE WITH HEAVY pieces of stone, and our wrists were bound to the armrests with chains that wouldn't break. Our ankles were locked together too, making us completely immobile.

Bastian had been the one to do it.

While Necrosis held us down, he secured each of us in place, giving us no wiggle room at all.

I'd never felt more hatred for someone in my life. I hated him more than Kronos somehow. I hated him more than every Necrosis combined. "I knew I was right about you, motherfucker."

He ignored me and checked my mother's restraints.

"I may die, but my brother will come for you."

He walked off without looking back, leaving me to simmer in my rage. Kronos had taken Elora's unconscious body into another room, and then we were escorted outside the castle. I didn't know what he was going to do to her…and I didn't want to think about it. I didn't want to think about anything. Reality was just too much.

Defeated, my mother just sat there, looking across HeartHolme to the gate that remained open, welcoming our attackers with open arms.

"Huntley's coming."

She was silent.

"He'll save us like last time. I know he will."

"Once Necrosis walks through those open doors, it'll be over. No amount of dragon fire will be able to fix it, not unless we burn our own people as much as theirs." Her voice was lifeless, as if she were just a hollow shell at this point. Her eyes were straight ahead, nowhere near me. "You should have let me die. And you should have died warning our men what's to come."

"I had to save you."

She turned to look at me. "Don't save someone who doesn't want to be saved, Ian."

"Huntley is coming. I'm not going to let you die when he's going to save us all."

"We can't rely on that, Ian. He could be dead for all we know."

"But I know he's not," I said. "I have faith."

She looked ahead once more.

"I didn't save you before…and I've regretted that every day since."

Her eyes briefly closed. "There was nothing you could do."

"There was nothing Huntley could do—but he stayed."

"And I wish he hadn't."

I'd never said the words to her before, and if we were about to die, may as well speak them now. "You've always preferred Huntley over me, and not because he's your firstborn. It's because you're forever bonded by that day…and I'm just the coward who tried to save my own neck."

She was quiet for a long time, letting me choke on the silence. "There's no preference, Ian. Your brother saw the version of me that I'm most ashamed of. He witnessed a trauma that doesn't escape my thoughts or my dreams. I pity myself, and then when I look at him, I pity him too. Yes, we're bound, but not in the way that I want. I wish he'd run that night. I wish he hadn't had to see me like that."

I stared ahead, trying to block her sorrow from my heart.

"I'm sorry if I've ever made you feel lesser than. If I've ever shown your brother preference, it's because he shares your father's likeness. I've never remarried, and that's because he's my one and only. Looking at your brother's face is like a breath of fresh air. It gives me courage when I have none. It gives me peace in war."

I stared all the way down through the open gates, seeing the fields beyond, hoping for a dragon to appear in the sky.

"You served HeartHolme well in my absence. You've taken care of the outpost for years. You've been a great son, Ian. I know your father would be proud of you. I'm proud of you as well—and I'm sorry I didn't make that more known."

Her praise meant a lot to me, especially since I'd never heard it before. She always expected the best. That was her minimum standard, so if I met it, there was no need for praise. "Thank you."

"I love you, son."

It was hard to say it back, especially since it felt as if what she was really saying was goodbye. "I love you too, Mother."

TWENTY-NINE

Elora

———————

When I woke up, I realized I was chained down.

To a bed.

My eyes opened, everything that had just happened hitting me at once, and then I focused on the face hovering above me.

Kronos.

My wrists pulled at the chains so hard the metal cut into my flesh. The sweat poured off me a second later, causing a burn so deep it made me cringe. "I'll kill you just like your little friend, motherfucker." I yanked hard again, and my body was tugged back to the bed.

Kronos stared with a hard expression, frozen just like a statue.

I knew my dagger had been confiscated, and with just my bare hands, there was nothing I could do even if I were free. I was going to die. And not just die, but lose my soul too.

His stare continued.

"What the fuck do you want from me?" I yelled, hoping my voice carried to anyone who might be able to help me.

His hand suddenly reached for my hair, as if to caress it like a lover.

I jolted away. "Don't fucking touch me."

"You remind me of Haldir's wife, Avice. Painstakingly beautiful."

Fuck.

"But she doesn't possess your strength. Your fight."

I'd just killed his brother, and he was coming on to me? "A fight that will kill you."

"Without your little dagger, there's nothing you can do to me." He smiled. "Where did you get it?"

I played dumb. "What?"

"Don't drop your feistiness now. Tell me where you got the Ice."

Bastian had abandoned me to this torture. He'd lied straight to my face and betrayed me. My family. I'd stuck out my neck for him when Ian wanted to kill him…and he'd made me look like a fool. I should tell the truth and get him killed. But for whatever reason, I couldn't. "Ice? I don't even know what that is."

His face quickly tightened into a look of rage. "Tell me."

"I found the dagger at a Plunderer outpost, alright? That's all I know."

His narrowed eyes scrutinized my face, tried to catch the lies in my eyes.

I seemed to have passed his test because he didn't press me. "We have two options. I can feast on your soul and have the most exquisite meal of my life. Or I can turn you, and you can be the Second Queen."

In either case, I lost my soul. If I were alone, that revelation would bring me to tears. Ian was probably already dead. Queen Rolfe had been eaten, no doubt. I was the last one left, and when Huntley arrived, he would see that he'd lost everything. "Kill me. I'd rather die than be bound to you." The most difficult part about this was the helplessness. I couldn't even fight back. I just had to lie there and wait for the end.

His eyes shifted back and forth between mine as the anger tightened the corners of his eyes. He straightened his back, and he continued his stare down at me. "You will be the Second Queen."

"I just told you to kill me!"

"Death would be a waste for someone as beautiful as you."

Now I wished I had my own dagger just to stab myself straight through the heart. I fought against the chains to break free, to slit my own wrists, to work my body so hard that I collapsed.

His enormous palm flattened against my chest, and he pinned me in place.

"No." I tried to buck him off.

He was so strong that it was no use. It was like fighting a mountain.

"Fuck you!"

His eyes glazed over before they brightened and turned a deep blue. They glowed as if lit from within, as if he were in some kind of trance. His body was stiff as stone, and he held me in place, the magic making my body weak.

It'd already begun.

Then a blade tip appeared straight out of his chest from behind. The blood oozed out, blue-gray like the ocean on a cloudy day.

I stilled in fright when I saw it, unsure what was going on. "What in the gods…"

The blade was pulled out and stabbed back in, hitting him in a different spot.

It was Ian. My brother had come for me.

Kronos was still for a moment, processing the stab wounds that made his body bleed. He was in as much shock as I was, probably because he had been in the middle of performing a trance. He jerked upright and turned on his assailant.

"Kill this motherfucker, Ian!"

Kronos pulled the knife out of his own body and attacked. I couldn't see past his body because he was a foot taller than the average man. Their bodies struck the wall, and then fists were flying. Kronos threw Ian's body across the room until he hit the opposite wall with a loud thud.

Ian righted himself quickly—but it wasn't Ian at all.

It was Bastian.

Kronos came at him with the bloody knife and aimed for his throat.

"No!"

Bastian ducked at the last minute and maneuvered out of the way.

Kronos pivoted back toward him. "You're a servant to the Three Kings. Bow so I may take your life." He came at him again, with a speed I couldn't even follow with my eyes.

I fought the chains to be free, but they were locked in place. "Don't you fucking die, Bastian!"

Bastian kept dodging and moving, sidestepping the blade at the very last second. With just one hit, he would be gone forever. The fight continued in the room until they disappeared into the hallway.

Now all I could hear was the sound of heavy footsteps, of bodies slamming into walls, an ongoing fight with no end in sight. Helpless, I just lay there, my eyes closed even though I couldn't see anything anyway. "Bastian...please."

The sounds stopped. It was quiet. The fight was over.

"Bastian?" My weak voice pierced the silence, afraid of the echo that would come back at me.

Nothing.

"Bastian...?" Tears already formed in my eyes because I knew the outcome without seeing it. "No..."

Footsteps sounded as they approached the room, the gait slow, like the victor was deeply injured. It must be Kronos, still bleeding from his stab wounds, and once he rounded the corner, he would finish me off.

A hand gripped the doorframe before he came into view.

Bastian.

Beaten and bloody, he was hardly recognizable, but he was alive.

"Gods…"

The sight of me seemed to invigorate him because he moved to the bed at a much quicker pace and got the chains free.

I was on him right away, my arms wrapped around him tightly. "Are you okay?"

Like he wasn't injured at all, he grasped me tightly, his chin on my head. "I'm fine, Elora."

I pulled away and examined his face, seeing the dark bruising around his eyes, the blue blood that dripped from his beaten eyebrow and the cut in his cheek. "What happened?"

"Haldir had already sent the other kings to Heart-Holme by the time I arrived. He dispatched me to join them. There was no way I could have given you a warning because we don't communicate with messenger birds. I had to play along until the time was right."

Now I felt like shit for assuming the worst.

"When I saw the look on your face…I wanted to die."

I dropped my eyes. "I'm sorry I didn't have more faith in you…"

His hand brushed my hair away with the same gentleness as the day he left. "Haldir is marching here with Necrosis as we speak. We need to prepare before they arrive. We'll need the dragons. If they aren't here, we won't stand a chance against Haldir."

"Huntley will be here," I said with a nod. "Let's go to work."

He moved off the bed.

I grabbed his arm and kept him in place.

He stared at me, his eyes searching my face.

"I love you." When I didn't tell Kronos the truth about the Ice, I knew. I'd hated myself for it because I'd given my heart to a man I'd thought didn't deserve it. It was a moment of heartbreak rather than joy. But now, it was a moment I would never forget.

He stared at me for a while before he gripped my face and kissed me. "I love you too."

———

The twelve Necrosis who accompanied Bastian weren't the twelve he'd originally intended to bring, so we had to kill them all. It was easy for Bastian to sneak up on each one and slip the dagger between their ribs. They crumpled one by one, and the castle was back to pure silence.

We made it outside and found Ian and Queen Rolfe sitting side by side, chained to the chairs outside the castle. The Necrosis that guarded them were killed from behind by Bastian. I got to Ian and started to remove his chains.

"Elora?" His voice picked up in excitement. "What's going on? How did you escape?"

"Him." I nodded to Bastian, who was loosening the chains around the queen.

Ian looked over and paled when he saw Bastian. "What…?"

"He killed Kronos and the others," I said. "The only reason I'm alive is because he saved me."

Once my brother was free, he was instantly on his feet. "So, the Two Kings are gone?"

"Yes," I said. "We killed all the Necrosis too."

Queen Rolfe was on her feet and already giving orders. "Elora, fetch me my blade."

"I grabbed it for you." I held it out to her in the scabbard.

A momentary glimpse of gratitude entered her features before she secured the blade to her belt. "Ian, take care of the gate."

Ian shielded his eyes and squinted. "They're closing the gate."

"They are?" I asked, turning to follow his stare.

Bastian returned to my side. "Necrosis has arrived. Prepare for battle."

———

"Go back to the forge?" I asked incredulously. "And do what?"

Queen Rolfe was rounding up the army and deploying them outside the city while Ian took care of the men behind the wall. Without Commander Dawson, we'd lost another leader to guide the soldiers. Ian grew irritated, wanting to focus on other things besides my protest. "Make more weapons."

"There's no more Ice!"

"Then make regular weapons."

"Ian, I've made more than we'll ever need. I belong here, in battle."

"No."

"No?" I snapped. "Who killed the Third King? If Queen Rolfe can fight among her men, so can I."

"She's a lot better than you—"

"Then fight me right now. See what happens."

Before Ian could yell at me, a hand gripped me by the shoulder. "I'll look after her."

Ian turned his stare on the man he hadn't fully accepted. "You want your woman out here? We've got the biggest army ever marching on HeartHolme—"

"And we need every person possible if we want to make it through the night," Bastian said. "If anyone wants to fight for their home, they should have the right. This battle only has two outcomes. Life or extinction. There will never be another opportunity to fight Necrosis. This is it. We either win—or we perish."

Ian drew a deep breath before he shifted his gaze to me.

"Ian, I know you want to protect me, but you can't this time," I said. "We've got too much at stake."

He released a heavy sigh, like he didn't know what to do. "No offense, man. But you look like shit." He looked at Bastian again.

"It looks worse than it feels," he said. "Besides, I've got all that adrenaline from killing the Second King."

Ian shook his hand. "Protect her—because I can't."

"With my life." He returned the gesture then stepped back.

Ian gave me a final hug before he walked off and got back to work. Right away, he started to bark out orders, telling the men to prepare the cannons, directing the archers to position the barrels of Ice arrows.

Bastian examined the closed gate for a moment, seeing Queen Rolfe organizing her army to fight outside the gates.

"What are you thinking?"

He was quiet for a long time, as if he hadn't heard me. "Haldir isn't going to stay on the field with the others. He's going to come straight here—for your queen."

"I made sure she has one of the strongest blades."

"I admire Queen Rolfe for her bravery, but all the courage in the world won't be enough to defeat him. I doubt she'll survive."

"I wouldn't underestimate her."

"I'm a skilled fighter and I'm Necrosis—and he almost ripped my head off my shoulders." He turned to look at me, his bruised face solemn. "I'm the one who should fight him."

"We have the dragons for that."

"We can't depend on that, Elora. Not until they're here."

"Well, I can help you."

"No."

"Two is better than one—"

"I'm not letting you anywhere near him. But you can grab a bow and shoot him with Ice."

I nodded in agreement. "That's a good plan."

"Hopefully we can kill him before his horde breaches the gate."

"What makes you so certain they will?"

A foot taller than me, he had to tilt his head down to look at me. The coldness in his eyes didn't come from his heart, but his sense of hopelessness. "Because there's way more Necrosis than last time."

———

HeartHolme was prepared for war.

The archers lined the walls with all the Ice arrows I could make. Soldiers were on the ground outside the gate, ready to fight the Necrosis that broke through the volley of arrows. Commander Dawson had been slain, so Ian took his place and issued our orders throughout the castle. Queen Rolfe was still and silent, as calm as she looked when she sat upon her throne. Night had fallen—and that was when we knew they were coming.

I thought the last battle of HeartHolme would be our final one, but I hadn't been nearly as nervous as I was now. There was a lot on the line, not just my family, but the man I loved—and his soul. The breeze moved across my face but not over my hair like it usually did. I pulled it back into a bun, something I almost never did, because I couldn't afford a single mistake.

Queen Rolfe had her thick hair interwoven with feathers, wound into a long braid down her back. It was elegantly done, but it was also functional. The black armor fit her body perfectly, covering every vulnerability but keeping its fluidity at the same time. She stood there with her hands together at her waist, waiting for the battle to arrive on her doorstep.

The scout called from the wall. "They're coming."

The bonfires in the field lit up their approach. "How many?" Ian called.

The scout stared for so long it didn't seem like he'd say anything. "Too many to count."

Fuck.

Queen Rolfe had no reaction to that. "I don't care how many there are. All we must do is buy ourselves enough time for Huntley and Ivory to join us. They'll light the skies with fire, burn their corpses to ash. I have no doubt my son, King of Kingdoms, will save us all."

An hour later, they crossed the field outside the closed gates, and Ian ordered the first line of arrows. "Make every arrow count. Fire!" The archers fired off their first line of arrows.

I was down below with Bastian, so I didn't see the effect of the Ice. My eyes were on Ian at the wall, and his lack of disappointment told me the arrows did their job.

Bastian stood several feet behind the queen. "She knows."

"What?"

"She knows he's coming for her."

I stared at the backside of the queen, seeing her standing there with her sword in her hands, the tip of the blade against the pavers at her feet. Her head was tilted back slightly, her focus on the dark sky.

Bastian unsheathed his blade. "Get ready."

"Do you see something?"

"No. But once he sees that HeartHolme has defeated his brothers, he'll strike when we least expect it. So expect it always." He gripped the hilt of his sword with both hands and watched the sky just the way she did.

The sounds of battle heightened as time went on. The archers continued to fire their arrows until the barrels were empty. I had the last barrel nearby, just in case we needed them within HeartHolme. The sounds of shouts and screaming became audible as our soldiers charged forward to the sea of Necrosis that waited for them.

I closed my eyes because it was too much. "Come on, Huntley…" The longer he took, the more Runes would die.

The screams of blood lust disappeared, replaced by the screams of the slain.

I could feel the loss already.

Without looking over the edge of the wall, I imagined what it looked like. An endless sea of Necrosis, ten to every one of us, a battle we could never win—not unless the dragons came. My breaths started to increase as the anxiety flooded into my blood. While everyone else felt adrenaline, I just felt terror.

Everyone I loved was about to die.

"Haldir approaches." He said the words clearly, loud enough for Queen Rolfe to hear.

I looked up into the darkness but didn't see anything.

"Get back, Elora." He grabbed my arm and gave me a hard shove.

Haldir came with the speed of a falcon, diving down straight for Queen Rolfe. It happened so fast she didn't even register it.

Bastian gave her a hard shove, getting her out of the way before Haldir could grab her in his arms. He lost his momentum slightly and fell to the earth with a thud that was louder than the battle over the wall.

Bastian didn't give him a chance to rise. He swung his sword down and struck him in the shoulder, trying to hit him in the small opening between the plates of his armor.

I snapped into action and readied my bow. The barrel of Ice arrows was next to me, and I nocked one to the string. I was a good shot, but instead of firing right away, I shifted the aim of my arrow left and right, their movements so quick.

Bastian and Haldir were locked in an exchange of blows that I could barely witness. There was a strike, a block, a combination of hits and spins that I couldn't see, let alone anticipate. Bastian held his own despite the bruising and exhaustion of his body. His eyes were focused, hardly blinking.

Haldir kicked him in the chest, sending Bastian flying back.

Haldir finally stilled for a moment, and that was when I fired an arrow at his neck.

It sank right into his flesh. He made a slight jerk before his head snapped in my direction. He spotted me a distance away, and the coldness that settled on his face was far more terrifying than the other kings.

Bastian was back on his feet, moving into his line of sight to block me from view.

Haldir turned his attention back to Bastian. "I spare your life, and this is how you repay me?"

"You killed me—"

"I gave you immortality." He was a different breed, a foot taller than Bastian, with a voice deep and sinister.

If a wolf could speak, that was exactly how it would sound. "I gave you the power of the gods."

"You took my soul and my afterlife."

"No need for an afterlife if this one never ends." He spun the sword around his throat and came for Bastian. "I'll finish what I started. And then I'll take the woman you're trying so hard to protect."

That spurred Bastian on, and he attacked with a new series of blows. Sword struck sword, the blue color of his Ice blade slicing through the night. Punches were thrown to force the other one off-balance. Bastian got a hard elbow to the face that made blood burst from his nose, but he didn't miss a beat as he kept going.

Watching them locked in battle made me realize Bastian was right. I didn't stand a chance.

I put another arrow to the string and tried to focus my aim. The men were moving so quickly that I couldn't get an opening. The other soldiers that jumped in to help were pushed back by Haldir, flying through the air and hitting the wall.

I fired an arrow, but it missed. It hit the wall and shattered. "Dammit!"

Haldir executed an impressive combo, hitting Bastian's blade repeatedly, and then struck him so hard he flew into the air and landed on the other side of the battlefield.

He didn't get up.

I lowered my bow and stared at Bastian's crumpled body, unsure if he was alive or dead. "Bastian!" My path to him was blocked—by Haldir.

He came right at me, his blade swinging, a grotesque sneer across his face.

There was no time to be terrified, no time to scream. I put that arrow to the string and fired. It struck him in the neck. I fired again, standing my ground because there was no escape. Closer and closer he came, until we were just feet apart.

I kept firing. "Die, motherfucker!"

He issued a horrible laugh and lifted his sword to strike me down.

I turned to roll away from the hit, but the blow never came. I turned back—seeing Queen Rolfe forcing him back with her spinning blade. She was my height, so several feet shorter than the man I would describe as a monster, but she spun her sword with such fury that she looked twice his height. I couldn't believe it.

Once Haldir recovered from the shock, he returned with his own offense, coming down hard.

Queen Rolfe used her shield to block his hits because the strength with just her sword wouldn't be enough. He hit her over and over again, driving her back the way she'd come.

I got back to work with the bow and nocked an arrow to the string. It was hard to get a shot, not when Queen Rolfe was constantly in the way. She was getting tired. I could tell. I'd never seen her strength tested like this.

Even though Bastian would be livid with me, I dropped the bow and unsheathed my own blade. I charged forward.

"No." Queen Rolfe shoved me aside and sent me to the dirt as she continued to fight.

I got up and came again, trying to slice my blade into the opening between his torso and his hip.

He struck my blade down and punched me so hard across the face I hit the earth. I couldn't roll out of the way, not when the world was spinning, not when I couldn't feel my hands or my face.

Then I saw her on top of me, blocking the blade that was meant for me. Her arms shook as she held back the weight, but she was losing. Her blade shook in her hand as he lowered them toward her, as Haldir forced the blade back toward her neck.

I grabbed my dagger and stabbed it into his leg.

He roared as the blade sank into the flesh of his knee, and he lost his force for just an instant.

It was enough for Queen Rolfe to get back to her feet.

But Haldir spun and stabbed his sword directly through her armor, right into her stomach, and impaled her straight through.

Everything stopped.

Went still.

I must have gone deaf because I didn't hear a thing.

She stood there with a brave look on her face, doing her best not to shuffle left or right, to face her death with as much bravery as she could. Her knees buckled, and she lowered herself to the ground, her breaths becoming deeper and harsher.

Haldir stared down at her, his grin disgusting.

"No…" I reached for my sword on the ground, but I knew I would never make it in time.

Haldir pulled out his sword and prepared to swipe her head clean from her shoulders.

Queen Rolfe looked him in the eye, unafraid. "Huntley…"

"Your son won't save you." He stood over her and readied the sword.

"N-n-ooo." She could barely speak. Her head turned slightly left as her chin rose, looking at the sky behind him. "But he's here to save everyone else."

ROOOOAAAAARRRR.

Huntley dropped from the sky out of nowhere and landed straight on Haldir just as Queen Rolfe collapsed.

THIRTY

Huntley

I recognized Haldir from the sky, saw his large form exchange blows with none other than my mother. Queen Rolfe took up her blade to a foe she could never defeat, but she did it anyway, did it for her people.

The army of Necrosis was far bigger than I ever anticipated. No fewer than a hundred thousand. This wasn't an army meant to conquer.

It was one to destroy.

The Teeth approached from the east, catching part of Necrosis off guard, but it wasn't enough to distract from the front. Even with two dragons, this battle would rage on for quite some time. "Tell Ivory to protect the wall."

Yes.

We flew over the castle, and that was when I saw my mother fall.

The blade stabbed her deep, right through the abdomen.

My hands went so weak I lost my grip on the pommel and nearly fell off. Storm redirected his body to catch me so I wouldn't spiral to the earth. "Noooo!"

She fell to her knees and looked up.

As if she knew I was there.

"Dive!"

Storm dove his body down and headed straight for the earth.

She dropped to her knees, and Haldir moved farther over her, ready to saw her head off her body.

Storm lifted at the very last minute so I could jump off and straight onto Haldir. "Tell Ivory what's happened." I fell through the air and landed right on his large body, making him drop to his knees and crumple to the stone pavers that lined the city. His body broke my fall, and I took advantage of the moment to stab my dagger straight into his neck over and over.

He released a roar and threw me off, sending me several feet away.

"Huntley…" My mother fell back, moving to her side to avoid the blade through her midsection.

Adrenaline as hot as lava sparked in my veins and gave me strength that I'd never felt before. Haldir had been a ferocious opponent that challenged decades of skill, but he suddenly seemed inconsequential. I had rage on my side, rage that couldn't be defeated by his smug grin.

"Sorry for your loss, *Your Majesty*." He spun his blade around his wrist.

I charged and performed a flurry of hits, striking his bracers then dropping to hit his greaves. I ducked several times and avoided the swing of his blade before I rose up and slammed my fist so hard into his face I heard the crack of his cheek. I kicked him back then slammed my sword on his bracers, cutting through the surface and revealing skin below.

"Huntley!" Elora slid her sword across the ground toward me. "Take my sword."

There was no time for questions, so I abandoned mine and took hers. It felt lighter than mine, and the blade sliced through the air as if it was as thin as a hair. Elora ran behind him to a man who had fallen near the wall.

Haldir circled me, his eyes combing my body for weakness.

The dragons roared into the night, their streams of fire lighting up the sky.

"You lost, asshole." I waited for him to charge, knowing he was waiting for the perfect moment. "You fucking lost, and you know it."

"Queen Rolfe is dead." He did a fancy swish with his sword. "I'm just getting started." With that, he lunged, his sword clanking against mine, hitting me so hard it looked like there were sparks.

Back and forth we went, striking and hitting, headbutting each other when we became too close. My body was tired, but the adrenaline was so strong that nothing could slow me down. I wouldn't stop until this motherfucker was dead.

Pyre came out of nowhere and grabbed Haldir by the shoulders. He slammed him down over and over, treating his body like a dead chicken, and then tossed him aside like his neck had been broken.

"Fuck yeah, Pyre." I rushed in, going for Haldir when Pyre was done.

Ivory slid off Pyre and rushed straight for my mother. Pyre took off, back to burning Necrosis outside the wall.

Haldir rolled away and got back to his feet, as if being thrashed by a dragon had little effect on his body. He came at me again, his blade marking my bracers, scratching up my armor, denting it in as he got closer to the skin.

"Ahhhh!" Ian came from behind and stabbed his blade deep in the back of Haldir's leg.

When he let out a scream, I charged forward and struck him right in the chest.

He punched me hard in the face then spun around to Ian, throwing him off like he weighed nothing.

We were both back on him, the two of us taking on Haldir together. Ian possessed the same rage I did, seeing our mother stabbed clean through. There was no amount of strength or skill that Haldir could possess that would challenge the fury drowning our hearts. We came at him hard—came at him together.

Ian got Haldir's left bracer off and sliced his blade over the skin, drawing blue blood. "How do you like that, bitch?"

I kicked him hard in the chest, denting the plate that protected him. I knew I'd hit it hard enough when his breaths didn't come as easily. It made the connection to his shoulder loose, so I stabbed my blade right through it.

Ian stabbed him again from the rear, issuing a maniacal laugh. "Fuck off."

"Wait!" Elora ran over, rope in her hands.

I knocked Haldir's blade from his hands and watched him fall to his knees.

"Don't kill him." She gave part of the rope to Ian.

I had no idea what was going on. "Elora—"

Ian immediately bound his wrists behind his back and secured them. Then he pushed him over and did the ankles. When Haldir tried to resist, Elora stomped on his face with her boot.

"What the fuck are you doing?" I asked, unsure what the hell I was seeing.

Ian kept going with the rope, tying his wrists and ankles together, wrapping the bonds all the way around his body so he could barely breathe. Elora kicked him in the face again, this time knocking him out cold.

"Huntley!" Ivory called for me.

I wanted this motherfucker dead, but I trusted Ian and Elora knew what they were doing. I ran to Ivory, positioned on top of my mother, who had gone pale in the face. Once I was close to her, the sadness was like a kick to the chest. "Mother, I'm here."

"My son…" She clasped my hand with hers, tears in her eyes. "My king…"

Tears already burned my eyes because this was the final goodbye. "Mother."

"I need your help." Ivory had her pack open, her essentials inside. "I know this is hard, but I need you to pull out the blade in one single movement. On my mark."

"You can heal her?"

"I…I don't know," she said. "I have an idea, but it might not work."

My mother's eyes remained on me, her hand squeezing mine.

"Alright. Let me know when you're ready." I had to release her hand—and it was the hardest thing I'd ever had to do. I gripped her shoulder and grasped the hilt, ready to yank it out.

Ivory closed her eyes and pressed her hands around the wound. She went still, sitting that way for a long time. The battle continued over the wall, shouts and cries spilling into the night. The dragons roared and burned Necrosis below, leading the Runes to release shouts of victory. I held my patience as Ivory focused, studying my mother's body so she could heal it as quickly as possible once the blade was out. If she didn't move quick enough, my mother would bleed out and die.

Ian kneeled next over her, clasping her hand in his, tears in his eyes. "I'm sorry I didn't stop him—"

"Son. I give you HeartHolme. I know you'll take care of our people—and rule with love in your heart."

He bowed his head, his breaths coming out shaky. "I love you."

A small smile moved on to her lips. "And I you."

"Now," Ivory said.

I pulled out the blade in a swift movement.

Ivory pressed her hands into my mother's abdomen and focused, her palms becoming bloody with the life that spilled out of her wounds.

Mother looked at both of us, like she'd never been so happy to see her sons. "I'm so proud...of you both."

Ivory continued to work, hunched over my mother's body as she put all her insides back together, attached the sinew, the tissue, the arteries. Minutes passed before she opened her eyes again and removed something from the contents of her pack. She emptied a bottle and poured it over the wound before she grabbed the cotton and began to wrap it around her midsection.

"Is she going to be okay?" I asked, needing that answer.

Ivory didn't look at me. "I did everything I could. It's out of my hands now. She needs to rest. We'll know in the morning..."

———

Haldir was locked away in a cell while we finished the battle.

All the soldiers who could fit on the wall watched the dragons fly over Necrosis and burn the ones that remained. All the Runes in the city piled up on the hills on the outskirts, watching the fire streak across the sky and burn their enemies to the ground. Once it was safe, we opened the gates so our men outside could retreat, but half of them had been lost in the attack.

It took the rest of the night and part of the morning for the last Necrosis to be destroyed or chased off. Pyre and Storm took off to hunt down the ones that had managed to slip away, to make sure there were no more Necrosis in this world that could turn anyone else.

My mother had been taken to her chambers in the castle so she could get as much rest as possible.

My home had been attacked for a second time. Ash was in the air just as it'd been at the Capital. The last month of my life had been spent fighting battle after battle—and I'd won every one. The fields outside HeartHolme were either charred or still actively burning, and the stench of melted flesh was repugnant in the air.

Ivory came to my side. "Pyre said they caught the last few that tried to escape. They're piling all the corpses onto the field now."

My helmet had been tossed away a long time ago. Not sure where it had ended up. The sword Elora gave me was still in my scabbard. The sword I'd wielded for years had disappeared in the rubble.

She studied the side of my face. "Are you alright, Huntley?"

The softness in her voice made me turn to regard her. "Thank you for healing my mother."

As her eyes shifted back and forth between mine, they softened. "You know you don't need to thank me for that…"

"I lost my father in a brutal way. I want to lose my mother to old age. I want her hair gray and her skin wrinkled. I want her to pass in her sleep—in peace. After all her sacrifice, that's what she deserves."

"And I think that'll still happen."

"You do?" I asked, my voice rising with hope.

She nodded. "If she's made it this long…I think she'll pull through."

I knew my mother would die with honor if she passed that day, but I still didn't want that for her.

"You have the blood of healers, so I think that's helped her as well."

Thank the gods.

Her hand went to my arm, and she looked me over, even though she couldn't see my flesh through my armor. "Are you okay?"

I was bruised and battered everywhere. I could feel it in my bones, feel it in my muscles. Once this armor was off my body, she would see all the discoloration, all the stress my body had endured this past month. Once the dead were burned and HeartHolme was safe, I wanted to retire to our home, to sleep in front of the fire and do nothing but make love all day long. But now, I had a kingdom to rule—and another battle to fight.

"Huntley?"

I gave her a nod. "What about you?"

"I'm fine." The ash fell on her shoulders, having been caught in her long strands of hair. The sun had risen in the sky, but the ash was so thick it was just a haze of red. It brought out the color of her eyes, made them look as if they were on fire. "I think we should talk to Elora."

My thoughts had been on my mother with such intensity that I'd forgotten. "You're right."

We moved through the rubble until we found her, sitting on a rock beside a man I didn't recognize. His face was beaten and bloody like he'd survived the battle of his life, and she was touching him gingerly as if he was more than just a fallen soldier.

Ivory stopped before we reached them.

I stopped with her, my eyes studying her face.

"I recognize him."

"From where?" I asked.

She stared a moment longer before she looked at me. "After we were attacked by Plunderers…in the forest."

My eyes narrowed. "Necrosis?"

She nodded.

I unsheathed my sword as I approached.

Elora noticed my movements, and she was quick to rise to her feet. "Put that away. Now."

"That man you're doting on—" I glanced at him past her shoulder "—is Necrosis."

"Yes, I'm not an idiot." She yanked the sword out of my hand and forced it back into the scabbard at my hip.

Necrosis got to his feet, a foot taller than her, standing at my height. He would be a handsome man if he weren't cut and bruised everywhere. "Bastian." He didn't extend his hand to shake mine, which was smart. "We've all had a shitty day, so let me give you the short version of this. I'm your ally."

"He's more than just our ally," Elora said. "He gave us the Ice to make all our weapons. He killed the Second King. He saved my life. It took a long time to get Ian to come around, so don't make me start over with you."

I watched my little sister's face, watched her basically threaten me without actually making a threat. "Why would Necrosis betray his own kind?"

"Because I want my soul back," he said. "And the only way to do that is to bring Haldir to the Bone Witch."

I looked at him blankly, hardly understanding anything he said.

Elora took over. "If we get her to remove the spell, it won't just release him, but it'll release anyone Haldir has ever turned. They'll get their souls back, and they'll be able to live the lives that were taken from them."

Now I understood why Ian had tied Haldir up rather than stabbing him through the chest.

"That was the deal you made," I said to myself more than anyone else. "You gave us the Ice in exchange for our help."

Bastian gave a nod. "And as you can tell, we fell in love in the process."

I'd noticed it a mile away. That was why I still wanted to kill him.

"So, I need your help with this, Huntley," Elora said. "I can't marry him if he doesn't have a soul. I can't have his children if he doesn't have a soul. My happiness depends on this." She pleaded with me. "And I know you'll do anything for me."

The first thing I did was turn to look at my own wife, a woman whom no one had accepted from the beginning. She was the daughter of my greatest enemy, but that hadn't stopped me from falling to my knees. I hadn't stopped fighting for her, and I knew Elora wouldn't stop fighting either. I turned to look at her again. "I'll help you."

Her eyes immediately softened. "Thank you."

"But if you want me to accept the man you love, you must accept the woman I love."

Elora stiffened once she realized her request was met with a condition. A hint of guilt moved over her face, like she remembered all the horrible things she said to Ivory, things that were unwarranted.

"She is your half sister, Elora."

Elora finally turned to look at Ivory. "Look, I know we're related biologically, but I have no connection to my rapist father, so I'll never see you as my half sister. No offense."

Ivory nodded. "None taken."

"But you're my sister-in-law…and I'd like us to be sisters in that way."

I hadn't expected my sister to say something like that, and clearly, Ivory hadn't either, judging by the look on her face.

"I'm sorry I was such a bitch," Elora said.

Ivory couldn't stop the laugh from escaping her lips.

Elora remained serious. "Now I know what it's like to love someone that everyone hates…and it sucks."

"It's fine," Ivory said. "You aren't a bitch."

"Come on. I was a total bitch, and we both know it," Elora said with a slight laugh. "Thanks for being cool about it."

"I have a brother, so I know what it's like to be protective. Don't worry about it."

Elora looked at me again, expecting me to fulfill my end of the deal.

"I'll help you in whatever way I can," I said. "But I don't have a lot of time. I need to return to the Kingdoms and keep my promise to the dragons."

"That's right," Elora said. "King of Kingdoms...how could I forget?" She had a teasing smile on her lips, like she would drown me in taunts when the time was right. "Let's wait until we know Queen Rolfe is well, then we'll depart. We all need to rest anyway." She looked at Ivory again. "Thank you for healing her."

"Don't mention it," Ivory said.

I looked at Ivory. "Let's wash up then head to the castle."

She nodded. "We've defeated Necrosis, but I feel like we didn't accomplish anything."

"Because we've been fighting so for long without taking a breath," I said. "It's just another battle to us. There's been no time to process any of it. We haven't even slept in the same bed for more than one night. And then my mother...unless she lives, this will never feel like a victory."

THIRTY-ONE

Huntley

_____

WHEN IVORY AND I STEPPED INSIDE OUR HOME, IT
didn't feel the same.

We'd only been gone for a few months, but several life-
times had happened in that time frame, and it felt as if I
hadn't been inside this house for years. I placed my
armor in the closet, took a bath, and then got dressed
again.

Ivory sat at the edge of the bed as she looked at me, her
eyes raking over the bruising of my body. The discoloration was everywhere because I'd been going nonstop
for weeks. Bruises were piled on top of bruises, like
paint layers on top of paint layers in a portrait.

"I'm going to the castle."

"Would you like me to go with you?"

After long consideration, I shook my head. "Get some sleep."

She got to her feet and gave me a passionate kiss before she let me go.

I gave her ass an automatic squeeze before I walked out.

It was afternoon now, smoke still heavy in the sky. Soldiers were still at the wall, cleaning up the ash and what remained of the dead. Cannons had broken parts of our walls, and the rubble needed to be cleared away so the gate could work properly again. Horses were spooked and needed comfort after all the terrible things they'd seen.

I made it into the castle and to her bedchamber at the top level. Asher usually greeted me, but he was dead now. When I'd lost my father, my world ended. I was a grown man with a wife, on the precipice of starting my own family, but if I lost my mother...my world would end again.

I moved down the hallway and walked through the open door.

She was in the bed, her hands folded together on her lap as if she were dead in a coffin. Her skin was still pale, hollows under her eyes. The blankets were piled high, and the fireplace crackled with heat like she was freezing cold.

Ian was there, in a chair at her bedside. He leaned forward with his arms on his knees, still in his armor like he hadn't bathed before he'd come here. Lost in thought, he didn't seem to notice me standing there.

I walked to his side and placed my hand on his shoulder.

He stirred at the contact, his head cocking back to look up at me. The duress quickly evaporated, and he looked defeated once again. "She hasn't woken up."

"Doesn't mean anything." I took the seat beside him. "I'd be asleep too if I weren't so worried."

Ian regarded her, releasing a heavy sigh as he did so.

I fell into the role of older brother immediately, my hand on his shoulder, my body made to support his. "I have faith in my wife. I have faith in our mother."

He stayed quiet.

"She hasn't lasted this long just to give up in the end."

Ian turned back to me. "Not killing Haldir…is the hardest thing I've ever had to do."

My hand lowered from his shoulder.

"But I did it for Elora. I did it because Bastian has done so much for us."

"You honored your debt. You did the right thing."

We both lapsed into a long silence. Sitting there, bound by our sadness, we waited.

———

Day had turned into night, and Ian had fallen asleep in the armchair.

My eyes grew heavy too, my head tilting sideways as it became too heavy to hold up. I jerked awake, my eyes on my mother, disappointed that she still wasn't conscious. My eyes moved to her chest, waiting for it to rise with a breath, and once it did, I felt the rush of relief.

I grabbed Ian and gave him a gentle shake. "We should get some sleep."

Ian blinked a few times then stared at Mother, his disappointment as raw as mine. "She's been asleep a long time…"

"Her body needs to put all its energy into healing."

We both gave her a final look before we stepped into the hallway. On the way, we ran into Elora.

"How is she?" She was in her normal clothes now, trousers and a long-sleeved shirt. But her sword was still on her hip.

"Hasn't woken up yet," I said.

"We've been with her all day," Ian said. "She's pale and cold, but she's breathing."

Elora gave a nod. "I'll sit with her next. You guys get some rest." She hugged each one of us, giving us a hard squeeze. "It's been so long since we've all been in the same room together."

We parted ways, and Ian and I walked through the streets back to our homes.

"A life without Necrosis…" Ian surveyed HeartHolme as we passed, looking at the buildings and the church in the center. "Hard to imagine."

"It's how life should have always been."

"You got the Teeth to fight for us? How did you manage that?"

"You can get a lot of shit done with two dragons." Saved hours of time normally spent on diplomacy.

He chuckled. "Yeah, I bet. What'd you do to Klaus?"

"What makes you think I did anything?"

Ian looked at me, the corner of his mouth up in a smirk. "Come on, Huntley. Did you rip out his entrails and feed them to Storm? Or did you carve out his eyes and force him to eat them?"

I looked forward. "Just a good old-fashioned beheading."

"Really? After what he did to Ivory?"

"I didn't have the time to torture him."

"So, now what?" he asked. "What will become of the Teeth?"

"In exchange for their help, I granted them a truce."

Ian didn't say anything, but his look said it all.

"Without Necrosis as their ally, they're the minority. If they stick to their lands, they should be no trouble to the Runes or anyone else."

"Uh, they still gotta eat people."

"They can eat animals."

"Seriously, why don't you kill them all?"

"Because I'm a just king."

"What if they attack us?" Ian said.

"So, what if they do?" I asked. "What's that going to accomplish?"

Ian turned quiet when he knew I was right.

"And let's not forget—I'm their king now."

"I guess."

"I still have to fight a war in the north. Might need them anyway."

He released a heavy sigh. "Forgot about that…"

"The last frontier."

"You have no idea what you're up against."

"Be that as it may, I made a promise. I'm a man of my word."

"Right," Ian said. "I don't remember you keeping your word when you butchered Ivory's father."

I shot him a glare.

"Not that I give a damn."

"I would have lost these battles if it weren't for Pyre and Storm. I must honor my debt."

"But what do we know about the north?" Ian asked. "Literally nothing. You're going into it blind."

"Be that as it may."

"It would be really shitty to make it this far only to be killed—"

"Let us celebrate our victory and rest. We can discuss this later."

Ian shut his mouth and looked ahead.

Our paths divided, and I entered the home where my wife was waiting for me. I walked up the stairs and found her asleep in bed, the fireplace now cold. I put on a few more logs and got the fire going again before I undressed and slid into the sheets beside her.

Her eyes immediately opened to look at me, and her hand reached for my chest. She grabbed on to me and pulled her body across the mattress until she was right at my side, her head on my shoulder. "Is she awake?"

"No."

She pressed a kiss to my shoulder. "Give it time."

I could feel her skin against mine, feel her completely naked figure as it pressed against me. It was an invitation, though one that I didn't have to acknowledge if I chose not to. But no matter my sorrow, her naked skin against mine was like a log to the fire. It burned me alive, formed an inferno in my belly.

I rolled on top of her, my thick thighs separating hers, feeling her warm sex right against my hardness. I didn't even know when the arousal had emerged. Must have been the moment I stepped into the room with her. My arm slipped under her lower back, and I lifted her hips so I could slide inside her.

Her eyes rolled back in her head momentarily, as always.

For a moment, there was no stress on my shoulders. It was just me and Ivory, the other half of my soul. It was hard to believe there was a time when I didn't love her, when she meant nothing to me, when she was just good in the sack. Now my heart beat for hers and only hers, even before she was my wife.

I'd die a million times for her.

She rocked with me, nails against my back, lips feeling mine. "I love you…"

I wrapped her legs around my waist and smothered her neck with kisses. My hips continued to thrust as I sank deep inside. The passion was as hot as the fire in the hearth behind us. "I love you too, baby."

THIRTY-TWO

Elora
―――――――

IT WAS THE FIRST TIME I'D SEEN QUEEN ROLFE LOOK weak.

Her skin was so pale, it seemed as if she'd been dead for hours. Even with the fire in the room, there was a chill that came from her cold bones. With her hands neatly folded on her chest, she looked ready to be buried in the cemetery alongside her fellow Runes.

I'd had a few hours of sleep, but that moment still felt as if it had just happened. Haldir chasing me down with a sword aimed at my neck. Queen Rolfe coming out of nowhere and saving my life. She held her own as long as she could—until she fell.

I would be the one in that bed if it weren't for her.

Or maybe I'd be dead.

I sat there for hours, wide awake because I'd slept all through the day. When I'd woken up, Bastian was still asleep, so I left him to continue to rest and I went to the castle. Commander Dawson and Asher were both gone, along with all the guards that had served her for decades. Now the place didn't feel the same. It felt like a bloody battlefield.

Hours later, her hand gave a twitch. So did her eyes.

I sucked in a breath then held it for seconds, hoping that my wish had come true.

She inhaled a deep breath first before her arm moved across the sheet. Her face immediately became hard with tension, as if all the pain struck her now that she was conscious. She woke with a start, her eyes snapping open.

I gave her a second to absorb her surroundings, to remember where she was and what had happened.

Her eyes settled on me and remained there for a while, her quick breaths slowing once again. Then her eyes moved out the window to distinguish the time.

"It's the middle of the night."

She shifted her body up against the headboard so she could sit up, cringing as she moved. "We won?"

"Yes. The dragons hunted down the Necrosis that fled. Necrosis is extinct."

"Good. Vermin…"

She seemed back to her normal self. "Huntley and Ian were here all day. But they couldn't keep their eyes open any longer."

"They should rest. They fought valiantly. What happened to Haldir?"

"He's in the dungeons. We're going to take him to the Bone Witch to break the spell."

"But you said you killed all the Necrosis."

"Bastian said there are some that still remain in their lands, including his sister."

Despite what Haldir had done to her, she didn't seem angry about sparing his life. "You're alright?"

Her question startled me. The silence trickled by. "Yeah…I'm fine."

"Good." She was back to her curt responses and silent authority.

It was hard to say the words out loud, and I wasn't sure why. "Thank you for saving my life."

With that, she looked away and ignored what I said.

That hurt a lot more than I'd expected it to. Probably because I was vulnerable. Probably because it had felt as if there was something between us for the first time.

Probably because it had felt as if she'd cared…for a fleeting moment. "I'll let you get some rest——"

"Elora." She turned back to me, the tension stark in her face. "I'm sorry for the way I've treated you all these years. I wish I were stronger. I wish I could get his face out of my mind every time I look at you."

My hands clutched together in my lap.

"It's not fair to you. You're a victim in this as much as I am."

We'd never spoken of this. Not once. Not ever. "Why did you keep me…?"

She held my gaze, possessing Huntley's blue and domineering eyes. "I didn't know who had fathered my child, my husband or my tormentor. Without knowing for certain, I couldn't take that route."

"So, if you had known…you would have done it."

She held my gaze for a long time. "I don't know, Elora. Once I'd felt life in my womb, I'm not sure if I would have had the ability to snuff it out. After you were born, I took a look at your green eyes and knew exactly what you were. I'd prayed that I'd had one final gift from my husband, another son or a daughter that I could love. But you weren't, so…I was devastated. I put the blame on you—the person who wasn't responsible."

The tears were held back because I refused to shed them, to look heartbroken.

"You're a lot like me, but I've always refused to see it. You're strong. You're brave. You're exactly the kind of daughter who would make me proud every single day. But because of the circumstances…I never acknowledged it."

I dropped my eyes to my hands in my lap, needing to break eye contact to keep my composure.

"But that motherly instinct is still there. It was there when I raised you instead of abandoning you to an orphanage. It was there when I saw Haldir come down on you and I put myself in harm's way. It's always been there."

My breaths turned deep and uneven.

"It's hard, to love the child that you were forced to have. It's hard to look in their eyes and see someone you don't love."

"I understand." I finally found the strength to speak. "If it were me…I would have struggled too."

A flash of softness moved into her eyes. "You're wise enough to see my perspective."

"I act like I don't care, like it's never bothered me that I haven't had parents, but it has…"

"I know."

"I don't know what I would have done without Huntley and Ian…"

473

"They're good men. Just like their father."

I gave a nod. "Wish I could have met him."

"He was a wonderful man. I still dream of him…every night."

A love that lived on after death. It reminded me of what I felt for Bastian.

"I want things to be different from now on."

I lifted my chin and looked up at her.

"I can't love you like a daughter, not the way I love Huntley and Ian. I won't give you false hope. I won't make promises that I can't keep. But I could love you in your own way, perhaps like a niece. Would that be okay?"

It was better than nothing. And it was real. "I've always wanted an aunt."

She smiled at me. Actually smiled.

THIRTY-THREE

Ivory

WHEN WE WALKED INTO THE ROOM, QUEEN ROLFE WAS sitting on her throne, still pale and feeble, but with her old strength in her eyes. She was in her usual uniform, the feathers in her hair, her majesty unquestioned.

Huntley didn't express himself with words. He did it with the change of his breaths, with the tightness of his jaw, the intensity in his eyes. He showed all the love he had for his mother when he rushed to her and cocooned her in his arms.

She gave a smile before she secured her arms around him, her eyes soft and a bit wet.

Ian did the same, coming to her on the other side.

The three of them held on to one another, a family.

I stood there and watched, grateful that I could do this for Huntley, that I could keep his family together. It wouldn't have been possible without her own resolve, without her refusal to die. Life and death were often separated by determination. Some people passed away because that was what they wanted. They didn't have the fight anymore.

She kissed both of her sons before she looked at me.

I was put on the spot with her gaze, frozen to the spot.

She pushed her arms against the armrests and forced her weak body to her feet. Huntley was there, his hand moving for her arm to help her remain balanced. He walked her to me, his eyes on her face the entire time.

Queen Rolfe stopped in front of me. "You defeated death with your magic. I'm still here because of it. You're a queen worthy of the crown—and I bow to you." She bent her body forward, giving me a slight bow. "Your Highness." She straightened again, looking at me with authority but also affection.

I had no response. None whatsoever.

Queen Rolfe seemed to understand I was speechless. "My injury cripples me, but I'm strong enough to discuss our next move. Let's congregate at the dining table—and plan our journey to the south."

———

Queen Rolfe sat at the head of the table while Huntley and I were on either side of her, across from each other.

Ian was there, along with Elora and Bastian. The servants placed an array of food in front of us, along with wine and the stronger stuff that Huntley liked. No one had celebrated our victory over Necrosis, not when Queen Rolfe had still been battling death over the last few days.

"Do you know how to find the Bone Witch?" Queen Rolfe asked Bastian.

Bastian's features screamed Necrosis. His high cheekbones. His stern jaw. The lifelessness in his eyes. "Yes."

"And how certain are you that she'll help you?" Queen Rolfe asked.

"Very," he said. "Necrosis is despised—even from within."

"How will we transport Haldir?" Elora asked. "The dragons?"

"I wouldn't allow him anywhere near our dragons," I said immediately. "We'll travel by horse."

"In a carriage?" Elora asked incredulously. "We'll have to release him to take care of his bodily needs. That sounds dangerous."

"I can give him a potion that will make him disoriented. He'll be able to complete simple tasks and communicate, but he'll also be confused and weak. We'll be able to transport him without issue." I turned to Bastian. "Will the remaining Necrosis give us any problems?"

"No," Bastian said. "Those that remained behind were too weak to fight or were responsible for other tasks. When they see us arrive, they'll know Necrosis has fallen. Those turned by Haldir will be free."

"And the others?" I asked.

Bastian remained quiet.

"We must kill them." Queen Rolfe stared at him. "We can't allow a single Necrosis to survive. They can turn more people, and in another hundred years, Necrosis will be in full power once again."

Bastian still didn't speak.

"You must understand this."

With Bastian's eyes still on the table, he gave a nod. "I didn't have a choice…I had to kill Kronos. Elora had to kill Vanquil. If we'd captured them, we could have freed more people…but it wasn't possible."

Elora's hand moved to his on the table.

"We'll take care of it," Huntley said. "Ian and I. You won't have to see it."

"We should bring more men with us," Ivory said. "Just in case."

"I agree, Your Highness," Queen Rolfe said. "Best to take at least fifty soldiers, all armed with Ice."

It was still weird to hear her call me that. "Shall we leave tomorrow?"

"Yes," Bastian said. "The sooner we do this, the sooner I can be free."

———

With Haldir constantly drugged and locked in the carriage, we made the journey across the open fields and landscapes to the south, where Necrosis territory lay. We didn't pass anyone on the trails, didn't meet anyone at the streams. It seemed as if the world was empty except for us.

"What about the Plunderers?" I asked Huntley as we lay down for the night in our tent.

"What about them?"

"Are you going to kill them?"

He shook his head.

"Really? Even though they're vile?"

"They're wild and savage because they had to be. They've fought Necrosis alongside us for decades. I don't personally care for their people, but I won't destroy them because of a petty opinion."

I lay beside him in his cot, seeing the beard thick on his face. "You're a good king."

"Because I was born to be one."

———

With the carriage attached to the horses, we couldn't move as quickly as we normally would, so we spent a solid week traveling south, encountering no one along the way. We were all exhausted and aggravated, and I got tired of having to force the potion down Haldir's throat while he was asleep.

We made dinner by the campfire once we were at the base of their mountains, finally nearing the end of the journey.

I sat beside Elora, the two of us eating the dinner she'd caught before the sun went down. "So…what's it like being with Necrosis?"

"I've always liked the bad ones, so for me, it's perfect." She ate the rest of the food on her plate then set it aside. "I've tested out a lot of different guys, but they've never felt right, not like it does with Bastian. And that's ironic, considering our circumstances."

I watched Bastian across the fire, watched him look into the darkness. "He's quiet."

"My brothers are quiet, so I'm used to it."

"I hope this works out for you. I can't imagine being in his shoes…losing my soul like that."

She nodded. "No one deserves that. I wish we could have saved them all, but Bastian's right, it wouldn't have been possible. Not with that army at our gates." She rested her arms on her knees and looked at me. "So, what's next for you guys? Other than challenging King Dunbar."

"I don't know… I guess ruling the Kingdoms."

"You guys will be so far away. Makes me sad."

"I know. Huntley is upset about it too."

"Are you guys going to have kids?"

"Huntley talks about it."

She watched me. "That didn't answer my question."

"He's a lot more excited about it than I am."

"And why aren't you?"

"I don't know… Maybe because the world has been in chaos for so long. It's hard to imagine a quiet life, you know?"

She nodded. "You're right."

"Huntley would knock me up right now if I were okay with it."

She released a laugh. "Sounds about right. He'd be a good father."

"I know he would," I said. "What about you guys?"

"We've got to get his soul back first. Then we'll see what happens."

"After everything you've been through, I assumed you'd get married at the first chance."

She shrugged. "He hasn't asked."

"Why don't you ask him?"

"I'm all about asking for what I want without apology, but something like that, he has to ask. I've come on pretty strong since the beginning, and I don't want to lay it on too thick, you know? Besides, I'm not in a hurry. Whenever it happens, it happens."

THIRTY-FOUR

Bastian

Instead of avoiding the main entrance to Necrosis, I walked straight up to it. The settlement wasn't fortified by walls and gates like HeartHolme and Crags of the Teeth, not when they were unchallenged in these lands. No one provoked Necrosis—unless they had a death wish.

In broad daylight, we walked along the path, moving farther through the hills and the mountains. We finally came across Necrosis along the path. They recognized me, but not the others, though there was no hostility because of it.

As if they knew.

We made it to the first settlement where the Three Kings had lived in their own castles, but the town was empty. A few Necrosis were spotted outside their homes, but it was a small fraction compared to what it'd been before.

I went to Haldir's black castle, where my sister would be waiting for me.

The carriage was still with us, and once we reached the entrance to the castle, we left the men behind to guard it. They displayed their Ice swords so no one would be tempted to intervene, not that it would make sense to attack anyway.

I walked up to the doors and realized I was alone.

I turned back to look at Elora. She'd stayed behind with her family.

She stared at me. "You want me to come with you?"

I nodded.

She moved forward.

Huntley's arm flung out and caught her. "Your sister is still Necrosis."

"Not by choice, but force." I walked back, extending my hand to Elora. "My sister would never touch her, and even if she wanted to, I would never allow it."

Huntley let her go.

Elora came to my side and placed her hand in mine, and we entered the black castle. The interior was quiet, the windows covered with black drapes. There were servants inside but very few. They greeted me wordlessly before they skirted into the corridors.

I moved to the top floor where the bedchambers were located. Her guard was there, and I asked to see her.

She stepped into the room a moment later, in a beautiful gown that Haldir would have asked her to wear, her dark hair long and down her shoulders. Her beauty was stunning, just the way Elora's was. Her eyes immediately dropped to our joined hands. Then they flicked back up, looking at me in confusion.

My heart was in my throat because I'd waited for this for so long. Dreamed of this moment. The moment I saved my little sister. I dropped Elora's hand and drew closer. "Necrosis has fallen."

Her eyes widened.

"I've captured Haldir."

Once she understood exactly what I was telling her, her breaths turned rapid, and her eyes glistened.

"Once I take him to the Bone Witch, we'll both be free."

She was always so poised and somber, sharing no hint of emotion even in Haldir's presence. She had to swallow all her sorrow and bottle it deep inside her. But now, she could break free for the first time, could feel every emotion as deeply as she wanted. Her breath hitched, and her sobs broke past her rib cage and reached the surface. She grabbed on to me as she sobbed, sobbed her heart out.

I held her in my arms and felt my own tears breach the surface. Every day I'd had to suffer, watching my sister be the prisoner of a man she didn't love, a man infatuated with her beauty but feeling nothing for her, for who she was. I hated to think of the nights she'd been subjected to, the hopelessness she must have always felt. "It's over…it's over."

———

Necrosis lands were as large as the Kingdoms. Once you moved past the mountains, the soil was fertile and thawed, the heat reaching the southern region in greater abundance than all the settlements to the north. It meant we had the best produce, lush landscapes of grasses and flowers, places too beautiful to be enjoyed by those who were dead.

We moved as a caravan, approaching the rock that could be spotted from miles beyond. It was easy to recognize even from the greatest distances because it was carved to look exactly like a snake rearing its head, his jaws open with fangs exposed.

My sister walked beside me, and she turned back a couple times to look at the carriage that contained the man she'd been forced to marry. "I can't believe you did it."

"I didn't do it alone. Without the Runes, this wouldn't have been possible."

"I had no idea you were undertaking all this..." She was still in one of her expensive gowns with pants underneath, her body adorned with expensive jewels to enhance her already goddess-level appearance.

"Couldn't risk telling anyone."

"So, it was just you."

"Others were part of the plan, but they didn't get the chance to leave Necrosis."

She already recognized the rock because she'd been there before. The Bone Witch had turned her before she'd turned me. Even though nearly two hundred years had passed, it was impossible to forget that change, when your soul left your body. "Elora loves you even though you're heartless and soulless?"

I gave a slight nod. "I don't understand it either."

"You didn't eat her—so you must love her too."

That was so obvious that I didn't comment on it.

She glanced over her shoulder again. "One of your men stares a lot."

"Which?"

"Has a black feather crest on his chest plate."

I turned to look at Ian, and sure enough, his eyes were locked on my sister. "He's harmless. Just an admirer."

"When this is all over, what are we going to do?"

"I'll return to HeartHolme to be with Elora. You can join me, if you like."

She stared ahead for a long time, somber. "I don't know where else to go. The lives we had have been gone for so long... I'm not sure how to start over. Everyone I ever loved has been dead for over a hundred years."

It was such a depressing thought. "I know."

"So, I'll accompany you...and try to start over."

Half a day later, we arrived at the cave. The carriage couldn't enter the cave, so we pulled Haldir out and dragged him across the ground by the ropes. He was still out of it, but he was aware enough to resist, to refuse to get to his feet and walk.

We were almost there, so this fight was futile.

Deep inside the cave, I found the Bone Witch, sitting in front of a fire of blue flames. As if she'd known we were coming long before we entered the lands of Necrosis, she continued to sit on her rock, her dwelling inside the cave modest. She came from a tribe of magical witches that gave the Original Necrosis the power to turn people because they'd been unable to do it themselves. Because of her, our population had grown to staggering numbers.

She was old, far older than I was, even though she still possessed her soul. While leaning on her staff, she rose to her feet, a deep curve in her spine from her abnormally long life. "I know why you're here."

"Good. Then that saves me the trouble."

We dragged Haldir in front of the fire, his heavy body sitting in the dirt.

My sister hardly looked at him, like their union of over one hundred years hadn't made her care for him in the least.

The Bone Witch stared at him for a long time. "The other kings?"

"Both were killed. Haldir is the final survivor," I said. "You don't need to fear repercussion. Once you release the magic, all those who are left that were turned by Haldir will be freed. And those that remain Necrosis… will be killed." I didn't feel good about it, not when they were people I knew, people who didn't have the same option I did because their kings had been killed. But Queen Rolfe was right. They needed to be wiped out for good. "Necrosis will be no more. They'll no longer be a threat to this world."

The Bone Witch stared down at Haldir. "Are you sure this is what you want?"

My eyebrows furrowed. "Why wouldn't it be?"

She stared for a while before she looked at me again. "With Necrosis finished, the balance of power will be forever changed. That will have consequences far beyond your limited sight."

I hated riddles. "Meaning?"

Her brown eyes stared into mine for a long time. "Have you heard of the Red Wolves?"

My eyes shifted back and forth, uninterested in this tale. "No."

"You haven't heard of them because they were wiped out nearly a thousand years ago. In packs, they would come to the villages and eat all the livestock, ravage everything throughout the winter months. So, all the villages worked together to kill every last one. What do you think happened?"

I stared.

"The Red Wolves were the only animals capable of eating Boiling Toads. I'm sure you don't know what those are either because a few hundred years ago, man created the antidote to stop the fatal poison from killing so many people. But once their predator had been elim-inated, Boiling Toads killed two-thirds of the population below the cliffs. Crops died. Famine spread. It was terrible. Even Necrosis suffered."

"What's your point?" I asked, growing irritable.

"Necrosis is the Red Wolves. And someone else will be the Boiling Toads."

"Who?"

She shook her head. "I don't know. But it will be someone—I promise you that. So, I ask again, are you sure you want to do this?"

I wanted my soul more than anything, regardless of the consequences. My sister and I both deserved to live the lives that were taken from us. "Yes."

She studied my face for a while, as if I might change my mind.

I never did.

"Then let's begin."

———

She completed the ritual, muttering incantations under her breath, slicing Haldir down the forearm to make him bleed into the blue flames. Once the flames exploded into an inferno and the wind picked up from nowhere, I knew the spell had taken hold.

Then I felt something else.

A tightness in my chest. As if my heart had grown three times the size and no longer fit in my body, I became uncomfortable, really uncomfortable. My breaths became shaky. Then it felt like I was drowning, like there wasn't enough air for my lungs. When I looked at my sister, I could see she felt the same way.

Then all the tension disappeared—and I took my first breath.

My chest suddenly felt weightless. My knees went weak before they became strong again. And then I felt it...a heartbeat.

My hand crossed over my chest, and I felt it with my own fingertips.

Thump-thump. Thump-thump. Thump-thump.

I used to feel only the sense of nothingness, but now, I felt everything. I felt the breeze across my skin, felt my lungs expand with every breath. I smelled the dampness of the cave. Felt everything with such vividness. I forgot how it felt to be alive...and now it all came back to me as if it had never left.

I looked at my sister, who was equally overwhelmed.

She rushed to me and held on tight. "Thank you..."

I gripped her closely and felt the raw emotions, felt the tears burn my eyes. I remembered the day Haldir kidnapped her from our village. I remembered how hard I tried to get her back, the sword that pierced my stomach. Even though it would cost my life, I still did what I could to save her. I was even damned to a worse existence than death—but it was still worth it.

But I finally did it. I saved her.

THIRTY-FIVE

Huntley

BASTIAN, ELORA, AND AVICE LEFT NECROSIS, WHILE Ivory, Ian, and I stayed behind.

There were very few Necrosis left, so we broke down every door and killed any that survived. Both men and women. I understood Bastian's guilt, but I'd fought Necrosis all my life, and I didn't feel an ounce of pity. Even if these Necrosis had never left their lands and engaged in warfare, they still fed the army, still made their weapons, still supported those that ate other people's souls to fuel their own immortality.

The Ice blades made the killing easy, felling them with a single swipe. But we worked up a sweat anyway.

Ian finished wiping the blue blood from his sword on the corpse before he wiped his own forehead with the back of his forearm.

"Are you going to make a move?"

Ian stilled at the question.

"You make it obvious."

Ian returned his sword to his scabbard, wearing a slight smile. "Do I?"

"A bit." I glanced at Ivory farther away, where she had just slain the final Necrosis. Even though she was capable of protecting herself, my eyes always kept track of her.

"Her husband just died…so I'll have to wait awhile."

"She didn't blink an eye as he burned to death. That man was never her husband."

"Are you saying I should go for it now?" he asked hopefully.

"No. You need to give her some time to adjust. But you need to make sure you're first in line."

"How do I do that?"

"Be her friend."

Ian made a disgusted look. "I hate that shit…"

"That's my best advice."

Ivory walked over. "I think that's all of them. We should meet the others."

I continued to stare at my brother.

She looked back and forth between us. "Did I walk into the middle of something?"

"Your husband is giving me romance advice," Ian said. "Not that I need it." He walked off.

Ivory watched him go before she turned back to me. "Bastian's sister?"

"You noticed too."

"The only time I've seen someone stare that hard is when you're looking at me."

The corner of my mouth quirked up in a smile.

"You know, now that Necrosis is gone...this land is available for the taking. It's warm, it's got great soil, the mountains are a natural defense. Maybe the Runes should occupy it."

"We've been at HeartHolme for thousands of years."

"Yeah...but it's a little cold."

"I'll speak to my mother. This is her territory, so she can decide what to do with it."

"Then let's get going."

We left Necrosis and joined the others at the camp. Now that Haldir wasn't holding us back, we would be able to return to HeartHolme twice as fast as our journey here. Then Ivory and I would have a short rest before we returned to the Kingdoms.

She and I sat together in front of the fire, our bellies full with the pheasants she'd caught.

"What's our plan?" she asked. "For King Dunbar?"

"We'll take our entire army and sail to their lands."

"But we've never been there. We'll go into it blind."

"You're forgetting that Pyre and Storm are both acquainted with the land. They'll be our guides."

"True."

"Our army is just a distraction for Pyre and Storm to do what they need to do. It's all on them, really."

"Will we take the Runes, Plunderers, and Teeth as well?"

I shook my head. "No. That would take far too long."

"By the way, we'll need to figure out a way for people to come and go more easily."

"I've thought about that. We can carve a path into the cliff."

"How?"

"The dragons. It'll be wide enough for riders and carriages to go up and down. It'll still be a long ride, but at least it'll make the journey possible."

"I wish we could rest, but now that Pyre and Storm did their part, I know they'll be anxious for us to do ours."

"I agree."

"But…we killed Regar, right?" she asked. "Wasn't that the biggest challenge?"

"I'm sure Dunbar has other dragons. And their mother will never be free until he's killed. I imagine I'll ride Storm straight to the castle, hop through a window, and kill him in his sleep."

"It would definitely be convenient if it went that smoothly…"

"We'll see. I suppose we should just enjoy our victory over Necrosis."

Her arms rested on her knees, and she stared at the fire.

I stared at it with her, everyone else getting ready for bed. Bastian slept close to Elora and his sister, and Ian was with the other soldiers on the other side of the clearing. Minutes trickled by, the two of us locked in comfortable silence. "I'm supposed to take my herbs tomorrow. But I'm not going to."

When she'd fully processed what I said, she turned to look at me. "We agreed we were going to wait."

"But this will all be over within a month. We'll either live or we'll die."

"There's still no rush—"

"What if I don't survive, baby?" I had the confidence to take the Kingdoms because it was my homeland. I was

499

fueled by rage and revenge. But this was a place I'd never been, and I was getting involved in a battle that had nothing to do with me. "You would still have a piece of me. You could rule the Kingdoms, and our child could take the throne once they're of age. Or you could flee to HeartHolme and raise our child with my family."

"Please don't talk like that."

"It's a scenario we have to confront. I know little of King Dunbar. And I know nothing about the place he calls home. I'll be attacking by sea, which already puts me at a great disadvantage. There are a lot of variables out of my control."

She continued to stare, her beautiful face tightened in unease. "Alright."

I met her look. "Is that a yes?"

She gave a nod.

"Then let's get to work."

THIRTY-SIX

Elora

When we returned to HeartHolme, it had been restored to its former glory. All the rubble had been removed. The stones in the gate had been repaired. The grass outside the city was still scorched, and there was a pile of ash where all the bodies had been burned. But everything else inside looked the same.

Once we entered the gate, Queen Rolfe met us. "Is it done?"

"Yes," Huntley said. "Haldir is destroyed—as well as all other Necrosis. Those that were freed after the spell was broken have asked to reside in HeartHolme. I gave them permission. All others were killed. I saw to it personally."

Queen Rolfe nodded before she looked at Bastian. "The spell worked?"

Bastian nodded. "Necrosis is extinct."

She released the breath she'd been holding, like she couldn't believe the war was finally over. We'd been enemies with Necrosis for so long, and now it was over forever. She probably didn't even know what to do with herself. "That is good news. I know you all must be weary. You should rest, and we'll speak later."

We disbanded and went our separate ways. Bastian and I headed home, but we weren't alone. His sister accompanied us.

Bastian took her to his home, which I still hadn't seen, and after he left her there, he walked in the door of my home. Once he was over the threshold, he stared at me from across the room as if he was seeing me in a new light.

I'd been hungry just a moment ago, but now that he looked at me like that, the thought of food vanished from my mind. My heart beat irregularly, as if this was the first time we'd been alone together. My stomach tightened in knots. My confidence waned.

He crossed the room and came at me hard.

I anticipated his kiss, but I still wasn't ready for his intensity. He grabbed my face and kissed me as he backed me up into the counter, and without wasting a single breath, he ripped my clothes from my body. He didn't even wait until we had the chance to bathe. He wanted to do this now.

I yanked his shirt over his head, and we barely broke apart long enough to allow me to do that. His hands went to my pants and got them loose, his mouth moving to my neck and collarbone. In a rush, we undressed, got down to our bare skin.

He knocked everything off on my dining table, the pot of flowers sitting in the center shattering on the floor, and threw me on top of it. His hands grasped my hips and moved me into position so he could get inside me with one hard thrust.

I moaned into his neck, loving his roughness, loving the way he loved me without restraint. His skin remained fair and unmarked by the hunger of Necrosis, and now I could feel the beat of his heart when our chests were close together. The heat of his body was greater than before, and it even reached his eyes, giving him a stronger look of vitality.

He gripped the back of my hair as he thrust into me hard and fast. "Fuck…"

We didn't have to stop. He didn't have to close his eyes and force himself to calm. He didn't have to stop himself from eating my soul.

We could just be together.

And that was what we did—all night.

———

When I woke up the next morning, I was wrapped in his warmth, his heartbeat like a drum against my ear. I stretched my arms and legs and looked out the window, trying to gauge the time based on the placement of the sun.

"It's afternoon."

"Damn…" I looked down at him, seeing that he was wide awake. "That was a long night."

He grinned.

"Being alive suits you."

He gave a deep chuckle. "You don't know how nice it is to be with you without wanting to kill you the whole time."

"Well, I'm messy, a terrible cook, and I hog all the blankets… So you might want to kill me eventually."

"Doubt it." He raised himself up and kissed me on the shoulder and the collarbone.

"Should you check on your sister?"

He shrugged. "She's fine."

"She's in a new place and doesn't know a soul but you."

He looked at me. "Are you trying to get rid of me?"

"I just feel bad, is all."

"I told her she wouldn't see me for a few days, so don't worry about it." He sat up in bed, his hard chest and tight abs revealed from underneath the sheet. "Did Huntley mention when he and Ivory are leaving?"

"No. But I know it'll be soon. Why?"

"I need to talk to him before he goes." He got out of bed and started to get dressed.

"Now?" I asked incredulously.

He smiled as he put on his pants then gave me a quick kiss. "I'll be back soon."

―――――

I threw lunch together in the kitchen, finding things that hadn't gone bad, and washed it down with a cup of coffee. As I sat at the table, a knock sounded on the door. I wasn't sure if Bastian officially lived here or not, but I was pretty certain he wouldn't knock. "It's open."

Ian walked in.

"Oh, so you *do* know how to knock…"

Ian ignored what I said and sank into the chair across from me. "Bastian here?"

I shook my head and picked at my muffin.

"Is he with his sister?"

"He went to talk to Huntley."

"About?"

I shrugged. "Beats me. So, what do you want?"

"Do I need a reason to visit?"

"After everything we've been through the last week, yes. All I want to do is sleep." Well, get laid too, but he didn't need to know that. "I'm surprised you aren't locked down in your favorite brothel."

"That's what I wanted to talk to you about."

"Your favorite brothel?"

His eyes narrowed in annoyance. "I want you to help me with Bastian's sister."

"Help you what?"

He gave me a meaningful stare.

"Hold on. Let me get this straight." I talked with my mouth full of muffin because I couldn't resist. "You give Bastian shit all the livelong day about being with me… and now you want his sister?"

"Not the same thing."

"Doesn't matter. But karma is coming to bite you hard."

"I have no regrets. He was Necrosis, and you were Necrosis food."

I rolled my eyes. "You don't even know her."

506

"And you know Bastian?" he snapped. "You guys met like two months ago."

I'd known the moment I looked at him, so that was a fair point. "I know she's super hot and everything—"

"She's the most beautiful woman I've ever seen. You need to help me make this happen."

"What if she's a bitch?"

"I put up with you, so I'm sure I could put up with her."

I stuck my tongue out at him. "I've only talked to her a couple times…but I can feel her out."

"Thanks. I don't want to come on too strong right now, but if I wait around, some other guy will beat me to the punch."

"I guess that's true."

The door opened, and Bastian walked back inside.

"Ian wants to bang your sister."

Ian turned his angry stare on my face.

Bastian faltered for a moment but continued on his way. "I'm used to it." He came to the table and sat beside me.

"What did you talk to Huntley about?"

He shrugged and never answered.

"Why won't you tell me?"

"I'll tell you later," he said noncommittally.

"Why later?" I demanded.

Ian grinned. "I've had to deal with this shit all my life. Good luck, man."

"*Good luck*?" I rounded on my brother. "Then good luck with her because I'm not helping you anymore."

"It's fine," Bastian said. "I'll give you an introduction."

"You will?" Ian asked, switching his gaze to Bastian.

Bastian dropped his arm over my shoulders. "Sure. You've defended HeartHolme from Necrosis twice. You protect your sister. You're loyal to your family. I think you're worthy of her—if she's interested."

———

Hand in hand, we walked to the church, the Temple of Adeodatus.

"What are we doing here?" Torches lit the pathways through the city. It was a quiet night, all the citizens already settled down after the battle that had threatened our very existence. We stopped outside the double doors to the temple.

"I'll show you." He opened the door and stepped inside, immediately admiring the large statue in the center that was also a fountain. Water splashed down from the top, the sprinkling accompanied by a playing harp we couldn't see.

Bastian stared at the statue in complete reverence.

I gave him all the time he needed before we moved on, past the monks working on their scriptures, and made it to the rear.

The priest was there—along with my entire family.

Huntley and Ivory were with Ian. Queen Rolfe was there too. Avice stood beside Ian, as if they had shared a conversation while they waited for us. I looked up at Bastian, eager for an explanation.

Bastian squeezed my hand to get my attention. "Once your brother leaves, I know there's a chance he won't come back. This could be the last time you're all together. I know how important family is to you, so I didn't want to waste this opportunity."

Now, I understood. "Is this too fast…?"

"It's not for me if it's not for you." He held my gaze with complete confidence, but if my answer was no, he would let it be. "Now that I have my soul again, you're the only person I want to share it with. I've never met a woman with such bravery and selflessness, who can wield a sword with the same bite as her words. There is no doubt for me."

I didn't feel doubt either. I just thought I should feel it… because everything was happening so fast. Once we did this, there was no going back. It was just the two of us forever. I gave a nod. "I love you."

"Then marry me."

———

With our hands joined together and the blessing of Adeodatus, the priest made us husband and wife, binding our souls together for all eternity. The sacred blade slit our palms so our blood would mix together. His was mine. Mine was his.

Bastian wore the same look of intensity as the day we'd met. It was piercing, deep, with the power to move all the mountains and the sea. He'd claimed me without the blessing of the gods, took my soul without the need of the priest.

Once it was done, I felt it right away.

Felt the invisible string that tied us together.

I didn't wear a wedding dress, but I'd never felt more beautiful. He made me feel beautiful every time he looked at me.

We said goodbye to my family and his and entered the humble home that I'd made for myself. Words weren't spoken. Clothes dropped like breadcrumbs through the house. We stopped to share heated kisses against the different pieces of furniture, from the dining table to the counter, and even the stairs. The journey to the bed took ten minutes because it was impossible to keep our hands off each other.

We finally made it to the bed, and his naked body sank into mine.

The instant we were connected, I felt the strangest sensation inside my chest. Peace. Harmony. Pleasure that was beyond the flesh. My body was satisfied, but so was my soul. It was now wrapped in his like a warm blanket on a winter night, sheathed from the dark and cold outside the front door.

I'd never felt so happy in all my life.

It wasn't the sex. It wasn't the hormones. It was so much deeper than that.

I knew he could feel it too—just by the way he looked at me.

THIRTY-SEVEN

Huntley

WE AGREED TO REST FOR A FEW DAYS.

Ivory and I remained in bed most of the time, making love between our naps, eating the food I grabbed from the tavern every night. She wasn't a picky eater, so roast beef sandwiches saturated in gravy were perfectly agreeable to her.

I skipped my herbs, so I knew I was fertile once again.

I knew it would happen quickly for us. We had sex so often, several times a day, that it was bound to happen overnight. I'd always wanted a family, but I'd never wanted one more than I did now. I'd watched so many people die, almost lost my own mother, and mortality was staring me right in the face.

My own mortality.

I wanted to leave something behind if I didn't return.

The morning of our departure, we packed our things and prepared to leave. We didn't need much since we'd be returning by dragon rather than steed. The journey would take less than a day. We'd be there hours before the sun set. Therefore, we didn't need to pack unnecessary items.

I took more time to rest than necessary, and that was because I dreaded the moment of my departure. Even if I defeated King Dunbar and fulfilled my promise to the dragons, Delacroix would be my home. I'd see my family sparingly, if I ever saw them at all. Our only connection would be the letters we sent back and forth.

We met outside the gate and on the field where the dragons waited for us. They'd both been properly fed with as many cows and sheep as they could eat. Whenever they needed water, they flew to a nearby stream.

My mother was as stone-faced as ever, but her eyes gave away her sorrow. "You're our king. We will serve you in all your wars if you call for us. I can lead the Runes as you claim Dunbar's life. Let me help you."

She addressed me as her king, but I only wanted to address her as my family. "I'll be alright, Mother. Please don't worry."

She took a sharp intake of breath, her hard features giving way.

"Continue to heal."

"I'm well enough to fight, son."

"I'll be alright," I repeated.

She released another heavy breath, powerless. "Is this really essential? You have no idea what you're up against."

I dreaded this war even more than she did. "A king always keeps his promise. The dragons have secured peace for HeartHolme and the Kingdoms. I owe them everything."

She still looked upset, like that wasn't a good enough reason. "Please write as soon as you can. I will worry nonstop until I hear news."

"Father taught me how to be king. You've taught me to master the sword. Don't lose your faith in me."

Now tears welled in her eyes as she embraced me. "Never, son." She squeezed me tightly, her face to my chest, her body shaking with her quiet tears. She held on to me for minutes, afraid to let me go and walk away, but she finally did. "I love you."

"I love you too."

When she stepped away, Elora came next. Instead of giving me a tearful goodbye, she just gave me a hug. "Kick ass, okay?"

I chuckled as I clapped her back. "You know I will."

When she pulled away, she kissed me on the check. "Love you."

"Love you too, sis."

Bastian shook my hand and wished me luck.

I saw my mother embrace Ivory with the same love she'd just shown me—and that meant the world to me. My mother said, "I know you always have his back, Ivory. Thank you for loving my son."

Ian came to me next, and he somehow seemed the most upset, even though his features didn't show much. He stood in front of me for a while before he released a sigh. "You sure I can't come with you?"

"I have all the men I need."

"But none of those men is your brother."

"I feel better knowing Mother has you around. It's hard enough for her to lose one son, let alone two." I clapped him on the shoulder.

He gave a nod. "Kill 'em all."

"You know I will."

"Your Majesty!" One of the guards ran straight from the castle, rushing downhill toward us at breakneck speed. "An urgent message from the Kingdoms!"

My heart just about exploded.

He had to skid to a stop before he barreled into all of us. So out of breath he couldn't say anything more, he just held up the scroll.

I was the one to snatch it. I unfurled it and started to read. "A fleet was spotted this morning. A hundred strong—with dragons. They sail from the north, and they're headed straight for us. We'll prepare for war, but by the time you receive this, the battle will have already commenced. If you're still alive, hurry back. We'll do the best we can. Ryker."

THIRTY-EIGHT

Ryker

I STOOD OUTSIDE THE CASTLE, MY CHILDHOOD HOME, the temporary king. The city looked the same, but now everything felt different. My father was gone. My sister was married to the man who had slain him. And the Kingdoms were under a different ruler. Once Huntley and Ivory returned, I wasn't sure what that meant for Effie and me.

Where would we start our lives?

Now I had no inheritance to support her. It had been taken from me. But then again, it never truly belonged to me in the first place. A sharp breeze swept up over the hills and hit me, pushing my hair out of my face and stinging my eyes. It was a clear day, a cloudless sky, but it was bitterly cold.

"Your Highness." One of the soldiers appeared behind me. "A family has come forward and wishes to speak with you."

I kept my eyes on the horizon, the world quiet in the afternoon. "I'm not hearing grievances right now." That was Huntley's problem. I was just there to oversee the Kingdom until he returned.

If he returned.

"It's not a grievance. They say Effie is their daughter."

I stilled when I heard his words and slowly turned to face him. "Bring them to me immediately."

———

I wanted to see them first, to make sure this wasn't a hoax before I got Effie's hopes up. I sat in the study as I waited for them to be brought to me, seeing Huntley's things on the desk because he'd dropped everything to conquer the Kingdoms.

They were chauffeured inside—and my heart skipped a beat.

It was her father.

Her mother.

And her sister.

We stared at each other for a long time, and without thinking about what I was doing, I got up and moved straight to her mother—and hugged her. We didn't share a conversation. Had no connection whatsoever other than her daughter. But Effie was enough to turn me emotional. I'd lost both of my parents, and I was so grateful she still had hers. "I'll go get her."

———

I didn't tell Effie anything as I escorted her into the room. Just told her I needed to show her something. We rounded the corner and entered the study, and she gasped so loudly it made the walls shake. Her hands cupped her mouth as she stifled a sob, overwhelmed by the sight of people she'd thought she would never see again.

She ran straight toward them and became cocooned in their love. Both parents hugged her, as did her little sister. Tears and sniffles filled the room, mourning their separation, rejoicing at their reunion.

I knew I wasn't a part of this, so I walked out.

———

I didn't see Effie for hours. She was still with her family in the study, probably updating them on everything that had happened, including her impromptu marriage. Her parents must have realized we were the interim king and queen of the Kingdoms, and that was when they knew it was safe to come forward.

I'd just returned to the castle from the barracks when a soldier from the aviary approached me. "Your Highness, news from Commander Brutus."

I didn't have a study to occupy right now, so I broke the seal and read it under the light of the torch. My eyes scanned over the letters, my heart sinking further as the message became clear.

We were under attack. "Fuck…" I read it again, my hand digging into my hair. Regar had been killed, and now there were repercussions for it. King Dunbar was sailing for the continent as we spoke—and the King of Kingdoms and his dragons were gone. "I've got to send a letter right this instance."

"Birds don't usually travel at night—"

"That's too fucking bad because they're going to do it anyway. And we prepare all the men for battle."

The terror on his face was indescribable. "Sir?"

"You heard me."

———

I sent off the letter to Huntley first. Hopefully, the battle against Necrosis had finished, and hopefully they won, because I didn't stand a chance without the dragons. I donned my battle armor despite the late hour, grabbed my best weapons, and prepared to leave.

But I had to say goodbye first.

Effie and her family had vacated my office at some point, so the next place I visited was the dining hall. The table was covered with a feast for her family, probably because they'd been beggars for the last few months. Her entire family had dropped weight they couldn't afford to lose in the first place.

I walked inside, no longer touched by their unexpected union.

Effie looked up at me, and once she recognized my battle armor, all the delight in her face vanished. "What's happened?" She slowly rose from her chair, her skin already pale at the revelation.

My helmet was tucked under my arm, and I was nervous even though I shouldn't be. Not nervous for battle. But nervous to leave her behind and never return.

When I didn't say anything, she left the table and walked up to me. Her entire family stopped eating and turned to hear the news.

I looked into her eyes before I spoke. "King Dunbar is sailing to the Capital as we speak. His intentions are clear—to conquer."

Her eyes widened.

"He has a fleet of a hundred ships…and dragons."

"Oh no…"

"I'm not sure if this is in retaliation for the death of Regar. Or if it's simply an opportunity to conquer the Kingdoms after we're exhausted from the battles we've already won. But it's happening—and I must go."

"What about Huntley?"

"I just sent off a letter, but I've received no news from him or Ivory. They may never answer the call because Necrosis won. I'm not going to depend on their victory." I wouldn't allow myself to think about it too deeply, because that would mean my sister was dead…or worse, turned.

"But…you can't leave."

"I'm the King of Kingdoms. I must defend it."

Her eyes were already red and blotchy from all the crying she'd done today. Now they watered once more. "I'll come with you—"

"No."

She cupped her face, overrun with tears. "This can't be happening…"

"Since we're on land, we have the advantage."

"But the Capital is destroyed after the battle. There's not even a castle—"

"Effie, we still have cannons and an army."

"And they have dragons—"

"We'll do the best that we can. And maybe Huntley and Ivory will show up."

She stared at the floor for a moment, taking a few breaths to stifle her tears.

I didn't want to leave her like this, but duty called me. "If King Dunbar wins, he's not going to hurt anyone else. Take the money in my room and start a new life with your family. It should be enough to buy you a home."

"Don't talk like that…"

I had to. "I have to leave."

"Right now?" she asked incredulously.

"I should have left thirty minutes ago. My soldiers are waiting for me."

At that, she really panicked, barely having enough time to process all of this, and now she had to say goodbye… possibly for good. She launched herself into my chest and held on tightly, even though she had to hug me through my metal armor.

I hugged her back, keeping a straight face because I wanted to make this as easy for her as possible. "I'll write as soon as I can." My hand moved into her hair, and I kissed her forehead, treating her like her family wasn't there watching.

She pulled away to look at me. "Please come back to me."

"I'll do everything I can, sweetheart."

We stared at each other for a long time, feeling each other's sorrow and unable to do anything about it. I was the first one to pull away. "I love you."

Her tears came harder. "I love you too."

―――――

The ride took several days, and by the time I arrived at the Capital, the war had already started. Smoke filled the sky. A dragon passed by so fast I wasn't sure if I even saw it. A cannon fired, and then a loud thud sounded, as if a building had just been demolished.

I gave my orders to the men behind me, sending them into the city and to the coastline where the ships would try to dock. I wasn't sure where Commander Brutus was, if he was still alive, but I made it to the turrets that were still functioning and found the cannons that the men were firing.

They had two dragons in their fleet, and their focus was on the cannons. They timed their attacks before they dove down and grabbed the cannon with their great talons and ripped it off the roof. The other would release a stream of fire and make everyone run for cover before they were burned to a crisp.

I found Commander Brutus in the chaos. "I just got here. I sent my men to the coastline."

"The armies of the other Kingdoms should be on their return journey. But I'm not sure how much of a difference it'll make."

I looked toward the water, seeing a few ships set ablaze in the harbor from the cannons, but there were far more untouched. The dragons were doing their job and making it impossible to sink their fleet. "If we kill the dragons, we have a chance."

"They're too fast. Can't line up a shot."

One of the dragons dropped down again, sending a stream of fire all along the turret. Commander Brutus and I jumped behind a wall to dodge the fire. We were spared, but most of the men weren't. "Are there other cannons?"

"On the next turret," he said. "But the roof is unstable. Why?"

"We've got to hit them when they don't expect it." I took off at a run, moving to the rear of the partially demolished castle until I found a path to climb. Stone jutted down from the wall, giving me just enough room to grip and climb. I was so heavy from all the armor, but the adrenaline was far stronger, and I made it to the top.

A few cannons were there, but more had been in place before the roof had collapsed. The foundation was shaky, and standing on it was probably suicide, but I found the pile of cannonballs and grabbed one.

That was when I spotted a chain on the roof, a chain that appeared to have been used to haul the cannon into place. I secured it around the cannonball then shoved it down the chute. I had to light the fuse before I could fire, and since the dragons were moving targets, there would never be an ideal way to time this.

I just had to go for it.

I lit the fuse then focused on the shot, always aiming for one of the dragons as he flew around, up and down, and then toward the cannon again. The cannon ignited and jerked back as it fired.

I was knocked on my ass.

ROOOOOAAAAAARRRRR.

I pushed myself up to my feet and watched the dragon drop from the sky. The ball had struck his wing, and then the chain had wrapped around his body and locked his wings against his sides. He fell hard to the earth, knocking over several buildings along the way. "Alright…one down."

THIRTY-NINE

Huntley

I COULD SEE THE SMOKE ONCE WE REACHED THE TOP OF the cliffs. We flew right over Delacroix, the city quiet as usual. But up ahead, the battle that would determine the fate of the continent was happening.

"You see that, Huntley?"

I looked at my wife. "Yes."

"Why are they doing this?"

"Because Rutherford told them my intention—to conquer the Kingdoms and Necrosis. They either think I'm distracted by Necrosis so my guard is down, or they think Necrosis has been defeated and it's their opportunity to conquer the entire continent for themselves."

"When will it end?"

"Soon," I said. "Very soon."

How many dragons do they have?

"Ryker didn't say."

Pyre and I will do our best.

"I know you can handle this, Storm."

"Do we have a plan?" Ivory asked.

"It's impossible to make one without knowing the conditions. But I assume the Capital is losing. They're unprepared for an attack. Their castle has already fallen. Their infrastructure if decimated."

Ivory nodded in agreement.

"You and Pyre will take on the dragons. I'll go after King Dunbar. The sooner he dies, the sooner this is over."

"Any idea what he looks like?"

"No. But I know a king when I see one."

———

The smoke turned thick, making it hard for us to breathe in the cloud bank. The details of what was happening below were difficult to discern, but the sounds of cannons firing were still audible, so the war wasn't over.

We only had one chance to use surprise to our advantage, so we dropped below the clouds and took a look at the battle. A gold dragon was flying near the turrets, blowing fire across the cannons and the men trying to load them. In the harbor, a third of the fleet was on fire, but a number of ships had already docked and there were invaders in the city.

A line of cannons fired from the ships, and Storm and Pyre quickly ducked out of the way to avoid the hits.

I looked at Ivory. "Stop the dragon. I'll take care of the ships."

"Alright."

I looked at her, perhaps for the final time. "I love you."

"I love you too."

I faced forward again and gripped the pommel. "Ready for this, Storm?"

I'm always ready to burn. Always. Storm flapped his wings hard and took off at neck-breaking speed, flying through the air quicker than the balls from the cannons. We flew to the coastline where the docked ships were allowing the soldiers onto land.

Storm swooped around and released a long line of fire, burning the soldiers that tried to invade the Capital on foot.

A line of cheers sounded from below.

You're welcome.

Storm moved to the next ship and released his fire, setting the masts on fire immediately. Once they fell, the ship would capsize and sink. He weaved through the different ships and set them ablaze, demolishing all their vessels without effort. Some fired their cannons, and I kept a close eye out so Storm would avoid getting hit.

Where's the king?

"I don't see him."

Only a coward lets others do his bidding.

"I agree."

Storm suddenly reared his head and spun his body back toward land.

"What is it?"

Pyre. He needs help. Storm took off at a sprint, flapping back in the direction from which he came.

I held on to the pommel hard. "What about Ivory?"

She's hurt.

My stomach dropped. Fear like I'd never known hit me so hard.

Storm glided low to the ground, finding the two dragons hovering just a hundred feet from the ground, locked in battle.

I spotted Ivory—gripped in Pyre's talon. She was unconscious, judging by the way her legs bounced around.

The dragon attacked Pyre, scratching with his large talons and biting his neck. Pyre was at a disadvantage because he had to hold Ivory and protect her at the same time. If he jerked too much, he could easily snap her neck.

Storm barreled straight into the dragon just like he had with Regar—and made him tumble out of the sky.

I wanted him to drop me so I could go to Ivory, but I had to wait.

Storm maneuvered on top of him and clawed him as they both fell to the earth. Claws ripped through scales. Roars pierced the sky. I gripped the pommel as we hit the ground, Storm on top. He bit down on the dragon's throat and ended it.

I slid off both dragons and hit the ground with a heavy thud. My knees buckled because of the momentum, and I lost my footing for just a second. I forced my body forward and ran as fast as I could. "Ivory!"

Pyre had opened his talons and gently laid Ivory on the ground.

I moved over her, seeing that she had, indeed, been knocked unconscious. She was still breathing, but I couldn't see the source of her injury. When I turned her over, that was when I saw the deep slash right through her armor, the mark from a talon. It had made it past her defenses to her flesh underneath. "No…"

"Ivory!" The voice emerged from behind me, delirious.

I didn't turn to look because I recognized his voice.

Ryker dropped to his knees beside me. "What's wrong? What happened?" He didn't need me to answer when he saw the wound in her side. "Shit…"

"Your dragons may have defeated mine, but your king will not defeat my blade." His deep voice sounded from a distance away, a voice I'd never heard in my life.

I looked up and saw King Dunbar in the flesh. His armor was bright red like the color of blood, and his blade was embedded with fire-red jewels.

His dark eyes were visible through his helmet, and he spun his sword around his wrist—an invitation to play. "When Rutherford told me your intention to defeat Necrosis, I couldn't resist the opportunity. Your armies are weary. Your cities burned. And if you've already defeated Necrosis, then you've prepared this world for my taking."

I didn't care about this battle anymore. All I cared about was my wife.

Ryker didn't seem to care either. "If I don't get her help, she'll die."

She needs a healer.

"Pyre, there should be a medic outside the Capital. Take both of them. Ryker, make sure she gets to the right person." I cupped her face and gave her a quick kiss on the forehead. "Don't die on me, baby." I left them there, unsheathed my sword, and faced the king in red armor.

He spun his sword around his wrist again. "My condolences." He grinned wide.

Storm emerged behind him, fire visible in this throat. *I'll burn him.*

Destroy the fleet. I'll take care of him.

Storm released a mighty roar before he took off.

King Dunbar approached me. "You're honorable."

"While Storm sinks your fleet to the bottom of the ocean, I'll stab my sword clean through your armor. Just practical." I sized him up based on the way he moved, what kind of footwork he had, his age, his muscularity. He seemed to be ten years older than me, give or take a couple years. I had youth on my side, but he had the experience.

"Not honorable at all, then." He launched at me with a speed I didn't anticipate. His sword slashed through the air, reflecting the fires from the buildings, giving a sharp glint whenever it moved.

I stopped his blade with mine and returned with several hits of my own, driving him back by sheer will. Now, I was used to opponents who were larger, nearly a foot taller than me, that had the strength of ten men.

King Dunbar was nothing.

He was forced to move farther back, putting all his energy into blocking my hits but unable to return any of his own. He became breathless, and the sweat on his forehead shone in the cracks through his helmet.

I kicked him back and watched him lose his footing and tumble to the ground. "You're disappointing for a king." At least this battle would be over quickly, so I could return to my wife—and hope that I still had a wife.

He pushed himself back to his feet and righted his sword.

"I'm not interested in ruling a land I can't see. There's only one thing that interests me. Give us your dragons—and I'll accept your surrender."

Still breathless, he stepped back, his sword held loosely in his hand.

I took gentle strides forward, my sword relaxed at my side. "Think of all the men you'll save. You've already lost both dragons you brought with you. Don't lose more life than you have to—including yours. I've defeated the Three Kings of Necrosis." I stopped, my stare burning into his. "You're nothing."

"What do you want with the dragons?"

"For them to be free."

His arm had gone slack at his side, the sign of surrender obvious. "You'll use them for your own benefit."

"I can't use them if I don't need them. Unlike you, I can take care of my own shit."

He looked away for a while, observing the smoke in the sky, listening to the cannons fire back and forth. "You do all of this...and expect nothing in return?"

"I made a promise to Pyre and Storm."

His eyes darkened as if he recognized their names.

"They fought for me—now I fight for them. And it wouldn't be for nothing, because if you try to invade our lands again, I know they'll fight for us. Any attacker that comes to our lands will be defeated by our allies. So, I guess it's not for nothing after all."

He stared at the rubies in his sword before he returned it to the scabbard.

"I need to hear your surrender." I wouldn't let him off that easily.

He forced the words past a clenched jaw. "I surrender..."

"Withdraw your troops from my land. When you return, tell your dragons they're free in my lands. If you keep any, I will know." I didn't waste another minute with him. I sheathed my sword and took off at a run.

FORTY

Ivory

IT WAS BLACK.

Ivory, can you hear me?

Darkness.

Ivory.

I felt my mind come into consciousness, felt the air in my lungs, was aware of the orientation of my body. I lay on something hard, maybe the ground. *Pyre?*

His voice grew louder in my mind. *Ivory!*

What's happening?

You were hurt. Ryker and I took you to a healer outside the city.

Ryker…? Where's Huntley?

He's here. I just told him that we're speaking. Can you wake up?

I'll try. I tried to push my mind out, tried to open my eyes, but nothing happened. *I can't...I'm too tired.*

And then it was black again.

———

Ivory?

I heard the echo of his voice. *I'm here.*

Can you wake up?

How long has it been?

You've been sleeping for three days.

Oh...are you sure I'm alive?

Yes.

This isn't a dream?

No. Please wake up.

What's happened...? The ground felt less hard now. But I couldn't feel my arms or my legs.

King Dunbar surrendered. What was left of his fleet left the Capital yesterday. He agreed to free all the dragons in his captivity when he returns.

How do you know he'll do it?

Because Huntley threatened to sail across the sea and kill all his people if he doesn't.

I tried to push my eyes open, but they were so heavy. I tried repeatedly, until finally, I saw light. My eyes opened to the morning light directly above me, along with Pyre's snout. "Pyre…?"

Ivory! He dipped his head and rubbed his snout into me, his scales hard and smooth against my skin.

I blinked a couple times before I reached my hand up and felt his muzzle. His hot breaths fell across my skin, warm and moist. I felt his scales, felt his warmth.

I asked them to keep you outside during the day so I could watch you.

"You've been here the whole time?" I asked in a hoarse voice.

Yes. There's nowhere safer than at a dragon's side.

"Where's Huntley?"

Restoring the Capital. I've let him know that you're awake, and he's on his way here now. He lifted his snout and released a loud growl.

"What's wrong?"

Just getting your brother's attention.

"Ivory?" Ryker ran over and kneeled down on the cot. "You're finally awake. I've been waiting for days." His face came into my view, and his palm immediately went to my forehead like he was checking my temperature. "Your fever finally broke."

A dragon streaked across the sky, and then a loud thud erupted a moment later. Huntley ran to me and kneeled, sliding across the grass slightly as he came for me. His arms pressed into the cot on either side of me as he held himself over my face. "Baby, you alright?"

"Yeah...I think so."

He grabbed both of my hands and guided me to a seated position.

"Her fever had broken," Ryker said. "I think the infection is gone."

Huntley checked the bandage around my midsection. "Looks like the bleeding has stopped for good."

"What happened?" I asked, not remembering the events of that day. I was on Pyre one moment, and then...everything went dark.

"One of Dunbar's dragons sliced you," Huntley said. "He hit Pyre hard, so you flew out of your seat. Pyre caught you before you hit the ground, but the impact must have knocked you out cold." His hands went into my hair as he kneeled in front of me, pushing the oily strands back to look me straight in the face. All the worry was written there, all the stress, all the terror. "I'm so glad you're alright."

Once I reached full consciousness, I felt it, the raw pain. It wasn't just in the area of my wound, but everywhere, like my body had taken a hard beating. "Storm is alright?"

"Not a scratch."

"Did we lose a lot of men?"

"Some," he said. "Not a lot."

"Ryker is okay?"

"I'm right here." Ryker gave me a squeeze on the shoulder.

I turned to look at him, seeing his features in full focus for the first time. "I'm so relieved…"

"I wasn't sure if you guys were going to make it in time," Ryker said. "You have no idea how happy I was when I saw Pyre flying through the skies. The war would have been lost without you. First, Necrosis, and now this… You must be exhausted."

Exhausted wasn't a strong enough word. "Effie?"

"I left her in Delacroix with her family."

"She found her family?" I asked in surprise.

He nodded, a slight smile moving on to his lips. "Yes."

"Oh, that's great."

Ryker circled his arm around my shoulders and gave me a gentle hug. "I'll give you two a moment. We'll talk later." He excused himself from where we sat together on the grass near the wall of the Capital. There were other tents around us, where the armies of the Kingdoms were stationed throughout the battle.

"Is it…really over?" I asked, unable to believe it.

Huntley just stared at me.

"You did it… You're the King of Kingdoms."

"And you're the Queen."

I didn't feel like a queen. I just felt like his wife. That was the only title I cared about anyway. "It feels like just yesterday when you attacked my carriage and chased me through the woods…"

"Really? Feels like another lifetime to me. Hard to imagine a time when we weren't this."

Husband and wife. King and queen. Soul mates. "Now what?"

"I sent a letter to HeartHolme reporting our victory. I said you were injured but very likely to pull through. I've sent the armies back to their Kingdoms so they can return to their quiet lives. The castle here will need to be rebuilt, but that's a process that will take at least a year."

"So…nothing, basically."

He chuckled. "We have a lot of stuff to do—but nothing that involves fighting."

I could still see Pyre above us, just sitting there. "It's the weirdest feeling, being finished. When we agreed to do all this, it seemed like an impossible mission. But we did it…"

Huntley stared at me, his hand resting on my hips, his eyes still a bit concerned. "I was thinking that we would live here, in the Capital, and allow Ryker to be the Duke of Delacroix, just as he would have been."

"You don't want to live in Delacroix? It's your childhood home…"

"HeartHolme is my home. But I can't live there anymore, so…"

"The Capital really is beautiful. You know, when it's not on fire and the castle isn't in ruins."

"Yes, I remember," he said with a smile. "Ian and I always loved our trips here. Chasing each other through the olive trees. Swimming in the ocean in the summer. Watching the sunset."

"I'm fine with that, if that's what you want."

"It'll take a long time to rebuild, so we'll stay in Delacroix in the meantime."

"And the dragons?" I asked. "Where will they live?"

Huntley shrugged. "Wherever they want. Harming a dragon will be against the laws of this land—so they'll be protected wherever they are."

PENELOPE BARSETTI

"And they can eat all the yetis."

Huntley chuckled again.

"I have an idea…what if we give them the Necrosis lands. It's huge, so they'll have their own space. They won't have to share anything with humans, even look at another human if they don't want to."

"Not a bad idea."

"You think Dunbar will hold up his end of the deal?"

"He knows he would have lost the battle if I hadn't let him surrender. And he would have lost, whether it was at our gates or his. I'm not worried about it."

I tilted my chin up and looked at Pyre. "What do you think? Will you still live here?"

If all the dragons are here, that's where I want to be.

"Good. That means we can still see each other." I reached for his leg and rubbed his hard scales, careful to avoid the horns that stuck out of his hide. "I think that's the best part of all this…"

FORTY-ONE

Huntley

ONCE WE RETURNED TO DELACROIX, WE RESTED FOR days.

Ivory was in bed most of the time, and I was right by her side. She had her meals in bed, and every time I changed her bandages, she looked better than she did before. Her injury wasn't enough to stop us from making love, especially when I could just take her at the edge of the bed with her ass hanging over the mattress.

She never asked me to take my herbs, so I didn't.

I was ready for a family, and I was certain she was ready too, whenever it happened.

Ivory was sitting up in bed reading when she abruptly dropped her book.

I'd been sitting there gazing at the fire, reflecting on everything that had happened in the last year. It was almost a year ago to the day when I followed her carriage and sabotaged her journey to the Capital. Now she was my wife. My queen. The future mother of my children. My eyes shifted to her. "Baby?"

"Oh my gods, get up!" She launched herself out of bed and grabbed whatever clothes she could find.

"What is it? What's wrong?"

She didn't answer me and tugged on her boots as she hopped around on one foot.

"Ivory?"

"Just come on!"

I threw on something as we ran through the castle to the outside.

"You shouldn't be running, baby."

"Whatever. I'm fine!" She made it outside the double doors into the afternoon light and immediately looked at the open field. She halted and brought her hands to her chest.

I followed her gaze—and spotted three dragons.

Three.

The third dragon was the same size as Pyre and Storm. With scales a beautiful red color, they looked like living fire. The red dragon rubbed its snout against Pyre's then wrapped its neck around Storm's in a gesture of affection.

I knew who it was. "She made it."

Ivory grabbed my hand with tears in her eyes. "Let's go say hello." We jogged down the path to the outside of Delacroix and across the large field to where the three dragons were getting reacquainted with one another.

Ivory walked right up to them. "I'm so happy for you, Pyre."

The red dragon turned her attention on Ivory before she lowered her neck and brought her head close to hers, getting a good look at my wife. Her eyes took Ivory in for nearly a minute before a deep voice exploded in both our minds. *I thank you both for my freedom. I thank you both for healing my sons. I thank you both for reuniting them with their mother. May the stars shine on you always.*

"You're very welcome," Ivory said. "We love Pyre and Storm...and we're happy they're finally happy."

———

I was sitting in my study when Commander Brutus knocked and stepped inside. "You have a visitor."

Tomorrow was the day of my coronation. Ivory would place the crown upon my head, the high sect of the church would bless my reign, and I would be the rightful King of Kingdoms. People had already traveled from all the Kingdoms to attend, the field completely full of tents and camps where people were waiting. The dragons stayed in their own area away from everyone else.

My first week as king was spent doing mostly nothing. I went into my study to find something to do, but right now, there wasn't much. Rebuilding the Capital was my biggest focus, but until it was finished being cleared of the rubble and broken stones, there wasn't much I could do.

So, I had no idea who had come to visit me. "Send them in."

Commander Brutus left, and a moment later, he returned with three visitors.

The first was my mother.

I stared at her from my seat, the same seat my father had occupied every single day, and our eyes locked for a long and deep moment. All the pride was written on her face. All the love written in her tears.

I came around the desk and embraced her.

She squeezed me tightly. "My son…" She cried in my arms before she pulled away and cupped my face. "I'm so proud of you. Your father is so proud of you." She gave me a kiss on the cheek before she stepped aside so my brother could greet me next.

"Ivory told us about the coronation."

"You came all the way here for that?"

"Wouldn't miss it, brother." He circled his arms around me and clapped me on the back. "I know Father is gonna be watching tomorrow, grinning from ear to ear."

I clapped him on the arm. "I hope so."

"You avenged him. The Rolfes took back their legacy. Because of you."

"Because of all of us."

He stepped away, and Elora came next.

"I'm really sad that I won't see you anymore, but I'm really happy for you." Her hands moved to mine, and she stared down at them. "You were the Forsaken King...but now you're the True King."

I brought her into my chest and embraced her. "King or not, I'll always be there for you. You're always welcome to stay here with us. Both of you."

"Thank you." She pulled away and let me go. "Might take you up on that offer…"

———

When I woke up the next morning, Ivory was gone.

551

I got out of bed and moved down the hallway, but I stopped when I saw something on the wall that hadn't been there before.

It was my father's portrait. The one my mother had found in the basement. The dust had been brushed away, and the paint still looked brand-new. My father's authoritative eyes stared back at me, as if he were there in the flesh.

My mother's portrait was beside his. She'd always been a beautiful woman, but in her youth, she reminded me of Elora. Utterly breathtaking. Another portrait hung next to it. It was a portrait of the four of us.

It should make me sad, but it actually made me smile.

I'd have another portrait painted like this soon, with my wife and children. It would grace these walls forever, capturing us in a happy moment in life, a moment before we passed on with time.

Ivory appeared in the hallway, wearing a full-length gown with jewels. "I was just about to wake you up."

I looked at the portraits again. "Did you put these up?"

"Yes…" She crept forward. "I hope you don't mind. We can put them somewhere else—"

"No. I want to see them every day."

"Oh good." She came to my side and stared at the pictures with me, of the perfect family I'd once had. "I'm excited for our own family."

I smiled. "Me too, baby."

We stared at them a moment longer before we broke apart.

"You need to get ready," she said. "Coronation is at high noon. You should see the crowd that turned up for you."

After I bathed and put on the uniform the seamstress created for me, I strapped my sword to my hips and left the bedroom. Through the castle I went, the same walk feeling different now. The staff was lined up and ready to serve me, and when I approached the first window, I saw the enormous crowd below.

There must be one hundred thousand people.

It was the first time I'd seen a crowd that size that I didn't have to fight.

A stage had been built at the bottom of the hill for the coronation to take place, and I walked down the path with my hand in Ivory's. The sounds of the crowd grew louder as we approached. Once they could see me, the cheers rang out.

I'd taken back my land, taken back my people, and now it felt like home again.

When I stepped onto the stage, the horns sounded, and the music stopped.

My mother was there, holding my father's sword by the hilt. Her eyes were misty but strong, and she couldn't resist the smile that broke over her lips as she regarded me. When I stopped in front of her, I kneeled, and she looked down at me with a shaky breath. "Huntley Rolfe, I name you King Rolfe, Rightful Heir to Delacroix, the True King of Kingdoms. Take this sword and protect us with your blood, sweat, and tears."

I rose to my feet and took the sword she presented. It was heavier than mine, heavy with wisdom and power.

Ivory presented the crown on a crimson pillow, and my mother took it gently then presented it to me. "Long live the king." I had to tilt my neck so she could place it upon my head, and on her tiptoes, she did.

The crowd burst into applause. The trumpets sounded. The sun shone brighter than it ever had. The dragons roared from their place at the edge of the field. All of us were bound by that moment, bound by that energy, bound by the hope we all felt.

———

Check out Penelope's new release!

About the book:

Enemies-to-lovers…to unlikely allies…to frenemies with benefits… 10/10 spice.

A horrible plague has swept the world.

Millions are sick. More are dying.

Except me. I'm immune.

I'm the only one well enough to defeat this plague and save my people.

Except one problem...

Kingsnake--King of Vampires--is intent on finding me. Without my people to feed on, he'll die. My blood is the only thing that will keep him alive.

He won't stop until he finds me.

Binds me.

And makes me his.

Order Now

Made in the USA
Las Vegas, NV
30 December 2023

83725834R10329